The Devil's Spring Holiday on the French Riviera

André Lwow

The Devil's Spring Holiday on the French Riviera

© Éditions Sydney Laurent – André Lwow
ISBN : 979-10-326-3365-6
Dépôt legal : Janvier 2020

"Good can exist without evil, but evil cannot exist without good."

St. Thomas Aquinas

"Evil is not a diffuse thing, it's a person. I want to say something that I am convinced: with Satan, we can not talk. If you start talking to Satan, you are lost; he is smarter than us, and he overthrows you, makes you turn his head, and you are lost. "No, go away!"

Pope Francis, in an interview with TV2000.

Chapter 1 - The Grand Master

In a miserable retirement home, like so many others in the towns and villages of the deepest province, a venerable old man was lying on a hospital bed. His waxy face showed a grimace of death. Sighing, he thought of his past life, which would never come back. Beside him, sitting on a stool, stood a beautiful young woman wearing a pink tunic, deep neckline, which highlighted her slim and graceful body. With a white, neat hand that wore many rings, she turned in a cautious gesture, the pages with the blackened edges of an old manuscript that came from the library of the ancient Greek city of Pergamos, famous since the night of time for treasures.

Seeing this old man in such shabby place, no one would have thought that they were once admired by famous people. Indeed, he was none other than the grand master of the Order of the Rose Cross, the very noble Order of the Garter and other religious orders scattered throughout the world. Not so long ago, his disciples, from the nobles of blue blood to President Jacques Sly, a man of the people who had been raised to the highest rank, spoke of him as they would have done with God and addressed him with solemnity and fervor: O Grand Master Polyus!

The great master Polyus had certainly lived much longer than ordinary mortals, but now he was in the throes of a long and terrible agony. His life had been too stormy for his soul to find rest in the afterlife. He had devoted himself to witchcraft and other dark practices, worthy of ghouls, vampires, and other demons whose existence is not officially recognized in this world.

Suddenly, the door of his room opened, to let Princess Jeanne and her friend Boris appear. The old man's battered lips stretched out a smile that was a bit distorted by the pain that gripped him, as if a clumsy hand had drawn a twisted mouth on his face. Nevertheless, he seemed to be alive again, so happy was he to receive a visit to this deadly place. In a hoarse 4voice, he greeted his visitors:

– Welcome! What a pleasure to have a visit! If you knew how bad I feel here... Oh, my God, I'm living a real hell! But, fortunately, my kind Margot distracted me a little from my horrible thoughts.

And he began to cry without restraint, impotent tears running down his cheeks.

– How are you, Master Polyus? —Princess Jeanne asked politely.

It was obvious that the master was not at his best, but she had found nothing better as an introduction. She tried to smile at him but could only sketch a pathetic grin, bringing out the wrinkles that had parched her face for years now, even if she tried to camouflage them under thick layers of various creams, at exorbitant prices, and White powder. The master was not fooled by Jeanne's false compassion. He knew that the witch would not mourn his death. Perhaps she even wanted to provoke him...

Jeanne had been a good friend of the Princess Grace, the very one who had married the old Prince of Monaco and who had died stupidly in a car accident on the road to La Turbie. The master suspected that Jeanne had cast a spell on Princess Grace and thus participated in her tragic end. The idea of being Jeanne's next victim made him shudder, but he did not show anything of his nervousness and replied with his usual frankness:

— Oh! My darling, I feel your impatience to see me dead, as you have been in the past with regard to a certain princess whose death you precipitated. Also, I will reassure you about my fate, by repeating the words of a gray-haired rabbi, although I am not a Jew: You will not wait for my death soon!

— Oh! Master, do you really think there was any spiteful hint in my question? —Princess Jeanne was clearly offended by the Magister— I loved Princess Grace, and I swear to I only well after her death found out the next day that the jealous husband ordered her murder and thus prevented his unfaithful wife from escaping to his lover in America.

Jeanne paused for a moment, then resumed, a strange smile on her lips:

— Besides, dear master, You have never had an unfaithful wife and daughter from a Hollywood actor. And in general, you have never been married and you never had your children! Your reference to the murder of my dear Grace is frankly inappropriate, for my poor friend has only harvested what she has sown: "Who is destined to hang herself is not drowning" as they say. Also, do not fear my curses, for I have no intention of using my powers on you. On the contrary, I wish you a long life, my dear friend!

After this tirade, all at once, she tried to smile again, without further success. If Stanislavski, the famous Russian theater director, was still alive, he would certainly have told him: "Alas, ma'am, I do not believe you!"

One might have thought that the grand master, in the grip of a moribund torpor, had not heard the sarcastic reply of Princess Jeanne. However, after a moment of silence, he replied in a weak but firm voice:

– Oh! Jeanne, to the Russians according: Simplicity is worse than theft! When you wish me, a long life, you vow that my agony and sufferings will be prolonged and be even more terrible! Your question: How are you, Master Polyus? –The master added, imitating her– is a sad stupidity!

And he continued to speak in his hoarse voice

– Jeanne, do not you see that I'm dying? Ah! What devil pushed me to listen to this vagabond Jacques who insisted that I settle in this madhouse?

He spat out those words like a flamethrower, and he was so angry that a flood of blood rose in his face, and his pale complexion turned red. Immediately, the beautiful Margot rushed forward, as quickly as a furious soldier throws herself on the barrel of a machine-gun, to appease him, but he pushed her away his gesture of his bony hand. He cleared his throat, and the spasms of suffocation faded. So, he resumed in a slow voice:

– You mentioned my role as a father... Well, no, ma'am, I have my only daughter, my love, is prefect of the city of Lyon and that I am very proud of it, even if she does not seem to care about me.

At these words, he began to cry again. His orbits, like two deep bowls, were filled to the brim with bitter tears. One could have gathered these holy terrors to sell them as relics in Jerusalem or elsewhere. Boris greedily detailed the silhouette of the beautiful Margot and plunged his gaze into the neckline of her nurse's smock slightly translucent tissue that hinted her pink breasts and vigorous nipples. Coming out of his lustful contemplation, he put his eyes on the old man and said to him:

– Grand master, anger seems to be beneficial to your health! Nervous irritation gives your face a healthy skin tone. So you look much better, and I see, thanks to the malice you live well for over a hundred years!

– Are you kidding me? –The old man interrupted– I am already over a hundred years old! And imagine that I would not die right away! But if you continued to talk nonsense, then, I may well die, carried away by a fit of anger, precisely! But let's go... I want to talk to you about something! Come near, my dear friend. I must whisper in your ear, because there is no other way to tell a secret... Do you understand?

And he pointed suspiciously at the walls of the room. Then he looked up at the white ceiling in a waiting attitude. So, Boris advanced towards the sick man but when he drew his face to the old man, he could not help but frown; in spite of the expensive perfume with which he had sprinkled himself, the grand master gave off a suffocating odor of rotten carrion.

Boris thought:

"According to the Bible, the body of St. Lazarus, before Jesus raised him up, stayed four days in a sepulcher, but obviously he didn't stink like that as this old man, who is still alive! I doubt what he wants to tell me... Is it really, does he ask me to bring him back to life? But I am not Jesus and he is not Lazarus! Certainly, the great master possesses powerful powers, which he has used to establish his authority in this world, but he is already more than a hundred years old! He will not be able to go against the laws of creation. Even if I understand him, that he does not want to die now!"

His inner reflections were suddenly interrupted by the old man who, as if he had heard Boris's thoughts and wanted to confirm them, said to him in a low voice:

– My friend, as you can see, my end is near. But I can not resign myself to dying now. I want to extend my life, even if only for a short time. I still want to enjoy the simple pleasures Mother Earth offers us, like walking on the banks of a lake or walking in the forest, a wicker basket in hand, to pick white mushrooms or lily of the valley... But for that, I need you. You are not Jesus and do not have the power to resurrect the dead but, with the help of another person, I know you will get there and you will achieve a brilliant result!

The old man paused for a moment, as if he wanted to give Boris time to assimilate the information, then went on:

— If you knew how bad I feel in this death place... I suffer terribly, I see only from one eye and, like you, I feel the smell of putrefaction emanating from my body.

This time, Boris was certain that the grand master was reading his thoughts, and he felt embarrassed.

— It's so degrading to see my beautiful wife being forced to clean the crap that sticks to my ass. And it's so frustrating that you can not make love to her anymore. It is a punishment as terrible as the one Zeus had inflicted on Tantalus, who, prey to hunger and thirst, could not access the food and water that was before his eyes. But still he suffered in the fresh air.

Boris did not pay attention to the vulgarity of the master and not knowing what to answer, he just shrugged and murmured with obvious clumsiness:

— Master, even the fruits, when the season is past, end up rotting on the branches of their trees. It's the law of life: nothing lasts forever in the terrestrial world...

— You'd better turn your tongue seven times in your mouth before talking! I'm tired of listening to your stupidities! —The master retorted hoarsely— I only want to get out of here, and you'll help me!

The voice of Polyus had taken threatening accents. So, Boris hesitated:

— How can I help you, master? As you rightly said, I am not Jesus, just as you are not Lazarus. And our current science does not know how to rejuvenate a body. Do you think that fountains of youth and other youth elixirs of folk tales actually exist? Or do you want me to invoke the Devil? And even if I get there, do you believe that the Devil needs your ugly and depraved soul so much that he would accept to offer you immortality in exchange for it?

– Are you making fun of me? –The old man cried furiously, straightening himself up.

As the master stared at him with an evil glow in his eyes, Boris suddenly felt a familiar pain assail his face. He then recalled an unhappy memory: at Avignon, during the Sabbath of the wizards, he was punished by the chief adviser of secret of the present President Jacques. Her name was Rosa but was nicknamed by the wizards "Thorn of Rose", she could become sharp in words, but also curses.

Sorcerers and witches came by plane from all over Europe and around the world to meet in Avignon for the solstice. It was before this assembly that because of an awkward word he had suffered the wrath of Rosa. He had felt, for the first time, this strange pain, as if a multitude of needles sank into his face.

Since that evening, on for some years now, he had the impression that a spell had infiltrated into him, as if a larva with an insatiable appetite was slowly nibbling at his soul. He felt his powers were diminishing, and he could do nothing against this curse. And today with it was the grand master who was inflicting this punishment on him: he had the sensation that beams of magic rays penetrated all the pores of the skin of his face. However, Boris did not see what he had said a bad witch to Rose, since he was very drunk then. And this time, it must be said that he had swallowed a good amount of alcohol before coming to visit the master.

Perhaps due to the alcohol had it a little too loose the tongue... It is not for nothing that one says: "What the sober holds to the heart is on the language of the drinker." Boris began to panic and tried to find excuses and to be forgiven for his lack of tact. Despite his efforts, his thoughts were too confused for him to find a credible justification. Everything was confused in his head: the words of his mother tongue were mixed with those in French, and he could not formulate any intelligible sentence. But suddenly, thank God, the old fool lay down and rested his head on his comfortable pillow. And, as if nothing had happened, he said to Boris in a calm voice:

– Do you think you know what souls please Lucifer? And do you think you know better than me what to do to get out of this situation? Margot will help you accomplish your mission.

– Margot? —Boris wondered, who did not see how this buxom young woman could be useful to get in touch with Lucifer, because it was the delusional plan that seemed to have fomented the master.

– Yes, Margot is my novice and even if she is no longer a virgin, her soul is pure. You see, I consider her as my goddess.

Boris could not help but let go of one more stupid thing:

– Master, you must be one hundred years older than her! I doubt that she lost her virginity with you... So, do not let her raise her so quickly to the status of goddess!

Understanding the impertinence of his words, Boris immediately pulled himself together and added:

– As for Lucifer, I must admit that I do not know much about him. I am well aware that popular imagery and priests draw us a completely wacky portrait of the Devil.

Contrary to his countenance, Boris looked at the grand master and saw that his last reply had calmed the anger that had seemed to have seized the old man again. If his left eye, blind and dull, expressed no emotion, his right eye, which saw perfectly, seemed to light up and stared with interest Boris. Also, the latter decided to drive the nail and declared, putting all his heart:

— Master, I swear to God that I did not want to offend you! I never laugh at poor and sick people and I will never have the idea of making fun of you, the great master of incomparable power, at the risk of seeing me slain on the spot. Alas, I often find it difficult to restrain my talkative character. This has been the case since my childhood: caustic words escape me and sometimes hurt people. But, if I can do anything to help you, you can count on me. Ask me what you want. And if I have to get Lucifer out of hell by pulling him by the horns, I'll do it! Go ahead, tell me what my mission is.

Boris preferred to stop there because he wondered if he had gone too far in his remarks. And if the lord of hell really existed? He had no desire to confront him! He had at first thought of a delirium of a dying old man, but Polyus, although he had not yet revealed his plan, seemed to have in mind to invoke the Devil himself. In any case, he had not contradicted Boris when he had made this assumption...

This man was dangerous, and Boris must not forget it. Suddenly, he remembered the presence of the Princess Jeanne, whom he had neglected, all busy as he was in quarreling with the master. He turned around and saw her, sitting on a plastic chair, all shaking, and displaying a frightened face. If she could hide in the closet, no doubt she would! Her uncontrolled thrills made her occasionally rise slightly from her chair, as if she were sitting on a bed of nails. Boris says to himself:

"Her face looks so horrified that it feels as though she's plunged it into the boiling water of a cast iron cauldron, or she's wearing a grimacing mask of ancient theater. She was clearly frightened by my insolent behavior and rudeness of words that I said to the great master of the Freemasons of the world. And now she is afraid by the words of the master of the masons or his reaction to my comments..."

Boris thought she was going to faint, but Princess Jeanne pulled herself together and managed to adopt a more normal attitude. At that moment, the master spoke calmly:

– My friend, Margot will give you the keys to my apartment in Cannes. You can settle there, the time you accomplish your mission. But I will ask you not to bring women home! You'll have to search my library to find the old book that describe the ritual that invokes Lucifer and the demons of hell. Boris blanched: he was now certain that he was not mistaken about the intentions of the master.

– Do not make that face! –The Polyus reared– I'll pay you for this job. As I'm stuck in this shabby retirement home, I can not do it myself. And Margot has to take care of me. So, as soon as you find them, you will bring me the old book here. I must admit that you inspire me with sympathy. You remind me when I was young: I was as insolent and impertinent as you!

At these words, he gave a straightforward smile as if he remembered something pleasant, and which put Boris in confidence.

However, this mission told him nothing of value, and he hoped that the reward promised by the master would be consistent, and he told him openly:

— Master, I will do my best to bring you satisfaction but I hope that you will keep your word and that the reward you have spoken to me will be up to the risks that I will take. I must admit that I am not very enthusiastic about putting my nose in the business of the Devil...

There was a certain weariness in Boris's words. He wanted to get out of this room that stank of death and old age. Admittedly, the displayed powerlessness of the master annoyed him, but the presence of this old skin of Jeanne also tired him. She was about twenty years older than him but was not what we could call a beauty, far from it! However, his excess testosterone pushed him very often to kiss, not without having drunk a few glasses of Armagnac beforehand, just to forget the ugliness of his partner. Moreover, each time, he took care to put a bottle of brandy on the bedside table, in case he had a moment of lucidity during their animal couplings. For there was nothing tender in their relationship.

Under her apparent coldness, Princess Jeanne turned out to be a real fury in bed! She urged him to be more violent in sexual acts with her. And when he rudely penetrated her at the open window, the Princess Jeanne screamed the words in Russian in all of Monaco, and at the end of the sexual act she drank a full glass of vodka Smirnoff! Of course, that all

Monaco had to hear because Jeanne's apartment was not far from the princely residence and Boris was happy to imagine that these illustrious neighbors heard Princess Jeanne shouting with lecherous words! Sometimes he imagined very funny scenes in which the prince of the Rock asked his butler to close the windows of his room to stop hearing Jeanne's groans of pleasure. Of course, Boris could no longer continue his vulgar relationship with the Princess Jeanne, to whom he experienced a strong disgust. And he had to put as much distance as possible between him and this shameless old woman. Finally, this forced stay in Cannes might be a good reason to say goodbye to always with the princess. Moreover, the master reminded him of his mission by saying:

— You should find, under the bed in my room, an old book that recounts the ritual of invoking demons. You have too absolutely!

Once again, Boris could not help interrupting Polyus:

— Master stop swinging like a cat-tail in March! You told me earlier that I had to look in the books of your library. And now you tell me that I will surely find one old book that lies in the dust under your bed and just to return it to you! What should I do specifically in your apartment? Be clearer in your instructions, if you want me to help you.

Fortunately for Boris, the ringing of the phone prevented the master from blaming him for his rudeness. Margot rushed to the phone, grabbed the phone and placed it against the master's ear. At once, the thunderous voice of President Jacques was heard; he spoke so loudly that everyone in the room could hear him.

– My master, –the president said– rumors are circulating that you accuse me of having shut you up in an asylum! While I managed to find you a place in this beautiful retirement home, where there are all the amenities, and where you are lavished the best care and where you can live happy days until your last breath…

Master Polyus, seeming to have a surge of energy, rudely interrupted this scoundrel of Jacques:

– Oh, my dear Jacques, I see that the words I uttered just now have very soon reached Paris! The cookies that your RG –services have installed in my room are decidedly very effective! These miserable voyeur insects carried my words on their wings to the Elysée! In vain and very prematurely you decided that it's time for the hyenas to shred the dead lion! But you omit one thing: I'm not dead yet!

After an anxious silence, President Jacques answered in an uncertain voice:

– Oh! Friend, how can you imagine that I have such bad intentions towards you? I know what I owe you: for thanks to you, I was able to climb to the top of the power of my country and now I work a lot for the good of the people!

– Oh yes, you have the pretension to think that I am your friend? Well, let me remind you that I am your master and that you are my slave! And I can assure you that your fall will not be long in coming: my best disciple, sinister Niko, will soon grab you your throne! Then it will be the people's court that will sentence you! Perhaps I will come to Paris myself to hang you by the gills with my own hands! –cried the master Polyus.

The wrinkled face of the grand master had turned a scarlet hue, so his white head with a wrinkled face resembled a withered red apple which was covered with the first snow. President Jacques hung up suddenly, and in chamber 7, there were sharp telephone beeps... By reflex, Boris looked around the chamber, looking for the "insects" that were watching them. He wondered if "these cookies" were equipped with cameras. Boris then felt a sincere compassion for the master and pointed out to him:

— You live here like a python in a vivarium! And is it really your tragic end was necessary to classify and expiate all the schemes you created when you were on top of power of the Masonic Lodge? In vain, the blood of so many innocent people have been poured out unnecessarily, and many countries find themselves bound hand and foot, under the thumb of your three-point brothers.

After the witch Rosa who cursed me, and after you who send me straight to hell, it is now President Jacques, the one who loves Mexican beer and the veal head with marbled, who will have me in the pollinator scope! And now, dashing guys special services around the world from the American CIA to the French DST will take care of me as a valuable sheep. In the past, the girls of MI6 gave me a hard time, and in this situation I would have preferred to deal with girls again!

— As long as I'm alive, Jacques will not be a problem! —The master said— And my son of a bitch Niko shouldn't give you any problems. Although, I can not vouch for him! Having said all this, master he stopped his sentence. His face froze in a grimace of pain and, seeming to lose his last strength, he slumped, inert, on the sheets of immaculate whiteness of his bed. A measuring device, connected to the master's chest, emitted an ominous beep. What caused a terrible stir in a nursing home and a crowd of people dressed in white robes rushed into ward number 7.

These doctors pounced like kites on the poor body of the grand master. Taking advantage of the great panic, Boris and Princess Jeanne ran out of the chamber in English without saying goodbye. But when he had reached the door, Boris met the green gaze of the beautiful Margot who, under his chestnut fringe, stared intently at him, as if to attract his attention.

"The beautiful witch that's here!" – He thought as she walked in his direction. Arrived at his height, Margot slipped into his hands a bunch of keys and a piece of paper. Then, without saying a word, she kissed him on the lips. As the saying goes, "For a mad dog, seven nautical miles is not a long detour! " Also, the same day, Boris went to Cannes, where he settled in the apartment of the master of the Masonic Lodge of the Rose-Cross. Disinterested in old book, he tasted the alcoholic beverages concealed in the master's cellar. He said to himself, not without pleasure, that every milliliter of these vintages should be worth at least a gram of pure gold.

After tasting the divine nectar from the time of Napoleon Bonaparte, Boris collapsed dead, and did not regain consciousness until the next day at noon. With great difficulty, regaining your consciousness, he then confronted with a dilemma, shared between his desire to have a good time and his conscience which dictated him to carry out the orders that

Polyus had given him: in other words, either he resumed his tasting of the alcoholic treasures of the grand master, or dive headlong into the dust of old books. While he was still thinking about what should do, it seemed to him that the bottles of old wine had suddenly turned into a line of soldiers. on a military parade ground, ready to serve their country at the risk of their lives. Therefore, Boris decided he would honor his word and bring his old books back to the master, if he was still alive. He began by looking under the bed of the room, where he found, indeed, a old book. Then he went to the library, which was full of a bunch of old books. He paled at the magnitude of the task that awaited him. How was he going to find the good books? As he flipped through the books without enthusiasm, he remembered that Margot had given him a piece of paper, which he had not yet read. Rummaging in his pockets, he found him and read the message. The young novice had made a list of all the books he had to bring back! Relieved, he undertook to gather all the works indicated. Once his task was accomplished, he decided to return immediately to the retirement home to bring the books to the grand master as quickly as possible. The days of Polyus were numbered, and he had already lost enough time the day before... No sooner had he arrived in front of the retirement home that he regretted his eagerness fulfill your duty to the dying Magister. In front of the main entrance to the building with a shabby facade, where President Jacques had locked up the grand master, two agents of the DST came at once to meet Boris and told him the tragic news: the great master Polyus was dead!

Despite the fact that poor Boris was still shocked by this announcement, they threatened him and jostled him a bit so that are demanding he will give them the keys to the apartment of the old Magister. Not having the means to stand up to these two agents, he had no choice but to give in, and handed them the keys.

He thought with a pain in his heart for all the bottles of great vintages he had left untouched in a beautiful apartment, and which now surely these two gorillas from the secret service will drink to his health!

Such a waste! He screamed in despair, both for the nectar of the gods that he would not have the opportunity to taste but for his sadness at the death of his master who will never again pay him for devotion to fulfilling a sense of duty! Tears rolled down his cheeks and a lot of thoughts jostled in his mind, so that he was dizzy and lost consciousness.

When he came back to him, the two agents were leaning over him, and they helped him up. Obviously, his tears of despair had touched the heart, though dry, of the two giants. One of them tapped Boris' shoulder, in a gesture of compassion.

Once the Russian was gone, he said to his sidekick:

– Who would have thought that a Russian could be so sensitive? Crying thus the death of an old man who, in any case, had already had his day... – And a careless gesture of the hand he wiped a lonely tear from his unshaven cheek!

Chapter 2 - The great magician

It was a terrible time! The dark sky, overhanging the seaside city, laid a moisture screed that penetrated every nook and cranny. Incessant bursts of the legendary mistral made passers-by bend and so shook palm trees and flowers, so that one felt that their sprawling roots would not resist and that this windy beast would tear them away off the ground. The beginning of March is usually not the most pleasant period on the French Riviera, but Boris paid no attention to humidity, fog or wind, so focused was he on the study from the ancient book of Lucifer. Indeed, Boris, for almost a month, worked hard to study the old book he had recovered in the master's apartment. It was Margot who had inspired him to continue his mission, despite the death of the master, because she wanted them to perform the ritual of invoking Satan anyway. She had convinced him by saying that before his death, the master had placed his trust in Boris and that the latter had to be worthy of a high degree of trust. Thus, Margot and Boris spent a lot of time together. The beautiful novice of the late master helped Boris to decipher the abstruse terms of the old book and introduced him to spiritual practices!

— ... so, you, my dear Boris, might attain a "higher degree of wisdom!" —she told him and gently stroked his face!

Boris sometimes had the impression of being in the very heart of the secret archives of the Vatican, to look at age-old book, which for many centuries was covered with mold and dust, and which revealed to him an ancestral knowledge. If the beautiful Margot was of great help in her learning of magical rituals and understanding of the mysteries of creation, she was also an excellent initiator and a great science connoisseur of the things of love, true love! Their noble sex lessons had nothing to do with bestial antics he picked up with Princess Jeanne. Margot made him gradually understand what a real relationship between a man and a woman was. It reminded him of values of respect and kindness that our modern times forget all too often. Every afternoon, Boris waited impatiently to find Margot, and like a good student he always wanted to receive his lesson of the day. The magic exercises and the amorous hugs overlapped and intertwined to form a their happy daily life. Like what Master Polyus had told him, Boris now considered Margot a goddess, that of love: she was his Venus. He could not bear the idea that she could be treated as a servant, humiliated by pompous Freemasons who took themselves for the masters of the world in their underground catacombs. Often, as he was going to bed, he was repeating himself like a mantra of words that resounded so sweetly in his mind:

"What is more beautiful in this world than the magic of love?"

During this very hectic time for him, a deep sense of love filled his fevered mind constantly. This it's a sweet sensation warmed his carnal envelope as well as his immortal soul and rekindled in him the flame of hope to know happiness. He simply resumed his taste for life. Indeed, despite the frightening side of his mission, life no longer seemed to Boris dark and monotonous. Margot's arrival in his life was like a flash of light in the deep darkness, and this flash had extended to form a luminous well at the end of the dark tunnel in which he had been too long blindly advanced straying very often from his great destiny — to be an omnipotent magician!

Margot had, in a way, set him on the right path, guiding him faithfully so that he would come out of that hopeless gulf in which he had locked himself up, like many unhappy bourgeois who yield to tempting temptations and excesses of this materialistic world.

After a month of intense study and practice, Boris gained confidence and achieved a level of magical knowledge sufficient to complete the Lucifer Summoning ritual. It was no longer a question of rejuvenating the master to prolong his life, but of resurrecting him from the dead. Boris had however often criticized the Utopian and delusional ideas of the great Polyus master. But now that he had been able to try the rituals of witchcraft, in spite of the disgust he felt for manipulating bats, rotten fingers, and other unsavory things, he told himself that the master's plan could actually work. He and Margot had therefore decided to perform the ritual on the night of March

12 to 13, 2005, at the bus station of the city of Cannes, where Boris worked as a guard.

He intended to take advantage of this intense moment of magic to cast a spell that would rid him of the curse that the old witch Rose had thrown at him in Avignon. During all his learning, he had felt the weight of this spell that poisoned his soul. He was anxious to be there and to honor the promises he made to Master Polyus before he died. Margot also showed a lot of impatience, and as the fateful date drew closer, she showed increased frenzy, both in her magical lessons and in her love affairs. She kept telling Boris that she wanted the magical ritual to succeed. Boris could only bend to the demands of his beloved because, as they say, "What a woman wants, God wants!"

Thus, the magician had decided to give himself fully to the fulfillment of his magical obligations, and thereby he tripled his magical abilities the study of the books of the master and bewitched of his mistress by the sensual caresses. He had to at any cost pull the Devil from his lair, although he only had the books from the dying master! Since he promised to help the master and even to go to hell himself to bring back Lucifer... At the time, he had thought that he was speaking there a simple joke intended to mollify Polyus, which he had somewhat irritated, but now he thought that this cynical joke took the air of prediction... At times, Boris suspected that Margot was so zealous to work for other reasons than honoring her allegiance to the master. Perhaps even his desire to bring back the master to life was motivated by the secret design to marry Polyus, which would allow her, the young novice, to sit down in the Masonic Lodge, this huge canvas of the spider that the master, like a black arachnid, had woven during his long life. It would be a great climb for Margot: she would become the lieutenant of the general with stellar epaulet! Had Margot been so considerate and kind to the magician, both in his witchcraft lessons and in the display of his charms, for the sole purpose of using the magical powers of Boris, in order to get his way? Boris refused to believe it and quickly swept away these dark ideas. The novice of the master had allowed him to discover a fascinating world, unknown to ordinary mortals; he could not believe that she had brought him to this point of knowledge of black magic by mere malice. It must be said that the beautiful Margot, during her initiation, repeated to Boris incessantly that she was impressed by her power, so that the magician had reached an excessive degree of self-confidence, which bordered on narcissism. Comforted in his vanity by his lover, he sometimes took himself for the most powerful magician of this world. Sometimes even when he looked at himself in the mirror, he thought he saw in his reflection, wide demon wings open on his back. Did he believe himself stronger than Satan himself? In one of Dostoevsky's novels, a poor student named Raskolnikov, weary of his miserable life and persuaded to be a "superman" like his model Napoleon, decides to kill an old pawnbroker with an axe so to steal it. He thinks he has the right to kill, given the superiority with which he believes himself endowed.

But once his wicked dream is completed, he will regret his act for the rest of his life. Unlike the hero of the novel

Dostoevsky, Boris did not intend to kill, but too would want to prove his omnipotence, by making a pact with the Devil, like Faust, in order to bring the great master out of hell. If he did, he would be even stronger than Napoleon!

A few days before the magic ritual, a question came to torment the mind of Boris: why did the secret agents of President Jacques take the keys of the master's apartment? Could the answer to this question be found in the French proverb "Look for the woman"? And the woman he was thinking of was obviously Margot, who could not ignore the actions of the agents. But why would she want to prevent him from accessing to the apartment of the deceased master?

Certainly, the cellar of the master housed many precious spirits for which Boris had a strong inclination. But this did not prevent Margot from regularly bringing Boris bottles of luxury alcoholic drinks confirming the veracity of the saying: "A nightingale does not feed on songs." Boris came to the conclusion that Margot did not want to deprive him of his passion for luxury wine, but she barred the keys to the apartment to control his alcohol consumption. And in this, Boris judged that it was in his right because, if he had access to the master's cellar, no doubt he would have spent more time in the alcohol than in the books! And that would have hurt their mission. Boris, prone to self-criticism, readily admitted that he could not have advanced so fast in mastering the magical forces if he had been drunk every day. However, in his dreams, he often saw himself in the master's elegant apartment, happily opening - with the help of a stainless-steel corkscrew and the ivory handle - lots of bottles of vintage wine, one after the other. But each time, as soon as he woke up, he chased these tempting ghosts silently repeating:

"Bad geniuses get out of my mind!"

On the appointed day, around eleven o'clock in the evening, when the last bus drivers left the bus station for their home, Boris remained in his watch-room and waited patiently for the beautiful Margot, who was to bring her all the necessary things the rite of witchcraft. But for a reason he did not know, she was late, which only increased his impatience to see her again.

His love for this woman was turning more and more into an obsession; he could not bear to be separated from her for too long and was ready for anything for her... even to dive into the abysses of hell to catch Lucifer in his magic nets like a fish, although it was to be feared that their evening business is more dangerous than a fishing trip! On the other side of the window of his box, the weather, once again, was appalling. Boris, alone in his sentry box, was beginning to worry about not seeing Margot arrive. Suddenly, the rain intensified, a flash of light illuminated the night sky with a dazzling zigzag and a roar of thunder echoed through the night. At the same moment, the door of the box opened abruptly, and Margot, dressed in a black and red coat, appeared before the dazzled eyes of Boris. The latter, all to his happiness to find his beloved, rushed to her and took her in his arms, covering her with kisses and malicious caresses. But Margot calmed her lover's ardor by pushing him gently away and saying:

— Boris, we'll do what you're thinking about later! For the moment, we must hurry. We are late!

Bewitched by the divine voice of his mistress, Boris let her away from him, not without regret, and Margot began to take out of her bag the objects necessary to perform the ritual. Boris looked with interest at the ritual trinkets that Margot was lining up on the table. The aesthete that he was particularly appreciated an old bowl made of gold and silver with, finely carved on its outer surface, a scene representing devils performing an infernal dance. Then, in a clever and professional gesture, he took in his hand a knife with a curved blade that was to be made of Damascus steel because it shone with a pretty moire blue.

But of all the things that Margot had arranged on the table, the ones that attracted Boris's attention the most were several bottles of irregular shape.

"These bottles may contain delicious wine from the master's cellar." – He thought, thirsty and he politely suggested to his beloved:

– Margot, my throat is dry. Maybe I could drink a glass of wine before we get to magical work? In addition, it will give me courage!

Margot ignored Boris's suggestion and continued, as if she had heard nothing, to arrange the last ritual objects on the table she had previously covered with a black cloth. She finished her installation by carefully placing golden candelabras. Within a few minutes, Margot had transformed the wretched guardroom of the bus station into a real witch room. Although it did not have the haunting atmosphere of a sacred grotto or an ornamented temple, this small room would suit their nocturnal ceremonial. After all, it is well-known that what matters is the candy and not the wrapper that envelops it!

For his part, Boris took Margot's silence for a consent to his request to drink old wine well before they began, so to conjure he grabbed a bottle and filled the goblets with wine. He was well aware that this witchcraft ritual could take a bad turn, but as the old saying goes: "He who risks his life thinks that the sea is knee-high."

When the clock struck midnight, everything was ready to begin the ritual: the wooden table, covered with a black cloth embroidered with golden Masonic symbols, would serve as an altar to Margot and the magician. Both were determined to go all the way until the desired result. Boris then grabbed Polyus' Old book, which he had brought with him and placed them on the table in front of the seven-branched tree-shaped candelabra so that they could read the magic formulas in the faint light of the candles.

Certainly, Margot's presence at his side reassured Boris, but he was a little worried about having to cut the palm of his left hand with the ritual knife.

He knew that this blood donation was necessary for the success of the ceremonial, because the powers of the other world like leeches caught the smell of fresh human blood. While Boris was trying to prepare himself mentally for the pain that awaited him, like a boxer before a fight, the beautiful Margot suddenly turned to him and declared in a solemn voice as if she were preaching in front of him as if in front of a huge audience:

– Ô great magician Boris, accept the sincere greetings of Grand Master Polyus. He offers you a powerful gift, that of the curse, that will make you one of the greatest wizards in the world! Due to his poor state of health, my teacher is not able to preside at this ceremony. Therefore, you will replace it.

"But is not Polyus already in the kingdom of the dead?" – Boris wondered but he did not share his thoughts with Margot, because this news was so unexpected that he gasped in surprise. In addition, for inexplicable reasons, his tongue seemed to be wooden, which did not allow him to say anything at all. He remembered the first words of John's Gospel: "In the beginning was the Word, and the Word was with God, and the Word was God."

In other words, it was through the word that God made creation and life appear. And from this it was clear that the Creator himself once thoughtlessly, thanks to only one stupidly stupid word, created the Earth with all the still abundant flora and fauna living on it. At times, Boris himself cruelly scolded himself for the thoughtlessness of some of his statements, but quickly calmed down with the thought: "If the Creator himself chatted at first, and then he thought, what claims could there be to me at all?" But at that moment, when for the first time in his life he tried to think something over before saying. Because the moment was too important for him to commit an strange act. For if he was not to create life, but on this night he will be forced to resurrect the already dead creation of God and for this to call the Devil from hell. And for the first time in his life, when Boris decided first to think, and then to say... Margo did not allow him to do this and literally rushed at him and kissed him passionately on the lips. The magician then felt a magical energy coming out of Margot's soft lips which began to penetrate him like some bitter nectar. The magic fluid was so powerful that Boris was dizzy and stuck in place.

"Finally you have received the gift of the curse!" —Margot said, as she pulled away from him.

— This pervert of Polyus put his filthy mouth on Margot's beautiful lips to transfer this terrible energy to her? —It was the first thing that came to Boris' mind, as his dizziness faded, and he regained his senses a little.

— This is so disgusting! — He exclaimed, before spitting on the floor, disgusted at the idea of exchanging fluids with the old master who, the last time he had seen it, gave off a terrible odor of putrefaction.

— Um yes! —Margot mumbled— He had to find a way to give you the gift.

— Polyus is not dead? —Boris asked.

This question burned his lips, and he could not hold it back any longer.

— Indeed, my master is still alive! —Margot said— But the doctors plunged him into an artificial coma. He sometimes comes back to him, shouts the word "Ritual!" And falls back into a deep sleep. That's how I realized that we had to do the ritual all the same. I had to insist that the doctors agree to wake him up for a few minutes so that he gives me his instructions and Magical Gift of Curse so that I can transmit it to you later.

— Why did you let me believe he was dead? —Boris exclaimed— I've been crying for a month! Besides, I know that it was you who asked the agents of President Jacques to take me the keys of the master's apartment! Do you know that there were, in his cellars, exceptional drinks, especially a cognac Napoleon I? Because of you, I could not even drink a glass in memory of the master!

Everything was mixed in Boris's mind and it was all over, because the great gift of the curse began to penetrate the soul of the Magus and therefore the offended lover could not put his thoughts in order or to express them.

— My master is still alive! —Margot said with an expression of genuine grief on the face— But death can strike him at any moment. We can not linger any longer; it would be fatal for him. The fact that Polyus is not quite dead yet will facilitate the ritual, but we have no time to lose!

She had uttered these words without compassion for Boris and it seemed that she was not ashamed of the fact that she had so cruelly deceived him - the Great Magician! Boris remained silent for he felt humiliated, betrayed, and insulted by the one he loved. She had given him a kiss of Judas! Now, Boris could not go back, because he promised to bring the work started to its logical conclusion.

— The master explained to me —Margot continued— that since he is still alive in between two worlds, we don't need to invoke Lucifer himself. We can call on a simple demon. It will be less dangerous. To do this, it is enough to cast less strong spells, by pouring less blood than we had planned.

Boris listened while continuing to drink wine. The alcohol was starting to make an pleasant effect on his psyche., but he could not help but ask his mistress:

— Are the secret service agents of Jacques Sly aware of what we are going to do?

— I do not think so. —Margot said— Otherwise they would have intervened to prevent us from bringing Polyus back to life.

— You still speak as if the master were dead! —Boris stammered.

— He already has one foot in the grave! —The beautiful novice retorted— the President Jacques has instructed Niko Sinister so that the men of the counterintelligence watch closely the grand master and while these fools are watching him, we will perform this ritual here in complete safety. I'm suspicious of this Niko for if he learns what we're about to do, he might send us a whole battalion of special forces! For now, our plan does not seem to have been discovered, so let's go!

In turn, Boris understood the reason why President Jacques had to prevent the revival of the great Master at any price.

The immense power of Polyus, who held many world leaders under his thumb, now was in him... So, the magician did not mind when Margot invited him to set himself up to begin the ceremony.

First thing Margot poured the contents of a vial into a cup: it was the black venous blood of the great master, whom she had herself taken from a vein of Polyus. She repeated to Boris that the fact that it was fresh blood, from a body still alive and not from a corpse, was going to make it easier for them. The two acolytes took each other's hands, then the magician opened one of the Old book he had brought back and read aloud a ceremonial opening spell. Margot grabbed the ritual knife and sliced the palm of her hand lightly, pouring only a few drops of blood into the cup that already contained the blood of the great master. Then she handed the knife to Boris, who seized it and carelessly made a long and deep incision in the palm of his left hand. He screamed in pain and poured a large amount of blood into the same cup.

– Not too much! –Margot stopped him– Do you want to bring Satan to our world?! I hope you did not put too much blood or the more you spill it, the bigger the demon will be.

In theory, the mixture of their three bloods, that of the master, of Margot and Boris, would make the demon that to be linked to them three and should answer their request and fulfill all their wishes.

But the more powerful he is, the harder it would be to master. And it was something like the bridling of a wild stallion. Margot looked at Boris reproachfully, then focused on the ritual again. She poured into two skulls set with silver and precious stones the contents of one of the bottles of wine she had brought. Then, with a graceful gesture, she removed her black dress, revealing her body completely naked. They arrived at the most enjoyable part of the ritual for Boris: he had to mate with Margot so that it turns into succubus, at least during the ceremony, to attract one of the demons of hell, whose lust is one of the favorite vices. While Margot poured a nauseating potion into the cup and mixed it with the blood of the three partners, Boris eyed Margot's skin, white as snow, with a lecherous look.

Margot looked like a porcelain doll. Boris also stripped to the goal and began rubbing his male device on Margot's buttocks, who continued to mix the potion. Then Margot recited a formula in a language unknown to ordinary mortals, which resembled the Chaldean. Boris began to caress the generous forms of Margot, who was gradually entering an erotic trance. The gorgeous and very seductive beauty leaned forward and went on all fours, like a panther, to offer his beautiful ass to Boris. The latter did not pray and began to penetrate deeply his mistress, who continued to murmur incomprehensible words. Boris could not refrain from thinking, jubilant, that the great master, in his semi-unconsciousness, was enraged at the idea that Boris was giving pleasure to the beautiful Margot in his place! This thought gave even more to Boris, who tried to keep Margot's excitement at its height, at the peak of this ecstasy.

The great magician grabbed one of the skulls that Margot had filled with wine and emptied it in one go, before handing the second skull to Margot, who also drank the wine greedily. Boris then had a thought that could easily have been attributed to Mephistopheles:

"The wine always makes you drunk and the women are always full of temptations!"

The beautiful Margot shouted with pleasure. At the same moment, the cup filled with blood and potion began to shake slightly. The mixture, illuminated by the flames of the candelabra, seemed to escape from the chalice, like smoke, and began to take the form of a human face with two horns. Boris thought it was a good sign and that the ritual was working. Also, he decided to open another bottle of wine and drank a large swig, before encouraging his partner in a peremptory tone that emphasized his dominance in this ritual:

– Do not try to resist the demon of hell! You must turn into a succubus to attract the devil, because he will want to abuse you like an incubus. At that moment, you will be able to catch it grabbing harder for his astral penis. That's what is written in magic books.

– Yes, I know! –Margot interrupted in an irritated voice– Enough talk! Stop drinking wine and take care of me!

– Woman, by what right do you give me orders? –Boris answered brusquely– I know what I have to do, and you have to submit to me! So, stop saying nonsense, because my desire for you might faint. And, to perform the ritual, it is important that my manhood does not weaken. I guess you would not want to be responsible for the failure of the ceremony...

With these words, Boris penetrated her with his penis even more violently, and Margot groaned with ecstasy, which was mixed with the words of the formula in the old language that she continued to chant in a low voice. Suddenly, outside, the rain redoubled and the wind became stronger. Boris even heard the displeased mutter of the Mediterranean Sea, not far from there, unleashing itself in furious waves. The horned form that floated in the air became more and more precise.

In addition to the clatter of raging outside, incantations and groans from Margot, Boris heard incomprehensible whispers in his head. He had the impression that his skull was going to burst, so much was the noise so oppressive. But the magician did not falter so much and continued to make love to Margot in regular back and forth. And when the fully formed paranormal face of the demon that flickered slightly in the air opened the fanged mouth, Boris thought it was time to cast the spell he had memorized in anticipation of this ritual. He pronounced the formula with a solemn voice. At the same moment, he saw Margot's beautiful body, whose white back sparkled in the candlelight, twisting like a snake, while his arms and legs moved in all directions. She seemed to convulse, and Boris wrapped her arms around her bust to support her as best he could. In doing so, he raised his head and saw the reflection of Margot's face in the window: her eyes seemed out, and his mouth was deformed into a large grin.

Suddenly, Margot threw her head back and uttered a heart-rending cry that ended in a dull, animal-like groan. Boris then burst into a nervous laugh, which he could not contain, as if he had smoked Himalayan weeds. This staging began to make Boris very uncomfortable, and he could not stop laughing, without knowing what caused his hilarity. Then, for fear of failing in his mission, Boris grabbed a new bottle of wine – a 1945 Mouton-Rothschild – and filled to the brim with a big cup made of skull.

This drink of the gods really turned out to be at a high level of quality, and, running down the throat of the great Magician, he was able to stop hysterical laughter. Boris continued to love Margot vigorously, and it must be admitted that he showed a great energy in the execution of his role in this very difficult ritual, the purpose of which was very noble!

He tried to ignore his mistress's moans and the voices he heard in his head, when he suddenly felt a pungent smell of sulfur. This nauseating smell reminded him of the hot springs of the Pyrenees, where he liked to go. The great magician thought, "Is it hell that smells so bad? Or is it the wine that starts making me lose my head? Because not only I have auditory hallucinations, but also my sense of smell seems to play tricks on me! Suddenly, he thought he saw a little squirrel-like animal appear in the room. Usually, after using several bottles of vodka, Russian people often saw such animals and among the Russian emigration talk about a squirrel was very popular and that were fashionable among Russian emigrants at that time.

He ran his hand over his eyes. The squirrel was no longer there. Did he have visions now? He realized then that the term "squirrel", in Russian, also referred to the "white fever". To chase away these bad thoughts, Boris poured another glass of wine into the skull-shaped cup; it was too good a vintage to drink at the bottleneck. As he swallowed his elixir, the magician thought:

"Apparently, this time I got drunk before seeing a little devil or I am having a bad dream but tomorrow everything will be fine!"

Suddenly, Margot shuddered and froze almost like she was attacked by tetanus because her beautiful body was paralyzed in a strange pose. Then, suddenly, a terrible spasm ran through his body. At the same time, the concrete walls of the box began to tremble like sheets stretched in the wind. The flames of the candles grew in size and took on a bright red hue. The beautiful novice in the throes of hysteria uttered wolf howls. The murmur in Boris's head became more intense so much so that he had the impression that his brain was boiling like chicken eggs that would be cooked in boiling water and that his cranial box like a glass in crystal was going to burst into a thousand pieces under the effect of sound waves.

Fortunately, when Margot's cries stopped, the magician's headache faltered. It was then that Boris realized that his left hand, which he had slashed with the ceremonial dagger, blew profusely. He grabbed his shirt, which he had thrown to the ground and wrapped it around his hand to stop the bleeding. The smell of blood mingled with the stench of magic potions and the sweet fragrance of Margot's Chanel perfume No. 5, which he continued to penetrate energetically.

This mixture of smells, associated with the sweat that trickled over the sensual body of the novice and the muscular one of the magician, was disgusting, so much so that Boris felt sick from it. He thought he was going to dump the contents of his stomach on Margot's back, but he managed to restrain himself. He noticed that the form of blood and potion, still floating in the air, now clearly resembled the horned face of Lucifer. The magician burst into irrepressible laughter at the thought that he had nearly vomited on the Devil himself! Unable to control his laughter, he could barely breathe, but he strove not to release the intensity of his thrusts in the privacy of his mistress who, after her screams, had dived into a silence total. Boris took another sip of wine, trying not to pay attention to the supernatural voices that continued to whisper in his head. Suddenly, Margot collapsed on the table. Boris had just enough time to push the ritual cup so that the head of his mistress, who banged against the wood of the table in a thump, did not bring down the precious chalice.

Seeing that Margot was not moving, the magician thought it was time for him to finish the sexual part of the ceremony. He intensified his back and forth in the body of his beloved and surrendered to enjoyment. As soon as he had discharged his male semen, which he had saved for three days in anticipation of the ritual, he felt a deep sense of relief and even the voices in his head fell silent. He wondered if Margot had not put any potion in the wine. He looked at his beloved with suspicion. At that moment, Margot regained consciousness and raised her head. She had a bruise on her forehead and was staring wide in front of her, a scene that remained invisible to Boris. In an exaggerated voice, Margot said to the magician:

— Do you see these ghostly shadows, with their long dresses and their hoods that hide their faces? They move and hold my master firmly by the wrists!

"Thank God, I do not see anything!" —Boris thought.

But suddenly, he heard crunches that echoed in his head, and bright circles appeared before his eyes. One of them, who glittered in an intense glow, seemed to approach Boris, who was dazzled. He could have said: "Amen! The phenomenon he was witnessing seemed to come from a supernatural power, but without understanding why, it was the word "Pass!" that came out, as if he had been in a poker tournament. Then he collapsed in his turn, unconscious. When Boris awoke, the first glimmers of dawn began to illuminate the interior of the box with their pale reflection. The wizard had a terrible headache, and his whole body was sore, as if he were under the wheels of a car.

Boris thought, desperate:

"The ritual did not work! The day rises, and the dark forces will join their kingdom of darkness. My colleague will not be long in arriving to take his turn. We must rid our entire from all this compromising bazaar and quickly clear the room".

He straightened up with difficulty and sat in a corner of the room. He then saw that Margot, still naked, was kneeling before the table and murmured in a monotone voice incomprehensible gibberish successive spells. He thought he could discern another voice, but he told himself that it was the alcohol that clouded his mind. Still, he was sure that what he experienced last night was real. Boris was about to tell Margot that they had to leave as soon as possible, when he suddenly saw a sort of diaphanous silhouette embracing Margot: the novice was not alone! But what was this strange form, that rubbed against his beloved? Margot and the ghostly figure seemed to perform a kind of dance. Boris's vision was troubled. "An infernal armband! Boris thought. The magician was dizzy, and as he felt faint, he heard Margot say:

– Okay! We accept!

Before Boris lost consciousness again, he had just enough time to catch a glimpse of Margot, who dressed quickly and ran away from the room, slamming the door like a farewell.

Immersed in the mists of a semi-unconsciousness, Boris tells himself that, contrary to what he had, thought the day before, he was not the one who dominated the novice: it was she who had used it all night and who was now throwing it away like a used condom. Boris did violence to regain his senses. He managed, not without difficulty, to get up and put on his pants, his shirt still wrapped around his injured hand. He began to clear the table of all ceremonial objects, which he put in a large bag.

As he finished putting the lodge back in order, a frightful thunderclap sounded sudden and lightning tore the sky. The siren of one of the buses parked in the parking lot began to scream.

Boris looked out the window and saw that the bus in question was on fire. Thinking that the vehicle had been hit by lightning, neither one nor two, he grabbed a fire extinguisher and rushed to the parking lot. Using ten fire extinguishers, Boris managed to extinguish the fire before it spread to other vehicles. The helpers soon arrived, as did Boris' colleagues, who were surprised to see him shirtless, with his bloody shirt around his hand. He told them that he had hurt himself by putting out the fire when one of the bus windows had exploded under the heat. Faced with these explanations, the helpers and his colleagues celebrated him as a hero; his intervention had averted a catastrophe. The firefighters, once they had completed their inspection of the incident, explained to Boris that, contrary to what he thought, it was not the lightning that caused the fire, but a short circuit created became ignition in the bus due to infiltration of rainwater in the electric shutter of the vehicle. Boris was somewhat relieved: he had believed for a moment that a supernatural power caused this fire! He retrieved his belongings from the box and headed for the locker rooms of the employees of the bus station. As he walked away, he turned around and noticed that the partially burned vehicle was decorated, on its periphery, with posters of Hollywood stars.

"The dream factory ignited! —Boris quipped, before continuing on continue your journey. Once in the locker room, the magician took a refreshing shower, then, using the products found in a first aid kit, he disinfected and bandaged the wound with his hand.

He took his civilian clothes in his locker and put them on. Finally, he returned to the guardroom to see how his colleague was doing; the fire had put the whole bus station in turmoil.

He looked at this little sentry box with a certain nostalgia; he had spent most of his nights there in recent months. After his days of magical study, this lodge everytime in the evening appeared to him like a sort of refuge. He ate there, drank and rested there. This time of respite allowed him to recharge his batteries, after the intense efforts he made for his learning of witchcraft. Boris would regret this place because he knew he would not come back... not after all he had been through that night. The great magician knew for sure that he would never return here.

He still remembered the sublime body of Margot which received great pleasure under his assault. The young woman, by its ardor and beauty, could satiate the sexual appetite of a whole battalion of soldiers, bring to life an army of the dead and even bring the Devil out of his dark den.

As he was about to leave the room, he saw under the table the ritual bowl, in which there remained a little potion, and a vial of holy water, which he had himself bought in the shop of religious articles from a Russian church, in case he had to fend off a demon from hell seduced by the talents of a beautiful sorceress. In his rush earlier, he must have forgotten to pick up these objects. Suddenly, the lodge phone rang and his colleague grabbed the phone and after hearing the message, repeated it to Boris: the director of the bus station wanted to see him on the report, about the fire.

Boris told his colleague that he could go to the principal's office and stay in the security booth until he returned. His colleague thanked him and hurried out of the room. Boris was able to take advantage of the absence of his colleague to recover the objects he had forgotten. He cleaned the cup with a little holy water and emptied the mixture under the porch of the security room. Then he stuffed the objects in his bag. His colleague had not returned yet and the magician thought he was going to wait for him in another room where the workers would usually drink coffee.

As he leaned over to get his bag, he was hit hard on the back of the neck. The blow was so brutal that he fell backwards and found himself sitting on the ground. He turned at once but saw no one. Who could have hit him? A little stunned, he saw on the horizon, above the shimmering water of the Mediterranean, a bright green dot: it was the planet Venus which shone, in the light of dawn, of a rare intensity.

Suddenly, beside the hut, where he had emptied what was left of the ritual cup, a diaphanous spectrum appeared out of nowhere. This strange creature, who seemed dressed in a dressing gown, reflected the first rays of the morning sun, straining the colors of the rainbow like a soap bubble. The ghost looked at Boris, leaning his translucent head to the side, and seemed as surprised as the wizard. He had to wonder what he was doing there, and Boris had no answer to give him. The latter had trouble putting a face on this figure because his head was so transparent that it was barely visible.

"Is it Lucifer?" —The magician wondered, somewhat frightened.

Boris suddenly came out of his stupefaction, stood up and ran to his car, parked in the parking lot. In the glove box, he took a disposable camera, in which there were still some shots to be made.

Boris wanted to immortalize this phenomenon and perhaps prove himself that he was not suffering from hallucinations. He returned to the ghost and had just enough time to take a picture because his colleague was coming back to him. Boris turned his head a fraction of a second to the latter who was challenging him, and when he looked back at the place where the spectrum was, it had almost completely disappeared. There were barely a few iridescent reflections that seemed to melt, like a snowman, under the rays of the sun. Boris's colleague, who came up to him, asked him what he was doing with his camera. A little caught off guard, Boris replied that he would like to be photographed in memory of the day he had managed to extinguish a fire. His colleague laughed and took the camera from his hands. Boris placed himself so that the spectrum appeared on the picture. His colleague took the picture, not noticing anything, just before the translucent form disappeared completely. Boris thanked his colleague and greeted him warmly. Then he went to his car and left the bus station. Disturbed by his long night of satanic orgy as well as by the ghostly apparition he had just witnessed, Boris had forgotten his bag containing the ceremonial objects under the porch of the guardhouse. But for the moment there was only one thing that worried him:

"What is the identity of the ghost that appeared to me? And what did he want?"

Perhaps the photos he took would give him some answers. Immediately, he went to a friend of his, who was a photographer.

The old man agreed to develop the film, and Boris accompanied him to the dark room. When the photographer developed the last two photos, he displayed a surprised look and scratched his head. He indicated to Boris a big bright spot on the first shot and another, less visible, next to the magician, on the second, which he described as "anomalies". The photographer examined the photos for a long time, before concluding:

– It's very strange all that! I do not see what could have caused these anomalies. This is the first time in my long career that I see something like this!

Meanwhile, Boris's colleague found the bag forgotten by Boris under the porch. When he opened it and found a lot of valuables, he thought it was the booty of a robbery and called the police. Two policemen came to retrieve the bag. Later, they searched their database for the origin of these strange objects. It was thus that the secret services were alerted. They immediately warned their superior, Niko Sinister, to whom had been informally entrusted the direction of a top-secret branch of the services of the RG. By order of the latter, special agents were sent to the guard room of the bus station where the ritual objects had been discovered.

After various analyzes, the experts concluded that a satanic ceremony had taken place in the guard room and that a breach had been opened between the world of the living and that of the dead, which was a clear violation of the country's security. Also, it was decided to destroy the guard box as soon as possible, and the bulldozers were not slow in doing their work. Then, the secret service chaplains purified the place by chanting prayers and pouring tons of holy water from the Grotto of Lourdes, where the Virgin Mary had appeared to young Bernadette.

Chapter 3 - The torments of the Homeless Poet and the first appearance of Voldemar

On the morning of March 21, 2005, the Saint-Nicolas church rose, majestic in the light of the bright rays of the Mediterranean sun. This masterpiece of early twentieth-century architecture was built by order of Tsar Nicholas II, in the street that was later renamed to his name and he himself was awarded the grateful church and awarded the title of Holy Great Martyr.

A young blue-eyed man, without special signs and tattoos, was sitting on a public bench in the garden, directly opposite the entrance to the church. It was Boris, the great magician. In the past, he was a lieutenant in the Soviet Union's Armed Forces Construction Battalion, which was disbanded in 1991, then a corporal of the French Foreign Legion. Ignoring the pious people who passed him by entering or leaving the church, he ate fried chicken with good appetite, whilst sipping a Guillotine, an unfiltered Belgian beer. He liked to come to this park, especially at lunch time, to enjoy the lush tropical vegetation and to feel closer to his native Russia, even though today he was there for another reason...

Boris suddenly broke away from the fried chicken as he saw one of his acquaintances: a middle-aged man with slanted eyes, tall, very thin and bald. This living mummy was heading for the church, and Boris, knowing the life-story this man, assumed that his friend already must have appealed to God more than once and lost a lot of weight due to the rejection of delicious food in the name of faith. This man was called Vadim Malevich. He was a poet emigrated from Russia. At the beginning of their meeting Boris called him "the Student" due to the fact that he read a lot of smart literature, then, later, Boris called him "the Homeless Poet", and very soon this nickname began to meet reality. Nevertheless, it had not always been so. Indeed, Vadim, having served for five years in the Foreign Legion, had first rented an apartment that was located on the outskirts of Nice, where he devoted himself to poetry. At that time, Boris also tried rhyme and discovered the literary works of the Homeless Poet. In turn the magician had been quick to give up the feather, so depressing was he to constantly linger over the vicissitudes of life! Whereas poor Vadim could not escape from the claws of his Muse and passion for writing idiotic poems took him away from the unresolved problems of life in civil society. So he smoked a lot of pipes full of Dutch-scented tobacco and by being plunged into a chimerical world, populated by the sublime words of Mandelstam and Brodsky, had disconnected from the realities of everyday life so much so that no longer paid rent. He was therefore expelled and found himself on the street. But fate had offered the poor man another chance, for he had found a job: a secretarial position for a Russian oligarch, Rashid

Selimovich Sardarov, who had just bought a sumptuous villa in Tanneron. This elegant mansion was located on a hill, overlooking an area of sixteen hectares of pine forest. Tucked into the Mimosa Valley and surrounded by the mountain ranges overlooking Cannes, to this day, this estate is becoming more beautiful every day thanks to the efforts of its new Russian owner and is already the best brothel for the richest Russian mafiosi, who have a good time there with the permission of the corrupt local authorities. Previously, this property had belonged to the famous Jewish writer Martin Gray. It was there that he had lost his family for the second time. Indeed, his Dutch wife and four children died in the fire of the mountains, in the autumn of 1970. In the distant past Martin Gray had lost his family for the first time during the Second World War: one hundred and ten members of his family lost their lives during this deadly conflict, including his mother and two brothers who were exterminated in the terrible gas chambers from Treblinka. During the same fatal period World history, a young man by the name of Joseph Ratzinger, enlisted by force as a volunteer, served in the ranks of the German DCA, which would not prevent him from becoming later the supreme leader of the Catholics, before giving up his pontifical function, probably discouraged by his futile struggle against corruption and pedophilia that gangrenes the Vatican and the Catholic Church.

But let us return to Martin Gray, who, despite these two dramas, found the strength to revive his life; having lost your another family in a fire, he remarried a third time and produced five more children. A married couple from the staff who lived and worked for a long time on the estate claimed that the owner of the villa had committed terrible wrongdoing from the field of pedophilia and molested in his pool a lot of minor children, and that the fire that had taken away his the second family was the punishment for his sins. This couple was not appreciated in the village, and the inhabitants did not give credence to their remarks, but personally, I will not question their exposure.

In any case, do not express mistrust to the words the accusations of this couple. Especially since many witnesses having stayed in the villa, reported disturbing phenomena, which may suggest the presence of avenging spirits. Among these witnesses, the Homeless Poet, who had worked for the new owner, was not stingy with scary stories. In particular, he said that every night ghosts wandered in the darkness of the park and demons appeared in the hearth of an old fireplace. He even supposed that these ghosts were at the origin of the terrible fire which had ravaged all the massif and that they had pushed, with their spectral hands, the family of Martin Gray in the flames. It must be said that, as strange as it is to say, if the greater part of the Tanneron forest was burned to ashes, the villa was spared; the family Martin Gray had been trapped while trying to escape by car. This villa, whose park had been arranged by Martin Gray, who had artistically and somewhat eccentric used to decorate of gravestones from Jewish cemeteries, had been bought by Rashid Selimovich, who hired the Homeless Poet as secretary.

The first months of work in the estate the Russian oligarch were the happiest of Vadim's life. In addition his former boss,

Andrey Russine, a graduate of the prestigious Moscow State Institute of International Relations, had lent him a small house, in which Vadim settled at the beginning of his service on the Russian oligarch.

Our Homeless Poet had, at that time, a decent salary and a comfortable home... until the day when everything had changed. Rashid Selimovich had accused Andrey Russine - an honest man in Vadim's opinion - of stealing a million and a half American dollars.

Bad people had forced Andrey Russine to flee and Vadim had to leave his home and had lost his job, because his friendly relations with Andrey Russine displeased the owner of the estate. So that's our poor Vadim becoming a new homeless! But Sophie, an employee of the estate with whom Vadim had a romantic relationship, and who had good relations with Rashid Selimovich, allegedly defended the Homeless Poet's cause. And thanks to this kind woman, the manor owner then allowed Vadim to moved to live at the stable; in exchange for this makeshift shelter, Vadim had to participate daily in the maintenance of the stables, and at night to protect them from strangers... without being paid, of course! Since then, the Homeless Poet lived in extreme poverty, having to do odd jobs to survive, in addition to his "forced volunteering" at the stables. However, he still hoped that Rashid Selimovich would one day offer him a job at the manor, this time paid. The manager of the estate of Baron Munchausen, a Frenchman named Marc Tirelle, told him moreover that when tensions had calmed down a little between Vadim and the rich businessman, he would try to convince the latter of to offer the homeless poet a decent job. But, as they say, "hope dies last", and the Homeless Poet could easily die from the illusions who supported his faith in justice and in humanity and decency. In fact, in this year 2005, the Homeless Poet had such an emaciated figure that one could only be surprised that he could still stand on his feet? He was exhausted and had nothing but skin on his bones. And it was at this same time that he began to have visual and auditory hallucinations. If at first he was somewhat disturbed, but eventually he got used to it and even got some comfort in these strange "presences" who persistently disturbed his blurred consciousness. Thirteen years later, in 2018, the Chinese Horoscope's Year of the Dog, the unfortunate poet, received another written refusal from Mr Mark Tyrrel - the estate manager Baron Munchausen, decided to seek medical treatment from psychiatrists to free him from those voices that constantly bothered him since 2005. That was what he would announce to Boris, in a telephone conversation on June 22, 2018.

This decision he was very hard to accept because, if some voices sometimes humiliated him and made him live a hell, then others brought him much joy, by recommending readings that allowed him to rise intellectually and spiritually, such as the works of Peter Teilhard of Chardin, Vladimir Vernadsky and Stanislav Grof, or the Tibetan Book of the Dead and the Veda. He was particularly interested in the experiences of impending death. All this might sound a bit mystical, but the Homeless Poet's interest in these subjects may have come from the fact that he himself came close to death in 2005, the Year of the Rooster on the Chinese calendar.

In fact, one day of that terrible year Vadim, by accident according to his words drank? caustic acid, used for cleaning the toilet. This made him very sick, and Sophie, his ex-girlfriend and lover, seeing him in such a worrisome state, told herself that it was perhaps the rats, who were in the stables, that had spread an infection. So she spoke to the head of the whole villa, by whose order were called brought in rodent extermination agents. They sprayed raticides everywhere, especially in the room where Vadim lived. None of his belongings were spared: his bench, his clothes, his dishes and even his stock of vegetables were impregnated with poison. But Vadim had not been made aware of poisoning specialists, and for several weeks he continued to live in this poisonous place and eat poisoned vegetables. And yet, he survived... When he learned that rat poison had been sprayed in his room, he thought that the acid he had drunk previously might have saved his life, by a kind of mithridatization.

This method involves ingesting small amounts of poison to be immunized. Russian spies know this process well: they could ingest a whole bucket of Novitchok, a very powerful poison, without even feeling smeared! This shed new light on the events of Salisbury in 2018...

But this poisoning case had not yet taken place at the meeting of Vadim and Boris, in March 2005, in front of the Saint-Nicolas Church and at that time the poet Homeless felt relatively good. It had been about three years since Boris had not seen the Homeless Poet, and he was somewhat shocked to see him so thin. The magician put aside a piece of delicious chicken, which he was ready to bite and called his friend, who was now on at the entrance to of the church:

– Vadim Malevich!

The Homeless Poet, surprised to be caught in this way suddenly, stuck his bald head deep into his shoulders. Then he glanced frightened all around him, before his tired eyes landed on Boris, who was smiling at him. The magician, who was still struggling to hold back the scathing remarks that came to his mind, said happily to the Homeless Poet:

– Since when do the Tatars frequent the Orthodox churches? Do not you have enough mosques?

Vadim, vexed, burst into flames immediately and replied scathingly:

– I'm Belarusian!

Boris knew that Vadim was an orphan and had spent all his childhood in Minsk. It was natural that he should consider himself a Belarusian. In the same way, Ivan, a black musician of the Foreign Legion Orchestra, called himself Russian, rightly, because he had been brought up in Moscow. However, Boris could not help finding in Vadim a certain resemblance to Chelubey, a Mongol warrior, immortalized by the famous painter Mikhail Avilov in his painting *Duel Peresvet with Chelubey at the Kulikovo Field.*

Not wanting to offend his friend any further, Boris retorted, conciliating:

– If a Russian peasant rubs me with sandpaper, he will turn into Tatar, but we do not need to rub a Belarusian to be Tatar!

This good word soothed the Homeless Poet. He approached a Boris with a faltering step and dropped onto the bench beside the magician.

— So, Vadim, everything is fine for you, as in the song "All is well beautiful marquise", even if I hope that you have not had the same misfortunes as those of this famous Marquise! —Boris joked.

But the magician did not have the pleasure of laughing at his joke because Vadim burst out with anger that he had probably retained for too long:

— That Caucasian donkey fired me! But thanks to Sophie, my ex-girlfriend, he allowed me to live in his stables.

Boris's face decomposed in a smile. The last time he saw Vadim the latter had a good job at the Baron Munchausen estate and conscientiously fulfilled the whims of the Russian billionaire. Things seemed finally to be all right for him... But, obviously, this respite had only been short-lived.

— Why were you fired? —Boris asked sympathetically— I know you enough to make sure you take your job seriously.

Vadim wiped a tear from his unshaven cheek, which he had accidentally let go, then explained in a sad voice:

— Two years ago, manager Marc Tirelle and I had to pick up the owner of the estate, Rashid Selimovich, at Nice Airport. But I had a setback and I arrived late. The Caucasian was furious and started screaming at me in front of everyone in the airport lobby. He told me that if I got on so well with my former boss, Andrey Russine, that he accused of embezzlement, it was because I too was a thief.

It made me angry and, without thinking, I said his: "If you really think I'm a thief, why do you keep me as a secretary? You would rather send me to hell! ".

He fired me on the spot and transferred to the stab:es! I should never have mentioned the Devil; it brought me bad luck! So, since then, I come here to pray to God and put a candle to Saint Nicholas, to make me forgive my sins.

– I find this story very strange: your boss fired you for a little argument, then finally he kindly allowed you to settle in the stables of his estate? —Boris wondered.

– I think that Rashid Selimovich was too angry... —Vadim replied— He hates Andrey Russine, and this same Andrey Russine is my friend. You understand? In addition... —Vadim hesitated— In addition, Marc Tirelle, the French manager, who is so nice that would not hurt a fly, told me that Rashid Selimovich has always had a preference for Yuri Kulachev, another of his employees, for if we are both former legionaries, he has more strength of character. And I can not contradict him because Yuri is competent and knows his job well. That's why this damn Caucasian gave it my place in the stables. But Yuri and Marc promised me that they would try to convince the boss forgive me for my insolence and re-hire me as secretary.

– I've heard a lot about this Yuri Kulachev. —Boris interrupted— He is a former athlete, a top swimmer from Moscow.

Russian legionnaires told that when he went on an run around the tropics, then he fixed lead weights to his ankles! They also said that in Guyana he did not seem to be suffering from the heat and could walk for hours under the hot sun, so much so that when his colleagues took a break in the shade and drank a beer, he refused to stop and told them not to drink beer but run with it in the woods and train. He also advised them to think about the future as well as what they would do in civilian life when they left the Legion. Despite his qualities, do you really think he will intervene in your favor with Rashid Selimovich? After all, he is the one who stole your work.

At this remark, Vadim stiffened and hurried to defend his former colleague:

— Yuri is a good man! When he says something, he does it!

Vadim thought for a moment and added:

— And then, Marc Tirelle gave me his word too! He is also a very decent person!

— Be careful not to trust too quickly good people, my friend! —Boris continued— Too polite people often conceal, in their affable manners, pernicious intentions. In his writings, Schopenhauer advises us to be wary of people who show too much kindness. But you, Vadim, are too naive: you only see the good in others, without trying to see their dark side. Leo Tolstoy, in his Tales for Children, teaches us that a tree trunk can be both straight and curved; it depends on which side you look at it! And it is for this reason that one must take the time to observe a person well before making a judgment on it by the external qualities of their behavior. Be careful of polite people!

Vadim did not answer, seeming to meditate on Boris' words. The magician wanting to know more about what had led his friend to be dismissed from his job as secretary, continued in a soft voice:

— Vadim, I admit that I am surprised that you arrived late at the airport. It does not look like you. You are always so punctual!

— I basically wasn't late! —Vadim exclaimed, as if he were hurt in his pride— Marc Tirelle and I arrived at the airport nearly two hours before the arrival of Rashid Selimovich. But while we were waiting for our boss, Marc received a message from the aircraft that was still in the middle of the road, telling him that our dear boss wanted his best assistant to be present when he arrive at the airport.

Marc thought about it and said in a very polite voice:

— Vadim, I can go get her assistant myself. But maybe you'd like to go? She's a very beautiful woman! And that would give you the opportunity to take a ride in Rashid Selimovich's luxurious car along the azur coast, and even in the company of a beautiful girl!

Vadim paused before and sighed deeply and with tears in his eyes he continued to speak nervously:

— You understand, don't you, what kind of girls are these assistants? They are very expensive prostitutes! But I do not throw the stone at Rashid Selimovich nor Marc Tirelle who made me go to get this girl. I am solely responsible because I have been weak. No sooner had Mark finished his sentence than I spun and ran headlong to the boss's car, a Cadillac! Certainly, I wanted to give satisfaction to my employer, but I must admit that I was dying to drive this car, along the coast, with a pretty girl by my side. And I can tell you that she was really beautiful, this assistant: my boss promised could have awarded her the title of Miss Russia! Tina Kandelaki, the Russian TV presenter, would have turned pale next to her! Oh, I did not have any misplaced intentions, believe me, but it's just nice to be in such good company. I had not been so happy since the cruise I made in Italy which I bought five years ago and I did not think that I would complicate my life like this with Rashid Selimovich's assistant.

"I already imagine the trap that closed on my poor Homeless Poet!" —Boris thought.

The magician smiled at his friend to encourage him to continue his story, which Vadim told with such passion, and the homeless poet continued to speak:

— When I arrived at the assistant's office, I told her of Rashid Selimovich's wish to see her at the airport. She agreed to come with me, but told me she needed to get ready. It is true that she was undressed and could not go out in this outfit. I told her that she had to hurry up, and she went to take a shower. I had to call and rush her several times. Each time, she replied that she will try to quickly finish taking a bath. When she finally came out of the bathroom, she wanted to have a cup of coffee. I almost despaired and already began to lose hope that this beauty would ever get to the airport!

She didn't even forget to sniff two thick tracks of "white snow". But when finally, we took the road, this beauty complained of nausea and asked me not to drive too fast. As soon as I accelerated a little, she began to moan and I had to go at the speed of a pedestrian. So I had no choice but to crawl like a turtle. As a result, we arrived late at the airport! And you know the rest: Rashid Selimovich, very angry, shouted at me and fired me!

"Marc Tirelle, who encourages this fool Vadim to go and get this girl in his place... The assistant who does everything so that they lose time... One would think that they have conspired for Vadim to get fired!" —Boris thought.

But the magician did not want to hurt the Homeless Poet by making him aware that he had been deceived by his boss. Boris also preferred to make the conversation more joyous:

— Vadim, I know you well and I know you say the truth when you say that you had no evil thoughts after you agreed to go get this girl! (Boris burst out laughing.) Remember, Vadim, the two happy girls Mimi and Lulu, the libertines we had met in a discotheque. Lulu had been harassing you a series of selective curses for two weeks because that evening you did not want to satisfy her desires and ran away from her without saying goodbye.

— Lulu? —Vadim asked— I do not remember this Lulu!

— How dare you forget Lulu? —Boris retorted— She was dark, very cute, with sparkling eyes and scarlet lips. It your friend Zozo who introduced you these two funny women. But the unbridled sexuality of Lulu embarrassed you and you refused to sleep with such a passionate woman!

— Oh yes, I remember! —Vadim exclaimed, hilarious— I had forgotten her name.

The two friends laughed as they thought back to that memorable evening. Then, Boris regained his seriousness and wanted to warn Vadim against the staff of the estate of Baron

Munchausen, who seemed to be playing with him a dangerous game. Carefully choosing every word, he told the Homeless Poet who was still laughing:

— Vadim, do you want to know what I really think of your misadventures?

Suddenly Boris paused because he noticed that a group of Russians bandits with a sinister look were watching them from a small distance. One of them approached the bench where Boris and Vadim were sitting and threw them a polite tone that sounded fake:

— My brothers, can I know what you are talking about?

Boris replied in the same tone:

— Well, brother, you will not believe me, but we are talking about poetry? We give glory to the immortal Leo Tolstoy!

The Russian seemed to think he was very strange or even crazy by this answer and, without saying a word, he joined back his group of friends. The thug's intervention had to frightened Vadim, so Boris decided not to distress him further by expressing his superficial doubts about the behavior of the employees of the estate. Then, the magician sighed sadly and said to his friend:

— I too lost my job. Just a week ago I was a night watchman at the bus station. In addition, my girlfriend, a Frenchwoman, flew away! From now on, I live on my boat, moored in the port of Antibes, away from the bustle of the city, like Diogenes in barrel.

Vadim held Boris's gaze and, with a malicious glint in his eyes, revealed to him:

– I know about your job! After you left, the management was looking for someone to replace you, and I got the job! I do not know exactly what happened, but everyone is still talking about you there! It is said that you extinguished a fire and that since that day you have never returned. Your bag was found in the in the guard's booth, and it was filled with a lot of strange objects. After this discovery, agents of the secret services sprayed the room with some kind of water, and then they immediately broke the security booth with a bulldozer. Some say that you did some black magic on the very premises of the bus station and you set the devil free. There are even some who claim to have seen ghosts... and others claim to have seen the Devil himself!

Boris was speechless in the face of this new information. In addition, he was unaware of the psychosis that had taken over the staff of the bus station. Suddenly he thought:

"I am not the only one to have witnessed these appearances! The poor employees of the station! If they talk too much about these paranormal phenomena, then will definitely end up in mental institutions"

Boris tried to calm the agitated flow of his thoughts. He was not to panic. The magician did not doubt that the visions of the employees of the station were related to the magical rite that Margot had accomplished that famous night.

Of course, the secret services had to have this in their line of sight and at least somehow respond! Besides, now he had an asset in his sleeve: Vadim, who worked at the bus station and who could keep him informed if supernatural phenomena would still be happening at the bus depot. In a surprised voice, Boris asked his future spy:

— What irony! Vadim, you got my old job!

— I need it, since I work for free in the stables of the estate. —Vadim sighed— I'm reduced to living with horses... My self-esteem has taken a big hit! Not to mention that Rashid Selimovich never misses an opportunity to humiliate me. Do you know what he calls me? The "Baron Munchausen", in reference to the name of the manor!

Vadim's voice trembled with spite.

— Do you also have strange visions? After all, you work where everyone sees something unusual? — Boris asked with a strange smile on his lips.

— I do not believe in all these nonsense! —The Homeless Poet hurried to answer in a sharp tone and it was clear that he was deceiving— Men do not need Lucifer's intervention to be evil!

— What do you mean? —Boris asked him— Are you referring to someone in particular?

— Rashid Selimovich ... his assistant... —Vadim stammered— It became clear that the theme of slavery in the stables was more interesting for Vadim than the devil in the bus station.

— His assistant or rather his mistress! —Boris retorted.

— When we were on the way to the airport, she kept caressing her stomach... —Vadim said blushing.

He was aware that he had betrayed a secret and by this had piqued the curiosity of Boris who could not help but exclaim:

— She is pregnant! Is she aware that you know?

– I think so, yes... –Vadim replied, sheepishly– When I asked her if she was planning to remain Rashid Selimovich's assistant, and what she thought about her life, she told me that in any event, her future and that of her child were already safe and well paid for many years to come.

– Vadim, that's why your boss fired you! –Boris exclaimed– Because you know, he put his mistress pregnant! Therefore he keeps you in his stables to make sure you will not repeat anything to anyone from his secrets.

– You think? –The Homeless Poet inquired in a small voice.

Vadim seemed very tired, and Boris preferred to reassure him:

– Do not worry my friend! The secret is well-kept with me!

– I trust you, Boris! –Vadim said– But can we talk about something else? This whole story is exhausting me!

The magician took advantage of the opportunity offered by his friend to return to the subject that interested him:

– You said you did not believe in the existence of the Devil, and yet you go to church!

The remark had the merit of restoring the smile to the Homeless Poet, who questioned Boris:

– Can you explain to me what happened at the bus station? Why did you leave your job?

– After what happened, I could not go back. And now, with all that you have told me, I think I did well!

It was a good thing that, after that strange night, I didn't reappear at the bus station! Otherwise these crazy workers would have burned me on the public place as at the time of the Inquisition, on a pyre made of bus tires, in place of fagots of wood!

— But then, everything that is said about you is true? — Vadim asked, puzzled— I did not know you practiced black magic!

— To be honest, I was forced to practice witchcraft. —Boris admitted— I just wanted to help a dying old man... This one Masonic Master, scared to death, asked me to perform a magic ritual to save him. At first, I took it as a game but then, the old fool had promised me a substantial reward. So I summoned a demon in the lodge of the bus station, with the help of Margot, my beloved girl. In the middle of the night the place was deserted, and we did not risk getting caught since the secret service agents didn't want to revive the supreme master!

Vadim showed his doubt and, for greater persuasiveness, somehow strangely blew his thin cheeks, but struggling to believe his friend. So, to convince him, Boris said to him in a thoughtful tone:

— After the ritual, a spectrum appeared, and I took a picture of its transparent substance! I have two shots where you can see a strange silhouette. And if I'm here today, it's because I'd like to show them to the local Orthodox pope, so he can tell me what he thinks of it.

— But how could you be stupid enough to forget your sorcerer's items in the dressing room ?! —Vadim noted sarcastically.

— To be more precise, I forgot them in the corner of the room. —The magician explained— The apparition of the demon occurred in the morning and while I wanted to photograph the phenomenon, one of my colleagues caught me camera in hand Therefore, I was a little confused and was forced to quickly leave the workplace.

— Do you think that the visions of the employees of the bus station are related to your ritual? —the Homeless Poet questioned.

— That seems quite probable to me. —Boris agreed.

— Then I think it would be safer to burn a candle in the name of St. Nicholas. —Vadim said staring slanting eyes in the sky.

Suddenly, a priest came out of from the door St. Nicholas Church. He was dressed in a long black robe and wore a large silver cross, hung around his on his chest. He was of average height and was about 40 years old. His hair was black and his beard curly and gray. A cloud of fragrant smoke had escaped from the religious building when the priest opened the door, giving the impression that he was coming out of a bathhouse.

— It's your lucky day! —Vadim exclaimed— Here is the pope! People say that he is the only one who does not steal here!

Boris looking at the servant of God with suspicion, then said to his friend:

— I still hesitate to talk to him. I learned about this pope, he comes from Greece. It seems that the Russian priests who ran this church before stole money and that the Greek pope was sent here to purge this church of these thugs. This priest is cunning, and I am suspicious of him.

When the priest passed them, Vadim looked at Boris. Trying to put his mistrust aside, the magician in a gentle voice said to the pope:

— Hello, Father! I need your valuable opinion on a very sensitive subject. Do you have a few minutes to spare for me?

The priest stopped and stared at Boris before answering:

— My son, I'm very busy today. But you can go to the church secretariat and make an appointment. You just need to provide a baptismal certificate.

This response irritated Boris sharply, who retorted to this church bureaucrat:

— Holy Father, are you kidding me? Do I need certificates and other permissions to seek the help of a man of God? I doubt that this kind of method corresponds to the teachings of Jesus!

The priest, paying little attention to Boris's statement, wanted to carry his way, but the magician stopped him by waving under his greek nose the two photographs he had taken at the bus station. The pope's eyes widened at the sight of clichés, and his face turned pale. The priest seemed and in a scared voice and stammering, he asked Boris:

— Where did you find these documents?

— I personally took these pictures, Saint Father! —Boris said softly— And now because of these two photos I may lose my job and... I am embroiled in a story that takes a very ugly turn. That's why I'd like you to help me understand what's going on.

— I do not see how I could help you! —The pope replied, who still seemed nervous.

The priest took the cross he wore around his neck in his hand and held it as a shield in the direction of Boris, while swiftly moving away from him, as if the magician had the plague.

— My father, —Boris explained— You certainly know more than I do about the Devil, since he is part of Christian literature.

But the servant of God did not want to listen to Boris's arguments. Still waving his silver cross, he took a few extra steps to the side, and he ran off toward his car. Boris followed him, but the priest rushed into big black car, parked in the church parking lot. The car roared its powerful engine like a mad beast, and the priest drove abruptly in reverse. Boris, who ran in the wake behind the holy father, almost found himself under the wheels of the car. The magician had just little time to retreat, before the vehicle rushed out of the parking lot like a wild bull against a bullfighter in the Roman theater, zigzagging and failing to overthrow, and almost crushing many believers who were walking in crowds to the temple! The poor people, frightened, jumped to the side as the black car passed, led by a priest with bulging eyes, terrified as if he had the Devil on his heels.

The pope, in his flight, forgot to shove the floor of his long clothes in the car, and a piece of it hung outside the cockpit, sweeping the dusty road. When he arrived at the exit of the car park, the priest braked suddenly and opened his door a fraction of a second, time to fold his robe inside the vehicle. Then he quickly closed the door and plunged down the main road, crunching the tires as if he thought he was Schumacher. Boris, stunned, watched as the vehicle swept away. For his part, the Homeless Poet had witnessed the scene sitting on the bench, without making a single gesture, paralyzed with astonishment.

Coming out of nowhere, an old man with gray hair, and of small height, appeared behind Boris. The stranger seemed to be nearly eighty years old and was very thin, but seemed endowed with an energy quite astonishing for a man his age. Facing Boris's back, the old man asked him, in Russian but with a terrible Estonian accent:

– What do you think, young man, this crazy pope runs to take their dose of "opium of the people"?

The magician did not even turn his head to see who was questioning him that way, his eyes still fixed on the road through which the priest had fled.

"Here! A supporter of Marx!" – Boris thought, thinking over the strange question.

At this moment, the church bell rang, calling the faithful to come and receive their crucified God. Boris turned to the church and found himself face to face with the old man who had not moved an inch. Boris detailed the man: he was dressed in a costume of another era, with a white shirt and a top hat, and leaned on a copper cane with his left hand with ivory pommel shaped jackal head. His eyes shone with a strange glow, and he stared at the magician smiling meaningfully. Boris was stunned because he had recognized his interlocutor.

– Master! –Boris exclaimed– But... how is this possible? Should not you be six feet under?

This apparition had destabilized Boris so much that he had forgotten all his propriety, but, realizing the clumsiness of his remarks, apologized:

– Pardon my rudeness, Master Polyus, but the last time when I came to the nursing home, I was told by the guys from the secret service that you died safely.

But the grand master already seemed to be losing interest in Boris. The old man looked around him and stopped to his gaze on the Homeless Poet who, still sitting on the bench and motionless, looked like a sphinx. Then, turning away from the magician, the grand master went to Vadim and asked him joyfully:

– Hello young man! Are you really living on the Tanneron estate? I went there a long time ago to visit an old friend whom God had worked hard for. Imagine a little: he lost twice his family! What a pain for this unfortunate writer! And yet, he managed to overcome these trials, showing exemplary faith, and even remarried the third time and had many children. I have a lot of respect and admiration for this man!

Boris, still in the shock of the sudden appearance of deceased Polyus, was watching the scene from afar: the old master, dressed in a costume that resembled one from a theater, had now sat down beside Vadim and babbled, making gestures of the hands. His legs were swinging in the void, because they were too short and did not touch the ground. It must be said that the grand master was particularly small in size and, with his face grimacing, it could have been compared to a leprechaun.

The Homeless Poet, at first surprised to be accosted in such polite and kind tone, gradually began to relax a little, listening to the old man's chatter, and even ended up smiling broadly, with his slanting Tatar's eyes stretching into an amused expression.

Boris finally came out of his lethargy and rather than stupidly standing there, in the middle of the parking lot, he decided to approach the bench where the two men were peacefully talking, in the shade of an old palm tree.

— Vadim, —The grand master continued— the Mimosa Valley is a wonderful place. The air is so intoxicating that you would like to slice it and eat it like caviar on toast. In the past, I have stayed there many times, and I each time had a wonderful time. But all this sweetness of life went up in smoke when a terrible fire ravaged the massif of Tanneron. And the family of this remarkable writer, the former owner of the estate of Baron Munchhausen, burned alive in the flames of a giant fire.

The old master began to talk so much and did not seem to want to be quiet, so he continued to monologue in an energetic voice:

— When I went to the Cap d'Antibes, I sometimes stayed at the Castle of La Croe. I was very well-received, and I liked very much going to this castle at the time when there was an English king who had preferred to give up hi throne, as he was in love with a bitchy American woman who had already married twice. This stupid king gave his throne to his brother even though he have could lived and ruled the British Isles without this American witch. Ah, the incorrigible romantic! But my best memories are those of Eastern hospitality when King Farouk of Egypt resided there. Although at the time it was rich Onassis who lived there and was just as happy. I was intoxicated with these dances, the cheerfulness of my friends and the beauty of their ladies until I would lose my head! My God, what a luxurious time! Alas, if the manor of Baron Munchausen resisted the fire, the Castle of La Croe was ravaged by the flames and abandoned for three decades. Fortunately, my friend Roman Abramovich bought it recently and will undertake pharaonic work to return the Castle of La Croe to its former splendor. I can not wait to go back to the castle, because Roman and I are in very close partnership and he will invite me as the best guest! Clearly, the Russians know how to revive the French heritage from the ruins! Because your boss, Vadim, also comes from Russia: Rashid... What his surname, again?

The grand master paused in his chatter to scratch his head with his right hand, before continuing:

– Forgive me, gentlemen. I think my senility is catching up with me! I can not remember the last name of Rashid, my disciple, and the owner of the Baron Munchhausen estate in Tanneron.

– Rashid Selimovich! –gently reminded him the Homeless Poet.

– Yes, that's it! He is from Dagestan, with legendary hospitality, lezgian dances and a bunch of delicious dishes, one can only lick his fingers! The old master continued enthusiastically. – Nothing to do with the French fat goose liver that gives me heartburn!

While the master continued to soliloquize, Boris watched the Homeless Poet, who listened with interest to the old man. The magician had always appreciated Vadim, in addition to his great culture, his good manners. As they say, "a good heart beautifies an ugly face", for it must be admitted that the Homeless Poet did not look good, his face was so emaciated and pale. Vadim's complexion was wilder than that of the grand master who was near death a week earlier. This observation made Boris wonder:

"Perhaps it is not the grand master? Because, to my knowledge, Polyus did not speak Russian. And he was far from being so talkative. The merry behavior of this talkative old man does not have much to do with the taciturn and contemptuous Polyus whom I knew. Yet, even if he seems rejuvenated, his face is that of the great master. The ritual must have worked, even though many things escape me."

Boris looked more closely at the old man, while mentally noting:

"I do not remember that the master was so small. And then, his eyes... his eyes!"

Boris had just remembered an important detail: when he had gone to see the grand master at the retirement home, his left eye was with white thorn and motionless in his orbit; then Polyus confessed that his left eye was blind. While the old man, sitting on the bench, seemed to have two eyes in perfect working order. Wanting to make sure, Boris approached the old man to better look at his eyes. The magician then noticed that if the right eye was a clear blue like that of Polyus, whereas the left was black and lifeless mowed to the left: it meant that he was wearing an ocular prosthesis! Continuing his "game of differences", Boris noticed that the master's clone had a beautiful baritone voice, like that of the ukrainian comedian by the name of Vladimir Zelensky, while the master Polyus was wheezing, because of the tracheotomy he had undergone. Boris was a little lost: this man looked like Polyus, but many small details suggested that it was not quite him... Also, Boris decided to take the lead and said to the old man in white:

– In my favorite book, Satan pretends to be the magician Woland. So, you can continue to talk about the moments of the moments you spent at the Baron Munchhausen manor and at the Castle of La Croe, you will not be able to make me believe that you are real master Polyus and in general, the writer Bulgakov in his book did not advise people to talk with strangers on the street.

The old man set his copper cane in front of him and put both hands on the ivory pommel, and looking at Boris with some admiration. Then he spoke:

– The Master and Margarita of Bulgakov is also my favorite book, young man. I see you want to play open cards on the table. Well, be it! I guess you want to know who I am... My name is Voldemar... or Voldemar-Polyus if you prefer, since now we are one.

In formulating his name, the old man had emphasized the first letter, which he had pronounced as an "F" instead of a "V": he had whistled a long "F", like the whistle of 'a snake.

– Your resemblance to the grand master is not a coincidence: did you really take his body! –Boris asked ironically, pretending to be joking.

– You're insightful, Boris! –The old man replied, insisting what he does really know the magician– who is he?

Voldemar even smiled triumphantly at Boris, who was beginning to wonder if he was going crazy. This whole story made him dizzy.

– You know my name! You own the memories Polyus, in addition to his body? —The magician inquired still in a mocking tone.

– I did not need to take possession of Polyus's old carcass for his memories. —Voldemar said— Polyus is my an old friend and I know him better than anyone. Besides, you and I have already met. Remember: when I appeared in my spectral form at the bus station, and you had the audacity to take a picture of me. It must be those photos that you showed to the pope, who nearly fainted! The poor priest before this incident, never scared in his life! Fortunately, the faithful who went to church did not see these cliches when you brandished them like an idiot! Ah, these faithful lovers of Christ who come to entrust to God their little daily worries... I hate them! They are blind sheep, unable to think for themselves. Do you think they come here to ask God to shed light on the universe? No, they are selfish cockroaches! They pray only in the hope that God will provide them with their daily bread. But what can be expected from these slaves of God? They are so weak...

"Maybe this double of the master somehow found out about the events at the bus station? Or is he an agent of the secret service?" —Boris involuntarily thought and for the first time took a serious look.

Suddenly, Voldemar turned to the Homeless Poet and shot him a look of reproach, before saying:

– You too, Vadim, you go to Christ to tell him of your worries that are worth more than a rotten egg!

The Homeless Poet, who until then had witnessed the exchange between Boris and the old man without a word, as he did not understand what was happening, dared to reply:

– How does this old man know so much about me? Is it you, Boris, who told him?

Vadim's slanting eyes stretched out in an expression of mistrust towards his friend.

– I assure you, no! –Boris affirmed– This is the first time I see this Voldemar, although I thought at first that it was my master Polyus! And, until today, I did not know that you came regularly to pray in this church. Besides, you heard him like me: he knows where the bus station is. He saw me and you there and now he is just mocking us both?

The two friends, during their exchange, had not paid attention to Voldemar and when they turned to him, they noticed, stupefied, that he had disappeared! On the bench next to Vadim, there remained only his copper cane with ivory pommel with a jackal's head.

– But where did he go? –Boris exclaimed– In addition, he forgot his cane!

Boris rushed into the middle of the alley that led to the church, trying to locate the old man among the faithful crowds walking in tight rows, more and more dense. Attracted by the house of God like sheep called by their shepherd, the people passed Boris skirting him from both sides like a river in the middle of which the magician was like an island turned out. The parishioners formed orderly columns, only deformed by the gap they were making to avoid Boris, who wondered how the old man managed to disappear so quickly? If Voldemar had not left his cane on the bench, Boris could have believed that he had dreamed this supernatural encounter. The magician turned to the Homeless Poet who had risen from the bench and was watching the crowd, also looking for the figure of an old man, dressed in a costume from another era and wearing a top hat. Suddenly, somewhere in the distance, the silhouette of the escaping old man flashed and Boris decided to make sure that the Homeless Poet also did. Fortunately, Vadim found himself where he was supposed to be - near the bench in the church garden. He in turn turned his head to Boris, and suddenly his slanted eyes widened, when they came across those of a huge black figure, mounted on a horse as dark. Vadim had the impression that this look was a bottomless pit that called him to throw himself into the abyss. In the grip of indescribable fear, he crouched and shouted to Boris in a falsetto voice:

– A black rider! A black horseman behind you!

As the Homeless Poet groaned in terror and returned his head to his neck, as if to avoid the mortal blow of Genghis Khan's sword, Boris turned around but saw nothing.

– Vadim, he's gone! —Boris said to reassure his friend, not knowing what Vadim had seen.

At these words, the Homeless Poet deftly rose from the ground to his feet and violently rushed into the crowd of faithful, pushing without hesitation the people who were in his way. He managed to slip in front of everyone on the porch of the church. Thus, as the doors opened, he was the first to enter the building, and to breathe the pungent smoke of incense. Boris saw him in the distance, as Vadim was about to step into the church: his bald head glowed in the sun, giving the impression that a shimmering halo was hanging over his head. This image was ephemeral because already the Homeless Poet had entered the building. At this moment, the bells of the church resounded to announce the office of noon. Boris preferred to leave, feeling that his friend had obviously gone mad and needed plenty of time to regain his senses. On his side, the Homeless Poet prayed that day with greater fervor; he did not know that the black knight was his first vision... the first in a long series.

Chapter 4 - The second appearance of Voldemar, in the church of St. Nicholas

Boris had finally returned home to his yacht *Adventure,* which had been docked in the port of the city of Antibes for three years already. Despite the fact that his boat bore name *Adventure,* little by little, the hull of his yacht was invaded by many shells and mollusks that clung to it firmly. Boris felt like his ship: chained prisoner of a life, and as if something prevented him from moving forward. A few weeks earlier, Princess Jeanne had offered to moor his boat in the port of Monaco, where she had found him a place at a reasonable price. But at that moment, Boris was under the spell of Margot. Between the pretty novice of the Grand Master and the faded princess, the choice was not difficult to make... He had refused Jeanne's proposal. Wherein, he did not know that Margot would let him down once the ritual was done. Now he was alone! Although, not so long ago, two passionate women pursued him. Now that Margot was gone, he could have called Princess Jeanne back, but he did not want her anymore. Lustful tricks of an old woman were nasty to him, especially since he had known the beauty of the amorous act with

Margot. Therefore, he preferred continue to live in a dignified solitude.

Thinking of his love conquests brought back to him a memory that dated back a few years already and that he and the Homeless Poet had evoked during their meeting in the garden of the Church of St. Nicholas. He plunged back into this memorable anecdote... That morning, Boris had gone, as usual, to a sports complex in Nice. After a workout, he enjoyed taking advantage of the sauna available to guests where he often met a colorful crowd, including Russian prostitutes who, after working all night in the cold, came to relax in a cloud of hot steam, while discussing the incongruous practices of their customers or complaining of violence of their pimps. But on that day, in addition to the usual prostitutes, Boris had seen an unusual couple arrive: Ineska, a woman of great beauty, was accompanied by Vadim, whom Boris had met at the Foreign Legion.

"This sexy girl came across of the bald, skinny Tatar." – He thought involuntarily.

Despite the fact that the scene was comical, she had somewhat worried Boris because Ineska had a sulfurous reputation. But Boris was content to greet them warmly, because he did not want to spoil the pleasure of Vadim or attract the attention of prostitutes.

Boris patiently had waited in the hot bath that girls, after a long chat finally come out to fresh air and as the Tatar followed the group of prostitutes to the exit, he was behind woe-lover and whispered in his ear:

– Vadim, I have to talk to you!

Vadim had hesitated for a few moments, reluctant to let the beautiful Ineska fly away. But he had finally resigned himself to join Boris, sitting on a sauna bench. Seeing that the Tatar was annoyed at having let his seductive prey escape, who had left with the group of prostitutes, Boris had explained to him:

— My friend, do you know that four former Russian legionaries finished behind the bars of the Nice prison after attending Ineska? Certainly, these guys were not the most recommendable, but do you want to be her next pigeon?

Vadim had been amazed, then, after a few seconds of reflection, that Boris saved him from big problems. So, to thank him, he had invited him to drink not only good beer, but also strong whiskey at his house that very evening. Boris visited Vadim and they in that memorable evening drank a lot of beer, smoked Dutch tobacco from pipes and talked about poetry. It was the time when the Homeless Poet still had a decent home, which he eventually completely lost, since for several months he no longer paid the rent. That night, Vadim had spoken of his youth: son of a teacher who had died while Vadim was still very young, he was an excellent student. In parallel with his studies at the University of Minsk, he gave literature courses to students — mostly female students — from lower classes.

— It was a beautiful time! —Vadim exclaimed, a touch of nostalgia in his voice.

— We are not so unhappy in France. —Boris had replied— We had great years at the Legion and to be reasonable, you can find a good Frenchwoman. But it is categorically dangerous to contact Russian or Ukrainian prostitutes.

Friendly conversation quickly flew by and at the end of it Vadim had made such an astonishing proposal to Boris and he almost choked on his beer: the Tatar, who was so timid, had proposed to his friend to accompany two french women, named Mimi and Lulu, to a discotheque swingers party! According to Vadim, these two women, in their forties, were in love with freedom and had decided to tour the libertine clubs of the French Riviera. Because they wanted to make new experiences and as they said: in order to "not die like stupid women". Vadim had presented things in a poetic way, speaking of a desire for freedom women rather than unbridled sexual desire. However, Boris wondered: "How Vadim found himself having this idea — to accompany these ladies in this kind of establishment? He feared that his friend, whose innocence had once again struck him that very morning, had been dragged into a scandalous story.

Also, he had questioned the Tatar:

— And how did you meet these funny ladies?

— It's my friend Zozo who introduced them to me. He usually accompanies them on their trips, but he is not available tonight. That's why he asked me to escort them in his place... —Vadim replied.

— I'm surprised Zozo wants you to replace him with his friends in this kind of practice. —Boris said and immediately felt a surge of new strength.

— To be honest, Zozo is an homosexual. —Vadim explained— I do not know the exact nature of his relationship with these two women, but I know he is very close to Lulu. It may be like Celine Dion's song "Ziggy, his name is Ziggy".

"Ziggy" and "Zozo", it sounds the same! – Vadim said with a spark in his eyes.

Boris still seemed hesitant, but, in truth, the idea of spending an evening in charming company did not displease him. Seeing that his friend was beginning to doubt, Vadim had tore off the seal:

– Come on, Boris, do not pull rubber! In addition, it would be nice to spin on the love bed with these pretty and very depraved women.

The argument had born fruit, and Boris had agreed to participate in the evening, not wanting to make Vadim languish more. So, they went to get Mimi and Lulu and had them first dined at a restaurant in Cannes, where Boris would often eat with Margot a few years later. The establishment was located opposite the world-famous Palace of Festivals for its cultural events, bringing together film and music personalities with rhinestones and sequins. Boris had immediately noticed that the two women were determined to spend a memorable evening. Mimi was blonde and had pretty gray eyes. Her figure was athletic enough, and Boris was not surprised when she mentioned that she was doing a lot of sport.

Mimi had strong character and Boris liked that kind of woman. As for Lulu, she was a brunette with mesmerizing sensuality. If the French were not already famous for their sex appeal, Lulu would be an exception to the rule: she was downright hot! And Boris would be well tempted by the pretty brunette but, finding that Vadim had no hooks with Mimi, which had too much of a character for the fragile Tatar, Boris had decided to abandon Lulu in Vadim's favor. He thought this brunette was more to Vadim's taste. But the rest of the evening would teach him that he was on the was wrong track because neither of the two women liked the thin Tatar; probably they were too extroverted for him.

At the end of dinner, a small hitch had occurred. When the waiter had brought them the bill, the girls had immediately pulled their wallets out of their purses, but Boris had stopped them saying:

— It's the men's duty to pay for the ladies!

— How so the duty of men? —Vadim exclaimed indignantly— Talk for you!

Boris, not wanting to argue with his friend, had paid the full amount, without specifying:

— I rectify already said: it is the duty of a real man to pay for the ladies!

Boris was unaware that the Homeless Poet was penniless and could not afford to pay his rent. Although Vadim was a very greedy person and in fact never paid for women. After dinner, the quartet had gone, as agreed, in a libertine club. But the atmosphere reigning there was not up to the expectations of both women.

It was not the right season because the disco was almost empty. There was only one old woman, approaching seventy, who had been hooked by a man even older than her, as well as an old prostitute with ten hungry Arabs which she gave them all in turn and they stood around her and waited to take turns kissing her in intimate places.

Our four lecherous had drank a few drinks, and Boris then suggested to Mimi to spend the night at home; this same night he had filled the sexual appetite of the pretty blonde, whilst Vadim had brought Lulu home and, courageously denying all sexual claims of the hungry woman, he had returned alone at his apartment. In the following days, Lulu, frustrated at not having got her way, had contacted Vadim many times, but the Tatar, with strong convictions, had not yielded, and Lulu had finally surrendered and loudly cursed Vadim for his vile disrespect for the woman!

Boris, coming out of his memories, thought back to what had happened in the garden of the Saint-Nicolas Church: first there was the priest who had fled when he saw the two photographs on which was pictured the spectral form, then the appearance of Voldemar who had taken the appearance of the great master Polyus. Boris then felt that too many questions remained unanswered and decided to return to the Church of St. Nicholas. Perhaps the Orthodox pope would have had time to regain his senses, and would be more inclined to give Boris some explanations.

The former legionnaire decided to go inside the temple and resolutely headed in the direction of doors the church. Usually, Boris did not like to enter religious buildings, except in Catholic churches, in the summer, to cool off a bit, because they were not infested with smoke incense, unlike the Orthodox churches. The few paraffin candles flashing here and there did not bother him. Sometimes he even thought that if Catholics had already agreed to switch from beeswax to paraffin wax, maybe one day they would put LED candles, more environmentally friendly than real-live candles then it will be good for saving the planet. Before entering the smoky atmosphere of the St. Nicholas Orthodox Church, which did not have benches to receive the faithful, Boris paused in the garden, where he had his habits. He liked to sit on a bench and, looking at the only Russian birch, to be sad about Russia. It had been six years since he not had entered an Orthodox church, and this time it was unknown as to why he was apprehensive about passing the threshold of the building. Finally the great sinner took a deep breath and decided to enter the church.

Once inside, Boris found himself a little confused, he began to look around. Near the altar there was a group of Russian emigrants who were praying fervently and the pope, whom Boris had briefly met before he fled, was walking in a circle before believers, waving a censer. Boris thought it was not time to bother the priest and, feeling uncomfortable with all that ceremonial he did not understand, decided to go out and come back to a better time. As he made his way to the exit, Boris jumped in surprise: he had just seen, standing in a corner, the grand master's clone. Voldemar was still wearing his old-fashioned costume and, leaning against the wall, seemed absorbed in his thoughts and did not notice Boris. The former legionnaire approached the old man and called out to him in a low voice not to disturb the faithful:

– Hello, Voldemar! Is it under this name that you introduced yourself the other day? Besides, you left so quickly that Vadim and I did not notice... In your haste, you forgot your cane on the bench, but I recovered it. If you want me to give it back to you, you can go to my place. I live on my boat;

it's called *Adventure* and it is docked in the port of Antibes, right in front of the customs building.

Voldemar, coming out of his inner reflections, had listened to Boris with interest and seemed delighted that his precious cane had been found, so much so that he uttered a cry of joy:

— Oh! Thank you, Boris! You're really nice and a true friend!

The faithful Orthodox turned to the two annoying violators of silence and gave them disapproving looks. One of them even gave them a mean look:

— Demons!

In order not to attract more the wrath of the parishioners, Boris invited Voldemar, with a gesture of the hand, to leave the church. The old man did not mind following Boris who was heading for the exit. As soon as they passed the door, the sun dazzled them and the pure air filled their lungs. They stopped in front of the church and Voldemar questioned Boris:

— Well, Boris, what were you doing in this church?

— I'll return the question! —The magician retorted— You are a very strange person and besides, despise Christians! What the hell are you doing here?

Voldemar did not appear to be embarrassed by this question and replied with disconcerting sincerity:

— During my absence, life on earth has changed so much! In cities, huge buildings were built everywhere. People always seem in a hurry. All this agitation makes me dizzy. But the churches have not changed: they are still majestic, and these are the only places where people stop running. They are havens of peace, where silence and serenity reign. When I am in a church, then I feel protected from outside excitement and can put my thoughts in order.

Boris was not interested in listening to Voldemar's torment. The magician wanted answers, and he did not hesitate to question his interlocutor:

— Voldemar, you said that you were absent. So where were you during your absence? And what were you doing?

These questions seemed to annoy Voldemar who replied, shouting:

— Ah, you want to know where I was! Well, I'll tell you: in Karaganda, Kazakhstan! In a deep coma! He had shouted so loudly that a group of pigeons, to whom an old woman was giving crumbs of bread, flew away.

— But stop screaming! —Boris snarled— How did you land in Karaganda? And why were you in a coma?

Voldemar seemed to have shut up like an oyster and Boris realized that if he wanted to get reasonable answers, then he shouldn't rush this crazy old man.

So, he resumed interrogation in a calm voice:

— Voldemar, why did you leave so quickly, the last time we saw each other? If not there had been your cane, I could have thought I dreamed our meeting!

— Oh, my cane! —Voldemar exclaimed— I am grateful to you for having kept it for me. This is my favorite cane! Without her, my knee hurts me so much because at night it groans so bitterly!

Boris could not help but smile at the old man's naivety and thought:

"This old man is really mysterious. Maybe he just lost his mind. And maybe I've lost it too! If it is, we will both end up in an asylum for mental patients. After what I did at the bus station, I am anyway labeled as crazy!"

The scene of the ritual then came back to him, and his face darkened as he thought of his beautiful Margot, whom he had heard nothing of since that day.

Seeing that Boris was deep in thought, Voldemar wanted to get his attention by saying:

— By the way, Boris, I went back briefly to your old workplace. Apparently, you made a big impression because I heard the director of the bus station, Mr Rode, talk about you. He was on the phone with a psychiatrist, a certain Serge Lunatik...

The news left Boris speechless. Noting his distress, Voldemar gave him a friendly pat on the back and said:

— My friend let's take a walk in the park. I think we still have things to tell each other!

Boris followed Voldemar, and they advanced in the path leading to the church.

— You know, Voldemar, —Boris said— it's a bit confusing for me to talk to the clone of my late master.

— And how do you know that your master is dead? — Voldemar asked, glaring at Boris.

— To be honest, I'm sure of nothing. I can only make assumptions. The last time I saw Polyus he was on the verge of death. Then, on the night of during the the ritual, Margot told me he was in a coma. And now, you are here! How did you take possession of his body? I'm forced to deduce that

Polyus is no more. The old man stared at Boris in the eyes and asked him in a very serious tone:

– Boris, what are you waiting for from life?

The magician was a little confused by this question and thought for a moment before answering:

– I do not think I can hope much of life now. Yet before, I was full of dreams and ambitions! But now I do not know what I want. Well... well, I'd like to meet Margot, my beloved. She was so sweet and so beautiful! I would at least like to know where she is and if she is fine. I know she played me and used me to perform the ritual, but I can not help but keep thinking about her. But why are you asking me such a question? How do you know my desires? And here again, I return the question to you: what do you expect from me?

– It's hard to explain, young man, –Voldemar began– but I feel connected to you. It seems to me that you are looking for something. And I am in constant search too. So, perhaps we can join forces finding solutions to the problems that torment us. In addition, you must have noticed that my French is quite limited; it is easier for me to talk to you than to the locals.

As Voldemar had just finished his sentence, a man, tall and athletic, approached them. Boris was surprised to recognize Zozo, the friend of the Homeless Poet. Voldemar hastened to meet Zozo. The two men spoke for a moment, but Boris could not hear what they were saying.

Suddenly, Voldemar turned to Boris and said:

– I have to go! Goodbye my friend! I will come to see you tonight, on your boat *Adventure*. Do not let me down. I believe we will live an incredible adventure and you will not regret it!

Voldemar followed Zozo and walked away from Boris.

In turn, the exhausted magician collapsed on a bench and threw his head back, swearing aloud:

– Shit! This old man has exhausted me!

– You should watch your language in front of the house of the Lord! —familiar voice exclaimed.

Raising his head, Boris saw a priest approaching him, who was mysteriously looking around the side all the time.

– Well, Father! Hello! —Boris said— I am very surprised that you now have decided to talk with me. The last time you ran away from me like scalded. But hey, since you're here, sit down! As they say, "There is no truth in your feet!".

The pope slightly raised his black robe and sat at the end of the bench, taking care to keep a certain distance between him and his interlocutor. Then he looked around, as if he wanted to check that no indiscreet ears were hiding somewhere, before addressing to Boris irritably:

– Can you explain to me why are you constantly climbing the church garden and what do you really need from me?

– To be honest, if I come to this park often, it's because I find it beautiful and relaxing! —Boris answered sincerely— In addition, being far from home, it is sometimes pleasant to meet and talk with fellow countrymen. And if I entered the church just now, it's because I was hoping to find you there. I thought you might be in better shape than last time to answer my questions. I would like to have your opinion as a specialist in a sensitive topic and on a tricky problem.

– Oh? –The priest replied, suspicious– I thought you were in cahoots with the band of thugs who roam around and who has been harassing me for several days!

– What thugs are you talking about? –Boris asked, puzzled.

– Well, men you were talking to right now! By the way, can you tell me where they went? As soon as I saw them get away from you, I went out the service door to join you. I just turned a second to close the door and when I turned around they were gone! Have you seen the old man walk slowly? It is not possible that they crossed the garden so quickly!

– If it reassures you, my father, –said Boris– this is not the first time this strange old man surprises me with his tricks. Every time he disappears like a wolf from a fairy tale; he is there in front of you and pffuu! For the second time he disappeared in the strangest way. Either it is a supernatural phenomenon that escapes us, or we both have hallucinations!

The priest frightened, looked around again and whispered to Boris:

– Maybe they are hiding nearby, and they are listening to us right now?

– Of course! –Boris quipped– The little old man swapped his ridiculous costume for camouflage and crawled on the grass with a spy microphone.

The magician was beginning to find this story distracting. It must be said that since the disappearance of Margot, he had the impression to get bogged down in an inextricable situation. And suddenly, the events were linked as unexpectedly as the twists of the series Santa Barbara:

Voldemar who wanted them to work together, and the pope who had initiated the conversation on his own.

The pope, a little ashamed to be so plump, spoke again, more conciliatory:

— Let's say you're not part of this gang of thugs, and you've only come here to talk to me. So, I'm listening to you. Tell me about your problem. Do it quickly because I have an appointment with the bishop to discuss the repairs of the church steeple. We are running out of money to finance the work. People are not as generous as they used to...

— No problem, my father! —Boris sharply interrupted the tedious words of the priest who was interested only in money— I will not hold you long! You already know my question: what do you think of the anomalies in the photographs that I showed you the other day? You did not have time to answer me since you fled. By the way, you almost crashed with your big car!

The pope fidgeted nervously and pulling his plump hands at the silver cross he wore around his neck. After a few moments of reflection, he replied in an agreed tone:

— Our Blessed Mother the Orthodox Church remains very suspicious of paranormal manifestations, especially when the only evidence their are fake photos. That is why we prefer not to comment on this type of subject. Go rather consult the Catholic priests! They are used to making money with these stories of apparitions: look what they do in Lourdes! We, the Orthodox, prefer to stay poor rather than to make a deal with Lucifer!

The pope had raised his voice a little at the end of his tirade and was preparing to get up and leave Boris in the air, when suddenly a voice came out of nowhere:

– Do you not fear to pronounce the name of the Devil thus aloud?

Boris and the priest in a single movement looked around: nobody!

– My father, –Boris said– You to have heard that voice, have not you? I will end up believing that we are really crazy!

The priest did not answer, paralyzed by fear. His face had turned olive green, like that of the shutters of houses in some villages of Provence.

Suddenly the voice was heard again:

– Forgive me, gentlemen, I did not want to scare you! But I could not resist the urge to join your conversation.

The two men had the impression that the voice came from the side of the church and both looked in that direction: but they saw no one! But when they both turned their eyes off the building with their eyes, they saw in amazement, standing in front of them, a little old man dressed in a funny costume: Voldemar!

The priest changed the color of his face, which suddenly became pale, as if fear had emptied him of his blood. Boris flinched, wondering how Voldemar was doing to appear and disappear like that, but quickly pulled himself together to challenge the old man:

– Tell me, Voldemar, is it the Kazakhs of Karaganda who taught you to move without anyone seeing you? Damn, will you tell us where you come from?

— From the Moon! —The old man laughed.

Seeing that the two men did not rate his joke, he resumed in a more serious tone:

— Young man, if you travel the earth as much as I have traveled, then perhaps you will understand that it is not because certain things are not visible that they do not exist.

This enigmatic answer left Boris perplexed. Voldemar hobbled over the bench and sat down between the two men. The old man stretched his arms to the sides, putting them on the back of the bench, as if he was sitting on his couch watching a movie. He was swinging his legs in the air, making of his black shoes sparkle in the sun. Suddenly, Voldemar put his hands on the nape of each of the two men although they were both at a great distance from him. Boris and the priest were surprised that old man was doing strange things, as some force pulled them both towards Voldemar and they were pressed against it on both sides.

They tried to shift from him but nothing worked: a supernatural force prevented them from moving.

The pope, his eyes wide with fear, exclaimed:

— But what do you want in the end? It's been several days since you harass me and I still do not know why! Are you blackmailing me? When will you leave me alone?

— When the truth has been restored! —Voldemar answered in a muffled voice— That is, when you publicly repent of your sins.

Boris, who understood nothing in the exchange of reproaches between the two men and said to the priest in a relaxed voice:

– Now, my father, do you believe me when I tell you that I have nothing to do with this man and his henchmen?

The priest ignored Boris's question and tried once more to free himself. He was moving in all directions, but he could not free himself from Voldemar's grip. The latter had to strengthen iron finger clamp on the neck of the pope because it gave a cry of pain, then finally stopped moving. Seeing that the priest had calmed, Voldemar spoke again in a softened tone:

– Father, I have heard you say that your church refused to make a deal with the Devil. This made me react because you must know that you are wrong: Orthodox, like Catholics, are quick to use treachery for the sole purpose of getting rich. I think it's worth reminding you about that you use a lot of trinkets to attract the generosity of poor naive people? Holy Tears, the Holy Shroud, the Holy Crown, the Holy Lance, and so on! We can also talk about the so-called miracles besides those already attested by the Vatican? The miraculous healing, the apparitions of saints, the statues that start crying! All those saints whose image you use shamelessly must tear their hair out when you see yourself playing with the candor of believers. These relics and idols are tools of evil! Admittedly, the different religions are opposed on theological or liturgical questions, but if you look more closely, you can see that in fact, they are much more alike than they seem. But still there is one thing that, more than any other, brings together Catholic priests and Orthodox priests... One thing you know well, father... Pedophilia!

At this last word, the pope's face decomposed and his arms sagged down his body. Lowering his head, he moaned miserably:

— I have already repented of all this before the Lord!

— Your prophet said: "Give to Caesar what is Caesar's, and to God what is God's!" —Voldemar replied— To repent before God is not enough. You must confess your sins to the justice of men.

Boris, disgusted by what he had just heard, did not want to be outdone and intervened:

— The son of my Ukrainian friend, who had dreamed of becoming a priest since childhood, went to study at the Kiev seminary. As a result, he came out totally devastated, so much so that he is now in a psychiatric hospital! His mother told me briefly what the priests did to him... horrible things, worthy of the worst movies from the category of black and vile pornography about masochists! These places of sin should be destroyed, as were Sodom and Gomorrah!

The priest, no longer able to cope with his own guilt, began to scream so loudly that Voldemar, surprised, loosened his iron grip. The priest took the opportunity to leap off the bench and was probably hoping to run away, as he had done the last time from Boris, but he was stopped in his flight by Zozo, emerging from nowhere. The peasant, who was about two meters tall and had a jaw of mastiff, planted himself in front of the priest, looked at him straight in the eyes and barked:

— Sit down!

The priest, frightened, had no choice but to execute himself. Voldemar then told him:

– Father, you are wasting your time running away. Last time, you left so quickly in your big car that you nearly crushed the faithful who came to seek comfort in the house of God. And now, would you like to escape somewhere again? Unfortunately for you it is already impossible to do because wherever you are, we will meet you again! And importantly, in your case, what you will not be able to escape your own conscience. It's easy to stupefy people with all kinds of standing stories, but it's harder to face the truth. Is it not, Father?

The pope did not answer. Boris thought it was time for him to bow. Besides, Voldemar had relaxed his grip on his neck; it must have been the signal that Boris could leave. The magician stood up, looked at the priest with a disgusted air and said:

– Father, you're disgusting! Whether by the justice of men, of God or even of the goddess Themis, your crimes will not go unpunished. You can still choose to do, finally, what is right. But this is not my business. I leave you in the hands of these gentlemen.

The pope remained silent; his eyes had lost all life. Boris started to move away and threw over his shoulder at Voldemar's address:

– My friend, do not forget to come see me tonight on my boat, to get your cane.

Then the magician went away, heading for the exit of the garden.

Chapter 5 - A pact with the Devil

Later that evening, aboard his yacht, Boris thought about the events of the recent weeks. It was unpleasant for him to encounter and to be faced with the clone of his late master, not to mention the fact that new master seemed to have rejuvenated, like Faust who was rejuvenated by mythical Mephistopheles.

Voldemar could have passed for the younger brother of Polyus. Admittedly, Boris had noticed physical differences between Voldemar and Polyus: the left eye, blind, of the grand master was dull and fixed, while Voldemar wore an ocular prosthesis, black color as one of Woland's eyes in *The Master and Marguerite* by Michael Bulgakov.

Except that, here Boris was not evolving in the imaginary world of a writer of genius, but he was in the real world, in which the dead do not usually come to talk with you in a park as if it was the most natural thing in the world! Boris did not know which saint to turn to for help. But the thing that intrigued him the most was the identity of Voldemar: who was really the one who had taken on the appearance of the grand master? Boris could see that Voldemar had supernatural powers.

Was he also a magician? Perhaps he practiced hypnosis, like Wolf Messing who with his abilities impressed Stalin himself? This could explain how Voldemar had held Boris and the pope against him, with a simple squeeze of the hand on the back of the neck. Or perhaps he was a magnetizer like the healer Juna who had treated Leonid Brezhnev.

Then Boris thought that Voldemar could just as easily be an eccentric old man, powerless, but rich enough to afford technologies, still unknown to ordinary people, that could rationally explain the old man's special abilities. And his resemblance to Polyus would be a mere coincidence, which would be more credible than this story of body possession. While indulging in these reflections, Boris had come down from his boat and was pacing up and down the platform in front of the customs building. Mooring his ship in this port began to cost his dearly, but in any case, his boat the Adventure was no longer able to go to the open sea. Boris sighed and tried to put his ideas in order. He wondered why he had twice met Voldemar in the garden of St. Nicholas Church. Suddenly, the magician burst out laughing, thinking back to how Voldemar had prevented the pope from running away.

– This time, the priest had not been able to escape. – Boris thought and remembered the scared face of the churchman when his foul secret had been revealed and how fear had seized his whole being.

The evening had already started, and the solar disk was gradually disappearing on the horizon, as if swallowed by the sea. The lights of the port were lit and shone the hulls of the ships. In the sky, gained by the gloom, we could see, through a thin cloudy veil, the first bleak light of the stars. The moon had to be hidden by a cloud because it was not visible. Night was slowly setting his black coat on the city and Boris was surprised that Voldemar had not shown himself yet. He was beginning to wonder if the old man had not mistaken him for a fool. But he reassured himself by saying that Voldemar seemed to be holding on to his stick and that, moreover, he had some difficulty moving without it. Yes, Voldemar would come, if only to recover his favorite cane. Reassured by this thought, Boris was getting ready to board his boat when he heard the sound of tapping on the bitumen, a bit like the sound of hooves but at a rate less sustained than that of horses. Boris turned in the direction of the slamming and saw Voldemar limping on the wharf.

The old man seemed to be making an effort to walk faster what his old age allowed him to do. As if he was in a hurry to get to his destination and Boris amused said to himself:

"This grandfather still has endurance! Young joggers should ask him for help!"

— You were waiting for me, my friend? —Voldemar asked when he reached Boris— Forgive me for arriving at such a late hour but important business has held me back. Ah, business, you know what it is! The old man did not seem more breathless than that, despite his brisk walk.

– Do not worry, I was not expecting you! –Boris lied– I like to stroll at night on the docks. But since you're here, let's get on my boat, have a glass of rum, and continue our conversation as started in the church's park. As Voldemar did not answer Boris suddenly laughed:

– You have seen all the colors complexion of this perverse pope! But I congratulate you for making that you forced this priest to confess his sins. I think that he will not dare to harm a child anymore.

Faced with Boris's congratulations, Voldemar made a funny face: Boris noticed in the light of the street lamps that the old man was blushing and looking embarrassed. Also, as if he wanted to avoid too much praise for himself, Voldemar motioned to Boris, with a wave of the hand, to climb first aboard the boat, *Adventure*. Boris, being on the stern of the boat, turned and extended his hand to Voldemar, but the old man ignored the outstretched hand of the magician and jumped aboard the boat with surprising agility for his age. Voldemar's heels slammed against the yacht's wooden floor..

Boris looked at the old man's polished shoes and thought:

"It feels like he's wearing horseshoes under his funny shoes, or as if he had hooves!"

Boris invited Voldemar to take a seat in the small lounge he had set up on his boat. The magician served them two glasses of rum from a bottle brought to him by Margot at the time, which seemed to him far too far away, back when the novice taught him black magic before she disappeared after the ritual on that memorable morning. The two men sipped their rum quietly, before Voldemar broke the silence with a serious air:

— I heard that the director of the bus station will formalize your dismissal. You should seize the labor courts to claim compensation. After all, you have prevented the bus station being totally burned down; you deserve a reward for this act of bravery on fire! After all, the French consider themselves a great nation, which means that they are extremely ungrateful. Whereas a cash reward clearly does not hurt you!

Boris thought for a moment: it is true that his finances were not at best and that to receive some compensation could save him the financial position. But after what happened in the guard's booth, he did not risk making statements so as not to worsen his position.

— Voldemar, I do not know what to say to you. —Boris said— Because I must admit that I left from work without leaving a signature in the working journal and now they will speculate on it. And then, they found my bag full of ritual objects and the secret services were warned. It might be more prudent for me to keep a low profile, even if the idea of spitting to the side at these idiots is tempting.

— My friend, —Voldemar said— you must know that your old boss, Mr Rode, is configured to be very up against you, so much so that one might wonder if your magic ritual is the only cause. Anyway, Mr Rode seems to want you locked up in a psychiatric hospital with strange aggressiveness. I already told you that I had heard him speak on the phone to a psychiatrist. Apparently, a member of the Cannes City Council would be in cahoots, because the psychiatrist assured Mr Rode that he would have no trouble getting your internment, at the request of a third party if the head of the city would guarantee this approach.

Boris was stupefied. He did not understand why the director of the bus station was fighting against him.

Frankly speaking, Boris admitted that because of his magical experiment, the secret service of France had spent some money on lighting holy water to cleanse the accursed place, but in return, agents received valuable cult objects made of gold and silver. But Voldemar was right: if Boris had not extinguished the bus fire, the damage would have been much worse. Mr Rode's reaction seemed disproportionate. But maybe the French government was involved in this matter, and Mr Rode was just a small pawn in someone's foul play?

Voldemar drank a few sips of rum before continuing:

– Ah, these French! As soon as you get out from accepted standards, they throw you away! They do not hesitate to use all kinds of tricks to get rid of their detractors. Moreover, Boris, you performed a real magic ritual! Therefore, you must be urgently locked up in a special institution, that is, simply neutralized! Take my word for it, Boris, I tell you: it would have been less detrimental to you to be an opponent of the Communist Party of the Soviet Union! The French can boast of their democracy, but here they have no morality. The satraps who govern them dictate the way they must live! One has the impression that the French still live under the regime of the Inquisition: they are afraid to end at the stake if they deviate from imposed standards! But the Germans are no better: they are programmed not to get out of the ranks. And I do not even speak about the Spaniards: certainly, they have the Mediterranean ardor, but it does not exceed the limits of their cranial box! As soon as we have to expose further to defend freedom, then they will either scatter like rats or hide like fat penguins. But back to the French: they are right to fear their leaders because the latter if they do not send their opponents to the stake, use equally cruel procedures. In particular, they send those who could harm them in a psychiatric hospital and stuff them with all kinds of narcotic substances until they are no longer able to think for themselves!

Voldemar had put so much ardor in his speech that Boris did not know what attitude to adopt. Therefore, the magician decided to lead the conversation in a different direction:

— Dear Voldemar, I do not know how best to call you according to your title? I do not know anything about you but I guess, in view of your manners, that you are of noble blood. You seem eccentric, through your costume of another era for example, but look at the millionaires who come strutting on the Croisette: they are much more eccentric than you! And unlike them you inspire respect by your charisma so much so that I could call you "Sire"!

Boris looked at Voldemar with a smile. He wondered if he had not done a little too much, but the old man seemed to enjoy flattery and how the turkey swelled with pleasure.

— If you like it, —Voldemar replied— you may call me "Sire". I am even flattered that you are raising me to this rank. But, if you respect my ancestry, I am the Count. And I will try to show myself worthy of the respect you show me, my friend.

Voldemar glanced at Boris: his pupils, including that of his black prosthetic eye, seemed to stretch like those of a snake. The magician, a little uncomfortable, preferred to continue the conversation:

– I was sure you were wearing a title! And you are a true count, not like that cheater of Cagliostro! Well, Count, can I serve you another glass of rum? May I suggest you stay with me for dinner? Returning to the port, after our meeting at the church, I stopped in a Russian grocery store, held by an Armenian. I bought Norwegian smoked salmon and dill cucumbers from Germany.

– Thank you for your invitation, but I have other plans for tonight.

But I would love to try more of this delicious rum. Boris poured rum in glasses, while Voldemar placed a cushion behind his back.

The magician was watching his guest: his gestures, the expressions on his face so manicured, almost overplayed, so much so that Boris wondered if Voldemar was not a theater actor. The old man's singularity greatly amused Boris, who had to restrain himself from laughing so as not to upset the Count, especially since the latter, after having settled comfortably, had taken a serious look on him.

– My dear friend, –Voldemar said– I would like to ask you an important question: if you received the visit of Mephistopheles or Woland, the character of Bulgakov, what would you ask in exchange for your soul?

— Only the Devil knows it! —Boris joked— You have already asked me about what I was expecting from life, earlier in the park.

Voldemar smiled and his eyes lit up strangely, shining like those of a cat in the dim light. Boris noticed once again, that his black prosthetic eye seemed to work better than he had thought.

— Ah, young people! —Voldemar exclaimed— They think only of women! This Margot seems to have bewitched you, as in the song: "She has the eyes revolver, she has the look that kills and she shot first! ". So you would be willing to sell your soul to the Devil for her? You would not rather want money, immortality, power?

— Count, why you look at me just as old Lenin looked at the bourgeoisie? Power does not interest me! Certainly, my finances are not at best lately but I do not miss anything and life offers me small pleasures from time to time. As for immortality... it seems to me that earthly life is sometimes worse than death. And then, if the director of the bus station succeeds and can lock me in an asylum, it would mean that I should live eternally among the madmen! I think I'd rather hang myself!

Boris got a little carried away, and Voldemar seemed annoyed by the words of the magician.

— If your desire is to know love, turn to God! —Voldemar became annoyed— This bit of love is not part of my field of action. So, ask me anything but not that!

— Today I asked the priest what he thought of the pictures I took at the bus station, he refused to help me. And now it's you who refuse to help me find my beloved! —Boris grumbled.

After this lively exchange views, the two men remained silent for a few minutes. Then Boris spoke again:

— Count, must I understand that you are Mephistopheles, the one who inspired so many great writers?

Asking this question, Boris smiled slightly, though Voldemar's offer and something indefinable in his appearance was demoniacal. But could Boris really consider that he was discussing very important topic with the incarnation of the Devil?

— My friend, are you sure you do not want anything else? —Voldemar insisted— Human emotions are beyond my comprehension, so ask me something more concrete.

— According to legend, if I make a pact with you, you will be my servant! —Boris smiled— In all sincerity, I appreciate you very much, count, but not to the point of spending my life with you, as Faust could do it! Especially that you do not believe in love! This means that our respective visions of life are totally opposed, which does not prevent me from finding you an excellent company, because our discussions are very exciting. But I do not think anything that you can offer me really interests me. Boris concludes his reply with a sip of rum. For the first time, the magician saw that Voldemar was truly disconcerted: he seemed to be searching for his words and glancing furtively at Boris. Then the old man reprimanded himself and said to Boris:

— You know, young man, currently I am less in search of so-called sinful souls than at other times. In this modern world, vice flows freely and my hell overflows with damned souls as if it is rubber! For example! The other day, arab sheikhs cheated my demons: by selling them fuel at an exorbitant price and thereby justifying the rise in its prices by the rise on the stock market oil! I can assure you that in the fact that these thieves will come to me in hell after their death, then they clearly will not be kept satisfied in my house! (Voldemar smiles, as if that's a good joke.) But today I don't want to talk for a long time about my work because for the first time in my eternal life I am on vacation! I just want to relax on this beautiful French Riviera, where I accomplished some pretty feats in a distant time. I like to remember my past glory with my old friends. Also, Boris, I will not insist further on selling your soul. I respect your choice and I even admire your tenacity. You know, I met a lot of skeptics, but all ended up throwing their beautiful convictions into oblivion to make a pact with me, too allured by my offer. I admit that I regret that you refused my proposal because your company is very nice and I was pleased to deal with you. I think you know Zozo? He's a complete fool! And his friend Lulu does not shine either by her intelligence. It has not been very easy for me to deal with them every day over the last millennia. Then some of my other demons are even worse! Your presence would have been good for me.

Boris thought for a moment since he was a little taken aback by this revelation and seeing Voldemar's grieving face out of compassion he I found a brilliant solution of a difficult task.

— Count, it's my turn to make you an offer! —Boris exclaimed— Dear Count, I see you more as the genius

Hottabych that is, kinda good sorcerer than the dark Mephistopheles (Voldemar raised his eyebrows at this remark). So, forget the traditional pact that we must sign with blood, or whatever. Even if I find life on earth very sad, I do not want to sell my soul, and especially not in exchange for things that seem superfluous to me and uninteresting. And besides, I think that my soul is not worth much because it seems to me that I lost the spirit because I am talking to the Devil! With all due respect, Count, your existence has not been proven in our world. So, maybe all this is just a hallucination and you're as crazy as me! (Voldemar widened his eyes a little more in the face of this assertion.) Anyway, I refuse to sign a pact with you because if it turns out that everything you say is true, I do not want to take the risk that you send me to hell! Moreover, no court will be able to confirm the legitimacy of our deal! Forgive my prudence but if I believe your words you are the incarnation of evil... You will understand that I take some precautions. That being said, I come to my offer: I propose to keep you company during your holidays, here on earth, and not in your hell! We could have fun, chat, meet people... in short, enjoy life! What do you think?

Voldemar's face had lit up with a broad smile. He seemed surprised by Boris's audacity, but obviously his offer did not displease him.

– My friend, you convinced me! I accept your offer! – Voldemar exclaimed happily.

Boris, to celebrate their agreement, again filled with old rum their glasses. They drank a few sips of rum, then Voldemar pouted and said in a thoughtful voice:

– There is really no animation in this port. Only the lapping of the waves and the clatter of the mooring ropes break the silence. This calm exhausts me! How about going back to civilization? My friend Roman Abramovich invited me to a party he is organizing here at Cap d'Antibes, to celebrate the progress of the reconstruction of the Castle of La Croe. We could have lovely meetings, therefore, we should not spend this magical night alone. The men of high society certainly have a lot of money, but they do not necessarily have what it takes to satisfy a woman in bed! Despite my advanced age, I can still give pleasure to women. And in case of failure, Viagra can fix it!

Voldemar concludes his reply with a loud laugh.

Boris smiled at him politely, a little embarrassed by the old man's words. The magician began to wonder if his companion had not lost the ball.

Boris thought, while looking at Voldemar with some distrust:

"The strange scene: an old man, who takes himself for the incarnation of the Devil and who obviously knows the beautiful world, is sitting aboard my poor boat which has a broken motor and doomed to stay in dock. Why does he want me to accompany him to this party? If he wants to find a dear geisha or geteru or even a courtesan, then, he can do it without me! May he take his cane and go to hell! Certainly, I agreed to join him in traveling, but I'm not obliged to follow him everywhere, like a dog! Does he intend to make me an object of experimentation, as Dr. Preobrajenski did with his dog?

Boris chased away all those thoughts that bubbled through his mind to express his reluctance, more diplomatically, to Voldemar:

– Count, we have reached an agreement and I promise you that I will keep my word. But you are clearly mocking me! We only found an agreement, but you offer me something incredible! Nobody will let us banquet to Abramovich! In addition, I do not even have a decent coat or tuxedo! And if I may your old-fashioned costume may be a bit too original for those good people from high society!

Voldemar seemed not to have listened to Boris. He was leaning nonchalantly against the cushion he had carefully placed earlier and stared at the stars, lost in thought. Suddenly, he shook his head, as if he suddenly remembered he was not alone, and said to Boris in a mocking tone:

– Forgive me, my friend! I was miles away! Did I miss something? Here! It reminds me of an anecdote: one day, one of my acquaintances told me that what differentiates a man from an animal is its ability to get lost in the contemplation of the sky. But when I repeated these words to a peasant friend, he told me that his cows, too, were looking at the sky, especially as the rain approached. So, are we really so different from animals? That is the question!

Boris, not allowing himself to be dismayed by the digressions of the old man, replied quickly.

– Rather than drinking rum with a former legionnaire, you'd better have tea with Kant! He would certainly answer that question better than me. However, I can repeat the thesis of many philosophers, including Aristotle, according to which man is distinguished from the animal by the fact that he is endowed with speech. On the other hand, one wonders what differentiates man from God, since he made us in his image.

Boris punctuated his tirade with a sip of rum.

— That's a very interesting question! —Voldemar rejoices— You know that one of my relatives calls himself "Son of Man" as well as "Son of God"; the assimilation between man and God is here manifest. But, for my part, these names reveal a contradiction. And I have spoken to the one I like to call my "bastard brother", given his troubled origins. I warned him that his inconsistent statements would eventually cause him trouble in public relations of a distant and very cruel era. Besides, history has proved me right since he ended his life on the cross. Two thousand years later, I still believe that its manifestations in the terrestrial world were a serious mistake. The proof look at the number of people who blew their blood for love for him! In my opinion, it was obvious that his Utopian ideas would be taken up by malicious people. But, as always, he did not want to listen to me! And we see the sad result: he is now adored by a horde of hypocrites and rogues!

With these words, Voldemar emptied his glass in one go and laid it noisily on the table. Then he stood up and said:

— While we are losing ourselves in philosophical conjectures, the guests of Roman Abramovich are getting drunk! So go join them, my friend, before all the pretty girls have flown away in other arms! Do what you consider necessary to do if you want, then accompany me! Life is made to have fun! We will have plenty of time to philosophize tomorrow because, as we say, "the morning is wiser than the evening".

Suddenly, Voldemar looked at Boris with a very stern look, and adopted the image of a pompous aristocrat.

Boris had to admit that, despite his small size, he exuded a certain majesty. It was not the first time great magician had seen Voldemar change his attitude so abruptly, and and did not object to him in anything. Not wishing to clash with his new friend, the magician decided to accept the count's invitation. So Boris got up and said to his companion:

– Count, I agree to accompany you to the *Big Blue*, Abramovich's yacht, which is a little further on the dock. And we'll see if the security agents let me get on board.

– Why do you want to go on Abramovich's yacht? – wondered Voldemar– The party takes place at the Castle of La Croe, at least in the part that has been renovated.

– Count, are you sure of it? – Boris retorted – Because I saw that there was a lot of excitement around the boat of your friend Abramovich today, as if a party was scheduled to hold a large banquet. And many security agents English forces against terrorists have surrounded the him ship.

– My friend, you are mistaken! –The count replied (Voldemar smiled, but at the same time from his right eye came an evil glow)– I do not appreciate when my words are questioned. The animation you observed on the port should not be tied to tonight's party. I can assure you that the evening takes place at the Castle of La Croe. I even have official invitations for both of us.

Voldemar winked at Boris, with his right eye, of course. Once again, the old man had gone from anger to humor in a split-second.

The magician merely replied with a slightly tense smile. Then the count continued in a softened voice:

— My car, a black Rolls-Royce, is waiting for us at the entrance of the harbor, and you'll find there, in the backseat, a suit tailored to you... and everything else you may need.

— But how do you know my measurements? —Boris asked intrigued.

Once again, Voldemar's mood changed dramatically: the magician's question seemed to have put him in a black rage. Boris, wishing to bring Voldemar back to better terms, laughed and said to him lightly:

— Do not get angry, Count! Understand me: I had a lot of information to assimilate today, and everything is jostling in my head. But be sure that I do not doubt the veracity of all that you have told me.

— Oh, my friend! —Voldemar retorted— You are not at the end of your surprises! Believe me, many adventures are still waiting for us! As Alla Pugacheva, my favorite singer, sings: "There are still a lot of things ahead of us... Oh, oh, oh! ". But we have lost enough time! Let's hurry, otherwise there will be nothing left to eat or drink!

— Well, Count, I'm following you! —Boris replied— But do not forget your cane!

Voldemar's face lit up when Boris handed him his precious cane, which he caught with obvious joy. Then the two men got off the boat and skirted the harbor, where small sailboats, luxurious yachts and glittering stars were moored to join the count's vehicle. During this short journey, many thoughts jostled in the head of Boris. The magician wondered if Voldemar was not fooling him. He had told him that he had received invitations for both of them, but why would the governor of Chukotka have invited him to a party? They did not know each other?

Boris had the impression to participate or rather to be the victim of the famous Russian show Cross Talk, where the animators do not hesitate to play the speakers. Also, Boris like St. Thomas was waiting to see to believe. When they arrived in front of the count's vehicle Boris was captivated by the magnificent black Rolls-Royce the latest model. This car, which made them a call of lighthouses, would have been worthy of an Arab prince! Arrived at the height of the vehicle Boris caressed admiring the body of the car and the doubts he had formulated in thought vanished immediately. The tall Zozo then got out of the car and opened the rear door diligently whence came a woman's chuckle. Astonished Boris approached and discovered not without surprise Lulu, the depraved quadragenarian he had met a few years earlier during the libertine club ride with the Homeless Poet. Seeing her still so seductive Boris regretted once again for having left her as a matter of courtesy to Vadim who had not even touched her. What a fool he had been!

– Surprise! – The beauty exclaimed.

Then she got out of the car jumped into Boris's arms and kissed him passionately on the lips. The past years had apparently not changed Lulu! And Boris had to admit that this kiss did not leave him indifferent even if he had a thought for Margot, as the poet Petrarch, in his time, could not help but dream of the beautiful Laure when he roamed the sinister streets of the debauched city of Avignon. All took their place in the Rolls-Royce, and Zozo started the race car that ran along the coast at a vertiginous speed. Boris then realized that he had not dreamed of everything that had happened: Voldemar was not the fruit of his imagination; he was real. Could it be that he was really the embodiment of the Devil, a kind of Mephistopheles or Woland? Except that, there we were not in a book but in real life and Voldemar was not a character of novel but a being of flesh and blood! Boris dismissed these thoughts, telling himself that he had to enjoy the wonderful evening that awaited him.

At this thought, his heart began to pound his chest like a bird squealing out of his cage and Boris thought:

"Few people are lucky to be invited to such a prestigious party! I have to enjoy! I know that Polyus also knew Roman Abramovich... Should I hope that Margot as a novice of the grand master, will be present too?"

While Boris was lost in thought, the Rolls-Royce left the main road and took a small street, which often had to see beautiful people. The car traveled a few hundred yards and arrived in front of the gate of the Castle of La Croe.

Chapter 6 - Ball at Abramovich, at the Castle of La Croe

When they arrived at the entrance of the property of Roman Abramovich, who suddenly got rich like a fairy tale marquis de Carabas, Boris was surprised to find that the security agents let them enter without difficulty into the courtyard of the Castle. Zozo, the driver, drove Lulu, Voldemar and Boris tp a large site not far from of the castle and went to park the Rolls-Royce where the guards had indicated. While waiting for Zozo to join them, the guests admired the castle and Voldemar, with the airs of a teacher, became to tell his friends a fascinating story:

– Historians consider that it is here that King of England, Edward VIII, abdicated his crown for a woman with light morals, in this castle which sheltered, from 1938 to 1949, his great love with Wallis Simpson, who before him had already divorced twice. He was so in love with his beautiful American that he preferred to give up the throne rather than live without her!

"I felt it was impossible to carry the heavy burden of responsibility and fulfill the duties that I have as a king without the help of the woman I love" —king said on the radio...

Voldemar was suddenly silent and kept silent for a few moments. Suddenly he laughed like a hunchback. Then, when he had calmed down a little, added naturally:

— That idiot in love got a little disappointed afterward in his family life. Every morning, he waited impatiently for his beloved to take down the sumptuous staircase and join him on the terrace to drink a cup of coffee. And Wallis seemed to take pleasure in making her lover languish. Waiting for his beautiful lady, he smoked cigarette after cigarette and drank brandy cognac. These hours of daily waiting made him crazy. One day, furious with his wife, he even said to me, "My friend Voldemar, if you want to see the effect of sharing a bed with a marble statue, I will lend you my wife! ".

Boris was beginning to get used to Voldemar's voluble digressions, and he was not surprised that the Count claimed to have rubbed shoulders with King Edward VIII, sixty years ago. Boris thought that Voldemar must have been a hundred years old, like Polyus, although he was particularly well-preserved for such an advanced age. After all, Mikhail Bulgakov, in his novel *The Master and Margarita,* had done even harder: his character Woland, who evolves in the 1930s, claims to have had breakfast with Kant, who died in 1804. At least, Voldemar remained in human proportions... or near!

Boris was still trying to find a rational explanation for what he was going through, because he had a hard time imagining these seemingly incredible things. And first of all, the fact that he is currently communicating with the real Devil! The skeptical nature of Boris caught up with him again. "Distrust is mother of safety," as the saying goes.

Voldemar, without paying attention to Boris' pensive attitude, continued with a carefree look to recount his memories:

— I have always loved this castle, built in the Victorian style. Whenever I come here, I feel at home. I have so many good memories: that's where I met Sir Winston Churchill, as well as the kings of Belgium, Italy and Egypt, and even the beautiful Helen of Greece, not to mention the western billionaires and Hollywood stars, including the muscular Schwarzenegger. In short, you will understand: people of high society! Ah, it was a beautiful time!

Voldemar showed great regret and with a mournful grimace continued, lowering his voice:

— Boris Berezovsky, the owner of the castle of Garoupe, and Roman Abramovich, the current owner of this wonderful of the Castle of La Croe, not worth a little finger of these illustrious personalities. If they have reached the highest levels of society, it is thanks to me! Yes, it was me who pulled them out of the mud in which they were bogged down! These are my serfs. Even if sometimes I wonder if I did well to choose them. And maybe it would be better for Russia if Roman Abramovich continued to produce rubber vibrators in his underground factory and have fun with his plastic doll! Finally, I began to respect Roman Abramovich because I see that the restoration work of my beloved castle have progressed well. Which means that Roman respected my orders.

Voldemar ended his monologue on this positive note and, seeing Zozo coming back, exclaimed:

— Ah, here you are finally! Demon, where the hell are you... you lost?

— Master, there was a parking problem! —The athletic Zozo justified himself— The place we were told was not worthy of your Rolls-Royce. I had to ask for another one more decent according to your status!

— Ah yes? That's how these miserable mortals receive me? —Voldemar cried angrily— Well, they'll see what a party I will give them today! Believe me, they will remember this evening for a long time!

Boris, alarmed by the old man's words, turned to him and saw, stunned, that Voldemar had changed his clothes, as if by magic! He had traded his old-fashioned outfit for a chic and a little more modern frock coat. But Boris was not at the end of his surprises because he noticed, scared, that he himself was wearing an elegant white tuxedo, without even having to change! He lifted his head and saw that Zozo and Lulu had also undergone a sartorial transformation: the big Zozo was now dressed in a well-tailored costume. And Lulu was more sensual than ever in a transparent dress that gave a glimpse of the splendor of his body, not to mention the sumptuous finery of diamonds that sublimated it and sparkled in the light of street lamps, as the garlands of a Christmas tree.

Boris had no time to wonder more about this impromptu dress changes because Voldemar, taking a solemn voice, announced:

— Dear friends, it's time to make our entrance! The owner of this wonderful castle and guests must look forward to us!

With that, Voldemar, leaning on his cane, made a quick step towards the main entrance of the castle. His three companions quickly followed behind...

Boris was still surprised inwardly with the physical form of the old man So he very quickly walked and this despite his lameness and old age. Once on the steps, he rang the bell and said to Boris, pointing to the building:

— My friend, you must have noticed that the facade of the castle still bears the marks of the terrible fire of which he was the victim... thirty years ago. However, I must confess: I insisted that this evening be held here, despite the fact that the work is underway. Because, you were right, Roman Abramovich wanted to organize this holiday on his boat Le Big Blue. You will soon understand why I insisted that the celebration be held at the castle, and I hope you will forgive me for not being completely honest with you, this evening in the port, on your yacht.

Boris did not protest and blame the count for his cunning behaviour. Moreover, even if the magician had wanted to say something, he would not have had time because a servant came to open the door and made them enter the hall. No sooner had they entered than the estate manager, as Voldemar introduced him to his companions, came to meet them without forgetting to do a curtsy.

The steward of the castle was clearly afraid and he was out of breath and the guests could see, that he gave himself body and soul to his work, thus justifying the miraculous salary that

Abramovich was to pay him. The man bowed to Voldemar and said in a quavering voice:

– Grand master, please excuse me for the mistake that was made in the parking lot. Mr Selimovich, a multimillionaire, made a mistake in parking and took your place. That's why the agent was forced to allocate not very good parking, which was not worthy of your rank, as your driver pointed out.

– Oh my God! I can still hear that name! Bring me to him, I want to see this man! –Voldemar exclaimed, borrowing the words of the Russian poet Sergei Iessenin.

Voldemar burst out laughing loudly, adding to the manager's confusion. Then, descending from the poetic summits to reach the land of common mortals, he added:

– I hope I have the opportunity to get to know Mr Selimovich better, but now I think only about the presentation of my magical experience and no one and nothing should distract me from such an important matter. This will be the highlight of the evening!

Voldemar's words worried Boris, but he quickly forgot his fears when, as they walked down a spacious corridor which was well lit by a giant chandelier made of Czech crystal. Then he saw his reflection in a huge mirror, hung on the wall and adorned with a frame in bronze: his tuxedo was perfect!

Boris thought: "No drop of champagne or wine should not fall for this wonderful suit great carved by the expert hands of a great Parisian designer!"

Boris had to pull away from his contemplation because a butler opened the door that gave access to a huge hall, where the party was taking place.

The four acolytes left the corridor decorated with antique-style moldings, to enter the ballroom shining with divine beauty and already full of people. A proverb says that "people are welcomed according to their habit and accompanied by their spirit," and Boris wondered if his beautiful suit would be enough to give the change.

The magician feared that his lack of culture and good manners would be noticed and ridiculed. He did not know at all how he should behave among this crowd of aristocrats on a spree chic life and dressed in the richest clothes of higher couture.

Voldemar signaled that he understood Boris' fears because he took him by the elbow and whispered in his ear:

— Do not worry, my friend! All these pompous puppets were, not so long ago, on the same rung of the social ladder as you. They were just lucky to have benefited from the bloody events of the early 90s. But you, unlike them, you have not been perverted by the perestroika of this filthy Mikhail Gorbachev. And I reassure you: we will not stay too long amongst this rabble and prostitutes, and we will leave immediately as soon as my ghosts have a little fun. They are bored in my kingdom of darkness and are sometimes nostalgic for their past life. A small trip to the terrestrial world will do them the greatest good!

Boris tried not to override Voldemar's mysterious remarks and followed the count, like Zozo and Lulu, into the ballroom, richly furnished and decorated. The room was spacious and high ceiling; the walls were adorned with elegant moldings gilded with gold leaf. The baroque and rococo styles merged to form a subtle and harmonious ensemble. Boris discreetly observed the crowd and noticed that the ladies were all very beautiful and that the gentlemen all had a carnivorous smile and they looked very much like predators.

Boris could not restrain himself from exclaiming:

– I am amazed! What splendor! People seem so rich and women are so beautiful!

Voldemar squeezed Boris's elbow tightly and whispered through his clenched teeth:

– My friend, you should behave as if you used to evolve in the upper class of society.

Boris nodded and replied with a detached air:

–I will do it, Count! But there are so many pretty girls that I'm dizzy!

– Well, my friend, –Voldemar whispered– choose the girl you want, and she will be yours for the evening. You can do everything you want and realize with it all your fantasies.

– Count, I find your offer a little strange and very tempting! I will consider it seriously but at the same time I will act strictly according to the situation. –Boris replied in a low voice too– However, I prefer to first look at how the party will evolves.

The quartet walked into the room, politely greeting the other guests as they passed past them, they nodded majestically with their heads. Small groups had formed among those invited for the evening, certainly out of affinity or interest. And because Boris imagined that all these good people were together to talk about business, more or less doubtful.

After all not so long ago, it was these same people who discussed their shady dealings over a good cup of Georgian tea in the depths of the Siberian forests when they themselves were the prisoners of the concentration camps. But listening them talk, Boris realized that he was mistaken: everyone was talking about the entertainment, the "black magic" promised by Roman Abramovich. He diligently followed Voldemar, feeling like a schoolboy wisely following his teacher's recommendations. At that time the melodies were linked together forming a pleasant background; Voldemar introduced him to many people, without failing to whisper in his ear some sharp comments. Boris often smiled respectfully. Although he was a little distracted by everything around him and he felt like a farmer discovering the "big city" for the first time! His heart was pounding so much that Boris feared for a moment that it would step out of his chest. So many things were jostling in his head that he felt like he had a lead helmet wrapped around his skull. The great magician had to concentrate to calm the surge of emotions that clouded his mind, for he did not want to attract the attention of all these aristocrats by staring too hard at them.

He breathed deeply and managed to transform the raging waves that submerged him, into in small ripples on the water more easily controllable. He was thus able to resume his observation magnificent meeting, in a more detached manner, which was called the "fair of vanities".

Most of the men were dressed the same way: expensive suits that shone in the light of the crystal chandeliers, as if the fabric had been coated with diamond ointment. The ladies who accompanied them, often much younger than these gentlemen, wore more heterogeneous outfits, but obviously their colorful toilets all wore the signature of a great couturier, such as Coco Chanel or Prada.

And these elegant women displayed precious jewels glittering with a thousand lights. The breathtaking beauty of these ladies shook Boris' soul and body, while the magician felt a mixture of respect and contempt to gray-haired, or already completely bald companions, who looked like ferocious animals ready to tear their victims to pieces.

Judging by the rounded cheekbones and protruding stomachs, it was possible to conclude that these guys had long been freed from concentration camps and prisons in immense Siberia. And now they were dressed in such sumptuous, preferred to relax not in the Crimea, and on the French Riviera, but they could not hide the carnivorous glow that illuminated their eyes: a pack of wolves!

Boris noticed that three men stood a little away from the crowd, clustered in the center of the room. They had something different from the other men in the room, a kind of charisma that marked their superiority. Boris immediately nicknamed them "the Archangels"; he did not know who they were, but after all, in the Bible we do not know the names of all the archangels either!

Voldemar approached Boris, and the magician wanted to ask him who these three men were, but he changed his mind, fearing that the count will begin to enumerate to him the names of all the bandits present in the hall at this gorgeous party, but Voldemar seemed to prefer to keep his close attention exclusively on the excellent ladies who accompanied these amine guests. However, he noticed Boris' interest in the trio and whispered in his ear:

— This chic party is informal, but still it makes a lot of important decisions. Politicians call such meetings "conversations without neck tie." While in the business world the legal spouses of modern gangsters are not allowed to negotiate and the girls in attendance play the role of a colorful export to satisfy the carnal pleasures of their owners or those who rented them as a beautiful car in a car dealership. These girls are here to look pretty, that's all! And they do it very well, by the way! Look how beautiful they are: most of them have won beauty pageants from Miss Tula to Miss Universe.

Boris dragged his gaze on the women and could only confirm with a nod the words of Voldemar and quickly brought his attention back to the three Archangels. Like all the men of the evening, they were elegantly dressed, but they seemed a little younger than average. They must have been about the same age as Boris.

The magician said to his companion:

— These three stand out, a little like three poplars standing proudly in the center of a clearing. I nicknamed them "three archangels of Michael".

At this remark, Voldemar let out a small chuckle and finally replied:

— This nickname is well found, my friend, because, indeed, unlike other participants in this Vererenka, this trinity has something else! For the moment, their pretty tails and wings have escaped the nets of justice. Many of their business partners have already made a stay in the safe areas of Russian prisons. But despite the fact that this holy trinity is purebred have not yet tasted the bars of a cage, that does not mean that they have no blood on their hands, but simply that, for the moment, they have shown themselves smarter than others. As you know, my friend, in Russia millions of dollars or euros can not be obtained without blood being shed. These Archangels have also sent many people to the afterlife. Besides, they are usually four. But the fourth thief, named Mikhail Khodorkovsky, found himself locked in a cage and it confirms the truth: "Wealth does not always protect against prison".

Boris turned his attention to one of the oligarchs, tall and thin. He pointed it out discreetly to Voldemar and murmured:

— The face of this high archangel seems to be known to me. Would not it is Mikhail Prokhorov?

— Good game! —Voldemar exclaimed as a proud teacher of his pupil—This arrogant shark has brought with him half a dozen damsels so little shy that you can find yourself kissing their feet before even exchanging a word with them. Mikhail Prokhorov is said to have a good taste for girls!

And Voldemar pointed out to Boris a group of young women who were gossiping happily as they chatted to ventripotent gentlemen.

The magician noted:

— It is true that they are very beautiful. These are carefully selected cultured pearls.

Voldemar seemed to like the picture because he nodded before adding bitterly:

— Usually, I understand guys like such as Mikhail Prokhorov but he has too much eccentric whims. Do you know that he regularly charter a plane from Siberia to Moscow just to get his favorite ice cream? And he always carries a bunch of prostitutes who feeds his Siberian delicacy! His arrogance will end up playing tricks on him and especially annoying my student Nicolas Sinistres, who hasn't got so many pretty girls yet. I know very well my son of a bitch, Nicolas, and I'm just sure that he will still punish Misha Prokhorov!

Then Voldemar nudged Boris to draw his attention to a man who was standing back with a young woman. The count gave his friend time to observe their new object of study and spoke again:

— You already know a lot about this little man, because it is the former boss of the Homeless Poet: it is the billionaire Sardarov Rashid Selimovich, owner of the luxury estate of Baron Munchhausen. The woman next to him is one of his girlfriends. Unlike his colleague Mikhail Prokhorov, he took only one girl to the party, because he tries to look modest in public. Although he has a whole flock of women who rival with ardor to win his favors. It must be said that he is not a simple Caucasian descended from his mountains to buy salt to put in his soup! It's not a harmless little Yorkie, but one of those wild dogs that gave their name to the Canary Islands. He is cut for the fight and is not afraid to face the wolves. Be wary of him because he could shred you as if you were one of those plastic toys that dogs are given. Besides, he is devilishly intelligent!

Voldemar stopped his presentation because the owner of the Castle of Croe had just made his appearance, descending a sumptuous staircase lined with a handrail of old style. As usual, Roman Abramovich was unshaven and his gray eyes expressed a sweet melancholy. On his thick lips was imprinted a mysterious smile, like that of Leonardo da Vinci's Mona Lisa. He was elegantly dressed in an English woolen suit, unpretentious even though his price was to be exorbitant, and was accompanied by a young woman with certain charm but classic beauty, not like those bimbos who this evening accompanied other less famous vampires.

Boris, after appreciating the elegance of Roman Abramovich's companion, turned to Lulu, who was provocatively sensual but short-legged. Admittedly, Lulu did not have the endless legs of supermodels but her curves were generous. In addition, her face was soft, with a slightly curved nose and scarlet lips that made them want to kiss them. But a detail, which Boris had not noticed until now, suddenly caused a shiver in his back: Lulu's eyes were so deep that the pupil could not be distinguished from the iris. The magician jumped because he had just realized that Lulu had exactly the same eyes as Zozo, who was standing next to her.

"These are demon eyes!" —Boris thought.

But he dismissed this disturbing thought, which might have spoiled this beautiful evening, as it would have done with a fly whirring in his ear. So, to silence his inner voice, he asked Voldemar the first thing that went through his head:

— Count, why does Roman Abramovich seem so sad?

– How can I explain that to you, my friend? (Voldemar for a while I was looking for the right word.) First of all, Roman Abramovich, because of his position in society, is obliged to keep people at a distance. You know, wealth attracts profiteers and since he has reached the top of the social ladder, he laughs rarely and constantly has a gloomy look on his face. But it is not the only reason. Because I must admit that I am no stranger to his constant sadness. Indeed, a few years ago, we made an agreement: I made sure he had the money and world renown he wanted and, in return, he offered me his happiness. In other words, I rejoice in his place of his successes, which I myself created, and he remains irremediably sad, although he has obtained the life he has always dreamed of. It must be said that at that time, I was in a difficult period: nothing made me happy; even when I was doing devilish projects, I could not celebrate anymore. That's why I had this idea to take someone's joy. Myths, inspired by stupid religious stories and relayed by writers, represent me as evil, a foul beast with monstrous horns, although I must admit that in recent years, an artistic trend returns a more flattering image of me. And I can not deny that evil is an integral part of me, but limiting myself to this aspect of my personality is ineptitude. Yes, I too can be depressed! Fortunately, thanks to my agreement with Roman Abramovich, I found my former spirit! Currently I have fun as a small child with his toys. In a way, I had to adapt to the changes taking place in the terrestrial world. For vice has so poisoned mankind that I no longer need to intervene to bring souls into my hell. Men condemn themselves, by their cruel and selfish behavior, to spend eternity in hell! Of course, there are still a few naive believers who still advocate for good, but they are fewer and fewer. It was for this reason that I sank, for a time, into boredom: I had little to do, and my hell filled up each day a little more. But now, this sad period of my existence is ancient history. I feel happier than ever and I intend to enjoy my spring break on the French Riviera! Besides, it's time to cheer up this evening. Did you hear the guests' conversations? They all look forward to the performance that Roman Abramovich promised them. So do not make them wait any longer and now step on stage!

Boris stared at Voldemar with a look that was both intrigued and worried. Voldemar smiled, savoring in advance the good trick he was going to play at this meeting of aristocrats.

The count, stifling a squeaky laugh, added:

– These oligarchs and their dolls think that I will do them a little trick of magic as they see on television! But, in fact, it is not them that I will entertain: on the contrary, they will serve as entertainment for my ghosts, who will soon be out of the chaos for the occasion.

Voldemar winked at Boris and, leaning on his cane, made his way through the crowd to position himself in the center of the room. Then he spoke in a loud voice to attract the attention of the guests:

– Ladies and gentlemen, the hour of dark magic has come!

At once, all the guests were silent and, visibly satisfied that this boring evening finally came alive, turned to Voldemar, who continued:

– First of all, I want to reassure you: I'm not going to kill you with an interminable speech. However, before beginning my demonstration, I would like to thank our host, Roman Abramovich, who has undertaken titanic work to restore this castle to its former splendor. Before a terrible fire devastated it more than thirty years ago, I had stayed many times in this house. Sumptuous feasts were given, just like tonight's. I know that the renovation is just beginning and it will take several years to erase all the stigma left by the flames and years of abandonment. There is so much to do, between the restoration of the building and the restoration of the garden, but I have every confidence in our friend Roman: he will lead this pharaonic project masterfully! When the work is finished, I hope that we will all meet again here to celebrate the resurrection of the Castle de la Croe №2!

Voldemar paused for a moment and cheerful applause rang out. Then the Count added in a more serious tone:

– I would also like to have a thought for those who could not join us. And of course, I'm sad about those who have left us forever but also to those who are detained for very different reasons, including Mikhail Khodorkovsky, who is languishing in a Russian prison, and Boris Berezovsky, who is in exile in London. My friends, let's pay tribute to to all our friends who for various reasons cannot be with this wonderful party.

Voldemar fell silent, but this time no applause came to fill the silence that had settled. In this way the guests tasted to do cynical allusions the Count. But that did not detract from Voldemar's enthusiasm, which resumed:

– My friends, forget for a moment the sad fate of some members of your community, and get down to business! I suppose you've already wondered if life after death existed. This is a vast question that scientists in this world have not been able to answer. Well, tonight I'm going to give you the irrefutable proof that there is a life after death. Because you will be able to see it with your own eyes. I personally invited to join us some friends who come straight from hell! I know that the different churches claim that staying in hell is atrocious, and yet you will see that my ghosts do not seem to be so unfortunate as that. I decided to bring the illustrious personalities who stayed in this magnificent house to the end of time, that is, to infinity! Ladies and gentlemen, I ask you to welcome, in a thunder of applause, the former owners of the Castle of La Croe!

Voldemar had pronounced the last sentence with an overflowing exaltation, but it was clear that no one shared his euphoria because once again not a single applause was heard in the heavy silence that reigned. Women glanced anxiously each other, and the men slipped their hands under their jackets to grab their handguns. No doubt all the guests thought that this old Count was good to lock up in an asylum for lunatics, and it would be better to bury him alive in the garden!

– Gentlemen, bad idea! –Voldemar exclaimed– The use of firearms, knives or other sharp blades is strongly discouraged. This kind of weapon has no effect on those who will join us since they are already dead. However, you could hurt yourself and your neighbors.

Worried about the turn of the evening, Roman Abramovich decided to intervene and act as if he were attending a regular show: he clapped his hands. The guests, surprised, turned to the master of the place who encouraged them to look like him. These good people hesitated a few moments, but then, not wanting to offend their respectable host, imitated him, at first softly, and finally it was loud applause that flooded the ballroom. Voldemar then bowed to the assembly in a grotesque reverence which provoked laughter and mockery. But the guests soon ceased to joke about the old Count who looked like a jester, for suddenly the huge Venetian mirror with the bronze frame on one of the walls of the hall began to wave like a wave, and shifting shadows appeared on the window, which began to increase as they got closer to the public.

First, two silhouettes finally came out of the mirror, and began to take human form. Faced with this supernatural phenomenon, some women fainted. Other guests, speechless, continued to applaud like automatons. But most of the guests were frightened, not knowing what to do. Even the most hardened men, those who had known the hell of the Siberian camps, shivered with fear. In certain looks, which were browsing left and right, we could read the thoughts that animated them: "Thank God, I'm not crazy! All the others seem to see the same thing as me!

Voldemar, not a little proud of his effect, began to present the two silhouettes from the beyond, whose features were now perfectly drawn:

– My friends, you have probably already recognized the first of our guests: King Edward VIII of Great Britain, later relegated to the rank of Duke of Windsor! Beside him, of course, is his wife, the incomparable Wallis Simpson! Let's welcome them with warm applause!

Voldemar spoke like an American presenter and seemed to take a real pleasure in seeing the astonished faces of the russian new rich with a halt in a heavy stupor could only frantically clap their hands.

– That's better! –Voldemar appreciated– I would ask you to greet our prestigious guests with such enthusiasm every time!

The Count was not fooled: the applause was motivated only by fear, the guests wondering what would happen to them if they did not answer his orders. And the power he wielded over those people who believed themselves so superior was not displeasing to him. Voldemar then turned to the ghost of Wallis Simpson and said bowing:

– Madam, you are lovely!

Wallis Simpson replied with a smile. It must be said that the American woman was not wearing a white sheet, as is often the ghosts, but an elegant dress in the fashion of the 30s.

In addition, this american diva was adorned with an impressive amount of glittering jewels, to make the young women who accompanied the Russian oligarchs dressed in luxurious outfits die from fierce envy.

– You can see for yourself that the so-called torments of hell have not changed the beauty of Mrs. Simpson! –Voldemar commented.

Another specter came out of the mirror under the astonished eyes of the audience. Voldemar waited for the vaporous figure to resume his human features and introduced him in turn to the still dumbfounded public:

— Ladies and gentlemen, we now welcome King Leopold III of Belgium! Applaud his Majesty more, please!

The guests in the same spirit as before had to focus in order to strike more vigorously in their hands. None of those present, except Boris, could stop, as they were all petrified with fear and could only clap their hands to express mute enthusiasm on their contorted faces. Voldemar remarked:

— My dear friends, do not you think that King Leopold is still a very handsome man? It has nothing to envy to King Umberto of Italy!

As Voldemar spoke, a new figure had advanced into the room and finished materializing. The Count pointed to her hand and said:

— And here is the mother of Leopold III, the gracious Elizabeth.

This time, Voldemar did not need to insist that the audience applaud; everyone had resigned themselves to playing the sinister game imposed on them by the old man. As a new figure had materialized, Voldemar immediately resumed:

— We now have the honor to welcome the sublime Helen of Greece, whose beauty is matched only by that of her illustrious namesake: the divine Helen of Troy, who was at the time considered the most beautiful woman of the world and who today inflamed with her charms all the demons of the Underworld, in which she languishes at the present time, so the husband of whom she betrayed still has not forgiven her traitorous wife.

While living people slowly came to their senses, Voldemar continued to present the ghosts that came out of the mirror, with the audience already at will becoming more eager to cheer each new paranormal apparition:

– Ladies and gentlemen, allow me to introduce you to the breathtaking Athina Livanos, accompanied by her first husband, Aristotle Onassis, and their two children: Alexander, who died in a plane crash, and Christina, who died at thirty-seven years in strange circumstances and according to the official version of the abuse of Coca-Cola soda.

Further, the chief leading the conference, in order to moisten a dry throat, drank a huge glass of champagne in one gulp and continued just as cheerfully:

– And here is the third husband of Athina: billionaire Stavros Niarchos, who was also, a few decades ago, the owner of the Castle of La Croe. And it gives us the pleasure to come to us with his third wife: the beautiful Eugenia Livanos, who is the older sister of Athina Livanos. Eugenia died in 1970, at the age of forty-three, from an overdose of barbiturates. The brave Stavros Niarchos then married, in 1971, the younger sister of Eugenia, Athina Livanos, the ex-wife of Aristotle Onassis. Alas, like her sister, Athina died of an overdose of sleeping pills, only four years after the death of Eugenia... The curse does not stop there as the son of Eugenia and Stavros Niarchos, Konstantinos, died of an overdose of cocaine: here he is joining us! Konstantinos Niarchos is the first Greek to have climbed Everest. Watch them, ladies and gentlemen! It's a wonderful family! True, their lives have ended in tragic and obscure circumstances, but their existence has been full of twists and turns. And you can see that if their relationships were not serene in their earthly life, they are now reunited in the afterlife and all get along very well. And then, the earthly epic of this family is not over yet: you have surely heard of one of the grandchildren of Eugenia and Stavros, who is called Stavros Jr. and seems to enjoy the company of actresses Hollywood. It must be said that he has to hold on: he loves women as much as his grandfather, whose beauty he has inherited!

After finishing the presentation of the Greek clan, Voldemar glanced at Roman Abramovich's very pleasant and charming companion.

Boris got the impression that the Count spoke to her telepathically. Besides, he ended by winking at her, with his right eye, as if they were accomplices of some secret. Then he returned to his horde of ghosts and threw himself into the presentation of another family, whose fate was just as tragic as that of the Greeks: the Kennedy. The transition between the two clans was easy for Voldemar to find:

– Now here is Aristotle Onassis' last wife: the charming Jacqueline Kennedy! You may notice that Jacqueline took on the appearance she had when she was at the height of her beauty, like all our guests from the other world ... and that's a chance for us! Is it not, gentlemen? Because it must be said that the ravages of cancer had, alas, altered the beauty of Jacqueline at the end of his earthly life.

Jacqueline Kennedy's ghost came forward to greet the audience, elegantly waving her right hand. Following her, appeared the specter of her first husband, John Fitzgerald Kennedy, to whom Jacqueline cast a distracted look of love, while she did not even deign to turn her head towards her second husband, Aristotle Onassis.

"All the rivalries of their earthly life may not have disappeared in the realm of the dead, contrary to what Voldemar asserts!" —Boris thought.

Of course, Boris, like all the other guests, immediately recognized John Fitzgerald Kennedy, Jacqueline's first husband and president of the United States. The brevity of his tenure had not tarnished his popularity, and even today, reports about the handsome American president were flooding television screens. Moreover, Boris just as easily recognized the two brothers of John Fitzgerald Kennedy, Joseph and Robert, whose ghosts appeared, followed by their sister Kathleen, all three dead, like their famous brother, in tragic circumstances.

Voldemar, as if he had read Boris' thoughts, said in a tone as enthusiastic as ever:

— I gave a little quicker representation on this famous family because I see that you know well the history of Kennedy and that you recognize them without difficulty. However, let me introduce Robert Kennedy's children, who are doing us the honor to visit us today: David, who died of an overdose, and Michael, who led a healthy lifestyle but died in a skiing accident. Let us note in passing that drugs are responsible for many deaths, although this tragic story with Michael makes me remember a wise saying: "Who does not smoke and does not drink will die in good health".

Voldemar proud of his joke burst out laughing before resuming:

— David and Michael are accompanied by their cousin, John Jr, the son of John Fitzgerald and Jacqueline, who smoked and drank, but who died in a plane crash with his wife and her sister, who join us just now. Once again, look like the the afterlife in my hell preserves well souls of dead people: these young women are of a prodigious beauty! Oh! And here is the proof: the divine Marilyn Monroe does us the honor of her presence! The famous mistress of John Fitzgerald Kennedy, with a wonderful voice, died in mysterious circumstances. And, speaking of beautiful voice, the greatest soprano of all time has just joined us: the sublime Maria Callas, who will make us the joy of singing for us tonight. Note that Callas was the mistress of Aristotle Onassis, here present. And to close this spectral parade, we welcome King Farouk of Egypt, accompanied by a part of the women of his divine harem.

Voldemar seemed a little tired of having talked so much. He grabbed a glass of champagne, which a pretty waitress handed on a gold tray. Then he spoke again to give some precautionary advice, but his voice was a little broken:

— Ladies and gentlemen, I hope you will not have the stupid idea, like St. Thomas in the New Testament, of doubting the real existence of our glorious guests. Do not try to push the blades of your daggers into their diaphanous bodies: this will not make them disappear and you could hurt yourself. Do not put your hands through their spectral envelopes: it's not very polite, and they hate it. If they come near you and speak to you, do not be afraid and behave as if you are talking to living people. Remember that you are all mortal and that one day or another, you will be like them. You all die soon, but if you still appear the opportunity to return to earth, you would not want the living to be disrespectful to you. Isn't it like that, dear friends?

Voldemar paused to allow time for the guests to assimilate his advice. Then, he concluded, crying out in a joyful voice:

– But, for the moment, ladies and gentlemen, you are still alive! So enjoy it! Enjoy the delicious dishes that Roman Abramovich has prepared for you, and revel in the tasty wines that are offered to you. You had been promised a prodigious party, I believe the promise was kept!

Suddenly the room fills with a haunting melody, carried by a magnificent voice: the ghost of the great Callas had begun to sing an operatic aria. The scene, which one would not have dared to hope in the world of the living, was unreal. But that did not seem to move the specter of Marilyn Monroe who, grumpy, made a scene of jealousy to his lover, John Fitzgerald Kennedy. But several ghosts intervened quickly and managed to calm the spirits.

Meanwhile, waiters in golden livery wandered among the guests, with trays laden with crystal glasses filled to the brim with vintage wine or Champagne Hector-Bastien! It was rare brand of champagne productions which is produced to this day great care by Chef de Cave winemaker Sylvain Espaullard exclusively by hand, not by industrial means and himself the only from grapes own registered vineyards in Les Riceys and so to speak: “from planting to bottle".

The reason for the denial of the use of famous brands was that famous brand Dom Pérignon is already out of fashion due to the fact that real gentlemen from Russia could not humiliate themselves to use products of industrial production designed for consumers of the lower class.

Also, respected guests were offered toast with caviar and other refined amusebuthes. Brought back to earthly pleasures, the guests relaxed gradually and some even dared to mingle with the beings from hell. The latter, moreover, took care to show their most respectful side, so that the living felt comfortable in their presence.

"Even dead, they kept their good manners, typical of the culture of Western countries!" — Boris says to himself.

The magician had already had the opportunity to see Voldemar's specter at the bus station, and he was relieved that tonight's ghosts look more normal, although the light diffused through the chandelier clearly shows the transparency of their bodies. Hardly had Boris made this reflection about it that Voldemar, with the prudence of the devil, ordered the servants to reduce the intensity of the lighting. Once this adjustment was made, it was almost impossible to distinguish the dead from the living. If the ghosts of the illustrious guests behaved in an irreproachable way, it was not the same with the demons Zozo and Lulu. These two, isolated in a corner of the room, were drunk like the damned and were smoking marijuana until the skin turns green. Although their behavior was not very decent, but very understandable, since only they, unlike other guests, still were able to enjoy this evening well. All living people and ghosts could hear this devilish couple laughing loudly and chatting animatedly, certainly making derogatory comments about the guests.

Boris looked approvingly at the fun that his demonic friends were having, and then gazed sadly at the well-educated audience who arrived in hopeless Russian boredom or in terrible English spleen, also burdened with eternal torment of hell.

Despite the supernatural presence of scandalous personalities, the party resembled to any social evening: everyone was overly courteous and the atmosphere very quiet, not to say deadly boring! People of high society can despise ordinary people. But on the other hand, the plebs knew how to have fun, while modern patricians in their joy began to look very much like frozen cod!

When Voldemar came to see Boris to ask him how he found the evening, the magician frankly told him he felt that the diabolical holiday was lacking in dynamism. The incarnation of the Devil nodded to Boris' criticism and gently snapped his fingers. Immediately, all the young women, who accompanied the oligarchs, ran to the next room, leaving these gentlemen alone with ghosts. But the aristocrats continued arguing as if nothing had happened, seeming not to have noticed the sudden absence of their riders.

— But look at them! — Boris exclaimed, bewildered — These men do not even pay attention to their beautiful girls running away! What kind of education did they receive? They are either bad guys or very good gays!

— Do not worry, my friend. —Voldemar said calmly— These ladies very soon will draw attention to them from a fun moment to another more tragic performance.

As soon as Voldemar uttered these words, the door of the adjoining room where the girls had flown, flew open. The damsels reappeared in the ballroom, waddling on twenty centimeters high heels, and dressed in long swirling dresses. This time, all the men turned to them and went to stand on the sides of the room to leave room for the girls. The latter then executed a French cancan furious, slamming their heels on the floor and lifting the sides of their dress and publicly exposing their intimate parts. It was better understood why this dance had long been called "heckling" because their heels made so much noise that one would have thought that the marble floor freshly laid would explode into a thousand pieces. And, in view of the suggestive antics performed brilliantly by the dancers, it was not surprising that at the time, the cancan was scandalous.

— It reminds me of the good old days which I spent on Montmartre in the company of my friends of artists: Picasso, Gauguin and of course Van Gogh! —Voldemar said laughing— Boris, do you see those beautiful dresses? Well, it's me who drew them, especially for the occasion. And I'm very proud of the result! These girls are beautiful and their cancan is prodigious! Nothing to do with the Lido shows where the dancers always seem sad and exhausted! These young girls in bloom demonstrate an inexhaustible energy! Yes, I am very satisfied...

Boris turned his attention to the dresses and noticed that they looked like cassocks, with this detail: the fabric had been cut in multiple places, in long and wide, so that the cuts revealed, with the movements of dancing, the white skin of the girls, and the lace garters holding white silk stockings. And these unbridled nuns did not seem to wear underwear... Their head was covered with a thick veil, a little like the Ursuline, which hid their sophisticated hairstyle. And they had covered their faces with a Venetian mask glittering with gold. At the base, the black color of the nuns' tunics symbolized the absence of passions and the renunciation of material wealth. Also, one could think that garters and white stockings, worn by the dancers, represented the transgression of good morals.

After all, if all the women who still continue to be born on sinful earth, had retired to the dark caves of the Pecherskaya Lavra in Kiev, or to any other monastery, the human race could not have been perpetuated. Rather than getting lost in tedious prayers, it was better to enjoy life! And these young dancers came to liven up the routine that sometimes darkens earthly life.

– These monastic tunics, – Voldemar explained to Boris – represent the submission of these girls to my will. And the rips in the fabric show that they want to free themselves from the shackles in which society is imprisoned. If I let Christians take power in this world, you would all end up living like in the Middle Age! Fortunately, in this world I can do what I like! My divine Father must have better things to do than to be interested in the little parties I organize on Earth.

Voldemar began to laugh, then, resuming a more serious tone, added while looking at Boris right in the eyes:

– Your world is imperfect, because it is built on the many contradictions of the Scriptures. If humans were able to shake off the hold that religions have over them, they could open up to new horizons.

Boris looked down for a moment to think about what he was going to say, and as he looked up, Voldemar was gone!

– What an annoying habit he has taken to disappear like that! – Boris grumbled.

Suddenly, the music stopped and the dancers moved away. Boris then saw Voldemar reappear, dressed in a cardinal's red cassock and wearing a cap of the same color. The Count took a few steps of dancing, twirling in his right hand his cane with ivory pommel with a jackal's head. His short legs were good for a man of his age! When he was certain he had caught the attention of everyone, he stopped dancing and began to sing, in a pretty voice, the famous chorus song:

"And I'm happy, I'm happy, I'm happy, I'm happy, I'm cuckolded, but happy." Beyond his incongruous choice of song, which was still in the same tone as the sultry dance of the young ladies, Voldemar had a powerful and clear voice, which Luciano Pavarotti himself could have envied. Decidedly, he was too fit for a centenary, and Boris gradually let himself be convinced that Voldemar was truly the Devil, and not a sort of conjurer.

But Voldemar did not have time to finish his vocal performance because dull moans, seeming to come from the ceiling, interrupted him. While the ghosts remained indifferent to these heart-rending cries and continued to talk to each other, all the guests froze instantly and looked up at the place from which the complaints seemed to be coming. They then saw the creature who had dared to spoil the beautiful atmosphere that had set in: the ghost of a young girl, wearing ragged rags, was chained to the ceiling. Her body was swollen and bore traces of deep cuts from which blood was oozing. Behind her the shadow of an executioner stood out on the ceiling: the hood that covered his head and the gigantic ax he held in his hands were discernible.

– You are born under a very sad star! –The girl cried in a hoarse voice– You prefer to have fun rather than trying to unravel the mysteries of the universe and love!

This feminine specter which displayed a sinister expression on her beautiful face surprised Boris and left him an unpleasant sensation. Voldemar seemed unhappy. He waved his hand, as if to chase away this apparition, and cried angrily:

– Again, this idiot could not help but come! It's always the same thing! She must always spoil my holidays with her jealousy!

Then, seeing that the guests were starting to panic, he resumed in a calm voice to try to reassure them:

– Ladies and gentlemen, calm down, please! There is nothing to panic! It's just Gretchen, the one that Faust fell in love with and which Goethe tells us about so well in his immortal work of art. Yes, yes, the same crazy and very sinful girl who chose to be on the chopping block under the executioner's ax, rather than run away from prison with my friend Faust who came to release her. And now she only complains and moans like a soul in pain. She never leaves others in peace! Ladies and gentlemen, do not worry about her: she's already dead, and she can not die twice!

He paused for a moment, as if to preserve his effect, then ordered in a loud voice:

— Executioner, do your job!

Immediately, the shadow of the executioner lifted his ax and made it fall with power on Gretchen's neck. The girl's head then fell from the ceiling and landed in the middle of the guests who shrieked in horror before rolling down the floor a few dozen centimeters like a fresh cabbage. The blood had spurted on the beautiful toilets of the guests who repelled by this terrible execution uttered horrified exclamations.

— Gentlemen, —Voldemar said enthusiastically— I hope that you are not badly hurt by the spatter of blood and the sight of the severed head of this damn thing! You all move in the business world in Russia. You are in the habit of shedding blood innocent people! After all, it is known that the death of one person is a real tragedy, while the terrible and premature death of millions of people whom you sacrificed for your enrichment is just statistical data!

Voldemar chuckled because he saw the puzzled looks on the faces of the gentlemen of fortune he had just targeted, then he continued in a softer tone:

— Ladies, Gretchen is no more dead than before! And if it can reassure you, know that every time the executioner cuts his ax on his neck this idiot spends the night with him and they engage in games much more pleasant than the one that we will play soon on this unforgettable night.

Reflexively, the guests looked up at the ceiling and saw that the silhouette of the executioner had disappeared, as well as the decapitated and chained body of the tortured. Then they looked down at Gretchen's head and realized that she was no longer there either. Seeing that the guests seemed reassured, Voldemar decided to explain the rest of the program:

– Now that we are all anointed with the blood of Gretchen, it is time that we resume the festivities. I propose a fun little game. The rules are simple: each man will choose one of the dancers dressed in nuns. Once all the men have made their choice, each of them will have to indulge in the pleasures of the flesh with the one he has chosen. And only after swinger-marriage relationship is tried that night, will young brides be able to remove their golden masks from their faces.

Everyone will then discover with whom they shared this moment of ecstasy. The winner, the king of the ball, will be the one who has chosen his true companion, despite their outfit that makes it unrecognizable, because it will mean that he has been guided by the power of love.

This lecherous game reminded Boris of the secret orgies in which he had participated, in private clubs, before meeting Margot.

But despite the fact that his beloved escaped that night, the great magician hardly imagined himself playing side games for adults without the accompaniment of his beloved Margot or indulging in lust with another woman. At the limit, he could have been tempted by Lulu, but she was drunk dead, lying in a corner of the room with Zozo, and was not one of the masked dancers. Boris thought that Mikhail Prokhorov, who had come with half a dozen young women, just obligated to share one of her seductive girls! And Boris had to admit that it was quite tempting to "steal" the wench of a Russian oligarch. Boris thought:

– After all, we're just applying our grandfather Lenin's advice that you have to share what you have with your neighbor! And Christian morality encourages us to share our excesses with poor people. Participate in an orgy without my Margot dislike me, but this redhead bitch ran away that night and I don't even know with which dog she spends her time today ?!

Boris was bogged down in conflicting thoughts, and he did not know what to do. Suddenly, an idea passed through the encumbered mind of the magician: "What if the Count wanted to trap me? To prove to me that true love does not exist and that my wish to find Margot which he refused to answer is ridiculous. After all, it's the Devil!"

While Boris indulged in these cogitations, the oligarchs had begun to choose a partner each. Voldemar had taken a seat on a gilded chair lined with purple velvet. He looked like a king on his throne. Behind him, his court, composed of diaphanous ghosts, formed a perfect semicircle. Voldemar and his ghosts watched what was going on around them in silence. Some oligarchs having chosen their new girl had already embarked on passionate antics. Remembering the pleasure of physical love, perhaps ghosts felt a certain nostalgia for their earthly life but they did not betray their emotions and feelings. While all the gentlemen seemed to have made their choice, two masked girls remaining without a partner approached Boris.

The latter had finally decided not to participate in the game because he did not want to fall into the trap of Voldemar.

So, despite the temptation of these two women, Boris just offered them a glass of wine and a cigarette. He explained to them that he was in agreement to discuss questions that concern them, but that it would not go further. He added that it would be more pleasant to talk to them if they did not wear their masks, because he could thus admire the beauty of their faces. One of the girls laughed, visibly charmed by Boris' speech and decided to stay with him. But the other girl preferred to leave and went to sit at another table, hoping that a hungry oligarch, after fulfillment of their wishes with the first woman, would need a second partner to satisfy their desires. The girl who stayed with Boris took off her mask, revealing a pretty face and brown hair, and sat down beside him. The magician had recognized one of Mikhail Prokhorov's courtesans; he served her a glass of wine, which she gracefully received with a smile of gratitude on her beautiful lips. Then the pretty brunette decided to start the conversation:

– It's a very strange game that takes place here...

– Not as strange as it might seems! –Boris said bitterly– On the French Riviera there are many establishments where one can indulge in this kind of practice.

– So, why do you not participate? –The girl asked softly.

– Because my girlfriend is not here! –Boris answered without going into details– If I participated by oneself, it would distort the rules of the game, since I have no chance to choose my partner with another girl. And then, I'm not an oligarch...

— Who are you then? —His interlocutor asked intrigued.

— I am a friend of Voldemar. —Boris explained— The one who orchestrated this evening (he nodded to the Count who was sitting on his throne a little further).

— Oh, that strange old man scares me! —The young woman said— If he is your friend, you must know who he is?

— Well... —Boris hesitated— Like his ghosts, he comes from the world of the dead and it's me who brought it out from hell to our world.

— How?! —The young lady exclaimed.

Her fingers adorned with golden rings began to tremble and, panicking, she collapsed on her knees in front of Boris, begging him for mercy:

— Please, do not hurt me! Please! I have a family in Borispol, Ukraine! I do not want my daughter to grow up without me!

Boris did not understand at first the reaction of the young woman who seemed very unhappy. Then he realized that the events of the evening had disturbed her and there was something she really scared: she had seen a horde of ghosts appears, not to mention the atrocious scene with Gretchen... And now he told him he that he pulled out the Devil from hell and returned it to life! Boris, embarrassed, tried to reassure her:

— Mademoiselle, come to your senses and look calmly at things! You have nothing to fear from me! I practice black magic but I am not one of those who murder young women with impunity. Go, miss, you must follow the path god pointed you.

The pretty brunette seemed stunned by the words of Boris who himself wondered where his last sentence came from, but she got up and went out of the ballroom, without taking a look at the orgiastic scene that was taking place in the house piece. From now on, everywhere, couples engaged in inflamed antics and groans of ecstasy echoed in every corner, while Voldemar and his ghosts watched, still and silent, the obscene spectacle. Boris wondered:

"Why did Voldemar organize all this staging, if it is for his ghosts to stay there, without saying or doing anything? When they were alive, were they so bored during their mundane nights? This would explain why participating in the party does not come them to mind: they have never used moments of erotic pleasure, even in their lifetime. Apparently, titles of nobility and wealth do not make one happy! These spectra are enclosed in a label that prevents them from having fun. Their money did not allow them to fulfill the dreams that they cherished so much that they plunged into a life of suffering, which has been perpetuated in the afterlife. To sum up, I think the earthly life of the aristocrats is so miserable that even after death they can not get rid of the rules that have always been imposed upon them. And yet, they are in hell... In heaven, it must be even more deadly boring!

In his thoughts, Boris did not immediately notice the bearded men, dressed in medieval costumes of hangman or jester, were changing the decor of the ballroom: now, in the middle of the room, were enthroned a nailed chair -- with nails on the surface of the seat, which is usually loved by Indian fakirs, and a cross of St. Andrew with leather straps at the end of its four branches, as well as a table on which were arranged torture accessories that had to have existed during the terrible Middle Ages.

The elegant ballroom looked like a sinister torture chamber of the Inquisition Court. But Voldemar thought that was not enough because he asked the bearded men to install, in addition, a wheel, a gallows, a sort of glass coffin pierced with holes and other strange equipment that would have inspired a feeling of disgust to any civilized person. But the guests tonight, who were slowly finishing their erotic session, were too intoxicated with sex to understand the stakes of all these macabre installations. All these good people were whispering to each other, watching the executioners and the jesters finish the assembly of the instruments of torture. It was at this moment that Boris came out of his thoughts and realized the change of scenery.

"What diabolical staging Voldemar has planned? —Boris wondered.

The magician was soon to have the answer to his question because the Count rose from his improvised throne and went to stand in the center of the room, in front of the machines of death. He waved his hands to ask for silence and, in a cheerful tone, announced the new scenario he had created so that those present in the hall do not have time to get bored:

— There was a time when people who did not share the chimerical point of view of the Church ended in such instruments of torture. Our nuns tonight have clearly sinned by indulging in lust! Gentlemen, you must punish them for their libidinous behavior! My jesters will give you costumes of different religious orders; you can choose the one that suits you best. Once you have taken on the appearance of worshipers of God, you will have to expel the evil that has taken possession of the spirit of the masked nuns, using the means at your disposal, concluded Voldemar pointing to the objects behind him.

That is why Voldemar had so many instruments installed: he wanted to torture all those women with dissolute morals! These people of high society were going to find themselves in absolute horror. Boris struggled to believe what he saw...

And yet, the oligarchs donned their monastic clothes without complaining. The vast majority of Russian businessmen chose the habit of the Dominicans. Some of their business partners, from the Orient, preferred the traditional costume of the dervishes. Rashid Selimovich, caucasian, was the only one to decide to dress in Sufi. The three men whom Boris had nicknamed "the Archangels" had disguised themselves as Jesuits.

Meanwhile, Voldemar had donned the white attire of the pope, and the bearded men had mounted a platform, upholstered in red velvet, on which sat an imposing desk in solid wood, adorned with black ribbons and wreaths. Voldemar placed himself in front of the tribune and exclaimed:

– I accuse these young nuns of having indulged in the seven deadly sins! They are witches and heretics! The tribunal assembled tonight must inflict exemplary punishment on them. At midnight, gentlemen, you can begin to punish these Ursuline's devils as it should. Jesuits, you will preside over this hearing. Take immediately the honorable places of the Inquisition Court! With that, Voldemar returned to his golden seat, his ghosts still sitting quietly behind him. And the three Archangels gained their place on the platform. It was a few minutes before the fateful hour and Boris, who had entrenched himself in a corner of the room, wondered with horror if the oligarchs would really dare to torture their companions. He felt like he was in a horror movie! As soon as the clock struck midnight, the three Jesuits ordered the nuns to remove their high-heels, dresses and shoes: they found themselves only dressed in garter belts and stockings, their faces still covered with their Venetian masks. The Archangels then appointed five penitents women and summoned them to appear before the tribune, accompanied by the men to whom they had given themselves a little earlier. One of the women being the one who had seduced Archangel Mikhail Prokhorov became the first victim of a trial and humane punishment and her judge and executioner went with her to the place of torture.

The two other Jesuits then enjoined to his brothers in Christ to choose the punishment which their their fallen women deserved. The five depraved women immediately were tenderly punished in the style of a soft and loving Catholic church. Two men dressed as Dominicans chose to lock up their two victims together in the glass coffin. Through the holes of the clear coffin they cut the women's bodies with sharp blades and poured hot wax on their thin and delicate skin. The two girls screamed and twitching frantically in all directions bumping into the walls of glass.

A third Dominican planted his unhappy girl bare buttocks on the nail chair and made her open her mouth wide. The man lifted his habit of religious abstinence and forced his penis in the mouth of the young woman, on the face of which big tears rolled. The fourth man, disguised as a dervish, tied his victim to a block of wood, her bust resting on the tray and her legs falling against the wall of the block. Then he hit the young lady's back and buttocks with his whip. The poor girl screamed in pain each time the staff slammed on her body. The fifth man, Mikhail Prokhorov, was the most zealous of the five torturers. He tied up with the help of two executioners his companion on the cross of St. Andrew. Then he carefully selected several objects on the table where torture tools were lined up and thrust them in turn into the vagina and anus of the young woman who was screaming terribly. No one spoke in the hall, filled only with the screams of the tortured and the sneers of their executioners. The five young women begged the men to stop, shouting that they regretted what they had done and would not do again sin and refuse to always work in the excursions of prostitutes. The other men silently observed their comrades, who were more and more eager to accomplish their misdeeds for the benefit of a great faith in eternal and unearthly love. They must surely be inspired by what they saw to how better and more sophisticated to cause terrible torment to other depraved girls when their turn came do divine justice on behalf of Jesus Christ.

The other girls, half-naked, were huddling against each other under the surveillance of several executioners in case one of them had the stupid idea of trying to escape. They cried in silence, wondering what fate would be reserved for them. A jester passed in front of them with a tray filled with ecstasy pills. The women grabbed handfuls from a tray of pills and swallowed them without question, hoping only that the drugs would allow them to better withstand the suffering they were going to endure. Same they were handed bottles of strong alcohol, which they did not take long to empty bitter contents and thereby disconnect from terrible reality. When the first five executioners judged that their victims had repented enough and had been sufficiently punished, jesters came to liberate them. But the victims of the Inquisitors were tormented to such an extent that they could no longer stand on their own and the executioners had to carry them to a corner of the room, where their victims were stacked one on top of another as if bundles of firewood. Then the three Jesuits on their platform called five new women. The latter, having seen what their friends in misfortune had undergone before, began to resist and executioners had to intervene to take them to the platform by applying brute force on them. One of girls knelt in front of her evening lover and begged him to spare her but the man just slapped her violently and told her to stop moaning. Besides, she was not the only one to repent even before the torture began. Most of the other women who followed demanded the clemency of their executioner, but none of the men showed the slightest pity. Some women even admitted acts of witchcraft they did not commit, but this made the ruthless monks only laugh. The torture session lasted for a time that seemed infinitely long to Boris. The magician could no longer bear to hear the screams of sorrow and the supplications of the young women whose faces were still hidden by the gilded masks. And he was disgusted to see the men show no compassion for those with whom they had previously shared a moment of sexual ecstasy. On the contrary, the executioners seemed to use ingenuity to find ideas of torture ever crueler. The oligarchs seemed inhabited by a furious madness which gave birth to a bad light in their eyes. They showed a disgusting sadism. The barbaric spectacle that unfolded before Boris' eyes made him think of the period of the Inquisition about which so many movies were made in Hollywood, when witches were burned alive in the public square before the eyes of enthusiastic commoners. The devotees wanted to let the people know what he was risking if he did not respect the precepts of the Church. These scenes of violence which had become almost banal, had only fueled a wave of terror and ignominious actions. The unfortunate victims often unjustly accused, might have repented of their so-called sins, but their fate was sealed anyway. The members of the Inquisition wanted to satisfy their barbaric impulses at any cost. Boris had the impression of being immersed in the heart of this dark period of history. When all the girls had received their punishment a heavy silence settled suddenly. The girls were lying in a corner scarcely conscious. Their bodies covered with bloody wounds formed a mass of swollen flesh.

"Such a waste! They were so beautiful and fresh just now!" —Boris thought.

The eyes of the young women were empty and inexpressive, like those of prisoners coming out of Vladimir prison or

Siberian detention camps. Suddenly, Voldemar demanded that the girls be brought to the center of the room. Some were no longer standing and had to be supported by the executioners and jesters. Then the Count ordered the men to stand each in front of their companion and remove the mask. It was then the general stupefaction! Out of twenty-one couples, only one was composed of a man and a woman who came together at the party: Roman Abramovich and his elegant companion ... a little less distinguished now. So only Roman Abramovich had the honor to personally torture his girlfriend. All the others had inflicted the worst abuse on the darlings of their friends.

— Bravo, Roman! —Voldemar cried happily— You can be sure that the love that unites you to your companion is sincere. Your heart was not wrong when you chose your partner. You gave me proof that love does exist. You are the king of the ball!

Voldemar hastened to put a gold crown on the head of Roman Abramovich, owner of the Castle of La Croe where a strange celebration had just taken place. Abramovich gave a tense smile; he did not seem very happy to have won that victory. But Voldemar was not upset: after all, Abramovich could no longer rejoice at anything, since he had made a pact with the Devil.

Chapter 7 - After the party

Once the king of the ball was appointed, the ghosts disappeared and the guests began to leave the Castle of La Croe, the men to support the young women who struggled to walk. Boris hastened to the terrace to take a great breath of fresh air. He needed it. The smell of sea iodine refreshed him somewhat. This evening had plunged him into an indefinable disorder. Of course, he had been fascinated by the appearance of ghosts: all those illustrious people who had materialized little by little, to resume human form, a little like the wax statues, exhibited at the Musée Grévin in Paris or Madame Tussaud's museum in London, which would suddenly come to life. Boris had also found it amusing to see all the wealthy Russian businessman show up with damsels much younger than them, as if their midlife crisis brought them a boost of testosterone. And before the evening turned to horror, the magician had not tired from admiring the beauty of the young ladies. Boris said to himself:

"Men, young and old, rich and poor alike, actually all aspire to the same thing: eat well, drink well and have a good time with pretty girls!"

As for the spectacle of torture that Boris had witnessed, he felt disgust for it, and at the same time it had revealed many things about human nature. The magician felt a little lost: he had wished so much that his monotonous life was alive and now that he lived full of adventures, he feared the turn that it was taking. At least now, Boris no longer doubted that Voldemar was really the Devil. The magician plunged into his thoughts:

"The Count clearly told me that he did not believe in love, so why is he trying to find evidence of the existence of love? It is very paradoxical, not to mention the fact that the methods he uses are abominable. We are far from the well-meaning ideas of the Church which preaches respect for the integrity of the person. Voldemar seems to have no morality, and his staging tonight borders on madness. And yet, he is devilishly intelligent. So why is he interested in love? Moreover, love itself is a paradox: it can disappear as quickly as it appeared! The Devil seems full of contradictions: is he a genius or a madman? It is said that "genius is elder brother of madness". So, maybe Voldemar has a bit of both, and that's not so bad!"

Boris smiled at this thought.

– Your reflections rejoice me, my friend! – A voice exclaimed behind him.

The magician was so surprised that he was interrupted as he turned quickly and almost punched Voldemar out of nowhere, standing behind him. Boris held his gesture in extremis.

— Count, you should not appear like that without warning, behind the back of people! —Boris snarled— They could have a heart attack! And then, are you listening to my thoughts now? That's another thing!

Voldemar did not answer, letting Boris' temper tantrum pass, who was quick to calm down and continued in a softened voice:

— Forgive me, Count, for having been carried away. But all these strange phenomena are somewhat disturbing.

— You do not have to apologize! —Voldemar answered— I must admit that the rules of politeness of the terrestrial world escape me. Humans know these principles innately. Their behavior is induced by ancestral and unconscious memory, and then by the education they received from their parents. In this, they make me think of ants which have a very structured society and who know, from their first day of life, what role they must play. But I did not learn anything from it! However, when I am in your world, I should conform to human behavior.

— I think it would be more appropriate. —Boris retorted curtly.

— And that's precisely why I need a companion like you! —Voldemar replied— Your presence at my side will help me better understand the rules that govern men's lives. Don’t we say that "two opinions are better than one"? Moreover, unlike many people, you are not a sheep, Boris! By this I mean that you do not believe everything you are told. You seek to understand things for yourself. This is a great quality, my friend, because too many people take for cash all the nonsense we sell them. Worse, some people, faced with the most obvious stupidity, will endeavor not to listen to what the very reason dictates, just not to deviate from the norm. Look, for example, at these wretches who bury themselves in the caves of the Pecherskaya Lavra in Kiev as if they were earthworms or moles, blinded by their naive belief in wacky texts. Thank God, you are not like those people!

— Thank God? —Boris smiled— It's a little surprising to hear you thank God!

— And why can not I thank him? —Voldemar chuckled— After all, he is also my Father! He created me to test the strength of the faith of Jesus and his followers. And, you have seen, he lets me do anything I want in the world of men! I thank him because I have fun. God is good, just loving and preaching forgiveness. Me, I am the opposite!

— But, in that case, Count, why did you punish the pope of St. Nicholas Church? — Boris asked intrigued Pedophilia is the height of evil! You who are the incarnation of evil, you should rather congratulate him for such acts, because he makes evil reign on earth.

— Here is an excellent question! —Voldemar exclaimed— What annoys me about pedophile priests is that they discharge their guilt on me! They indulge in their evil deeds, and then go to pray to God saying: "Forgive me, Lord! Because the Devil pushed me to sin! ". Well, no, I refuse to be associated with that! It is not me who encourages them to abuse their young sheep. It is they who decide to behave this way. Men tend to discharge their responsibilities to me. But do you really believe that I'm interested in your daily small pettiness? Let's see! My ambition is much bigger! The living that I take under my wing are people of power, those who can really spread evil around the world. Did you see, Boris tonight what kind of people surrounding me? And I could name other more prestigious names, such as Alexander the Great, Napoleon, Mao Zedong, Hitler, Stalin and Putin. All the "great bad guys" in history have lent me allegiance, and they still have followers. So, you can well imagine that the escapades of a little depraved priest, lost in a miserable orthodox church far from his native country, do not interest me! It's too easy to take all the actions of people on my back!

— However, it is said that "the Devil is in the details". — Boris noted— In other words, small malignancies are also evil.

— Certainly, but all ordinary meanness is are not my fault. —Voldemar said— Evil is an integral part of the human being and I do not need to intervene so that this dark part is expressed.

— If I understand correctly, —Boris said— it is not the acts of the pope that you reprove, but the fact that he does not assume that he is the only one responsible for his sins. And that's why you forced him to confess his guilt.

— Absolutely, my friend! —Voldemar agreed— This priest betrays his God, by not respecting his precepts, and dirtying my name, by blaming me. He may repent, but I will not forgive him this offense. I am not God! Because you must understand, Boris, that these cockroaches, who say they commit bad deeds because of me can hurt my big project. Evil, so that he can reign on earth, must not be rude. On the contrary, it must be subtle, as in the pacts that we spend with me. And this is where I agree that indeed, "the Devil is in the details," because it must creep discretely and then explode in all its splendor.

As he said these words, Voldemar's eyes began to shine with a cruel glow that sparkled in the darkness. Boris, seeing that his interlocutor was starting to get excited, preferred to divert the conversation:

– In spite of all the things with which men overwhelm you, do you know that they lend you a comic power? (Voldemar puzzled, opened his eyes.) Yes, Count, there are jokes about you. My favorite is this: a man arrives in hell and is greeted by the Devil who tells him, pointing to three doors: "You will have to choose the room in which you will stay for eternity". The man opens the first door and sees a group of people balancing on the head, on tiles. The man said to himself: "It must be painful to stay on such hard ground. I will try another door". The man opens the second door: people are there too in balance on the head, but this time on an old floor all damaged. The man said to himself: "The floor is full of splinters. It must hurt a lot. Let's try the last door". The man opens the third door: this time, people sit on chairs, but they have shit up to their knees. The man says to himself: "To spend the eternity sitting on a chair, even with shit up to the knees, it is more bearable than to remain in balance on the head". He returns to see the Devil and announces that he chooses the third room.

– Very well! –the Devil replied– You will spend eternity there.

The Devil accompanies the man to the third door, and when he sees everyone seated, exclaims: "Hey! The coffee break is over! Everyone on the head! ".

The joke amused Voldemar, who laughed heartily. Then, catching his breath, he remarked to Boris:

— This is the proof that we must always be careful when we reach an agreemen... especially with the Devil! American friends told me a similar joke, except that it is Barack Obama who arrives in hell and that, among the various punishments that are presented to him, he sees Monica Lewinsky make a treat to Bill Clinton, which does not seem to him not be too painful torture. Also, Barack decides to choose this punishment, without inquiring further on the conditions of the punishment ... so that he finds himself forced to take the place of Monica!

Voldemar laughed a long time at his typical American joke. Boris almost regretted having thrown the Count into the field of humor because his joke had made him think of the orgy that had taken place a few hours earlier and the macabre scene that had followed. Seeing that Boris seemed preoccupied, Voldemar asked him kindly:

— My friend, something is wrong? Come on, tell me what is tormenting you.

— No, all is well... —Boris hesitated— But I was thinking about what happened tonight. Do you believe that the oligarchs and their young companions will be able to resume the normal course of their lives after experiencing such traumatic events? Between the ghosts and the staging that turned some into executioners and others into victims of the Inquisition...

— My friend, you are mistaken if you think that this is the first time that these men and women have lent themselves to sadomasochistic games. —Voldemar answered— Admittedly, this may be the first time that these businessmen have abandoned themselves so much to their sadistic tendencies, but in their daily lives they behave like real torturers with those around them. I only highlighted what they really are, in the deepest of themselves, both men and women elsewhere, because they let themselves be treated as less than nothing every days that God does. But if I had chosen to turn the tables, women into executioners and men into victims, do you think women would have been more lenient? When we offer humans the opportunity to express their dark side, they do not deprive themselves! The barrier between evil and good is tremendously moving. It is to verify this idea that a few years ago, I urged prominent psychology professors at Stanford University to carry out a highly successful experiment that consisted in reproducing conditions of detention in prison. Participants were selected for their mental stability and did not have any particular provision for violence or submission. They were randomly divided into two groups: prisoners and guards. The roles could have been exchanged. The first day of the experiment was rather quiet, but the next day the guards began to mock and insult the prisoners. And the cruelty of the jailers grew crescendo: from starvation to sexual humiliation. And yet, no prisoner left the experience, as if, in spite of the violence that they underwent, the prisoners accepted their fate. They respected the precept of my brother Jesus Christ: "If anyone strikes you on one cheek, present him also the other". Only one prisoner denounced the cruel behavior of the guards, but when he was punished for his rebellion, no other prisoner supported him. And the guards, they, loved so much this feeling of domination that most of them asked to work overtime! The teachers and I, who watched them with cameras installed all over the prison, were fascinated by the changing behavior of the participants. Prisoners were showing more and more signs of emotional turmoil, and guards were becoming more and more sadistic, so much so that the experience was cut short. This observed phenomenon, that morally good people become bad if given the opportunity, has been named the "Lucifer effect". But I want to make it clear that I did not intervene in this experience, either in the minds of the jailers or in the prisoner who tried to rebel.

For religious and believers always reproach me for having risen with my fallen angels against my Father. But what should I have done? Let my Father behave like a tyrant without reacting? My attitude is only a reflection of human nature: when you enslave humans, most will submit, but some will resist. And you have seen that tonight, all the participants in my experience have submitted and played the role that has been assigned to them... all but you! Like what, we may have more in common than you thought. All that to say that you do not have to worry about the oligarchs and their companions because they have only expressed their true nature, especially that they, unlike the participants in the

Stanford experiment, are not what we would call "good people": the men were already, before tonight, true sadists and the women of prostitutes subjected, ready to do anything to attract the generosity of their pimp. They believe that because they have a lot of money, they have the right to do whatever they want. And what happened tonight will not change anything.

Voldemar completed his long soliloquy, watching for the reaction of Boris, who had listened with interest. But the magician did not know what to think of all this, so he just said:

– Count, your demonstration is very interesting, but it requires reflection and I must admit that I am too tired to formulate an intelligent answer. I'm sorry to give you a miss but I'm tired. Zozo, your driver, and Lulu are drunk dead: I saw them get into your Rolls-Royce and collapse sleep on the back seat. But, if you wish, I can take the wheel and take you back to where you are staying. I can even suggest you spend the night on my boat, although the cabin is a bit small for both of us...

– Do not worry, my friend! –Voldemar interrupted– I suspected that the evening would end well and I had planned a place where we could spend the night comfortably, without the need to hit the road again.

– Do you want to sleep here at Castle of La Croe? –Boris wondered– The building is still in very bad condition. I am not sure that there is room for us, nor that Roman Abramovich wants to offer us hospitality.

– No, we're not going to spend the night here. –Voldemar said, displaying a mysterious smile– In fact, leaving the

Castle of La Croe by the main entrance and along the road on the right, we arrive at a small discreet entrance that opens on the estate of Mr Berezovsky, the castle Garoupe. Rumor has it that Roman Abramovich often visited Boris Berezovsky on this road. It must be said that they were very good friends and it is no coincidence that they have neighboring residences. Indeed, in 1998, Boris Berezovsky, Roman Abramovich and Tanya Yeltsin were taking a boat ride in the gulf that is right in front of us. It's dark but in broad daylight, we have a beautiful view of this terrace. Alas, this beautiful gulf is tainted by dirty money circulating here. In short, it was during this trip at sea that the trio discovered the Castle of La Croe. Under the charm of the building, Boris Berezovsky, who has garnered a staggering amount of greenbacks which he has given Russia, wanted to buy the Castle of La Croe for his girlfriend Tanya, but someone told him about the history of this area and told him that he was cursed because he only welcomed fallen kings and unfortunate billionaires. Even to Onassis, he did not bring happiness. As a result, Boris Berezovsky turned away from the Castle of La Croe and preferred to buy the neighboring castle, that of Garoupe, whose restoration work was less important. However, he urged his business partner, Roman Abramovich, to buy the Castle of La Croe. But we must believe that the curse of the Castle of La Croe has spread to the Garoupe, since Boris Berezovsky has fallen out of favor with the Russian government. While his accomplice, Roman Abramovich, as you can see, is prospering well under my protection. Like what, it's nice to give ourselves to the Devil! Although Abramovich can no longer rejoice in his success...

As far as Berezovsky is concerned, his fervor for Judaism offended me so much so that I sent him into exile in London, where he languished in the English fog. Of course, he regrets having betrayed me and even converted himself, but I do not intend to forgive him for his behavior. As they say, "Beware of a tamed wolf, a baptized Jew, and a reconciled enemy." When I was staying at the Chateau de la Garoupe, her mother, an old woman, was preparing breakfast for me every morning. She behaved with me as if I were her son. She is not present at the castle at the moment but she gave me her consent for us to spend the night.

– In Mikhail Bulgakov's novel The Master and Margarita, the demon Koroviev hints that Woland lives in Nice all the time, where he has his own "bad castle". The castle of Garoupe would it be your "bad apartment", dear Count? —Boris smiled.

– My friend, there is inevitably some truth in the novels! – Voldemar answered mysteriously – Writers are always inspired by real people or events that have taken place in reality. And the talented Mikhail Bulgakov is no exception to the rule: he did not invent the character of Woland based on the wind!

Boris did not know how to interpret this last remark. In any case, Voldemar did not give him time to wonder further about the question because he took him by the elbow, saying:

– Come on, my friend, it's time to go to Garoupe Castle. We can relax by the old fireplace, around a nice glass of wine, before going to sleep. You will see more clearly tomorrow because, as they say, "the morning is wiser than the evening".

Leaving the Castle of La Croe, Boris glanced at the Earl's Rolls-Royce, still parked in the parking lot, and was surprised that he no longer saw Zozo and Lulu, who had to emerge of their ethyl sleep.

Voldemar and Boris went on the asphalt road. The magician was exhausted and hoped they would not have to walk too long.

— You are very quiet, my friend! — Voldemar pointed out — Do you still worry about the oligarchs and their companions? If it reassures you, the human mind is so made that it transforms reality when it seems too ubiquitous. Some guests will simply wipe this evening out of their minds, and others will say that they have had a very strange dream. In any case, they will not hold me true to what happened tonight.

Boris smiled at the Count to signify that he had understood, even though he wondered how it was possible to forget such an evening.

Voldemar directed Boris towards a gravel driveway at the end of which the Count opened a gate which gave direct access to the entrance to the castle of Garoupe. On the porch, Zozo and Lulu seemed to be waiting for them. When they saw them arrive, they rushed to meet them and exclaimed with enthusiasm for Voldemar's intention:

— Master, your show tonight was wonderful! We don't know how to thank you for giving us such a good time!

Voldemar, obviously flattered by their praise, humbly stopped them with a wave of his hand and said:

– I'm glad you enjoyed the evening, but our friend Boris needs some rest. Let's go relax in the living room.

At this they all four entered the house, and Voldemar immediately led them into the salon, where a magnificent chimney was enthroned. The Count fell into a leather chair and sighed:

– Ah! Here I am finally at home!

Then, turning to Zozo and Lulu, he threw them:

– Serve us a good glass of wine. And you, Boris, do not stay here! Take a seat in the chair next to me.

Boris complied, while Zozo and Lulu handed each of them a glass generously filled with a vintage nectar. Voldemar took a sip of wine, then began to monologize, as if thinking aloud:

– At least here, I do not have to bear the living, who constantly complain and never enjoy anything. They live in the past, always repeat the same mistakes, even if they repent, and fear to look at the future they see only through a thick veil of fog. However, the modern world offers them many facilities, but they do not know how to be content because they want more. Personally, I do not need much to be happy. I love old houses because their sturdy stone walls give me a sense of security. I like moments like this where, comfortably seated in a soft armchair, I can let my mind sail, watching the flames crackling in an old chimney and enjoying a good wine in a crystal glass of Baccarat. I can spend hours there, as when I lose myself in the contemplation of an impressionist painting. Modern men pride themselves on the progress of their society, but are all their inventions better than before? For my part, I prefer a leg of lamb well roasted molecular cuisine! The living say that God created the food, but it is I who created the kitchen, just to tempt them and make them succumb to the sin of gluttony! And it's the same for everything: they praise God when they are in good shape but, when they go wrong, it is on me that they reject the fault! Except when their last hour has come: there, too, they pray to God, to attract clemency. And when I offer them the freedom to get out of the shackles in which society locks them up, they often prefer to stay there! They are so used to being slaves to God or their rulers, as was the case with Caesar who was a real dictator, that freedom frightened them, and they imprison themselves, perverted by their stupid beliefs.

They are blinded by the prejudices that religions inculcate and lie to themselves, because it is simpler than looking in the face of what they really are: selfish beings whose choices are motivated solely by their personal interest. Even those who predict the end of the world do it for their own sake, because they think they'll get God's help when that day comes! But how can men still believe that God wants to help them for anything? It must be remembered, however, that it was he, the Creator of all things, who chased Adam and Eve out of paradise for a small fault of nothing at all... a fault he himself caused by creating the conditions conducive for it to be committed! So, after that, how can men believe that if they repent of their sins, God will welcome them to heaven? If they think that the Creator will receive repentant murderers and pedophiles with open arms, they will put their finger in the eye! Humans see evil everywhere, even where there is none. They always expect the worst, as if they were hoping for misfortune to happen to them. Yes, I have the impression that people feed on evil, so that they do everything to create it, more or less consciously. In Europe, during the Inquisition, the Church did not just burn the witches alive, it also eliminated the cats, because it considered that these animals were Satan's henchmen, simply because they did object of pagan cults. As a result, because there were fewer cats to hunt them, the rats proliferated, so much so that they transmitted the plague to the men. These horrible epidemics have been generated by the Church, not by me! And what about the brown plague, this disease of the mind? Admittedly, Hitler was one of my followers, but it was the men who chose to put him in power. And God did nothing to prevent this tyrant from executing his evil plan! Where are the scientists in all this? They should have the means to oppose beliefs that are not based on anything concrete. Yes, but here they are: they are afraid to expose the truth! It must be said that the Church did not hesitate to silence the too wise thinkers: look what happened to poor Giordano Bruno... In fact, as soon as we push the reason, superstitions settle and poison people's minds. And these false ideas have nearly destroyed human civilization on several occasions. Then, I wonder why the Church has opposed me for centuries: for it is crueler than all my demons together! Religions are a dangerous virus: they creep discreetly into the minds of men and wait for the right moment to destroy those it has infected. To understand how much religion makes its followers sick, one only has to look at what people are able to do with this insidious infection: they do not hesitate to kill in the name of their God! This has always been and will be again. It is said that it is I who do evil, but when we look more closely, we realize that I am far from being the only person responsible for the torments of humanity. And then, unlike religions, I assume what I do! For example, I am reproached for having instilled temptation into the minds of Adam and Eve, although it was God who created the Tree of knowledge of good and evil. Well, yes, it was I who prompted Eve, then Adam, to bite into the forbidden fruit, and I do not see what I did wrong! If I had not intervened, God would not have chased Adam and Eve out of paradise and humanity would not have existed! Yes, I tested the strength of faith of my brother Jesus, but if I had not done it, he would not be idolized today by millions of people! The worshipers of Christ should rather thank me rather than accuse me of all evils: without me, the legend of Jesus would not exist! And the Christians might have chosen Hinduism or animism... At least they would not have sent so many poor people to the stake! Oh, how men are deceived and deluded. Paradise, Adam and Eve, all these stories have been turned into charming fairy tales, but the truth is quite different...

Boris took advantage of Voldemar's catching his breath to intervene:

— Count, I have the impression that you are looking for excuses! It makes me think of a Russian joke... Tchebourachka, a small animal with big round ears, announces to his friend the crocodile an incredible news: "Old Shapoklyak gave birth to a strange animal in the hospital, with such a long green body, like yours, and with big ears, like me.

Do you think we have anything to do with this? ".

— I do not seek excuses and do not claim to be responsible for any of the misfortunes that fall on men! —Voldemar replied— It is obvious, as in your joke: I am the Devil and, therefore, I sow the evil. But I just stress that neither God nor men are exempt from all responsibility in the difficulties of earthly life. And sometimes I need to put all these things in order in my head so that I can have clear ideas. Rethinking what happened in the past helps me keep my goal in focus. You know, I'm eternal, and when you've been living so long, it's sometimes hard not to lose the thread. Now, it is essential that today and tomorrow, I continue in the same way.

Voldemar paused for a moment to take a sip of wine, then concluded:

— I think it's time you went to bed, my friend. Tomorrow we will go to the bus station to see what your old boss is cooking up. I want to tell you, Boris, that you impressed me tonight: during the orgy of the oligarchs and their companions, you did not succumb to the temptation, when two beautiful young women came to solicit you. In doing so, you have provided me with proof of the existence of love, because I know that if you refused to abandon yourself in the arms of one of these creatures, it is because you did not want betray Margot. What is so special about you that you deprive yourself of the pleasures of the flesh?

— I can not really answer this question, —Boris sighed— because love is not a rational feeling. Margot made me feel things I had never experienced before. And since she disappeared more than a month ago, I can not fill the void that her absence has left in my heart. Of course, I do not remain insensitive to female charms. For example, I find Lulu's overwhelming sensuality very disturbing, but even if I let myself be tempted by her, I know I would not feel the same osmosis as with Margot.

And it would have been the same with the girls of this evening: these young ladies, who charge for their services, could not bring me the slightest tenderness or the slightest passion. And now that I know what men have done to their partners, I am all the happier because I have not succumbed to temptation. These oligarchs are really Philistines who have no other aspiration than to have money and power. Finally... I can comfort myself by saying to myself that, without really wanting it, I incited one of the young women who had accosted me to leave. In a way, I saved her from torture.

As Voldemar did not comment, Boris decided to end the conversation:

– Well, Count, as you suggested to me, I am going to bed. The events of this evening have exhausted me. Fortunately, the wine has somewhat purified my mind. Good night, Count!

Chapter 8 - The Pope's death at the Vatican

– I thought we had to go to Cannes bus station? –Boris asked, as the count's Rolls-Royce took a different direction.

The magician was not in a very good mood because Voldemar had woken him up, saying they had to quickly get on the road to settle an urgent matter. Boris had followed him reluctantly, wondering what another plan was still fomenting his evil companion. Now he was in the Count's luxurious car with Zozo driving and Lulu clung to him like an Egyptian cat.

– We must go to the Vatican as soon as possible. – Voldemar said.

Boris preferred not to ask questions and turned to the window to watch the landscape scroll. Meanwhile, Pope John Paul II was obediently waiting for the Reaper with a scythe to come and get him. His breath was wheezing and he was moaning. The sheets of white silk that covered him were impregnated with his sweat. Lying in bed, he stared at the frescoes ceiling of a great Renaissance painter with his expressionless eyes, as if trying to discern something. A clock chanted, in a monotonous melody, the last seconds of the long life of the pope. The deaf rattling of the pendulum prevented John Paul II from getting to sleep, but he had preferred not to ask the staff to stop this breaker of silence, because he was waiting for an important visitor, and he feared, without this regular noise, to sink into a sleep from which he would no longer emerge. This visit would be decisive for his future. Perhaps some people would find it ridiculous to talk about the future for a dying old man but others would understand without a doubt that life in the other world is of paramount importance.

Death had wanted to seize him a little earlier, but she had been asked exceptionally to leave a few more breaths of oxygen to the dying person and to come back for him later. The Reaper was not used to being lenient, but she had no choice but to meet the requirements of the Dark Master. She had gone a little further, but was watching in the dark for the moment when she could do her work. The pope had also felt the favor that was granted to him: a pain had awakened in his legs numbed by osteoarthritis and, while he could not move them for a while already, he had managed to unfold them completely, which gave him unspeakable relief. He had thought then: "My guest must not be very far..."

Many people had gathered to pray under the Pope's windows; they wanted to accompany, by their religious fervor, the vicar of Jesus Christ until the moment when the Holy Spirit would come to take him to the gates of paradise, where Saint Peter would welcome him with open arms.

But other people were desperate to see that the pontiff did not seem in a hurry to join the celestial kingdom. The slow agony of the old man, lying on his deathbed, annoyed many people in the Vatican. The fact that the pope so long resisted the call of death intrigued them and put their nerves to the test. Those who had hoped for a quick end were gnawing their brains, eager to see the end of this tragic episode of the reign of a Pole in the Catholic Church.

"This dirt of Poles clings to life! They said to each other. Would he hesitate to join the Almighty? Or he decided to fuck us to the end! "

These reflections, the successor of John Paul II also made them. Cardinal Ratzinger was standing in front of a mirror, trying on the papal costume he was planning to put on soon. As he placed the papal miter on his white hair, he suddenly thought he saw in the reflection of the mirror the face of a pig instead of his own! This vision made him jump and the miter fell heavily on the floor covered with a Persian carpet silk. Ratzinger watched as the headdress rolled over the carpet, as if she wanted to get away from him.

"Oh! It's a bad omen!" —The cardinal thought.

He then used a large glass of red wine from a bottle whose label indicated that it was a New castle of Pope. He drank a large swig of this nectar and felt more relaxed. He told himself that he was not going to be impatient: his predecessor would eventually win the afterlife. However, the pope clearly did not seem to be in a hurry to pass the weapon to the left, much to the chagrin of his bishops who had been waiting so long for this moment when they would be rid of this importunate who had, throughout his pontificate, been asking for forgiveness for the crimes committed by the Church in the course of history: the Crusades, the Inquisition and other abominations. These public repentances had shaken the foundations of the Apostolic See, which rested on the dogma of the infallibility of the Church: by recognizing the errors of the latter, John Paul II challenged this inalienable principle!

Cardinal Ratzinger was quite right, however, because neither the prayers of the believers gathered in Saint Peter's Square, nor the thousands of paraffin candles they lit would change anything: the pope was dying indeed!

And the crowd, like all the Catholics in the world, were well aware that the outcome was inevitable, but they could not resign themselves to abandoning their shepherd to his fate. They wanted to support it to the end, like faithful sheep, and they would not rest until a tiny breath of life animated John Paul II. In order to the pope received extreme unction, one of his compatriots Polish cardinal, had approached to receive last confession, he had pointed out the door to him, with a stern gesture. As well as to the religious who prayed at his bedside, like flies swirling over a carrion he persistently waved his hand pointing toward the door. It must be said that the poor pope had undergone a month earlier a tracheotomy which rendered the use of speech almost impossible.

In the end, the clergy had come to respect the wishes of the Holy Father and had left him alone. Since then, the Pope had stared at the ceiling and listened to the clock ticking its last hours on the ground, throwing a glance at the golden-leafed door from time to time, hoping to see it open. And finally, the doorway should appear the silhouette of his mysterious visitor. He could not leave in peace until he saw it! John Paul

II was so subject to the will of this mystical man that he absolutely had to speak to him before joining the heavenly countries.

The Pope looked away from the high ceiling of his spacious room to look at the gilded frames hanging on the walls covered with natural silk, which represented portraits of previous rulers of the Vatican. He thought that his portrait would soon be added to this series. Then he put his eyes on the huge Venetian mirror, which sat in a corner of the room, and saw in the reflection the rich decorations that surrounded his red velvet four-poster bed hemmed with golden brocade. All this luxurious refinement, which stank of wealth, was disgusting to John Paul II. This outrageous elegance hid a treacherous ugliness, like a barrel of honey in which tar was poured his loneliness. The pope sank gradually into deep despair. He wondered what had been the meaning of his existence and doubted he had done all he needed. This feeling was amplified by the fact that Parkinson's disease had dug holes in his memory, such as bark beetles eating away at the bark of trees. His spirit, once brilliant, had too many whites spots, and the dying man was trying to gather his fragments of memories to reconstruct the thread of his long life.

When the bells of St. Peter's Basilica sounded midnight, a Rolls-Royce appeared in front of the Vatican's main door, under the watchful eye of guards dressed in costumes from another time. A strange trio came down from the luxurious car. The one who seemed to have authority over the other two was an old man, wearing the black cassock of Catholic priests and wearing a white plastic collar around his neck, symbol of purity and humility: it was Voldemar, of course! Following him, it was hard to recognize Boris, who was dressed in a dark brown monk's robe, with a hood that he had folded over his head. Beside him stood a nun, wearing the traditional Ursuline habit, which was none other than Lulu. Although the monastic tunic was very strict and devoid of any aesthetic appeal, Lulu remained very beautiful, with its elegant silhouette, and, this time there were no complaints about the decency of her robes. Zozo, as a driver, was forced to stay in the car.

Hardly had the three accomplices come down from the vehicle when a cardinal rushed to meet them. The man was very thin and his white hair indicated an age already advanced. Out of breath, he leaned up to the hand that Voldemar handed him and kissed the Count's signet ring. When he straightened up, then murmured in a worried voice, looking around him as if to make sure no one was listening:

– Oh, great master! We looked forward to you. The Holy Father seems not to want to leave our world without receiving your holy communion. He refused to confess one last time in their sins.

The cardinal then turned quickly to one of the Swiss Guards and ordered him in a grand tone:

– Drive us to the room of His Holiness Pope John Paul II.

– Let's hurry up! –Voldemar exclaimed– Oh, Lord! We can not let His Holiness leaves the earthly world without having absolved him of all his sins!

They followed with a rapid pace the Swiss guard who led them to the door of the room of the dying pontiff. The cardinal led them into the room, then withdrew on tiptoe, shutting the door behind him. Voldemar without saying a word pointed to Boris and Lulu a corner of the room where two old armchairs framed a small round marble table, on which sat a silver decanter and crystal glasses. Voldemar motioned them for a drink. Lulu complied immediately and, once the glasses were full, they began to taste the nectar. Boris immediately recognized the delicious and fragrant Polish brandy, which conjured up the image of plum fields in his mind. The monk and the nun showed serious faces of circumstance, even though Lulu quickly engulfed the contents of her glass. She seemed to enjoy the liquor of Krakow a lot. Boris, who wiser sipped his drink, wondered if he was ready to drink this before the pope, but he reassured himself by saying that, in the state he was in, the Holy Father did not would not report. Lulu grabs the carafe again, taking care not to clink it against the silver tray. No doubt there would not be a drop of the famous plum moonshine. Meanwhile, Voldemar had approached the bed in which the pope lay and sat in a chair at the bedside of the dying man. John Paul II had not moved since the arrival of the trio, and if it was not the slight movement of his chest, one would have thought that life had already left him.

Voldemar, in a voice tinged with sadness and bitterness, exclaimed:

— Oh, my old friend, what these fiends did to you!? I can not believe these damned dared to pierce your trachea! They intentionally deprived you of the word just before your death.

Is it really would they have been afraid of the last wishes that you could have expressed?

It is important, however, that you confess in conscious sins and in innocent delusions as long as you are still part of the world of the living, for you do not know what path will open before you when you come to the kingdom of heaven. Once you leave us, it will be too late to repent. Sinners who join the hereafter without having expiated their faults while still alive, not may well kneel before God and ask for forgiveness, the door of Paradise will remain closed to them. But I will make sure that you can express yourself, because to me, my friend, you can speak freely!

At these words, Voldemar's eyes lit up for a moment in a strange light. At once the pope opened his eyes and, turning to the count, exclaimed:

– Oh! Spirit of evil, you came to me! I waited for you!

The pontiff seemed surprised to be able to speak so distinctly. Visibly moved, he added:

– It is true that the impure Spirit has great power over the physical body. But I am grateful to you for giving me the opportunity to express myself before I leave this world.

– Certainly, I have the power to act on the bodies of men but, believe me, I can also affect their souls! –Voldemar became annoyed– Do you not notice that your mind is clearer and you have recovered your entire memory? And, to thank me, you call me Impure Spirit! But who are you to define what is pure and what is impure? If you were so pure, your Holy Spirit would have already manifested! Instead, I came to your bedside, and now I have to listen to your hypocrisy and hear the next to insults!

– Do not be angry, I beg you! –The pope replied– I have called you impure Spirit out of habit, because they are terms used in the sacred texts, which I have read and re-read, having regard to my function.

– My old friend, rest assured, I am not angry with you! –Voldemar interrupted– That would be unfair on my part, given the sad situation you are in. It would be cruel of me to be mad at you, but still... Well, let's get to the point! You wanted me to receive your last confession before you left this world. So, I'm listening to you ... my son!

In saying these last words, Voldemar almost burst out laughing. Apparently, he took a liking to his role as priest confessor, and therefore he managed to restrain himself.

– I have already publicly and repeatedly asked for forgiveness around the world for the errors committed by the Church: Crusades, wars of religion, the Inquisition, the extermination of Protestants, the genocide of the Jews, the violent evangelization of the people of America, the various divisions and intrigues of the Church... –The sovereign pontiff said as in a pre-memorized text. It was obvious that he had some difficulty in breathing properly but he continued– Before me, no religious authority had shown such honest repentance.

Voldemar smiled as he listened to the pope's words, as if he had known beforehand that John Paul II would say him this speech and slammed it sardonically:

— My friend, you made me listen the same speech you made during your entire pontificate? Do you think that admitting your mistakes in front of me will change something in your fate that awaits you in the afterlife? Do you hope that I intervene on your behalf before the Almighty?

The measuring Pope of Rome clearly evaded sincere repentance: it was, of course, what Voldemar expected from this interview.

— If it reassures you, —Voldemar said with a grin— when you are dead, it is indeed this mumbo-jumbo which will appear in the obituary for you. Already all newspaper articles will extol the courage you have shown in recognizing the faults of the Church. But do not count on me to sing your praises because they are not simple errors that the Church has committed, but real crimes against humanity, for which there is no limitation period! All those who profess your religion are criminals, you in mind, because that amounts to approving all the crimes perpetrated by your Church. You deserve to be all judged for these crimes, alongside the Nazis and Stalinists in a kind of on the bench of the Nuremberg trial. So, I do not see why your speeches of repentance should be praised, since that did not stop you from taking the lead of this deadly Church and still hide her next crimes against humanity! You should rather repent of having been stupid enough to believe all the nonsense told in the scriptures! No other religious order diverse world religions has shed so much blood to impose its chimerical ideas. Look at the Hindus for example: it is nearly four thousand years since their religion existed, and they never wanted to exterminate other religious communities! But you Christians have not hesitated to kill all those who dared to contradict you. And now that murder is widely reproved by modern society, you have had to find other ways to satisfy your cruelty. So, you have attacked your young sheep, whom you have misled by showing the same immorality as the inhabitants of Sodom and Gomorrah! May the monks and nuns indulge each other in the pleasures of the flesh, why not! But why are you annihilating the life for innocent children, whom their parents have entrusted to you with confidence? So, Holy Father, what do you have to answer to that? That it is the Devil responsible for all these perversities? If I have heard you confession very much about the tragedies of history, but I found you not very prolix on the issue of pedophilia and did not condemn their colleagues for their prelude against an innocent childhood! Yet, as the saying goes, "the little cat knows who has eaten the meat". Of course, it is easier to ask forgiveness for sins committed in the distant past that can hardly be held directly responsible, rather than confessing those that are happening now under your rule. And what about the corruption that plagues the Vatican? Again, I found you very cautious about this issue, which will remain long on the agenda. On the other hand, I have heard you, on several occasions, denigrate me – the Devil! But I remind you that it was God himself who created me and that I only did the task he assigned to me. So, would you dare to question the validity of the Creator's will? Alas, your successor who was part of the German DCA during his youth will certainly not do better than you. If he will be very annoying, then, I will find a way to drive him out of the Holy

See, and I will replace him with a cardinal whom I already have spotted and who seems to like to talk about me nice things. I really love being called a great thinker!. Although I do not care what kind of people think of me, this Argentinian cardinal could make a good recruit to spread my ideas among your herd of naive sheep, which will contribute to my plan to make the evil prevail Earth. Men are so easily influenced: one day, one can make them believe one thing and, the next day, one can make them swallow the exact opposite of what they were told the day before!

Voldemar caught his breath before concluding:

– Well, you will understand, I did not come to receive your last confession, nor even in the name of our so-called friendship, for I never considered you anything but my slave. If I wanted to be present before you left to heaven,it was only because I wanted to show the Vatican to my friend Boris. Now I want to say goodbye to you, Holy Father! Go with God!

At these words, the pontiff creaked and burst into tears. When he recovered, he asked Voldemar, in a voice steeped in sadness:

– So, does that mean we will never see each other again? But, please, let me enter my Father's house!

This time, Voldemar could not help but burst out laughing, before saying:

– Your father! Do you really take yourself for Christ? I imagine Joseph, the patriarch of the Bible, imploring his brothers when they sold him: "For pity, let me go back to our father! ". Even on the verge of death, you're still so funny, my friend! But, you see, even if I wanted to, I could not open the door of paradise because I do not have the key! And I have already explained to you why I will not intervene in your favor with the Creator, especially since I am not empowered to judge who can access the kingdom of heaven. However, you will always be able to introduce yourself to the door of paradise and you will see how you will be welcomed! But, sincerely, I doubt that God will accept you by his side. You are very likely to end up in hell, where I will take care to avoid you because I have sufficiently heard your whining during your earthly life. Well! I lost enough time with you. I do not need you anymore: you can die. Death has already shown great patience with you.

The sovereign pontiff did not try to restrain Voldemar, and even seemed relieved to have been able to hold this conversation with the count, although she did not give the results he hoped for. As soon as Voldemar and his companions left his room, John Paul II finally found sleep.

A few hours later, when the last agony of agony took hold of him, the pope, his brow covered with sweat, began to groan:

— Let me enter my Father's house!

He repeated this phrase throughout the day following Voldemar's night visit. This leitmotiv of the dying man made a great noise in the corridors of the Vatican. When this information was reported to Cardinal Ratzinger, who was sitting in a salon with the personal physician of the Holy Father, he exclaimed:

— Even dying, he can not help but be noticed by eccentric statements!

Suddenly, the cardinal was silent and, visibly perplexed, turned to the doctor to whom he asked:

– Tell me, doctor, how is it possible that our Holy Father, who has undergone a tracheotomy and is connected to an artificial ventilation device, is able to speak? Especially that he is unbelievably talkative! ...

– Well ... –the doctor answered, embarrassed– I can not explain it in a scientific way because I have never seen such a case. I would say ... it's a miracle!

At this answer the cardinal's eyes widened in amazement. Immediately, the future pope called his secretary and ordered him:

– Give the following message to everyone who has heard the Pope's ramblings: no word to anyone! It's an absolute secret! If that were known to the whole world, then it looks like it's the work of the Devil...

That evening, Pope John Paul II relieved took his last breath...

Chapter 9 - Death of the Prince of Monaco

For their part, Voldemar, Boris, Lulu and Zozo had taken the road again and their chic Rolls-Royce behaved like a racehorse of purebred breed who had a good rest before the next race.

— Let me enter my Father's house! —Lulu imitated unfortunate pontiff, laughing.

— My dear, a little respect! The pope is living his last moments. Tonight Death will come and get him. —Voldemar said, in a tone that seemed really pained.

— Oh, master, if we have to mourn every time we visit a dying person, we'd spend our time playing mourners! In this case, it is better stay in hell! At least there, there is something why cry plenty! —Lulu answered casually.

— In this case, next time, I'll cry about my dying friend! — Voldemar retorted, annoyed. Although I was hard on him earlier, because that's my devilish role, but I must admit that I enjoyed the moments I shared with John Paul II. He was in good company and his conversation was very interesting. It is not a man like the others who same will die today but he was not like those sheep blindly following their shepherd and the stupid doctrines they are taught. Yes, the Pope and I were very different, but we talked a lot, and he understood what I told him. He tried to raise awareness, but his hands were tied because he was surrounded by vile and hypocritical people who prevented him from doing everything he wanted. So, yes, his impending death is painful to me. I will lose a precious ally in this world. I knew in advance that he would try to escape my hell but, given his proximity to me, it is certain that the gates of paradise will not open for him. How sad! John Paul II was a good servant. That's why, Lulu, I will not allow you tell out disrespect him. But, if you want to go back to hell, I'll send you there with pleasure!

Zozo, who usually remained silent, hands on the wheel and staring intently at the road, decided to protect his stupid girlfriend:

– Master, without Lulu, we would be bored a lot on earth! So, please, do not send her back to hell... Oh! Mamma mia! These Italians drive as badly as the Arabs in Marseille! Look at this idiot behind: it seems he wants to get in! If he wants to die, I can help him!

Boris looked away from the beautiful scenery behind the window and asked Voldemar in a detached tone:

– Count, do you often take possession of the body of the grand master Polyus?

– My friend, do you think I change my body as actors one changes clothes? – Voldemar smiled.

– I was just it seemed curious that... – Boris replied, who still hoped to finally get some answers to the questions he asked himself— In fact, I could not help but notice that the cardinal who greeted us at the entrance of the Vatican immediately kissed your ring. In other words, he recognized you without difficulty. I conclude that he already knew you as Polyus.

— Superb deduction, my friend! —Voldemar exclaimed— Well, yes, I've sometimes asked Polyus to lend me his body. But I think it's the last time because it has already exhausted all unthinkable resources.

And although Polyus has used every conceivable means to conserve his body, I can only note that his fleshly envelope has come to an end.

— And, in exchange for the loan of his body, what have you offered to the master Polyus? —Boris continued.

— In exchange? —Voldemar wondered.

The Count thought to tell that he could have seized the body of Polyus without asking his opinion and without compensation. However, he understood that Boris needed encouraging answers, and he decided to satisfy curiosity his new friend a bit:

— All the time that I remained in possession of the body of Polyus, his fleshy envelope did not age and even rejuvenated a little. It is for this reason that Polyus has been able to live as long, much more than an ordinary human being. In addition, this extraordinary longevity strengthened his credibility in the eyes of his henchmen, who could only believe in his supernatural powers. But time eventually caught up with the body of Polyus, and his vile followers took the opportunity to lock him in this horrible retirement home. What nonsense!?

They all hope to take the place of Polyus and my damn children, Nicolas Catastrophe and cunning Jacques, are trying especially hard in this ignoble deed! Although they don't even realize that I'm talking to the Masonic Master, they deal personally with me or on following my instructions!

— It was an honest bargain! —Boris readily admitted— The master could not have kept his place so long without your help.

Boris thought: "It's not surprising that the vacant place of the master Polyus attracts so much lust among the top leadership of the fifth French republic".

Preferring not to push Voldemar too much into his entrenchments, the magician decided to change the subject and asked him:

— Count, where are we going now?

— Our plans have changed due to the impending death of an important person who will follow a few days after the death of the Roman pontiff.. —Voldemar replied— We must visit the Prince of Monaco!

Boris did not understand why the death of John Paul II forced them to go to Monaco. The Count had to seize the perplexity of the magician because he added:

— It will be more practical that the Prince of Monaco goes out soon. The pope will die in a few hours and tomorrow, people will flock to Rome to pay homage to the deceased pontiff. If the Prince of Monaco dies in the coming days, the French who will go to Rome will, on the way back, stop in Monaco to show their respect to Prince Rainier.

Voldemar had spoken almost joyfully, as if he was proud of his organization. Boris, however, remained wary of this down-to-earth explanation.

But the magician did not have the leisure to question himself further because the Count exclaimed:

– Ah, that will do the business of Nico Sinister, all this traffic between France, Rome and Monaco! For sure, people, on the road, will commit offenses, and the police, greedy, will stick fines at arm's length! But it is not these agents who are to blame, because they are only executing the orders of their boss, because Nico has already more or less taken the reins of the state and blows to President Jacques what he must do. And, believe me, this sinister Nico has no morals. No wonder Americans like it! He is one of my cruelest serfs: it is for this reason that I chose him to be the next French president. But I'm suspicious of him because I know he will not hesitate to betray me at the first opportunity. We will have to go and visit him in Paris but, for the moment, we must go and deliver the Prince of Monaco from his sufferings. People show themselves as they really are when Death comes knocking on their door. That's why I like going to see them in person on their deathbed, even if, often, I receive only the ingratitude of their share!

– It is said that Grimaldi are struck by a curse. Is it true? – Boris asked. The death of Princess Grace was indeed a tragedy...

Evoking the tragic love story between Rainier and Grace made him think of his own relationship with Margot. Boris knew he had to forget her, and maybe Lulu could help him, especially since she seemed to be asking for nothing else! Often, she stuck against him in the backseat of the Rolls-Royce.

"Yes, but Lulu is a demon! —Boris thought— Finally, it is not so different from humans because half of the women are witches! The others are laying hens submitted. (He chuckled at this thought.) It is not for nothing that the Emperor Napoleon said: "All women are whores except my mother! But do not forget that my mother is also a woman". And the French of today do not think differently. They simply express their thoughts below the belt with more delicacy, like the great Victor Hugo: "The man has received from nature a key with which he goes up the woman every twenty-four hours". "

— That's one of the reasons I love France, especially its south coast! —Voldemar exclaimed, as if he had heard Boris's thoughts— And I love Monaco too. If it is I who put the pontifical tiara on the head of the Pole, it is also I who put in the arms of the prince of Monaco the American, certainly commoner but very beautiful. It was a nice present that I gave him there, and yet he mistreated the elegant Grace all the time that lasted their marriage. I will have to organize a confrontation between these two. Because if I knew that John Paul II would try to escape my hell, the Prince of Monaco, after his death, could be tempted to join his beloved...

Voldemar paused for a moment, then finally answered Boris's initial question:

— With regard to the curse of the Grimaldi family, it is the strict truth! To understand why bad luck is beating on the Grimaldi, we must go back to the Middle Ages. It was at this time that Francois Grimaldi seized the Rock, showing cunning: he disguised himself as a monk to enter the fortress, then brought in his army. It was me who blew this idea to him, and I even accompanied him, disguised myself as a monk, during this incredible adventure! It is for this reason that two monks appear on the coat of arms of the princes of Monaco. As for their motto, "With the help of God," it is a biting irony when one knows the truth, does not it?

Sincerely, I very much doubt that God and my brother Jesus appreciated that we used the religious robes of their servants to seize the fortress of Monaco. But neither me nor they are not responsible for the curse that hangs over the Grimaldi. God and Jesus are too good to do this kind of thing.

— So who started this curse? —Boris asked.

— As often, the answer to this question is in the proverb: "Look for the woman"! —Voldemar replied, laughing.

The count caught his breath and told, with obvious pleasure, the rest of the story:

— Cunning Francois seduced a young Dutch woman, then left her unceremoniously. Maybe he had real feelings for this lady but had no choice but to separate from her. This is something commonplace in history, as sung by my favorite russian singer Alla Pugacheva: "No king can marry for love". Faust was also forced to leave Gretchen, while she was pregnant, because he had killed his beloved's brother. Then, Gretchen, desperate, killed their child and when Faust wanted to free her from the prison in which she had been locked up, she preferred the executioner's ax to Faust's love. But let's go back to the Dutch girl, who also took the treason of Francois

Grimaldi very badly. Mad with rage, she threw her lover with these devilish words: "None of the Grimaldi will be happy in marriage! ". Maybe this curse has touched me too, and that's why things of love escape me! It is also during this episode that I was injured in the left leg. The pain I still feel today makes me think of Francois Grimaldi all the time. The latter eventually sank into madness: to avenge the curse thrown at him by the Dutch witch, he accused many young girls of practicing black magic and sent them to the pyres of the Inquisition. In particular, he burned another of his mistresses alive, and it is said that she too would have sent him a curse. But, for my part, I had already gonc to the Pyrenees to heal my leg injury by bathing in the hot springs of the mountains. That's where I met Guillaume Bélibaste, a Cathar preacher, who will also end up at the stake. It was awful to see the beautiful land of the troubadours with fire and blood, simply because Catholics did not like to be contradicted by the Cathars. The latter recognized my powers as demiurge and, therefore, my right to dominate the world, in the hope that their souls would then be liberated and that they could thus reach paradise. Stop talking about sad things! Let's go back to Monaco! If some Monegasques are unhappy in marriage, which is not my competence, rest assured that the thirty-three thousand inhabitants of this small state are very successful in business! They are good recruits for me! It is also said that the Monegasques have some morals somewhat dissolute! But it’s hard for the rich to find joy in life, since they already have everything. Therefore, they are engaged in debauchery in order to somehow raise their spirits. Life without intrigue is equivalent to death for them! Of course, some religious fanatics still blame me for to induce them to lust, since, according to the Bible, it is because of me that Adam and Eve found out what their genitals did for them! It is for this reason that we were all three chased from paradise. But we must not forget that it is the Creator who endowed humans with a sex. They are therefore entitled to use it as they see fit! Without sexuality, the human species would soon be extinct! Have you noticed, my dear Boris, that most dictators encourage their citizens to unite and start a family? To better lock them in a straitjacket, no doubt!

— We say that when we get married, we go "the rope on the neck"! —Boris replied— And I must admit that I agree with that!

Voldemar drained half a bottle of cognac Napoleon I, which he had taken out from under his cassock and gave a grunt of satisfaction before speaking again:

— I love my old Rock and its famous casino, that the Monegasques could build thanks to my advice. It was not by chance that I sent Polyus to Monaco, when I had him appointed Grand Master of the Masonic Lodge. That way, I first came from hell to visit his body, it gave me the opportunity to immerse myself in the festive atmosphere of Monaco. And then I liked living in Monaco so much that I often began to use the body of my favorite Polus!

Taking advantage of the fact that Voldemar was silent for a moment, Boris intervened:

— And I do not doubt that you are a good companion at these festivals. Do you know that even religious representatives say that you are charming and courteous? And that's precisely why they are afraid of you: you are so intelligent that it is easy to be tempted by your beautiful words!

Voldemar replied with a mysterious smile. At this moment, Boris saw a road sign and exclaimed, happy:

— We have just left Ventimiglia! To come back to what you said, Count, I am a little astonished at the portrait that you drew of Monaco. I stayed there for a few months and I must say I got bored. I found the inhabitants of the Rock too wise and affable. Therefore I was very happy to return to Nice where you can still meet prostitutes on Promenade des Anglais.

— My dear friend, —Voldemar said with a malicious glint in his eyes— it is because you have only seen the surface of it. I would say that you saw the packaging but you did not suck the candy! You are not the only one to have this impression because it is not easy to penetrate the heart of the Monegasque society.

The inhabitants of the Rock belong to the high society, and they are used to adopting a refined behavior. But, believe me, under their carapace collar mounted, hide passionate personalities and very heterogeneous. I have too many memorable memories in Monaco, and it will take a hundred years to tell them all! I could introduce you to many interesting people. However, this time, I will not visit my Monegasque friends because most of them belong to the Masonic Lodge and, as Polyus is officially in a coma, it would be too difficult to introduce myself to them under the guise of their grand Master. Moreover, I may encounter some difficulties to enter incognito in the princely palace, because everyone there knows Polyus. In addition, they have surveillance cameras everywhere! But I must go to see Prince Rainier.

Boris thought for a moment, then declared:

— Count, I could distract you, diverting the attention of the palace guards, which would leave you free to sneak in discreetly. I advise you to keep your priest's clothes: they could help you to go unnoticed, since it seems normal that a priest comes to the bedside of a dying person. And then, I do not doubt your power of persuasion. On the other hand, Lulu will not be able to accompany you. Forgive me, Lulu, but you're less credible in your role as a nun... You can wait in a bar sipping a cocktail.

Lulu seemed to rejoice at the role assigned to him by Boris. She glanced at the magician and hugged him, purring like a cat. Boris asked Voldemar to give him a few days to better prepare his plan, a delay that Voldemar granted him without difficulty because the announcement of the death of John Paul II, who had finally died, had created a great stir on the Rock. So it was better to wait for things to settle down a bit, and an order was given to the Angel of Death to wait a few days before visiting the old Prince.

Three days later, Boris announced to his companions that he was ready to carry out his plan. He wanted to act the next morning, very early, because there would be fewer people in the palace likely to recognize Voldemar... or rather Polyus! Zozo and Lulu groaned a little at the thought of having to get up early in the morning, but the count chopped off and agreed with the arguments of Boris. It was at the first light of dawn that Zozo parked the Rolls-Royce in the underground car park near the Oceanographic Museum. They left the parking lot and took the narrow streets of the old town to reach the main square facing the palace, where Prince Rainier was dying slowly. On arriving at the square, Voldemar went straight to the statue of Francois Grimaldi, nicknamed "the Cunning", who was represented wearing a loose monastic robe and ready to pull his sword out of his scabbard. Voldemar, moved, greeted the founder of the principality with a voice filled with emotion:

– So we meet again, my old friend!

– Count, what for are you talking to the statues now? – Boris quipped in surprise.

– I feel nostalgic, my dear Boris. –Voldemar said and wiped a lonely tear from his face with his hand. I shared so many strong moments with him...

– But you just came from hell where can you see your friend Francois at any time? - Boris was clearly surprised at the Devil's grief he saw.

– My friend, I am crying for the old time, when we were having fun as real bandits from the highway but after he betrayed me, I do not want to see him again! –Voldemar cried out– I do not forget that he sent many girls to the stake, pure souls who did not have time to taste the pleasures of sin. But nobody tried to stop it, quite the opposite! That was the business of the Inquisition. And then, the crusaders did a lot worse than him. I remember the Crusade, sponsored by the

Vatican, against the Cathars of the city of Beziers, nearly a century before our tour de force in Monaco: twenty thousand people have died there. I remember the cruelty of the chief of the Crusaders, Father Arnold Amaury. When the soldiers asked him, "How to distinguish good faithful from heretics? He replied: "Kill them all, God will recognize his! ". And Father Amaury, in his report to Pope Innocent III, did not seek to conceal his crime, since he wrote: "Neither the years, nor the position, nor the sex have become their salvation! ". Forgive me, my friend, for rehashing these old memories. It must be believed that senility is watching me! But the bloody massacre of Beziers still haunts me. My hell could be paradise next to what happened at that time!

And this carnage was motivated by the fact that the Cathars considered me the creator of the earthly world. They were not wrong because it is me who shapes this world as the way I want to see him. And no crusade launched in the name of Christ will ever change anything: evil reigns on earth. Even if the devotees of Christ still sometimes horrify me, the Catholic Church has lost its fight against me and exhausted uselessly. Look what her state it is today: just as moribund as Polyus! And yet Christians have fought for centuries to kill anyone who dared to contradict them. This was also the case of Protestants. More than three hundred years after the massacre of Beziers, the Spanish duke of Alba launched a great campaign in the Netherlands to exterminate the Protestants, and he was no less cruel than his predecessors. It is because of all the horrors that have been perpetrated on earth that the Apostle Saint Paul called me, in his wacky texts, the "god of this century"! And yet, I am not responsible for all the atrocities committed on earth. The proof: men, very often, kill in the name of God ... and not of the Devil! But no one reproaches anything to the Almighty or his Son, who did nothing to prevent all these massacres. Well, be it! May they stay in their heavens! Me, I'm very good on earth! Ah, my dear Boris, I let myself be carried away by my memories, and here I am in a moody mood!

Voldemar sighed and glanced at Boris, who merely gave him a slightly tense smile. Then the count asked the magician:

– Explain to me your plan, my friend, so that I may enter the princely palace. I want to be sure that we have not omitted any details.

– It's very simple! –Boris replied– I intend to distract the guards by showing them the most incredible thing I have in my possession: the pictures I took of you at the bus station! I had time to make a copy. For sure, it will create a nice fuss and you can take the opportunity to see the prince.

– Ah yes! The photos of my arrival on earth! –Voldemar exclaimed.

– That's it. –Boris confirmed– I understood that your appearance is related to the ritual that Margot and I did in the bus station lodge, and this certainly explains why you took possession of the body of Polyus, since this ceremony was intended to bring him back to life.. You should not expect to be brought back to earth in this way because you seemed as surprised as me. Is it not, Count?

Voldemar showed a mysterious smile but did not breathe a word.

— Well! —Boris continued— Since you do not want to answer my question, let's go back to our mission of the day. I'll show the cliches to the guard on duty in front of the entrance, and it will be up to you to play. I admit that I regret not being able to accompany you, not because I absolutely want to meet Prince Rainier, but because I worry about you, Count. If you ever get spotted...

— Do not worry, my friend! — Voldemar reassured him. — I do not risk anything, but I can not say as much for you! Once I have seen the prince, I will come to your rescue.

— Well, it's time to put our plan into action! —Boris says.

With these words he went to the guard who was standing behind a barrier. Whereas Zozo and Lulu moved to a bar not far away and Voldemar stood near the entrance to the palace.

When Boris arrived at the height of the guard, he brandished the photographs in front of him and, without a word, significantly winked at him. The guard, a little surprised, glanced at the cliches and widened his eyes wide what foreshadowed the commotion of combat! The guard shouted "Alarm! ". Immediately, a squadron of security guards arose and surrounded Boris, handcuffing him and taking him unceremoniously to an office in the basement of the palace.

Meanwhile, seeing that the guards had deserted their posts, Voldemar, disguised as a monk, slipped into the entrance of the palace. He immediately took the direction of the prince's room, with a quick step but taking care to show a serene face. For his part, the guards had begun to question Boris about the origin of the photos. The magician making an innocent face and told them that he did not know where did this come the anomaly from the cliches and, precisely that the authorities of the principality could give him some answers for we are talking about the tribal curse of the Grimaldi clan. Boris's explanations did not seem to convince the guards, but the guards did not have the opportunity to continue interrogation the magician further because a man — obviously the chief of security — entered the room and announced that Prince Rainier was asking to see the man who came to visit him to show him paranormal photographs.

The guards appeared astonished at the state of the prince's health, but executed the order without flinching and escorted Boris to Prince Rainier's room. When the door was opened, the magician found Voldemar sitting at the bedside of the dying man and murmuring inaudible words in his ear. The Count turned his back on the guards, who seemed to think it natural for a priest to be there. The security chief invited Boris into the room and closed the door behind him. Boris, not wanting to disturb Voldemar in his last interview with the prince, saw a marble table in a corner of the room, on which stood a bottle of brandy. He went immediately to drink a glass, which he swallowed in one go. The nectar made him crazy after all these emotions. But suddenly, Boris gasped in surprise: the ghost of a beautiful woman had just appeared in the room! Boris recognized the sublime Grace Kelly in all its unearthly beauty! The ghost beautiful woman then said in a soft voice, taking the Prince's hand, which is lying on his deathbed:

— I came to get you, my dear husband!

The Prince's face, which seemed barely able to breathe, lit up in an instant. He wanted to sit up but his head slumped down on the pillow.

Voldemar grabbed another cushion and placed it gently under the prince's head, so that the latter could see his wife better, in its spectral form. Certainly, in life she was even more beautiful, but she was also good in astral form!

– Oh, Grace! You came! If you knew how I missed you! – Rainier exclaimed in a weak voice filled with tears – You have to know that I did not want you to die. On the contrary, I wanted to keep you near me ... by all means! But my agents misunderstood my orders... Forgive me, my angel! Forgive me and take me with you!

– I forgive you, of course! – The ghost of Princess Grace replied – Besides, I didn't reproach you, neither for my accident nor for our problems of couple. I also had my share of responsibility. Our lifestyles were too different. But it's past! We will have eternity now to love us. My husband, follow me to eternity!

At once the specter of the princess disappeared, and the prince's body gave a long sigh, before subsiding forever and ever!

Voldemar then turned to Boris and said to him:

– Do not hang around here! We urgently need to escape from here unnoticed!

He took the direction of the door, caught the bottle of cognac on the table and hid it under his cassock. Then, he showed a punctuated look, opened the door and announced, bowing his head, to the guards waiting in the corridor:

— Prince Rainier has passed away.

The guards, alarmed by the news they had yet to expect, rushed into the room. Voldemar nodded discreetly to Boris, and the two men hurriedly left the palace, unhindered. Once in the open air and at a reasonable distance from the princely residence, Voldemar exclaimed:

— Oh, love! Always love! Humans will drive me crazy with their overflowing feelings! Have they all lost their minds? — but then, he remembered something and with a grin adding. — Apparently this old sly man did not know that Princess Jeanne was in the next room when he ordered the detention of his wife and youngest daughter. It was difficult to understand ambiguously. Or maybe because of senility, the Prince forgot everything?

Boris did not answer because he did not want to dwell on the subject. After what he had been through, the magician had more and more difficulty in contradicting the Count when he expressed his resentment of the feeling of love. The reunion of Grace and Rainier had awakened in him painful memories: his beautiful Margot, who had vilely abandoned. Boris pulled himself together and pointed out to Voldemar:

— It is you, have you not, who intervened to have the guards take me to the prince's room? I tortured my head for three days to foment a plan that was useless!

— Think again, my friend! —Voldemar exclaimed— Your help has been precious to me. You were ready to sacrifice for me! What a beautiful proof of friendship!

Zozo and Lulu, who had seen them, left the terrace of the cafe where they had settled and joined their two senior acolytes. Then the quartet returned to the underground car park and climbed into the Rolls-Royce.

— Zozo, take us to Paris! —Voldemar ordered— I have to go see Nico Sinister, who is having some difficulties to finance his election campaign. Then, Boris, after returning to Cannes... we will take care of the director of the bus station of Cannes. Once all these worries are settled, we can enjoy the festivities of May 1, before I go back to my hell where I can warm myself in front of my fire. I love coming to earth. It's very entertaining but I can not linger too long here. During my absence, my demons could burn all my hell! And then, as the saying goes: "Nothing is worth your home". On this words, Voldemar took from under his cassock the bottle of cognac, stolen from the prince's room, and took a long sip from the neck. Then, he handed the bottle to Boris, who did not pray, to swallow a large swig good brandy, before exclaiming:

— Forward for Paris! Perhaps we will have time to go to the Red Mill. Although the atmosphere of this cabaret does not equal the exuberance of the party you organized at Abramovich, in his Castle of La Croe, it remains one of my favorite of memories in Western countries!

Chapter 10 – On the road to Paris

The road to Paris was going to be long, but that did not bother Boris... The magician had finally yielded to Lulu's advances, and both were indulging in all kinds of carnal pleasures on the backseat of the Rolls-Royce. At first, Voldemar, sitting in the front passenger seat beside Zozo, who was driving in silence, seemed amused by the situation. Whereas Voldemar even took pleasure in watching, in the rear view mirror, the acrobatic tumults of the two lovers, worthy of the most daring postures of the Kama-sutra. Then, after a while, he began to tire of hearing the moans of the hellish couple. Boris could hear him grumbling with annoyance, and suddenly felt himself too tired. The evil Lulu was insatiable! Of course, Boris did not forget Margot so far, but there are certain physical needs that man must satisfy. And the magician had to admit that the beautiful Lulu turned out to be a skillful mistress, although there was not, with her, that osmosis he felt when he shared intimate moments with Margot. Boris sighed and poured himself a big glass of brandy, which he added with a slice of lemon. He slumped against the leather bench's back and, sipping his drink, lost himself in his memories, peopled with images of his beloved.

The magician came out of his thoughts: apparently, Voldemar was tired of being silent, and his the tongue itched! Boris told himself that he need to dispel the loneliness of the count and engage in conversation, but he was not sure what to talk about. Of course, he was tempted to ask him a whole lot of questions about hell and life after death, but he preferred to do nothing about it. He doubted that a mere mortal like him could understand all those things that went beyond human understanding, and he did not want the Devil to make fun of him. Also, Boris preferred to fall back on a subject less metaphysical but which encumbered his mind for a moment already.

– Count, I apologize for disturbing you, –Boris began– but may I ask you a few questions?

Voldemar shrugged his shoulders but Boris knew that his companion was delighted to be able to untie already hardened tongue.

– I would like to know, –Boris said– why you are so attached to the body of Polyus. You told me that before the bus station ritual you had already many times borrowed the body of Polyus, but I find it strange that you choose the carnal envelope of an old man, whereas you could take on the appearance of a young man, fit and attractive. And then, I suppose, saw your spectral shape disappear before my eyes at the bus station. After all, you could make yourself invisible, to wander among people and whisper them all sorts of demonic things and move freely around the world.

So, why embarrass yourself with a old body somehow envelope? Besides, you can come to earth whenever you want, so what was all this ceremonial we did with Margot? Was it just folklore to impress the gallery? Boris was silent, wondering if his questions were not too indiscreet, but Voldemar did not seem at all annoyed by the magician's questions. The count took a serious look, to better conceal his satisfaction of being again the center of attention of his companion, and took time for reflection, before answering:

— Indeed, I can take possession of anybody, and this is not what is missing here on earth! I can even look like a poodle or a goat! But when I come into your world, I like to mingle with men and get to know them, and so it's easier by taking on a human appearance. Being invisible is fun, but you can not get in touch with people. As for the reasons why I have chosen and on several occasions, to borrow the body of Polyus, from many other and more attractive bodies.

First of all, it's part of our market: he lends me his body and I'm trying to slow down the aging process of his flesh. Which brings me to another reason that explains my choice: Polyus has lived for a very long time on a human scale and, since he has worked with a lot of important people, I have been able to easily meet the figures who have marked history of several past centuries. Moreover, mortal people do not even realize that they are talking directly with the Devil himself. And then, you see, I have a certain taste for luxury and Polyus, because of its position as grand master of the Masonic Lodge, lived in opulence. Also, every time I go to visit people in the guise of Polyus, they welcome me by deploying all their wealth and with much friendliness, which is far from displeasing me! And do you want me to give you a secret, my friend? Polyus and I have the same sartorial tastes: we both like to wear well-made costumes and, thanks to him, I have been able to experience the evolution of French fashion through the decades. Ah, my dear France! She has not been out of trouble during her history, but I have always found her life to be good, compared to other countries where life is much sadder and miserable. You know, it's very funny to see how the customs evolve quickly. You must have noticed, my dear Boris, that I am not insensitive to what men call "sins", and it is a joy for me to be able to feel the happiness of surrendering to vice. And, if I do not understand the feeling of love, I nevertheless feel a certain attachment to the people whose company I appreciate. It is therefore nice to find them when I return to earth. As for your sorcery ritual, it was not useless: it helps strengthen the compatibility and symbiosis of my soul with the body of my host. But I do not think in the base, Polyus had asked you to bring me, the Devil ... is not it? You had to be zealous and shed a lot of blood on their own initiative or by negligence.

Boris's cheeks flushed. Indeed, he remembered that evening he had slashed his hand and Margot had scolded him because he had shed too much blood in the ritual cup.

The magician preferred to avoid the delicate subject of this last night spent in the company of his beloved, who had fled in the early morning, and asked Voldemar:

— Where and on what occasion did you meet the master Polyus?

— At the Paris fair! —The Count replied, laughing— At that time, Polyus lived in Germany, specifically in Berlin, and worked in a branch of the Ottmar Mergenthaler company, the inventor of the Linotype, a very innovative printing machine at the time. Despite the fact that Mergenthaler died, not wanting to reveal his typography method but that did not prevent his invention to be a huge success and a sensation in major European cities. It is precisely to to make good money on this printing press that Polyus had gone to the fair of Paris. Alas, the Parisians were suspicious of the quality of printing leaflets that Polyus presented: no stains, well-formed letters and perfectly aligned... Such book test could only be the work of the Devil! Therefore, they suspected him of a relationship with me and decided to torture him en the Inquisition, and poor Polyus would have finished at the stake! Then he admitted that he uses a certain mechanism for printing books and demonstrated it in public. All the same, the crowd was threatening, and people could even hear religious fanatics whispering, "This guy should be arrested and taken to the fire!". But Polyus did lead the way and with courage, continued his demonstrations, and very soon the rumor spread that a man was selling a "devil's machine". People even found respectful to him a nickname: Dr. Faust! Some began to say about him: "Dr. Faust is smart and rich as the Devil!"

When this rumor reached my ears, she drew my curiosity: who could be associated with me? So I went to meet him, and we sympathized very quickly. At the base, Polyus did not have magical powers, but as he was very intelligent, he learned very quickly how to use black magic. In addition, since he allowed me to take possession of his body from time to time and I performed witchcraft tricks in his appearance, his reputation as a great sorcerer grew steadily over the years.

— And that's why you put it at the head of the masons? — Boris asked.

— That's right! —Voldemar agreed— You must know, my friend, that I created Freemasonry to counterbalance the Vatican. If not, the Catholics would eventually destroy all Europe, and it would be the Russians, the Chinese and the Arabs who would have taken possession of the territories of the Old Continent. Of course, I had begun to counter the Catholic Church before creating the Masonic Lodge because, in the dark Middle Ages, Christian ideology was spreading everywhere, like a metastatic cancer. Men may not know it, but it's thanks to me that Europe has survived. And saving the Old Continent was not easy, believe me! Catholics have shown great determination to try to establish their supremacy, by sending witches, heretics and scholars to the stake, but also by organizing pogroms against Jews and Protestants. I still remember the night of St. Bartholomew... What a horrible massacre! And this only because some believers preferred to refer to biblical texts rather than believing everything the Vatican decreed. But have all the atrocities that the Catholic Church committed really helpful? We can ask ourselves the question when we see the number of people who today are turning away from religion. The Church is dying, and John Paul II carried with him, in his death, the last remnants of the true Christian faith.

Voldemar was silent and Boris thought he'd better start the conversation again, if he did not want Lulu to jump on him again. Also, the magician, while continuing to sip his glass, said:

— The Vatican massacred the Protestants because they saw in the Pope the personification of the Devil! And the followers of Protestantism have not hesitated to massacre Catholics! But both of them burned witches equally at the stake.

— Certainly, —Voldemar said— But compared to the Protestants the cruelty of the Vatican knows no bounds. However, there was a time when I had fun in Rome, when the Borgia family, with my help, seized the Holy See. Ah, that was my hour of glory! I knew the dolce vita! It was at this time that I founded the first sect of Illuminati in Spain, which allowed me to meet Alexandre Borgia, whom I later put on the pontifical throne. I have many times possessed the body of Alexander Borgia, and some things that are attributed to him are in fact my fault! I can tell you, my dear Boris, that at that time, I dusted off the dark corridors of the Vatican ... and especially the sleeping rooms! But, alas, there is not much left of this remarkable curia. So I let the Church destroy herself, because in today's society people are more free and the strict and depressing principles of Catholics wear them out and no longer seduce them. Men have nothing to do but to know that Jesus fasted for forty days in the desert to test his faith and save mankind from the sin into which it was sinking. Today, people prefer to eat sausage, ham and I do not know what else, rather than to deprive themselves of food under false pretenses. And then, the leitmotiv of "We harvest what we sow", which means that people must pay attention to everything they do, seems anachronistic nowadays. Apart from a few fanatics, men no longer see the intervention of the Devil everywhere. They want to enjoy the benefits that are offered to them, without constantly wondering if it's good or bad. They want to have a happy life, simply!

— It seems to me that you are no stranger to this change in human morals. —Boris said— After the Renaissance, you changed tactics: instead of creating fear, you decided to show yourself more attractive, offering men greater freedom that was not displeasing to them, given the restrictions that their imposed the Church. So, little by little, people have seen God as a real tyrant, compared to your permissiveness.

— I do not think I'm responsible for the degradation of God's image. —Voldemar said— The Church has done very well alone! But I must admit that allowing men to enjoy earthly pleasures, even to excess, is one of my favorite tactics. And if men are so easily tempted, it is because it corresponds to their nature. Take the example of sexuality: humans feel the need to satisfy their desires, so it is more pleasant for them to go to principles that allow them to indulge in the pleasures of the flesh, rather to have to impose an abstinence against nature. Look at the Catholic priests: even they feel the sexual desire. Then, as their Church forces them to go against their nature by imposing continence, they use all kinds of means to silence their impulses, such as self-flagellation or fasting, which lowers the production of sex hormones. Note that it does not work every time, since many religious state their desires on young children. Thank God for not having put such nonsense in the minds of animals! They respond to their instinct and know that reproduction is essential to preserve their species. Alas, religion has perverted the minds of men who, not knowing how to think for themselves, have gone against their instinct of reproduction. The most telling example of this state of affairs is Spain: at a time not so long ago, there were so many devout people who rejected sexuality that the very survival of the Spanish nation was threatened. Moreover, it is amusing to notice that the women of the countries which did not undergo the pangs of the Inquisition are very beautiful, as if they had not had to wilt to escape the repression of the Church. Whereas, in countries that have had to deal with the barbarism of religious, the beauty of women has faded. These ladies, in particular, have gained weight, especially in Germany. In Ukraine, especially in Dnepropetrovsk, and in the Czech Republic, women have lost none of their beauty. It is said that it was because the empress of Russia, Catherine the Great, sent some pretty, shy little girls as well as many prostitutes and witches to comfort their Cossacks to the western end of her territory. Be that as it may, the beauty of women can also have perverse effects: in Dnepropetrovsk, there is a big problem of sex tourism and, in Russia, women are so beautiful and so intelligent that they have difficulty in to find a man worthy of them.

Is the fault of Lenin and his Bolsheviks, who advocated gender equality and allowed women to learn. But it may be a lesser evil when you think of all the girls who were burnt by the Catholic Church!

– You are often distressed by the actions of the clergy, – Boris interjected, not without provocation– but could not you have fought more effectively against these abuses? After all, you are the Devil!

– Do you think I have not done enough? –Voldemar replied irritably– I liberated humanity from the tyranny of the Creator! And, unlike my brother Jesus, I did not seek to impose my principles on earth. I leave men free en choices. Yes, it is true that I sometimes interfere in the affairs of this world. But do I really have a choice? If I release my attention, devotees of Jesus will jump at the opportunity to seize power, and they will destroy the human race with their propaganda about the benefits of Platonic love! And besides, although I adore the exuberance of men, I sometimes have to come to earth to restrain them somewhat, because my hell is overpopulated. But I willingly admit that I also stay in your world for my only pleasure. The company of my ghosts and my demons is sometimes exhausting, and I find communication with people very refreshing. This is why I can not stand that clerics denigrate humanity and even hope for the end, since they are waiting for Armageddon, the Apocalypse or thc cnd of time, no matter what they call it. Fortunately, these fanatics are fewer and fewer. Even if other scourges have appeared lately, such as communism, radical Islamism or nationalism, which are very likely to destroy countries that until then were doing well. But, rest assured, I remain vigilant and ensure that these viral calamities do not turn into a generalized pandemic. We have already seen, through Christianity, what damage can cause extremist ideologies! Besides, have you noticed, my dear Boris, that religion is imposed where people are unhappy, by selling them the hope of a better life after death? Happy people do not need to abrade the mind with such nonsense and forget God, except perhaps in certain traditions or when the hour of their death approaches. Look at the Japanese: they did not let the Judeo-Christian octopus spread its tentacles on their islands, and they are happy! God is a vector of discord and misfortune.

— And the Devil is a peacemaker! —Boris exclaimed laughing.

Voldemar would have liked to answer this ironic comment of the magician but he saw, through the windshield of the Rolls-Royce, a magnificent castle overlooking a limestone massif, typical of Provence.

— We will have to put an end to this exciting conversation, my friend! —Voldemar said— My friends masons were warned of my passage in the vicinity and drew a banner bearing the emblem of the Masonic Lodge at the top of the tower. It means that they hope for my visit. I will answer their invitation.

Voldemar watched the castle, in ruins, with admiration. Boris seemed a little disillusioned by the program announced by the Count. The magician decided to make a proposal to Voldemar, hoping to escape a boring meeting:

— Count, I must confess that the prospect of listening to your fellow masons blowing their nonsense on Solomon's temple does not delight me more than that. You could drop us, Lulu and I, in the village of Lacoste. We would enjoy it lunch a good restaurant. I know this village well because I lived there for seven years, and it would please me to walk again the streets that the Marquis de Sade borrowed once.

— Oh yes, the Divine Marquis! —Voldemar exclaimed— I remember him well! He was a talented writer, but he did not do all the libidinous things he described in his books. Perhaps he was inspired by the unbridled manners of the monks of his time! In any case, I have a lot of admiration and respect for him.

As they entered the village, Voldemar turned to Zozo and ordered him:

— Zozo, stop the car here! I will not force our two young friends to accompany us to the castle if they do not want to. Besides, I understand them! These masons also tire me. But as it is the last time that I take the appearance of Polyus, it is also the last time that I will see them, at least as Grand Master of the Lodge. So I have to make this last effort, even if I blame them for playing scavengers around Polyus, waiting impatiently to take his place. I will have to find a way to not lose the control of the Masonic Lodge. Come on, young people, come down and have fun!

Boris and Lulu complied, delighted to be able to escape Voldemar's inquisitive eye for a moment. Boris and Lulu chose to go to a traditional restaurant, not far from where Zozo had dropped them. The establishment was welcoming and picturesque. They sat in comfortable wicker chairs. Boris decided to take a closer look at Lulu; he knew her pleasant body and her skill in the things of love, but he knew nothing of her life.

— Lulu darling, what are you doing with your time when Voldemar located is in his hell? —Boris asked, smiling at his companion.

— Well, I defend the interests of my master by practicing the occult sciences for politicians, be they mayors, deputies or senators. With the intention of placing the followers of Voldemar at all levels of society. Magical rituals can help rally voters or motivate them to go to the polls, for example. — She told him in a serious tone.

As Boris seemed interested in what she was saying, Lulu continued her explanations:

— I can also use magic to neutralize the opponents of the followers of the master. Sometimes I even infiltrate the opposite camp, to make it fail better. These little pedestrians see only fire! But what amuses me the most is when our opponents also use a magician. Some of these fools call "white wizards", but they are charlatans because white magic does not exist! Only black magic has real power. Of course, there are different levels of magic, and you can be sure that these "white wizards" do not have great abilities and that they can not in any case make the weight against real wizards. It's even more interesting when we have to face followers of black magic.

— It does not surprise me that politicians use every means to achieve their ends. —Boris remarked— Even in their oratorical jousting, they do not hesitate to use fallacious arguments to counter their opponents. But back to what you said.

So, you want all politicians to have their magician white, medium and even black, to amuse you and confront your powers in a sort of esoteric battle? I imagine that with your exceptional talents, you must make a mouthful of those who dare to oppose you!

Lulu smiled at the compliment and answered naughtily, while stepping at Boris under the table:

— Know that my skills in politics and magic are matched only by my talents in sex! But, I reassure you, I am serious in my work and think it's possible to combine business with pleasure. I have a whole team of wizards who help me in my missions. Sometimes our opponents launch magical attacks that we did not foresee, and we must redouble our ingenuity to respond effectively. And we never lose at this little game! I feel a lot of satisfaction when I see our candidates reach the positions they wanted ... or when Voldemar has awarded them.

— But I suppose that in exchange for your services, you ask for a counterpart? —Boris asked— Have all your candidates sold their souls to the Devil?

— Oh, yes, it is the master who chooses the candidates and, therefore, in exchange for the power they will get, they must offer him a part of themselves and give him allegiance. The pact is more or less restrictive for them, according to the importance of their political responsibilities and the power of the magic rituals that we must perform. Some people rely too much on the rituals of witchcraft, without realizing the consequences for them: the more they abuse, the higher the price to pay. Look at John Fitzgerald Kennedy: thanks to the master, his rise was dazzling, but his soul had become so black, by dint of calling all sorts of demons, that he attracted the hatred of his detractors, with the outcome that we know. Before him, kings were also carried away by the whirlwind of power, so that they lost their heads ... literally as well as figuratively! As soon as we have to bring demons out of hell to perform certain rituals, it becomes dangerous for our candidates. But what do you want? There are people who love to be applauded by jubilant crowds that they lose all measure and are willing to sell the souls of their parents in addition to theirs, just to know a little longer the success. Often such upstarts are very similar to those sentenced to chopping off their heads, as they climb too quickly up the stairs leading to the scaffold. Then they grimace before the public and lose their heads in the rays of glory. And when their heads cut off with a knife, the guillotines fall into wicker baskets, then in the crowd you can hear the cry of their followers mixed with the laughter of ill-wishers.

— There are still things you can do without the consequences being so tragic. —Boris asked.

The waiter brought them the flutes of champagne that Boris had ordered. It was nice for the magician to chat with Lulu. He discovered her in another light and found it very interesting.

Lulu swallowed her glass of champagne in one go, before answering Boris's question:

— With simple rituals, it is possible to increase the charisma of a candidate or to reduce that of his opponent. It is very effective because it is essential that a politician know how to seduce the voters. Rituals become more complex when it comes to influencing the opinion of a large crowd. But, you know, it's not just politicians who use magic to be successful. Why do you think Marilyn Monroe and Grace Kelly were so much adored before ending up were they so tragically lost to society? Because they had invoked far too many demons to establish their popularity! There was so much darkness around them that only bad luck could happen to them. Brigitte Bardot also used witchcraft, so much so that she lost her reason! So many women and men of genius could not reveal the full extent of their value because they gave in to the ease they thought they found in magic... What a waste!

The more Boris listened to Lulu, the more he blamed himself for having seen in her, until then, only an expert and voluble lover. He would have liked to apologize to him, but that would be like telling him he had mistaken her for a brazen idiot! So, he preferred to be quiet, and once the waiter had brought them two beautiful rare entrecotes and a vintage wine, he invited Lulu to continue talking to her about her and her life. The meal was held in a pleasant atmosphere. Lulu seemed happy to have shared this moment of complicity with Boris and, when they saw the Rolls-Royce in front of the restaurant, she whispered tenderly to him:

– Thank you, Boris, for this wonderful moment! You are an incredible man!

And it was by cooing like lovebirds that they joined Zozo in the car. The driver told them that Voldemar's meeting with the Freemasons would soon be over and that they would have to wait for the Count in front of the castle. The few minutes of waiting before the heavy stone walls of the old castle did not bother the magician in the least: Lulu had found something to occupy her gentleman! She rubbed her velvet skin against his and let her sensual tongue slide over Boris's body. The latter, encouraged by Lulu, fell headlong into to amorous passion. For the first time, he did not think of Margot while he was plundering Lulu. Maybe the moment they shared at the restaurant was no stranger to this change of mind. Boris congratulated himself on it; he was beginning to forget his beloved and felt a deep sense of relief, as if he had freed himself from these unconscious burdens love.

The two lovers barely had time to put their clothes in order for Voldemar appeared, coming out of the castle accompanied by a group of Freemasons, dressed in elegant tuxedos decorated with colored ribbons and crimped gold stars of diamonds. The three-point brothers did not hold back their tears when they said goodbye to their grand master. Obviously, Voldemar had announced to them that they would not see him again or, more precisely, that they would not see Polyus who, for more than a century, had worked at the head of the Masonic Lodge to make the world order prevail. And now he is tired and terminally ill will die in a few days. In parting, the great master, not restraining the tears of great chagrin, said to his stone masons:

— It must be acknowledged that we had done a good job: we had greatly helped to purge Europe of imperial and royal dynasties, archaic, to establish governments advocating the ideas of the Illuminati and had also sent the Vatican cockroaches to the closet, though have not yet managed to get rid of it altogether.

Then, their grand master —seriously ill and on the verge of death— as he just had told them — rushed quickly, as nimble as a young man, inside the Rolls-Royce.

Voldemar dashingly jumped in the passenger seat next to Zozo, and gave goodbye one last hand to the group of masons. As Zozo started the vehicle, he exclaimed, echoing the terse words of the Russian cosmonaut Yuri Gagarin:

— Here we go!

The powerful engine of the Rolls-Royce propelled a car on the asphalt, leaving behind a plume of smoke that enveloped the Freemasons who remained on the road for a long time, unanimously lobbying their dying master, which made the quartet laugh. They took the direction of Paris, where they hoped to enjoy the excitement of the city. They remained silent for a moment, then finally Voldemar sighed:

— I will miss Polyus! He did a remarkable job.

— Count, why did you choose Polyus to take the reins of the Masonic Lodge? —Boris asked, who did not want Voldemar to relaunch him on the subject of romance when he was just beginning to mourn his story with Margot— From what you told me about him and you're meeting, he did not seem predestined to take on this role. You could have chosen, in its place, one of the Freemasons already well integrated in the order.

— I chose Polyus because I had full confidence in him. — Voldemar said— And I have never regretted my decision because he has demonstrated a loyalty without fail during all these long years. I could count on him to watch these scoundrels' politicians. These, as soon as they reach the high office, the power circling them head, and they want more, even betraying those thanks to which they arrived there. Gandhi was right when he said, "There is enough in the world to satisfy the needs of man, but not enough to satisfy his greed." That is why it is essential to keep an eye on the policies, especially that my Freemasons are not lacking in money and that some intriguers might be tempted to take control of this nest egg. Also, I will have to quickly find a replacement for Polyus, but it is a very important job and it is not easy to find someone reliable.

— Master! —Lulu asked him— Can I submit a candidate for the position of Grand Master of the Masonic Lodge?

— Of course, my dear Lulu! —Voldemar answered— Your opinion is precious to me. So, tell me, who do you think able to take such an important post??

— To Manu! —Lulu exclaimed— You know, it was this young person who asked me to introduce him to the occult sciences. It was Priestess Rosa who introduced him to me and who told me that he was destined for a great future. Currently, he works at the General Inspectorate of Finance, but he has not hid me his ambition to enter the Rothschild Bank and penetrate the arcane of the Stock Exchange, which would be a plus to grow the treasure of the Masons.

— I see who you want to talk about. —Voldemar said— I am closely watching the evolution of this young wolf. But at twenty-seven, he still seem very young to become Grand Master of the Lodge, although he is the same age as Polyus at the time of our meeting. To tell you the truth, Lulu, I thought to keep him to put him in the French presidency in a few years. Once he has exercised this function, if he gives me satisfaction, I can consider putting him at the head of the Masonic Lodge.

— Count, —interposed Boris— why don't you give Polyus's post to Nico Sinister?

— Certainly not! —Voldemar exclaimed— Nico is a trickster and I have no confidence in him.

— But you told me you wanted to make him the next president of France! —Boris pointed out.

— That's right, —Voldemar said, softly— In two years, Nico Sinister will be elected president. It is the current President Jacques who has insisted that I choose Nico as his successor. And I can not deny that he's very good at everything he does, but I'm suspicious of him. However, I decided to give him a chance to prove his worth.

— But, in that case, Count, —asked Boris— why did you say that you wanted Manu to become president, since you decided it would be Nico?

— For Nico Sinister will not stay long in power, my young friend! —Voldemar answered— I said that I had decided to give him a chance, but not that I wanted him to take a permanent place at the head of the country. Nico is too aggressive and rude. He has the madness of grandeur and sees himself as the new Napoleon. As soon as he is in power, he will want to upset the established order and will attract many enemies. Of course, it is necessary to dust off from time to time the high spheres of power, which tend to fall asleep on their laurels, but it is not about going to war against the whole world! It would be too dangerous, and the French will understand it soon enough. That's why Nico will not have to stay too long in power. As for Manu, he is not yet ready. I reserve it for myself in a few years. He is courteous and masters the art of seduction. I already met him on a Sabbath, and I was able to measure all his qualities. Here! I remember he came with a woman much older than him. Decidedly, I will never understand the manners of love of men! Seeing that Voldemar was, once again, drifting on the subject of love, a point always difficult to address for Boris, the magician preferred to relaunch the count on political questions:

— Count, you used the term "war". Do you think the situation is so bad?

— But the third world war has already begun, my dear Boris! —Exclaimed Voldemar— Radical Islamism is already taking hold everywhere in the world. And that is going to do the business of Nico Sinister. For the war against terrorists will provide him with an opportunity to justify his repressive policies and his attacks on democracy. He will try to pretend to be a vigilante who wants to clean up society by fighting mafia, drug trafficking, illegal immigration and prostitution. This will provide him with the pretext to give the police unlimited powers, so that all demonstrations of discontent by the people or opposition parties will be repressed. He will not hesitate to use the insidious plot of wiretaps to better counter those who oppose him. Moreover, he has already begun to apply these methods in the various positions he has held. In order to establish this police state, he will rely on the religious authorities but also on the terrorists themselves, those he will say he wants to fight! Because, under the guise of wanting to fight against the soil of radical Islamism, he will be able to engage in inept wars alongside the Americans. He will use the hegemony of the United States as proof that the military interventions he will launch will be just and necessary to preserve the security of the French people. He will take himself for a real little Napoleon! To finance all these operations, he will not hesitate to appeal to other tyrants, such as Muammar Gaddafi and Bashar al–Assad. Which is quite funny, because he will send his armed troops later to Libya and Syria! But Nico Sinister is not at a contradiction! Watch as he castigates the immigrants, while he himself is the son of a Hungarian immigrant! The fact that his father had to flee Hungary because of the advance of the Russian army during the Second World War may explain why Nico has complicated relations with the Russian authorities. But I'm sure he'll be able to put some water in his wine, because he is ready to do anything to have more power. For him, "the end justifies the means"! Moreover, one may even wonder whether the liaison he had with President Jacques's daughter was not a trick to enter the circle of the French elite and to win the good graces of Jacques. Certainly, he has managed to rise to the highest spheres, but his pronounced taste for luxury will eventually discredit him in the eyes of all. I tell you, my dear Boris, Nico Sinister will provoke his end. Like all tyrants, he spends his time blaming others, never questioning himself. Even when one highlights his mistakes, Nico always finds excuses to discharge his responsibilities: it is always the fault of others, and never his! This mentality can only lead to the fiasco.

— Well, Count, I feel that you have chosen the worst president that can exist! — Boris exclaimed laughing.

— To tell you the truth, President Jacques and Polyus insisted that I choose Nico Sinistre as future President of France. Polyus did not have a great sympathy for him either, but he felt he was the only one who could succeed Jacques. As I have always trusted Polyus, I agreed with him, especially since I have to admit that Nico Sinistre has a certain talent for making evil prevail on earth. But it is too unfriendly and it can not drag on in time. Anyway, for the moment, I do not have any other candidates likely to replace Nico. So I have to do with what I have! After all, this is not the first time that France will be led by an incompetent! In a few years, I will be able to place Manu at the head of France. It will be a lot more fun for me to work with this young wolf, especially since I really appreciate his partner who is older than him...

In pronouncing this last sentence, Voldemar smiled and rubbed his hands. The count's thoughts were clearly moving away from the political questions!

"Rumor has it that Manu loves not only mature women, but also men," Lulu burst out laughing. Master, I believe that the Elysee Palace will become, under his reign, a place of unbridled sexual practices!

— Well, as the proverb says, "Charbonnier is master at home!" —Voldemar smiled— It will only be necessary that we make sure that the dissolute manners of Manu do not interfere with our great project.

– Every time you are in his body, you will feel the consequences of his dissolute life with men and especially in the anus! –Lulu laughed.

– I'll wean him off this bad habit! –Reluctantly, Voldemar answered him and involuntarily rubbed his back on the surface of the car seat, apparently unintentionally imagining these strange sensations...

Our companions continued to chat for the rest of the way. Outside, the weather was good, and traffic on the highway was not dense in early April. The quartet was happy not to have had to deal with traffic jams, especially when approaching Paris where the road has the reputation of being constantly congested by a myriad of vehicles idling.

Chapter 11 - In Paris

They arrived in Paris at night and went directly to Place Vendome, at the edge of which stood a magnificent building that had hosted many personalities, monarchs to film stars through politics and billionaires.

— Welcome to the Ritz! —Voldemar exclaimed enthusiastically— It was here that Coco Chanel, the remarkable seamstress, who was part of my followers, spent a part of her life. She even died there, in her luxurious suite where she had received her friend Serge Lifar —dancer of Russian origin— These two were doomed to gémonies in the post-war years and even had to go into exile in Switzerland because, during the Occupation, they had chosen to collaborate with the Germans. During my various stays on earth, I lived for a long time at the Ritz. Although paradise is not my cup of tea, I could go back to Ernest Hemingway's words: "The Ritz is the last before heaven".

After leaving the Rolls-Royce in the hands of the valet, the four companions entered the hotel. Their entrance did not go unnoticed, for all the staff came running to welcome the

Count. The hotel manager arrived last because he almost had a heart attack when he saw Voldemar and had to recover from his emotions. Indeed, as a member of the Masonic Lodge, the director had heard that the master Polyus was in a coma, on the verge of death. Also, the surprise was great when he saw Polyus introduce himself, happy and and indecently rejuvenated, in the hall of the hotel.

– Grand Master! –The director cried, advancing to meet the newcomers– What a surprise to see you! Forgive me for being late to welcome you, but I preferred to go first and ask my employees to prepare your favorite sweet the "Coco Chanel", as well as the "Imperial" and "Windsor" for your companions.

– Perfect! –Voldemar agreed– Zozo, my driver, will take the "Windsor" suite. He deserved it because he drove all day. And the two lovebirds will settle in the "Imperial".

Voldemar glanced mischievously at Boris and Lulu, then asked them naughtily:

– I think you will not mind sharing the same room, right?

The couple giggled at this ironic remark. Voldemar turned back to the hotel manager and ordered him:

– You serve a meal in my suite. While waiting for it to be ready, we'll have a drink at the Hemingway Bar. All your cocktails are excellent, but I particularly appreciate the "Side-Car"!

With that, he went to the bar together with by his three acolytes. The Freemasons present turned to the passage visibly surprised to see wandering the great master who was said to be dying! They discreetly questioned the director of the establishment who could not answer their questions, for he himself was surprised by this surprise appearance. Yet he had seen some strange things here! But that was beyond his understanding! In order not to arouse further curiosity, the quartet did not linger at the bar and, after drinking a cocktail, immediately went to the suite "Coco Chanel", where the table had been set up. They waited under the bell for dishes from the L'Espadon restaurant, whose fine cuisine was famous throughout the world and was honored with two Michelin stars.

The four companions took their places around the table and began to eat. They opened their appetites with a crayfish bisque, sprinkled with flaked almonds and parsley. Then, as a starter, they savored a Caesar salad, topped with a honey sauce and slightly grilled toast and fat duck liver. Then, they continued with the main course: pork chops, accompanied by new potatoes and a sweet sauce with fried onions. Hungry Boris in just a few seconds swallowed all these delicious dishes famous not only for their taste, but also for scanty portions. Therefore, the magician could safely say that the food was excellent, as he suggested, but the quantity was catastrophically wanting.

Involuntarily experiencing a crisis of nostalgia, Boris thought:

"I'm not convinced by gourmet cuisine. I love to eat at the table, copiously garnished a peasants whom we met during of our campaigns! I love too much good and tasty food to appreciate the bourgeois cuisine — so-called "refined" cuisine.

But as they say: "Do not come with your rule in the monastery of others". "

Boris concludes his reflections aloud, to make his companions understood what he was thinking for so long:

– I understand better why the rich Parisians are so meager! The restaurants of the capital seem to put just enough quantities so that their customers do not starve or did not starve to death, but nothing more...!

Bursts of laughter, far more numerous than the number of guests, followed Boris's remark. The magician was surprised to hear all these different voices and asked Voldemar:

– Count, would you have invited some of your ghosts to join us?

– Indeed! –Voldemar answered– Three of my ghosts have been sitting with us since the beginning of the meal, but I asked them to stay invisible and be discreet so that you would not be disturbed during the meal ... even if it seemed frugal! If you agree, they will materialize to accompany us while we eat dessert.

Boris nodded in agreement, and the first specter to take human form was Coco Chanel's.

– The presence of this great lady of fashion will not surprise you, my friend, –Voldemar said– since it was in this suite that she lived during her lifetime. I allowed her to come back here whenever she wished. And, to be honest, she resides much more often in this suite than in my hell. Suddenly, the two other ghosts materialized, which Boris recognized without difficulty: Princess Diana and her lover Dodi Al-Fayed.

Boris greeted these unusual guests with a friendly nod.

— What a wonderful table! —Voldemar exclaimed, delighted— Here are gathered: a living person, three ghosts, two demons and the Devil himself! We have to celebrate this!

Voldemar stood up, grabbed a bottle of champagne from an ice bucket and served four cups. He kept one in his hand and handed the other three to his traveling companions. Then, his eyes lit up a brief moment with a strange glow and, as if by magic, flutes of champagne appeared in the hands of the three ghosts. Everyone raised his glass and Voldemar said:

— I make a toast in honor of the beautiful ladies who honor us tonight with their presence.

— Allow me to complete your toast, master! —Lulu intervened— I would like to thank the only one living men around this table for bringing you to earth. Without him, we would not be all together tonight! And, thanks to him, I rediscovered the pleasures of the flesh! And in general, I felt like a full-fledged woman in the literal sense of the word! For my knight Boris!

— Lulu's right, my dear Boris. —Voldemar said— If, during the magical ceremony at the bus station, you had not shed so much blood in the ritual cup, I would not have appeared. Margot did not stop you in time! Otherwise, we would not have met. And a bottle of holy water was also welcome. Unfortunately, the Master during his delirium forgot to tell his novice Margot about such a trifle, which is holy water from the Christian church... But thank you for giving me the opportunity to enjoy these beautiful spring holidays. To my friend Boris!

— Glory to Boris! —All the guests, including the ghosts, screamed in chorus, and then rang out applause.

The magician also decided to make a toast, and when it came to him to speak, he, as expected of a former military man, stood up and said:

— Men, alas, continue to see the world through blinkers: they prefer to deny the existence of what they do not see rather than question their vision of the world and recognize their ignorance. Some even are so embittered that they fall into a violent nihilism. But I remain hopeful that one day men will be more open-minded. That is why I would like to toast in the name of friendship between the inhabitants of the terrestrial world and those of the afterlife!

— To friendship! —Lulu exclaimed, applauding— And to love!

The three ghosts also simulated cheerful applause, but, suddenly, all suspended their gestures, because Voldemar had frozen and seemed lost in his thoughts. Realizing that everyone was staring at him, the Devil came out of his thoughts and wanted to revive the festive atmosphere by explaining:

— Forgive me, my friends, but the fact that Lulu talked about love has plunged me into my thoughts. I still do not understand what this feeling is that seems so dear to humans. But the words of Boris made me think: it's not because I do not know love that it does not exist! Just as it is not because the living do not see ghosts that they do not exist! Especially that many living men and some women have given me evidence of the existence of love. So, I join my voice to your wishes:

— To love!

— To love! —The table repeated.

And all the guests raised up off their champagne glasses, including the specters, even though they were no longer endowed with bodies, and all that they let appear was nothing but a chimerical image.

The four traveling companions then discovered the dessert that the Ritz had reserved for them: marbled cakes, accompanied by custard. Boris silently nodded at the small size of the portion dishes. He preferred, this time, to keep his thoughts to himself because everyone was chatting happily. He swallowed his dessert in two bites and took an apple from the basket of fruit that sat in the center of the table. While biting hard in the fruit, Boris said he would have liked to take advantage of the presence of the three ghosts to satisfy his curiosity, but he was afraid to sound too indiscreet. So, once he had finished nibbling his apple, he said cautiously:

— Ladies Coco and Diana, Mr Al-Fayed, it's an honor for me to meet you and share this moment of conviviality with you. Dear Diana, let me ask you one question! I see that you speak perfect French.

Princess Diana's ghost nodded, while Voldemar burst out laughing and explained to Boris the reasons for his hilarity:

— Ghosts understand any language, they speak at least Arabic. Of course, when they are in front of living people, they try to speak in human language.

— Well, in this case, I will ask my question in Russian! — Boris smiled—Diana, is it true that you said to your butler

Paul Burrell, shortly before your death, that you feared for your life?

— Yes, that's right. —Diana answered— But if you think that Charles ordered my murder, you are mistaken...

Boris jumped because it was the essence of his thought. Voldemar did not lie when he claimed that ghosts able to penetrate people's minds. Moreover, Boris was not long in having the very illustration of the telepathic communication that the Count had mentioned because he felt a thought, which was not from him, crossing his mind, in an intense way:

— Charles would never have had the courage to commit such a crime.

Diana smiled at the magician, who nodded to indicate that he had received the message. The evening did not go too far. Lulu was more and more pressing: under the table, she ran her hand on the thighs and crotch of the magician. Also, Boris took advantage of a blank in the conversation to take leave of Voldemar, Zozo and the three ghosts. While getting up and greeting the guests, he grabbed a bottle of champagne on the table and some fruit in the basket, a snack that would surely be needed to regain strength during the night. Lulu slipped her arm into the hollow of Boris's, and the two lovers quickly joined the "Imperial" suite that had been assigned to them.

The night was indeed hectic for Boris, and not only because of the insatiable Lulu... Once he had fulfilled the wishes of his mistress, he saw, between her half-opened eyelids, the diaphanous silhouettes of Princess Diana and Dodi Al-Fayed who wandered in the "Imperial" suite. Although he had become accustomed to the presence of ghosts and was not afraid of them, this ballet of vaporous specters had kept him awake, and he could doze only out intermittently.

Also, in the early morning, Boris abandoned the idea of finding sleep and decided to get up. He was careful not to wake Lulu who, curled up like a cat, did not seem to want to leave Morpheus's arms. Then he went down to Bar Hemingway, where he ordered a coffee.

The magician had heard a lot about Hemingway, the famous writer who had given his name to the bar, but had not read any of his works. However, Boris knew that Hemingway had frequented the Ritz, where he had left a memorable memory. The name of this author inspired him, and he promised himself to take the time to discover his books. Despite its famous name, the establishment was similar to all other bars in Paris, apart from the tariffs consumption that were breathtaking. Although Voldemar would settle the bill, Boris preferred to settle for two cups of coffee and a basket of pastries. Once his breakfast had been swallowed, he went outside. At this early hour, the street was deserted and the Parisian air was not yet infested with the unbreathable smell of car exhausts. Boris thought it was the perfect time to walk around the capital, but he had hardly taken a few steps before a car stopped at his height. What was his surprise when he recognized Voldemar's Rolls-Royce, in which his three companions were sitting, and Lulu, smiling, signaled him to join them.

"But how did they get ready so fast? Lulu was still asleep when I got out of the room!" —Boris thought.

The magician decided to put aside his questions and got into the vehicle. The other three welcomed him happily, visibly ready to embark on new adventures. Boris responded to their enthusiasm by greeting them with enthusiasm. Zozo restarted the car, roaring the powerful engine and disturbing the morning quietness of the streets of the city.

— So, Count, where are we going today? —Boris asked.

— Well, my friend, we accompany you where you have been invited! —Voldemar answered— By the way, I still want to congratulate you for your wonderful statement last night: it was very moving to hear you toast in the name of friendship between our two worlds.

— And where am I invited, Count? — Boris marveled, ignoring Voldemar's congratulations.

— Boris, why have you been so shy for so long? —Lulu chuckled tightly the wizard— You are a member of the UMP and you were invited to the congress that is being held today, on the occasion of the nomination of Nico Sinister as a candidate for the next presidential election. A breakfast will be organized before the declaration of the president of the UMP.

— Ah yes! —Boris exclaimed— Now that you remind me, it's true that I received an email invitation a few days ago. I had completely forgotten! Had I know were awaiting we a breakfast, I would not have eaten so many croissants at the Hemingway Bar! But how did you know I was invited to this congress?

— Sometimes, chance does things well! —Voldemar replied, a mysterious smile on his lips— Since I too must go to this mceting to settle some points with my follower Nico.

As they rushed past the Sainte Genevieve church, designated since the French Revolution as the "Pantheon," Voldemar shouted to Zozo to stop the car. The driver braked abruptly, ignoring the rules of the road. Fortunately there was nobody behind them, otherwise they would have created a pileup wrecked cars!

— Forgive me, my friends, —Voldemar said— but I would like to pay homage to my valiant followers who are here.

With these words, Voldemar left the Rolls-Royce and walked briskly toward the entrance of the eighteenth-century church. Boris, now accustomed to the whims of the Count, followed suit. They both silently advanced to the doors of the building, which they found closed. But that did not discourage Voldemar from assuming the role of history teacher to explain to Boris:

— Before sheltering this famous monument, the mountain Sainte Geneviève, then called Mons Lucotitius, welcomed Roman monuments, especially the arena of Lutèce. At the beginning of the 6th century, the monastery of the Holy Apostles was built on the orders of Clovis, the first Christian king of France, and his wife Clothilde. This monastery was renamed "St. Genevieve's Church" because, according to tradition, St. Genevieve often came to pray there. Destroyed by the Viking invasions and the pangs of time, the church gradually fell into ruin. It was not until the eighteenth century that King Louis XV decided to rebuild the church of

St. Genevieve, following a prayer he had addressed to the patron saint of Paris, while he was seriously ill: if St. Genevieve saved him, he would have an abbey erected in his honor. When he was reestablished, the King of France kept his word and laid the first stone of the building, although the Duchess Marie-Anne de Châteauroux, his mistress, died soon after, under strange circumstances. This neoclassical building features an antique-inspired facade with Corinthian columns and a stone dome. Although the Parisians strongly criticized the aesthetics of this building, he was chosen, during the French Revolution, to welcome the great men who have marked the history of France. This choice was motivated by the fact that the church, just completed, had not yet been consecrated. The revolutionaries had not yet cut off the head of Louis XVI when they buried their first heroes, who were also my followers. If, originally, the church was built to house the shrine of St. Genevieve, it was destroyed during the Revolution, and the bones of the saint were burned, to be eventually replaced by those of many famous people such as free-thinkers Voltaire and Rousseau. For my part, I consider it only right that this building was desacralized, because the Church had made tyranny prevail for far too long. The nobility and the clergy, with their unjust taxes, had plunged the French people into total misery. It was time for the people to rise up! The Revolution is one of my greatest achievements. But enough of these old memories! Let's listen to what Nico Sinister has to say! I think we'll have a good time, my dear Boris!

Voldemar and Boris climbed into the Rolls-Royce, which Zozo had not moved, even as cars lined up behind her, leading to a concert of furious Klaxons. A few minutes later, the car stopped near the building where the congress was held, in front of which Communist demonstrators were holding banners demanding the resignation of the right-wing government. The executives of the UMP, wearing a badge on the back of their suit, entered the building wisely, not troubled by the vociferation of the demonstrators. Our four companions entered the room where the meeting was held. As the grand master of the Order of the Golden Rose-Cross ascended the central alley in the company of his three henchmen, one of Nico Sinister's partisans hastened to greet Voldemar with a bowed bow. Boris immediately recognized Francois Fillon, Minister of National Education. After exchanging a few words with Voldemar, Fillon joined a group of deputies on the right. The Count then explained to Boris that he had chosen Fillon to be the next prime minister. The magician thought that indeed, Fillon, by his education and his speech, had the stature to occupy this ministerial position, but he had found his attitude vis-à-vis Voldemar too affected. Suddenly a man, who presented himself as Nico Sinister's secretary, came to meet Boris and whispered in his ear that the grand master was expected in a separate room, to their left. Obviously, Nico Sinister's secretary had thought that Boris was Voldemar's special advisor! The magician was amused and remarked that the great Zozo could be said to be the Count's bodyguard, and that Lulu, with her strict tailor and rectangular glasses, which she had taken out for the occasion,reminded a secretary from an adult movie. Boris conveyed the message to Voldemar, but not wishing to interfere with these political questions that bothered him, the magician pretended a pressing desire not to accompany the Count to his secret rendezvous with Nico Sinister. Boris thus respected the famous saying: "Too much curiosity gives more inconvenience than pleasure". With that, Voldemar went into the room designated by Boris, and the magician dragged Lulu, who was beginning to catch the leering gaze of these gentlemen, to the toilet, where he satisfied an urgent need other than the one he had mentioned in front of Voldemar. Then the two lovers joined Zozo in front of a long table overflowing with pastries and various drinks. Croissants were crispy at will, from one of the best bakeries in France, the small village of Tuchan lost in the foothills of the Pyrenees. Boris indulged in greed and swallowed several pastries, which he washed down with a variegated cocktail Monaco. Then he drank two San Marco espressos, which he found delicious. Finally, the magician felt himself ready to join the followers of Nico Sinister, who had sat quietly waiting for their favorite candidate.

The secretary of the president of the UMP come to talk to Boris but he kept looking nervously at the door where secret negotiations were going on between Nicolas and Voldemar and the magician jokingly told him:

— You fear that the secret services KGB come to spy private conversations your the boss with my friend Voldemar?

Alas, Boris's remark did not have the desired effect: far from laughing, the secretary turned pale, then fainted. Fortunately,

Boris managed to support him over the shoulders. Security guards intervened quickly to evacuate the secretary who was gradually regaining his spirits. Boris and his two companions, not wanting to draw more attention to them, went to sit at the back of the room where members of the UMP which were getting bored, while nibbling French pastries or discussing things and others jokes from political life.

Suddenly, the door of the room where Voldemar and Nico Sinister were talking to each other opened on the fly, and the future President of the Republic appeared, all smiles. He was greeted by a concert of applause. He walked up the aisle, clutching his hands here and there, and climbed onto the platform where a desk with a microphone had been placed. Voldemar had left the room after Nico Sinister and, spotting his companions, motioned them to join him. As Nico began to show his faithful companions his plan of action for the next two years, Boris, Lulu and Zozo discreetly slipped away. They were walking fast because Voldemar was already out of their field of vision. Lulu, perched on his high heel Louboutin, stumbled several times, but Boris avoided him falling every time.

"But where has this damn Count gone yet? —Boris thought— I know he is the Devil, but he could still spare us his sleight of hand and especially the speed of their legs!"

Finally, the trio found Voldemar waiting quietly in the hall, with a satisfied smile, as if he silently boasted of his success in the political meanders. Zozo continued on his way to get the Rolls-Royce. Outside, police contained the growing crowd of protesters. Suddenly, a roaring Rolls-Royce came to stand right in front of the entrance of the building, showering the clinging Communists with smoke, which literally covered the crowd of protesters with a black cloud. Voldemar and the two lovebirds rushed into the vehicle, which started again and, as swift and elegant as a cheetah, took the direction of the south of France. After a few minutes' drive, Boris, no longer holding it, asked Voldemar:

– Count, forgive my indiscretion, but what have you discussed with Nico Sinister, to isolate you for such a long time? We have almost lost hope of seeing you again!?

– To be honest, –Voldemar said– not much interesting! You did well made not to come with me. You would have been bored. Nico renewed his total fidelity and presented me his campaign plan for the next two years: the same speech that he serves his supporters at this very moment! That's why I did not want to stay. Nico is a big talker and a nice speaker: it does not surprise me that he manages to wind up so many people! For my part, I told him to wait a little longer before going public with his candidacy for the presidential election. He must not reveal his cards immediately to his opponents. Only the cadres of his party, gathered today, must be aware ... even if the whole of France already suspects its ambitions! To make him wait, I promised him that he would have the post of Minister of the Interior in the next government of Dominique de Villepin. After all, he has already held this position and has never really left it, since President Jacques has entrusted him with top secret missions in counter-intelligence services. I also assured him of the financial support, for his campaign, of Muammar Gaddafi, in exchange for a non-intervention of the

French army, alongside the Americans, in Libya, even if I know in advance that Nico does not will not keep his word. I also advised him to change soon a woman, for the benefit of a beautiful lady who will represent France elegantly. It may be the only one of my advice that he will respect! In any case, I am sure he will not even keep the promises he makes to the French people. The latter will return the favor! Anyway, I'll let him lead France briefly ... not too long because he would be well able to lead the country to bankruptcy! But let's put aside, for the moment, these political considerations. Because once we are back on the French Riviera, we will have a lot of things to do: solve the problem of shenanigans that operates your former boss, the director of the bus station in Cannes, and we hitch the preparations for the Sabbath of May Day. On this occasion, witches and wizards from all over the world will land in the Tanneron Massif. They must have a nice party, but it will be tedious because the demons of my hell are not very disciplined.

Lulu and Zozo burst out laughing at this last remark.

Chapter 12 - Resolution of the conflict with the director of the bus station of Cannes

When the four companions were back on the French Riviera, Voldemar embarked on active preparations for the May 1 Sabbath. According to his plan, the assembly it was supposed to take place on a mountain in the Tanneron Massif, not far from the Baron de Munchhausen estate. In the world of witchcraft, this event was of paramount importance and was world-renowned. This is why Voldemar wanted everything to be perfectly organized, especially since President Jacques and a few other eminent political personalities from the Old Continent would be present.

It was shortly after their return from Paris that Boris received a summons from the director of the Cannes bus station. The mail meant he had to sign documents to make his dismissal effective. On being informed of the convocation, the magician was angry at first and refused to go to the rendezvous, but Voldemar told him, with a strange smile, that he could go without fear. Boris calmed down and, encouraged by the Count, decided to go to the interview with his former boss. So, on the set day, Boris went to the headquarters of the security company SPS Safeguard, located in Mougins, one of these small towns, perched on hills, which welcomed many rich people wanting to live not far from beautiful Cannes and its colorful festival.

Mr Rode, the director of the bus station of Cannes, had an office in this security company with which he worked to supervise guard the station. It was there that he had chosen to invite Boris, rather than in his office of the bus station. Maybe he was feeling safer here, far from where the satanic ritual had been?

Zozo parked the Rolls-Royce in the car park next to the headquarters of the security company. Boris stepped out of the car and walked slowly to the industrial building, typical of the 1960s. The magician, who had been here when he was working at the bus station, noticed some changes: the old glass door of the entrance had been replaced by an armored steel door with a small skylight to control visitors. The windows were now provided with iron bars. All around the building was equipped with many surveillance cameras. Boris amused himself with this excess of caution and thought that it was surprising that the site was not surrounded by a row of barbed wire and that snipers were not posted on watchtowers with machine guns. Was it's like consequences the ritual he and Margot had performed that had so scared the director of the bus station? Boris then thought of that famous March night when he and his beloved had indulged in a strange ceremony. He remembered Margot's naked body perfectly well, then his disappointment when she ran away, before the fire broke out and Voldemar, in its spectral form, did not appear for the first time. Boris expelled these memories and presented himself before the armored door, which was opened to him, after he had presented his convocation, by a secretary who accompanied him to the office of Mr Rode. As he entered the room, the magician thought it was time to put an end, once and for all, to this episode of his life. In any case, his job as night watchman at the bus station was very poorly paid. Mr Rode welcomed Boris coldly; he did not even shake his hand and merely pointed to the chair facing his desk with a wave of his hand. The magician sat down and watched his former boss: he was a man in his forties, tall and fat. He wore an elegant suit, and on the back of his jacket glittered a trilobed cross of gold, a symbol of his belonging to the Masonic Lodge. Mr Rode, who had remained standing, spoke in a tone almost threatening:

– Before we talk about your dismissal, I would like us to mention a strange event that happened at the bus station on the day of your departure.

– Oh yes, I guess you mean the bus fire! —Boris replied with a smile— Perhaps you would like to give me a medal to congratulate me on this act of bravery? Because if I had not intervened, the fire could have spread to other vehicles and even to nearby buildings. In fact, I want to point out that the extinguisher I used to extinguish the fire was defective. I had to do it several times before I managed to make work old fire extinguishers. You should have your security equipment checked.

– Do not take me for a fool, Mr Lvov! —Mr Rode cried— You know very well that I was not referring to the fire! And I do not appreciate your comments: would you be threatening me to send the security control service to the bus station? And I do not see how your behavior is heroic: you should have called the fire department immediately! No one gave you permission to put out a fire at a bus station yourself.

Boris preferred not to reply to this last remark, tinged with obvious bad faith. The director knew perfectly well that if Boris had not intervened before the arrival of the firemen, the damage would have been much greater. Mr Rode understood without difficulty the meaning of Boris's silence, and, in order not to lose face, immediately went on:

– Let's put aside this fire story and come to the point. I would like you to explain to me why, after we found your bag filled with strange trinkets, special agents intervened to destroy the lodge, and why many of the employees of the bus station had madly need the intervention of psychiatrists.

– I'm not aware of this. – Boris retorted calmly – Since I left my post at the bus station, I have not set foot there. I do not see how I could be informed of the secret service or mental health activities of my former colleagues.

– Still, there are many things that make me think you're no stranger to all these events. – Mr Rode continued – First, you left your job, without warning, just before the employees started having hallucinations. Then we found your bag containing esoteric objects. And then I was told that on the morning of the fire you had photographed the surveillance booth. Admit it's strange...

– Mr Rode, – Boris began – there is nothing strange about everything you mention. The items you found in my bag were just decorative. And if I took a picture of the lodge, it was because I wanted to show my mother where I had worked for several months. As for the health problems of the employees, I think that the explanation is in their working conditions: they are exhausted because of all the overtime that you impose on them! You make them work two hundred and twenty hours a month, instead of the one hundred and forty regulations! It is for this reason that I myself decided to leave my post: I was tired of working during long sleepless nights, for a pittance. I think you should be lucky that none of your employees have started proceedings against you because you are exploiting them. Ah, if Lenin was still in this world and saw how you treat your employees, he would have launched a vendetta against you!

— As you go! What are you hinting at the communist rebellion? —The director exclaimed.

A silence settled. Mr Rode, understanding that he would get nothing more from Boris, decided to attack on another subject:

— As I was somewhat surprised by your defection, I inquired about your career and I learned that you were fired from your previous job at Security Shop because of your very bad character.

— That's wrong! —Boris exclaimed, irritably— I was fired from Security Shop unfairly! Three years ago, on the night of 7 to 8 May, Greenpeace activists set fire to the Villeneuve-Loubet dump near Nice, where I worked as a security officer. They wanted, by this act, to denounce the sanitary scandal: the hills are transformed into giant garbage dump! But they did not measure how much it was a real powder keg! When I took my service in the early morning, I immediately noticed the white smoke coming out of a pile of garbage. I approached and saw that a fire was already spreading and immediately phoned my boss, who shouted at me because I was bothering him on a holiday! Convinced that I was dramatizing the situation, he forbade me to call the fire department and ordered me watch evolution in fire. But I told him loudly that it was all-important and then I immediately called the firefighters, who took two days to extinguish the fire, with tons of water. The situation was serious because if the fire had reached the toxic waste warehouse, the entire landfill would have exploded and the ecological consequences would have been disastrous. The pretty town of Nice would probably not have been spared polluted by a wave of toxic filth as how the volcano Vesuvius once covered the city of Pompeii with ashes. Yes, I saved the city of Nice from an ecological disaster! And and in gratitude, I was fired because by calling the fire department, I disobeyed an order from my superior! That's the real story and by nature I am a very peaceful person! If don't wake the beast inside me...

— And you think I'll believe you, Mr Lvov? —Mr Rode, who still had not sat down, became angry— You're still trying to pretend to be a hero, who proved himself in the fight, putting out the fire on bus at the bus station! I spoke to the director of Security Shop, and he told me that you had shown insubordination. So, do not be surprised to once again be fired from all your jobs!

— Speaking of that, —Boris continued— You did not even signify my dismissal until I received the summons for today. I am not sure that you have followed the legal procedure.

— And you, you respected the law by deserting your post? —The director retorted— You are sick, Mr Lvov, seriously ill! Your behavior is dangerous, and you must be treated before your actions cause irreparable damage.

— Mr Rode, thank you for worrying about my sanity. — Boris smiles—but I suggest you monitor yours too.

Curiously, the director returned his smile, as if he wanted to coax him, then he said in a soft voice:

— Do you know that secret services are interested in your case? If you tell me what happened in the lodge of the bus station, I may be able to intervene on your behalf...

— Dear sir, —Boris said— believe me, it is better for you that you know nothing... As the saying goes: "He who knows a lot sleeps little".

He concluded his reply with a malicious wink, which enraged the director.

— We have nothing more to say to us! —Mr Rode cried— Go see my secretary; she will explain the formalities that you will have to perform. You will receive a summons from the labor inspectorate for an interview with a psychiatrist. If you do not attend this appointment, you can be sure that you will be in big trouble. We are not in Russia here! You have endangered national security, and you will not be able to escape as easily!

Mr Rode had the foam on his lips and looked at Boris badly. Whereas the magician continued to wear an ironic smile.

— But what makes you smile, damn it? —Mr Rode irritated— Definitely, you are really crazy!

Boris did not answer right away. He took the time to choose his words and asked his former boss:

— Mr Rode, did you hear about me before I worked for you?

— No, I did not know your existence! —The director replied in a scornful tone.

— So you do not know my past, before I become a security officer? —Boris continued.

— I only know that you were part of the Foreign Legion.

— Indeed! —Boris confirmed— But you are far from knowing everything... You do not even imagine what I can do. People who pick on me always end up regretting it. I can assure you that you will remember me throughout your miserable existence. You and your acolytes make me think of the members of the Inquisition, except that instead of burning your detractors alive, you lock them up in an asylum! You treat people as if they were sheep: they must stay wisely in the flock, otherwise you let go of the dogs! Or rather, you stuff them with drugs to reduce them to vegetables! But if you think I'm going to let you do it, you put your finger in your eye! As you rightly say, we can not break the law without suffering the consequences. And I'm sure your employees would have a lot to say about their deplorable working conditions. With that, I'll see your secretary. Good luck, Mr Rode, because you still do not know everything that awaits you...

— And, besides, you threaten me! —Mr Rode roared.

Boris got up from his chair and, without a word, came out of the room, slamming the door. As he made his way to the secretary's office, a thin employee came to meet Boris and told him:

— Forgive me, sir, but I have surprised the end of your conversation with M. Rode. Am I to understand that you are going to do something for us, the employees of this tyrant?

— I promise you nothing, —Boris said— But I will do everything in my power out of harm's way to myself from the consequences of a conflict with this parasite. I think that this will make your life easier.

A glimmer of hope lit up in the man's gaze, which shook hands with Boris, thanking him. Then the magician went to the secretary's office. He knocked at the door and was very courteous to the young woman, whose name was Christelle. She was pregnant, and he did not want to scare her. Despite her pregnancy approaching the end, she was very beautiful. Her face resembled that of a porcelain doll. The secretary informed him that she had sent him by post the papers concerning his dismissal and that Boris would have to return them signed. She added that she had also sent him his summons for an interview with the psychiatrist of the labor inspectorate. Boris thought that Mr Rode had lied to him: he had pretended to have some papers to sign for him.

Whereas in fact the director wanted to call him to come here and try to extract information from him. But what did he seek to know? Boris thanked the secretary, and she accompanied him to the security door, which she opened by dialing a code. The magician wished Christelle a good day and left the building.

"Finally in the open air!" —Boris thought.

As he walked along the building to the parking lot where the Rolls-Royce was parked, he heard Mr Rode's familiar voice coming through the open window that was not far from his desk. The bars of the windows may have prevented thieves from entering, but not the voices to go out!

Obviously, the bus station manager spoke on the phone and gave the order. His deputies for work immediately came to talk to him in office. Boris looked around him and, since he saw nothing suspicious, decided to stay about by the window ajar to listen to the conversation that was to follow. Moments later, he heard that someone was knocking on the door of his former boss's office.

— Come in, gentlemen! — Mr Rode said in a nervous voice — And sit down!

Boris glanced discreetly through the window: he saw two men of about forty, meager and not very tall, like many Frenchmen. They stood very straight almost and clearly demonstrated their attention to a future conversation. Great magician wondered if they were not former gendarmes. He also saw Mr Rode, who was standing next to his desk, as in his interview with Boris.

— Well, what are, Dear Sirs, you waiting for to sit down? — Mr Rode asked annoyed voice.

— Boss, — said one of the deputies in a hesitant voice — it would be impolite for us to sit while you, our superior, are standing...

Suddenly, Mr Rode began to cry with heavy sobs, like a child. His two deputies seemed dumbfounded and did not know what attitude to adopt regarding to their boss, who was in a bad mood.

— Gentlemen, —Mr Rode sobbed— it's hard for me to sit down. It hurts me too much...

Boris heard the director blow his nose, then he said:

— I have to tell you a terrible story. But I can not find the words to describe what happened to me. It's so humiliating... (Mr Rode sighed and kept silent for a moment.) Last night, a strange couple burst into my room. I do not know how they managed to enter my home, without raising the alarm, because my house is equipped with a high-performance security system and a security door with tamper-proof lock. Anyway, I found them at the foot of my bed! The man was very tall and very strong: a real gorilla! The woman was pretty and dressed provocatively and something like a little monkey. Even before I had time to realize that someone had entered my room, the gorilla threw himself on me! He lifted me up as if I were as light as a feather and turned me back on the bed. He plunged my head into my pillow, almost choking me, and forced me to get on all fours. I could not do anything to defend myself because he held my hands and pressed his elbow very hard against my neck. Then the woman introduced me into a huge plastic dildo, saying, "So, you bastard, you are slapping your secretary? Except that you made her pregnant! And now, you refuse to recognize the child!". And she continued to drive the plastic penis into my anus, more and more deeply, over and over again, still vituperating: "Take this, bastard! It is for all the women that you treated like vulgar prostitutes!". I do not know how long it lasted, but I felt it was an eternity. It was only in the early morning that they left, as suddenly as they had appeared. It was as if they had evaporated in the air! Since then, I've been bored and I cannot sit...

Mr Rode spoke quickly and without stopping, as if he was in a hurry to finish. His two assistants said nothing and lowered their eyes. They did not seem more offended than that of the rape suffered by their boss.

– Why do you stay without reaction? –Mr Rode continued– My ordeal does not shock you? Looks like it's not the first time you hear such a story.

The cheeks of the two deputies flushed, and Mr Rode asked, suspicious:

– Gentlemens, I order you to sit down!

The two men, with a sad look, shook their heads.

– Gentlemens, you, too, have trouble sitting down. –Mr Rode said– You received the same visit as me and suffered the same thing!

The silence of the deputies was eloquent confirmation. They did not even try to deny. The director thought for a moment, before concluding aloud:

– But why did they take both of you... too? Gentlemens, would you have, like me, an affair with with my beloved Kristel? The two men nodded in the affirmative, fearing their superior's reaction to this news.

–If we think about it, –Mr Rode continued– it's a good thing: the probability that I, the father of Kristel's child, has just been divided by three! And maybe we're not the only ones to have fun with her! Gentlemen, let's see if other men in the office have a hard time sitting down! And tomorrow we will go to church together to repent of our sins!

Boris saw the three three familiar guards heading to the doors of the main office. The magician bent down and hid behind the bushes to avoid being caught suspected in the act of espionage. This overheard conversation had been rich in information! It was the least what is director and his two subordinates could say! Christelle, the secretary, had an affair with his boss Mr Rode, but when she announced his pregnancy, this hypocrite refused to acknowledge his possible paternity. And the two deputies were no better: they too could be the father of Christelle's child and these three bastards had abandoned the poor woman, pregnant to the mercy of fate!

"Ah, bastards! —Boris thought, indignantly— They only got what they deserved!

Apparently Zozo and Lulu visited each of the potential fathers, to punish them for their heinous behavior... and certainly it was revenge too which I was not capable of!

Mr Rode and his bastards can continue to scheming against me but... Now, I have a way of pressing against them! If ever Mr Rode will try to piss me off, I will make this whole story public!"

With that, Boris hastened to the parking lot, where Voldemar and his demons were waiting for him wisely, leaning against the hood of the Rolls-Royce. As soon as the magician arrived at their height, they pressed him with questions in a relaxed manner. Then Boris told them everything: his interview with Mr Rode, who had tried to find out what had happened in the lodge of the bus station; the appointment of the labor inspectorate that awaited him the interview with the psychiatrist; the conversation he had caught between the director and his two deputies, and the conclusions he had drawn from it. When Boris specified that the three men had some difficulty in sitting down, the four companions tried to keep their seriousness but their faces betrayed the hilarity that which they held back with great difficulty, before it broke out completely in the form of an explosion laughter.

They all left in a hysterically laugh that they had a hard time to restrain. Voldemar, Zozo and Lulu seemed very proud of the twist of fate they had played to the director and assistants. Voldemar, holding belly, said between two bursts of laughter:

– My dear Lulu, you gave us a good demonstration of what feminine solidarity is!

Once they had calmed down, the Count gave the starting order:

– By car, my friends! When they were installed in the Rolls-Royce, Voldemar added:

– My dear Boris, we had a good time today, and I think that your next interview with the psychiatrist will bring you some surprises... But, for the moment, we have to go to the Baron Munchhausen estate, because celebration the May 1st Sabbath will be held at night near the House belonging to our beloved Sufi Rashid Selimovich. So I have to discuss organizational details with him. I hope that Rashid Selimovich will not be reluctant to participate in the preparations for this event, because I know he is still a follower of Sufism – great doctrine of the monastic modesty of life – . The celebration of May 1 is a symbol of the solidarity of all the oppressed on earth, that is, the proletarians and witches who have nothing to lose but their shackles. Whereas our Sufi is an exploiter who revived along with other oligarchs like grebes in the vast expanses of the devastated Russia. My friend, I will borrow the beautiful Lulu to go talk to him, because Selimovich will be more conciliatory in her presence. Boris looked tenderly at Lulu and took her hand, which he kissed, to express his gratitude to her: the nocturnal visits she had given to Mr Rode and his assistants were doing the magician's business! Lulu smiled at him and gave him a soft kiss on the lips, while Zozo started the vehicle and headed towards the Tanneron Massif.

Chapter 13 - The follower of Sufism

As our happy quartet approached Baron Munchhausen's estate, Voldemar sighed deeply and spoke in a voice full of nostalgia:

— I want to tell that in 1970, the wife of Martin Gray Dutch-born and their four children lost their lives trying to flee the terrible fire that ravaged the Tanneron Massif... What a tragedy! It makes me think of the story of poor Job, which my heavenly Father has allowed me to put to the test to devotion to faith in God. This good man lived in present-day Palestine. He was a good family man, loved by his children. He had many flocks and servants. He was very rich and powerful, respected by all, so much so that his fame had spread beyond the borders. That is why I said to my Father, who praised his slave Job's piety, that if he lived in misery, then he would certainly be less pious! After all, when one lives in opulence, it is easy to praise the generosity of God. But when you are poor, do you want to thank the Almighty for the suffering you endure? This was a simple remark, but my Father took it literally and asked me to take away all of his riches from Job, to see if he would continue to praise God's virtues. Then, I made a series of disasters destroy his breeding. But even once he was poor, Job continued to pray fervently to God. So, I blew a violent wind to destroy the house, which roof collapsed on ten children, seven boys and three girls, all of whom died in this drama.

Then, as if that was not enough Job got leprosy. And yet, despite all these trials, he kept the faith and never cursed the Creator. Although, I am partially responsible for the misfortunes that have afflicted poor Job I want to say that I regret having persecuted him. Also, I can not help but make the connection between the story of Job and that modern martyr of faith of Martin Gray: the two have lost everything that is, relatives and friends of their people, personal property and real estate, but still found the strength to continue living. For it must be remembered that Martin Gray had already lost his entire family once, during the horrors of the Second World War. And as a mockery of the victims of this monstrous massacre, the former Nazi legion warrior Austria led the Vatican.

As far as Old Testament Job is concerned I am not the only one responsible because it is my Father who wanted to verify my theory that it is more difficult to have faith when one lives in misery and that allowed me to test the strength of Job's faith!

I gladly admit that I should not have doubted Job's piety but people too often forget that it was my Father who oversaw this experience bird's-eye. God likes to check that men believe in him. Job is the only one whose faith he has experienced. He even charged me to tempt his beloved Son. And since then, it is in honor of Jesus that Christians sacrifice a lamb at Easter to thank him for diverting them from evil. At least, if we believe the scriptures...

Because it must be said that there are less and less right on earth and even if it puts me on the back maybe all the tests that God Jesus and the Holy Spirit subject men just to ensure their love are not unrelated to the fact that men are sinking deeper and deeper into vice. Although, Job proved to me that selfless Faith in God existed!

I am not sure that everyone has as strong a faith as he does or the resilience of Martin Gray. The nature of man is so made that he always doubts and that does not change over the centuries.

The Rolls-Royce arrived in front of Rashid Selimovich's mansion silencing Voldemar for a moment before he laughed again and admired the building like a kid glancing at a delicacy:

— How lucky he is, our great Sufi Rashid Selimovich live in this wonderful home! The French do not have the same housing problems as the Russians especially in Moscow. Rashid Selimovich had a fine nose! So that by buying the estate of Baron Münchhausen he saved himself from the terrible torment of housing disorder and the grunts of his wife. Rashid Selimovich does not profess the Torah: he is a follower of Sufism, which is a current of Islam that preaches love and harmony with the aim of rising spiritually and opening up to the beauty of the world as the sacred lotus opens to the glow sun!

In a way, he is a free man because thanks to this doctrine he has freed himself from Judeo-Christian dogmas ignorant and selfish. But Selimovich is also a brilliant businessman who has made a fortune in oil and is present in every stock market in the world. He is married to the beautiful Marianna but that does not prevent him from honoring his young and busty friends. He has earned so much money that he has ensured the future of his descendants over many generations. He bought medieval castles, luxury villas and even hunting estates all over the world from Siberia to the African savannah. The actor Ivan Okhlobystine nicknamed him "the Muslim Angel" but, for my part, I doubt that Selimovich is an angel! It seems to me rather that his only god is money! I would even say that he is as far removed from Sufi values as Caesar, the emperor of Rome, was from the Platonic precepts! And the way he treated your friend the Homeless Poet proves to us that he has somewhat forgotten the notion of love of neighbor. And we know that in truth, he is a follower of the Devil! And of course, the lame and one-eyed Iblis is his best friend and assistant in his suspicious deeds.

At this remark, Voldemar winked with his black eye prosthesis at Boris, then resumed:

— My friend, as I explained to you earlier, I am going to borrow Lulu because I hope that she will be able to coax our pious Sufi to accept without hesitation to participate in the organization of the Sabbath, May 1st. Meanwhile, you can go visit the Homeless Poet, who lives in the stables of the estate. I must admit that I do not have much sympathy for this Vadim, because I do not like weak beings who let themselves sink into a life of misery. As for his literary talents, it seems to me that these are only the delusions of a madman. All the same, one thing intrigues me in the story of the Homeless Poet: why does Rashid Selimovich keep it under his control? While he exploited it by making it work without paying, but he still offers a roof... Selimovich is a billionaire, he could very well pay someone to clean the manure in his stables! And I do not think he agreed to house Vadim just due to the simplicity and grandeur of its Sufi soul.

As the saying goes: "Everyone defends themselves to do nothing out of interest and it is the interest that makes everything do". Here! We will try to find out more about the subject! I'm talking heart to heart with Selimovich and you with the Homeless Poet.

Boris did not have time to give Voldemar the information he already had about Vadim's relationship with Selimovich, as the count had already got out of the car and taking a hand Lulu was walking towards the door entrance to the mansion. For his part, Boris took the direction of the stables, where lived the Homeless Poet since already two years. When the magician entered the two-storey brick building, he was assaulted by the disgusting smell of horse dung. He wrinkled his nose, thinking: "It smells so bad that you could die asphyxiated! I wonder how Vadim does to live here! "

Holding his breath, Boris climbed the concrete staircase to the second floor, where he arrived in a long corridor with doors on either side, as in a barracks. Boris hesitated for a moment because he did not know in which room lived Vadim.

But, suddenly, he heard a familiar voice, coming from behind one of the doors, declaiming a poem:

"When Death answers my prayers
And creeps near me, to take me near
the birds of the cemetery,
then, by grace, I will find the faith!

With a pretty bouquet of flowers,
begging for mercy,
I will present myself before the Lord
who will silence all discord.

But the Devil is still in the round.
Laughing, in his garden infernal,
he creates the vile passions of our world
and invites the Grim Reaper to dance at the ball! "

Boris listened to the poem in silence and mentally said that it must be a text of the Homeless Poet. The mage sincerely imbued for the sadness that emanated from these few verses and thought:

"Is Vadim still shocked by the hallucination he had in the park of St. Nicholas Church? He was terrified after his terrible vision of the black rider! And, what's more, it's the same day he met Voldemar, who is not reassuring either! "

Boris was very worried about his friend and sighed with sadness as knocked softly at the door, which opened all by itself under the impact of his blows. The magician entered the room and was first struck by the misery that reigned in this room with very spartan furnishings. Then, Boris stopped on the silhouette of the Homeless Poet, sitting in front of a small wooden table, in a corner of the room. Vadim was even thinner than usual, and his bald head and bloodless face were of a grayish color, just as dull as the complexion of a corpse. Boris, terrified, could not refrain from shouting:

—Oh! Vadim, how are you! What happened to you? What did these monsters do to you, who treat you like a slave? The rumble from computer keys and screen glow stopped, but Vadim was still looking into a black screen as a picture of his namesake artist Malevich "black square"... And in his glass eyes expressed only terrible mental anguish.

— It's true I'm not at my best, —Vadim said weakly— Demons dance constantly before my eyes and I hear strange voices in my head. They humiliate me incessantly and reproach me for my bad actions. In addition, it has been almost three weeks since my stomach refuses to keep the little food I swallow.

— My friend, did anything happen to make your health deteriorate so fast? —Boris asked, sympathetic— You did not go so bad a month ago when we saw each other in the church garden.

— Yes, something happened... —the Homeless poet murmured, never taking his eyes off the screen— Three weeks ago, I accidentally swallowed a caustic acid, which I used to wash the toilet. I felt very bad, but I did not tell Sophie, my ex-girlfriend. But since she always looks after me, she noticed that I was sick. She was afraid it was the rats that infected me.

The stables are full of these animals. So she summoned the sanitary prisoners who sprayed rat poison everywhere, including my room and vegetables, which I store on my shelf (he nodded at the modest shelf that bordered the room wall). But since they came in my absence, and Sophie forgot to tell me about it, I continued to eat poisoned food for more than two weeks. I just found out yesterday that rat poison was sprayed in the stables, because the cleaning ladies had come to clean the other rooms. They asked me to clean up the empty stables, because new horses with riders would soon appear, and that they should not poison themselves. At first I did not understand what they meant, so they explained everything to me. And then I understood why I thought my vegetables had a strange taste and why I felt so bad for more than two weeks.

– But why didn't you go to the hospital? —Boris asked, worried.

– Because I heard Sophie tell Marc Tirelle, the manager of the estate, that I should be taken to a psychiatrist. If I had been to the hospital, one of Rashid Selimovich's doctors under the hood could have taken advantage of it to lock me up in an asylum, and I do not want to be injected with all sorts poisons into my veins!

– And after that, do you still think that Sophie is watching over you? —Boris wondered desperate for his friend's naivety.

– Of course! —Vadim retorted— You know, when we both worked at the estate, we were very in love and we even wanted to get married! But when Rashid Selimovich sent me away I preferred to leave because I did not want to drag him into misery with me. And yet she still intervened in my favor for Rashid Selimovich to accept that I stay in the stables.

The Homeless Poet had finally turned away from his screen and looked at Boris who was frightened to see that his friend's eyes had returned to their sockets like those of an undead.

— Vadim, it's time for you to open your eyes! —Boris said panicked— If Sophie cared for you, she would not accept that you live in these miserable conditions and that Selimovich exploits you by making you work without paying you!

— You're wrong, Boris! —The Homeless Poet retorted— Besides, Sophie recently offered to pay me three hundred euros a month for the work I do at the stables. But I refused because I do not want her to give me charity. And then, it's been a month since I took your place at the bus station. I should be getting paid soon and things will get a little better. While waiting to receive my pay I had the idea to grow cannabis on a hill a little further to sell it to the rich visitors of Rashid Selimovich, but when he knew it, he is came to see me and ordered me to stop my business. He told me that if he finds out that his son smoked drugs he would hold me responsible and charge me a lot of money. So, I gave up my project... It was the first time in two years that Rashid Selimovich had spoken to me!

Boris did not know what to do to help the Homeless Poet because he refused to face reality.

— In addition, —Vadim said— the other day on the way back from the bus station, I hit a big black dog on the way. The poor animal did not survive ... and my scooter either! Now, I have to walk to work or hitchhike when I meet a good soul. I hope that soon Rashid Selimovich will agree to take me back to the field. Marc Tirelle told me that he would try to convince him.

Hearing his friend's words, Boris decided to try one last time to open his eyes:

– Vadim, I think it's not thanks to Sophie that Rashid Selimovich has allowed you to live here. She only executes the orders of her boss. And if Selimovich is so anxious to keep an eye on you, it's not because he plans get you back to a decent job one day but it's because he wants to make sure you do not go tell Marianna, his wife, that one of his mistress from escort is impregnated. He keeps you here just to watch you, Vadim. And this poisoning story doesn't reassure me about what it is willing to do to make sure of your silence. You must leave here, my poor Vadim!

– And where do you want me to go? –The Homeless Poet answered with bitterness– I have nowhere to go! And then, I'm sure you're wrong. Rashid Selimovich just wants to punish me because of our debate at the airport. But when he sees that I have not betrayed him he will take me back to the manor and everything will be in order.

– It's not for nothing that we say that "hope gives life". – Boris sighed.

He approached Vadim and put a friendly hand on his bony shoulder. Then Boris took leave of his friend because it was pointless to insist: Vadim was deluded and Boris did not know how to make him listen to reason. Vadim tried to escort Boris out of the stables like a guest escorting his guests on the doorstep of his house.

Leaving the brick building they came face to face with a woman of about thirty years, with rather crude features. Immediately, the face of the Homeless Poet was illuminated and he exclaimed happy:

– Sophie! You came to see me!

Vadim performed a kind of dance step making him look like one of the "dancing men" of the new eponymous starring the famous Sherlock Holmes and he hugged Sophie in his bony arms. The young woman's face twisted into a disdainful grin which made her even more unfriendly for Boris. The magician even saw that she was squeezing her right fist as if Vadim's embrace was a real torture for her. No doubt, if she could she would have slammed her clenched fist into the face of poor Homeless Poet.

When the latter released his embrace, she took a normal attitude, gave a hypocritical smile to Vadim and turned to Boris to say:

– Monsieur, our bosses have finished their conversation and the Count has been waiting for a little while already.

– The Count is not my boss, –Boris retorted dryly– but my friend. If I asked him for a service, he would not hesitate to return it to me. But, unlike you and your boss, I'm not the style to abuse my position to harm others...

With these words Boris gave Vadim one last nod and headed for the manor.

When the magician arrived near the villa, he saw Voldemar and Lulu accompanied by a small man whom he recognized immediately: the owner of the estate of the Baron Munchhausen himself! Boris had seen Rashid Selimovich at the party at Abramovich's Castle in La Croe. He remembered him dressed in Sufi, whipping a poor young woman and Boris smirked. This time, the Caucasian was dressed in a most ordinary costume and seemed in great conversation with Voldemar who was waving his hands while talking while Lulu stood a little behind. When Boris approached them, he heard the Count say:

– Dear Rashid Selimovich, I thank you for this fascinating discussion which has enlightened me on the precepts of Sufism in the Middle East. In particular, I very much appreciated that you shared with me the teachings of the wise Tijani and his disciple Sidi Tahar.

Voldemar reached out to Rashid Selimovich and shaking his hand asked him:

– By the way, how's Vadim? I saw im recently in the park of the Saint-Nicolas church of Nice and we briefly discussed.

Rashid Selimovich seemed a bit destabilized by this question. He obviously did not understand why Voldemar who was so powerful and respected around the world was interested in this miserable Vadim. But Selimovich recovered and replied in an affable tone:

– Dear Voldemar, I did not know you knew this so-called Baron Munchhausen who lives in my stables! I sometimes ask my servants for news and they are always told me that he is well. He sometimes helps to clean the stables. Sophie, one of my employees, who know him well told me that he smokes cannabis. I do not like it but what do you want? He is an artist! His presence in my stables does not bother me. So, if it comfortable for him to stay in my stables I have no problem letting him write his poems on my property.

– Well, it's very generous of you! –Voldemar said barely concealing his ironic tone.

Then the Count pointed to Boris who had stopped at a reasonable distance from the trio and presented him to the owner of the house:

– I present you my friend Boris who does me the honor make to company for me a during my stay on the French Riviera.

Rashid Selimovich looked at Boris suspiciously and only gave him a polite nod. The magician was relieved because he would not have liked to shake hands with the torturer of his friend Vadim. An awkward silence settled in but luckily he was soon broken by the engine 's sound of the Rolls-Royce approaching them. Zozo was well aware of the uneasiness of the situation and was intime!

While driving towards the vehicle Voldemar offhandedly told Rashid Selimovich:

– See you soon, dear friend! I am delighted that you have agreed to host the Sabbath participants. My first guests will arrive in a few days and I trust you to welcome them as yours dearest guests.

Voldemar, Lulu and Boris got into the car and the Count gave Rashid Selimovich a last wave of his hand while the Rolls-Royce as swift as Pegasus took the direction of the exit of the estate leaving behind a cloud of smoke. As soon as they left the property Lulu visibly delighted her eyes sparkling exclaimed:

– Master, this Sabbath is going to be a success! Everything is perfect: the ceremonial place in the Tanneron Massif is away from the city so as not to disturb the lives of ordinary people and now we have even found where to house witches and magicians!

– By the way, Boris, – Voldemar said, interrupting Lulu – what did you got to know about the situation of the Homeless Poet?

Boris described the miserable conditions in which Vadim lived and related the poisoning he had suffered and the reasons why Rashid Selimovich kept it at hand.

– It's lucky, Boris, that you came across the Homeless Poet in the church garden. Without that you would not have known that he was staying in the stables of the Baron de Münchhausen estate and you would not have been able to intervene.

– Alas, my intervention did not have the desired effect, – sighed Boris – I could not make him listen to the voice of reason. He still believes that Sophie is watching over him and that Rashid Selimovich will eventually take him back to the manor.

Chapter 14 - The courageous psychiatrist Serge Lunatik and a foretaste of Walpurgis night

Boris had preferred to go alone to his appointment at the psychiatrist because he did not want Voldemar to be tempted to intervene by sending his demons along with a few hellish surprises to amuse the doctor in his own way. He had seen what the Count and his henchmen were capable of with the director of the bus station and his deputies. Certainly, these thugs deserved what had happened to them but Boris feared that if too many unfortunate events would happen to the people he met it would eventually fall on him. As Serge Lunatik's office was right in front of the Palace of Festivals, Boris decided to walk a little on the Croisette before going to his meeting. He had to think about this situation. He sat down on the terrace of a cafe in the shade of the magnolias and ordered a beer, just to put himself in the right mood before going to the psychiatrist. He did not know what to expect from doctor: Should he lie on a soft couch and deliver his intimate thoughts to Dr. Lunatik or just chat about nothing?

At the appointed time, Boris went to the psychiatrist's office located on the second floor of a luxurious building. He sat down in the waiting room and as he would have done for a simple dentist appointment flipped through a magazine that was three years old. Boris did not have to wait a long time because a few minutes after his arrival the cabinet door opened and let appear the athletic silhouette of a handsome man with sad eyes. His faded blue gaze was so melancholy like that of a sad clown that Boris thought for a moment that the psychiatrist would begin to cry. But the doctor advanced towards Boris held out his hand to him whom Boris energetically shooked and said to him:

– Hello. Mr Lvov, I suppose?

– Hello. That's right, doctor, –Boris confirmed.

– Follow me in my office.

They entered the cabinet adjoining the waiting room and the psychiatrist offered Boris a comfortable chair in which the magician sat and the doctor was sitting on the other side of the table. Boris was relieved not to see a couch in the room!

Serge Lunatik asked Boris:

– So, what brings you?

– To be honest, doctor, –Boris answered– it was not me who wished to see you, it was my former employer who imposed me this consultation following my dismissal.

– There's a reason your former boss thought you needed to see a psychiatrist! –Serge Lunatik replied in his melancholy voice.

– Well, honestly, doctor, –Boris retorted– Why did the boss send me to you for a consultation? I just know that since I left my post some of my former colleagues have had hallucinations as in a kind of collective madness crisis. As a result of this astonishing phenomenon maybe management wanted to check the mental health of all its employees but I did not have any abnormal vision. I think rather that my former boss has a tooth against me, I can not explain why but I chose to come anyway so as not to aggravate the situation.

— You had no hallucinations, do you say? —The doctor inquired.

— There were no hallucinations! Not in one eye, that is, neither in the left nor in the right. The same thing is with my ears. Although in fairness, I have to tell you... Well, I recently met an amazing character whose name sounds like the bad guy in Harry Potter. It's an old man a little crazy but I assure you it is real! — Boris laughed.

— I'm not used to my patients laughing and joking. —Serge Lunatik said— I wonder if I should not worry about it.

— Oh, then, in this case, if you prefer I can make a funeral head! —Boris exclaimed, who immediately displayed a pouting lips— If I had known I would have dressed in black and come with a bouquet of chrysanthemums!

— Are you making fun of me? —The doctor retorted and somehow viciously bared his American jaw studded with beautiful and even teeth from a ceramic doorway.

Noting that the features of the psychiatrist's face had become tense Boris decided that better would be do not annoy the nervous doctor and try to bring him back to better feelings:

— Forgive me, doctor, if I gave to you the impression that I was making fun of you. It was not my intention. It must be said that the situation is a little disconcerting for me because I do not know what I'm doing here. This may explain why I do not behave like your usual patience. And then, you know, everyone mens reacts in their own way to the unpleasant situations they encounter. For example, I heard that the Vikings did not consider the funerals of their loved ones to be sad. It was rather an honor for them to accompany theirs to the realm of the dead. We are far from the mourners of ancient Rome! You see, we all react differently according to our culture, beliefs and experiences.

– All this is very interesting but I would like you to tell me about you. –The psychiatrist interjected– Your face is known to me... I think we met several times at the restaurant in front of my office. Each time you were accompanied by a pretty young woman. Is she your fiancee?

At the mention of Margot –with whom he was pleased to go to that restaurant of which the doctor was talking – Boris tensed and replied a little curtly:

– My friend is gone... But I do not see how this information can help you to judge my mental health. You want to send her to an asylum too?

–I am far from this idea! –Serge Lunatik exclaimed surprised at his patient's reaction– Because you think I want you to be interned in a psychiatric hospital? You need to know that I am not one of those psychiatrists who lock up their patients with the slightest strange symptom. But I deduce from your remarks that you are in a transitional period of your life which should not be easy to manage: your girlfriend left, you lost your job and you make new encounters... (The doctor marked a hesitation.) What is the name of the old fool you mentioned earlier?

— His name is Voldemar, —Boris said— but again I do not see how it can help you diagnose my mental state.

— Yes, Voldemar... —The doctor murmured suddenly lost in thought.

Boris was beginning to wonder what was the meaning of this conversation which had neither tail nor head. After a few moments of reflection Serge Lunatik spoke again:

— Well, M Lvov, I think I can say that you have bipolar disorder.

— Sorry? —Boris surprised, stunned— And how can you say such a thing after a few minutes of discussion?

— Well, your behavior since you walked into my office! —The psychiatrist replied— At first you were happy almost euphoric. Then, you have suddenly become serious and you are lost in digressions. And finally, you got upset for no reason when I mentioned your girlfriend. It seems clear to me that your mood is very changeable.

— But, doctor? —Boris replied— it has been two months since I have been in an excellent mood! Certainly, I had a little trouble to forget my ex-girlfriend, but now I'm perfectly fine!

— Yes, those times when one feels euphoric are characteristic of bipolar disorder! —Serge Lunatik explained. — They are always followed by long periods of depression. One day, you feel so good that you feel like you can walk to Biarritz and the next day you feel so bad that you lock yourself in a casino to spend all your money. (Boris raised his eyebrows at these incongruous examples.) Yes, Mr Lvov, the consequences of this disease are diverse and varied. It is for this reason that it is essential to control the symptoms. I will prescribe a treatment that will reduce your mood swings which consists of three different pills to be taken each after the meal: in the morning, you will have to take a pink pill, at noon a yellow pill and in the evening a blue pill.

While listing this colorful treatment the doctor wrote his prescription under the bewildered look of Boris who did not know what to think. He had no intention of ingesting all these anxiolytics!

Also he pointed out to the psychiatrist:

– Doctor, all these drugs are they likely to affect my efficiency in my work? I work in security and I need to be fully awake to ensure vigilant surveillance. For now I am unemployment but I intend to resume working as soon as possible. Would not it is better for us to see each other again so that you can make a more accurate diagnosis?

– Oh! You no longer have to worry about the job! –Serge Lunatik replied– I will declare you unfit and you will receive a comfortable pension. The priority is your health. And indeed, we will have to meet again to see if your treatment is right for you. If necessary we will adjust it.

– I do not need to work anymore ?! –Boris exclaimed– Well, I did not expect that... In a way, this disease is better than nothing!

All in all doctor and patient seemed satisfied with the conclusion of this interview. As he was taking leave of the psychiatrist Boris squeezed his hand so much, so that Serge Lunatik was unwittingly distracted by the pain in the wrist, but still found the strength to smile politely. In turn, the magician, blurred in a wide smile, said to him in a cheerful tone:

— Thank you, doctor... or maybe I should thank Voldemar?

Serge Lunatik pretended not to have heard Boris's last remark and took him to the door of his office.

Once outside, Boris decided to go immediately to get the drugs that the doctor had prescribed. Along the way, he sang a verse from a Foreign Legion song as he felt he had won the battle against his former boss:

"Against the Viets, against the enemy,
Where the war is raging
Soldiers of France, soldiers of the country,
We will go back to the lines."

He entered a pharmacy and came out a few minutes later and looked with puzzled eyes at the boxes of medicine that lay at the bottom of a small paper bag and said to himself:

"Satan Voldemar! He had told me that he would not intervene with Serge Lunatik but he could not help it! I saw the psychiatrist's hesitation when he asked me about Voldemar. I'm sure it was the Count who asked him to find a pretext for me not to work anymore. Because I know that I do not suffer from any bipolar disorder! Bah! After all it's not bad to be able to live without having to work. Some people kill themselves all their lives in order to have an miserable retirement pension. "

Then he decided that deserved to relax a little. So he went to buy a bottle of cognac and a lemon in a supermarket and then settled on a bench to contemplate the blue waters of the Mediterranean. He did not even have the opportunity to open his bottle because suddenly he heard that he was being asked in a happy tone. He turned his head and saw the infernal trio: Zozo, Lulu and Voldemar who seemed drunk! They went on performing a few dance steps and laughed loudly! When the three happy fellows reached Boris, then Voldemar slumped on the bench next to the magician.

– You drank or what? – Boris asked.

– The first witches have already arrived for the May Day Sabbath! –Voldemar explained– So we had to welcome them with dignity! We tested their flying brooms. You should have seen that!

– Count, you lied to me! –Boris interrupted.

Voldemar fell silent and looked serious while Boris continued:

– I know you had a deal with Serge Lunatik, when you promised me to do nothing. Now I am considered unfit to work because, supposedly, I have bipolar disorder! Come on, admit that you went to see this psychiatrist who, moreover, is clearly depressed. He would need to consult one of his colleagues!

– My dear friend, –Voldemar answered– I had a little discussion with this Czech psychiatrist. You were lucky: he was very accommodating. It would have been much more difficult with a French doctor who always very much on the issues of professional ethics. As the saying goes: "Of two evils one must choose the least". If I had not made an arrangement with this psychiatrist, he would have had no choice but to take into consideration the fact that you performed a sorcery ritual at your workplace! In your opinion, would that have happened for a perfectly normal behavior or for the actions of a madman?

Boris sighed and crossed his arms over his chest, scowling.

— My friend, —Voldemar said— when you agreed to perform this ritual you must have known that it would not go unnoticed!

— Basically, I only had to go to carry books to the grand master! —Boris retorted— And Polyus had promised me to pay me consistently for this service. Subsequently, when the master fell into a coma Margot used all her charms to convince me to help her to perform the ceremony so that I could not refuse. Result: I did not receive a cent and my beloved flew away! I did it all for nothing... The only thing I got was to meet you, Count!

— So, you still have some satisfaction ... since I'm sitting next to you! —Voldemar smiled— And then you're going to receive an allowance from the state albeit modest but it will not be worse than the miserable salary you were getting when you were working at the bus station. Some people would dream of being in your situation rather than being forced to work like mad men until the dawn of their death! You have achieved the feat of being declared unfit for work in less than five minutes while some workers are trying all their life to get the same thing to no avail.

— I understood your argument, —Boris said— but I'm still categorized as bipolar now... It's not nothing!

– If you had been dealing with a French psychiatrist, – Voldemar said– you would have been diagnosed with schizophrenia and you would have ended up in a psychiatric hospital!

– Did I get into such a hopeless situation by participating in this magical ritual? –Boris worried.

– My dear friend, you are so naive! –Voldemar exclaimed– Didn't you notice that you were observed during our visit to Paris? Of course, the secret services are watching you! It is time for you to face the facts: after all that has happened, you will never back your ordinal life again. I advise you to go green in Avignon after the Sabbath of May 1st. You know, in the old days it was the Church that imposed its rules and in order not to be contradicted by it silenced the scientists. But today as the Church has weakened it is science that has seized power in a disproportionate way. Now, if a psychiatrist says you're crazy and you have to lock yourself in no one will dare to contradict him on the pretext that his diagnosis is based on scientific certainty and that the latter can not be questioned. No one is immune, not even President Jacques. Science, especially through psychiatry, makes the world reign a new kind of Inquisition with internment and antidepressants. Yes, science is presented as carrying the one and only truth. But one day, like religions, it too will be discredited. The Church has condemned herself by cruel repression. In the last century fascism reigned for a brief moment but again he committed suicide himself because of the horrors he committed during the Second World War. It must be said that Nazism to commit its massacres was largely inspired by those perpetrated by the Church. No, it was not the Nazis who invented Jewish ghettos or mass exterminations for racial motives, although it must be admitted that they did it very well. In short! All that to say that all the dictatorial powers end up crumbling one day and science will not escape the rule.

— Science is easily manipulated and we can make it say what we want! —Boris intervened— I was able to see it earlier during my appointment with the psychiatrist: I hardly said a few words and now I am condemned to pass for a madman!

— You know, —Voldemar said— Serge Lunatik took a risk by going against the will of Mr Rode, your former boss, by not taking into account the fact that you were indulging in black magic. The authorities could fall on him! After all, this is a matter of national importance and the fact that you, my friend, communicated with the Grand Master of the Masonic Lodge can threaten many political figures, including the President of France. Indeed, in your hands there may be a lot of secret information or even the entire personal archive of Master Polus, but we will talk about this later. And as for our brave psychologist Serge Lunatic, then I will watch over him and protect him from problems with the Masons. It's part of our agreement.

— He could have made me lie down on a comfy couch and listen to me talk about my life. —Boris grumbled good naturedly— It would have been more credible and I wouldn't have realized that you were conspiring with him.

— My friend, —Voldemar retorted— you seem to confuse psychiatrist and psychologist: it is not the same thing! The psychologist makes you talk to try to find what in your experience could create discomfort in you.

The psychiatrist on behalf of science decrees like in the tribunal formal diagnosis that can not be contradicted nor ke, that is, his verdict is final and not subject to appeal! The Psychiatry is based their conclusions on so-called symptoms without trying to understand the causes. I tell you, Boris: Psychiatry is nothing but a repressive organ of the state. Modern democracies can no longer use violent repression, so they have invented another way to silence their detractors... That would have been called "heretics" in another era. In the Middle Ages, people who did not respect the precepts of the Church were sent to the stake.

In the time of Stalin or Hitler the dissidents went to extermination camps or on shot or in gas chambers. Today opponents of power are locked in asylums and fed with psychotropics in full. And it is not known who is more fortunate – a century-old heretic at the stake or to a modern dissident in the soft room of a psychiatric institution?

When one is reduced to the state of vegetable, death may seem to you a less heavy penalty. But I want to reassure you, my friend: I will look after you personally. I have enough followers within the authorities to avoid such a tragic fate. Whoever wants to attack you will have to deal with me! Also, do not worry about your future, my dear Boris. Nothing untoward will happen to you, I promise you that. By the way, at the expense of the personal archive of my friend Polus... – Voldemar, looking closely at the sides, whispered something to Boris's ear and added in full voice. – Here in Cannes not only the walls have... but now, I am for you, Boris, completely calm for now you have in your hands as a trump card - a real Joker!

— Thank you for your concern and here I am reassured! — Boris replied in a slightly disappointed tone— I fully trust you, Count.

— Is it really do you have any other choice but to trust me? —Voldemar smiled— I know, my friend, that you do not like being labeled as bipolar but what other solution did I have? After all, you could get into a psychiatric institution, because it has taken an important place in modern society. Also, I myself used it the best so that it does not harm you. Believe me, I am doing everything in my power to counter this new inquisitive power, because I know that science is the new weapon of the authorities and that it is likely to deviate to a mass repression, as has did the Church. But thank god creator, what paranoid abuse in the past led to her loss the way power over the minds of their loyal subjects.

Today, now that peace has settled in Europe, fewer and fewer people are going to church on Sunday. There are still some fanatics who will listen to the preaching of the servants of God and commune with the body and blood of Christ. Sometimes they will confess and repent of their sins. But these faithful practitioners are scarce nowadays. Today, men are free to believe or not to believe, to worship the god of their choice ... and even the Devil! The Church can no longer force people to praise the Lord, and no one in Europe is in danger of being executed for blasphemy.

In our enlightened age, can be recognized as crazy those release fanatics who dare to claim publicly are both like Saint Angela of Foligno, which claimed to feel the suffering of Jesus during the Passion and and caused terrible humiliation to herself.

Today, the list of schizophrenics may include those who, like Saint Catherine of Siena would be forced to a life of asceticism and would say to receive the stigmata of Christ or who like Mary Magdalene Pazzi would fall into long periods of spiritual ecstasy or those who like St. Catherine of Genoa would argue that he It is possible to live without eating material food simply by feeding on spiritual energy and at the same time absorb the larvae of flies and other insects. Besides, it is now forbidden to torture people. Sexuality is no longer considered a capital sin much to the chagrin of the Catholic Church who at one time liked to burn the genitals of women with boiling fat. There have even been cases of voluntary castration like Origen who castrated himself thus thinking to conform to the sacred texts such as this one: "If your hand is for you an reason for falling into sin then cut it off! " I'm not talking about my half-brother, the bastard, who offered the sinners to tear out eyes if they seduce them!

Ah, modern psychiatry could do a lot of useful things in ancient times and now my enemies would be even fewer on earth!

Voldemar paused for a moment to catch his breath and added:

— Here! It reminds me of Van Gogh's story. This renowned artist had originally intended for the priesthood but the Church did not want so that he literally lives by biblical rules. Nevertheless, he tried to live according to the biblical canons and eventually went crazy and cut off his ear to himself! — Voldemar burst out laughing.

Once his hilarity subsided, Boris spoke:

— Me too, I am considered crazy but I did not cut off my ear ... nor male pride which besides have always faithfully served me. After all, it is not for nothing that a Russian saying says: "If we make love, we die. If we do not do it, then we die too. Better to make love and die then".

— My friend, I'm glad to see you have found your good mood! — Voldemar rejoiced sincerely.

— Ah, do not talk about my mood, the Count! —Boris retorted— During my interview with doctor Serge Lunatik I wanted to joke and he told me that my euphoric mood was a symptom of my bipolarity!

— That's interesting because being in good spirits has not always been very well-received by the Church. —Voldemar said— For example, in the Middle Ages it was believed that a loud laugh moved away from God and brought closer to the Devil! This is why the Church recommended laughing discreetly. Moreover, Jesus never laughed at all and it is said about it in the holy bible!

Today I have the impression that laughter remains highly regulated. Fun are allowed when you are at home, on weekends or when you participate in events that elicit a joy shared by the greatest number as in sports events, for example. As for the believers, they have the right to sketch a smile at the end of the mass after having communed with God. But, on the other hand, there are situations where it is simply forbidden to be in a good mood. For example, it is very bad to laugh at a funeral, in a court ... or during an interview with a psychiatrist!

Voldemar laughed and Boris rolled his eyes from a fit of laughter.

— It is true that psychiatrists are rarely gay lurons! — Voldemar continued— At the same time, this can be understood: they spend their days being confronted with the dark vicissitudes of man. In the work of psychiatrists you can always find food for depression or what would to go crazy! By dint of listening to dozens of delusions from crazy people a day they are overloaded and become crazy in their turn. So, to get rid of their patients as quickly as possible they found the solution to stuff them with drugs. Madness is very common among psychiatrists and is a kind of occupational disease. Therefore, it is not known who uses psychotropics more - are they themselves or their clients?

— I was surprised when Serge Lunasek, telling me about the color of the pills, licked his lips so sweetly. —Boris decided to insert his word into the long monologue of the drunken interlocutor.

Voldemar nodded in agreement and continued:

— What is admirable in this profession is the solidarity that binds psychiatrists to each other, a solidarity even stronger than that which unites women so that they always support each other and that we will never see a psychiatrist question the diagnosis of one of his colleagues. As the saying goes, "unity is strength". And Serge Lunatik, who is in a depression is no exception. While you, Boris, are alone, that is why it is useless for you to contradict the diagnosis of Lunatik. You would run the risk of upsetting the whole profession which would be dangerous when you know how powerful psychiatry has become in modern society. The mere signature of the mayor of the city on an internment form could have led you straight into a psychiatric hospital. Do you understand why it was important to neutralize this Machiavellian process? Now that a psychiatrist has declared you simply bipolar and unfit for work no one will dare question his diagnosis and any danger of forced internment is discarded. Fortunately the only thing that dampens the heat of psychiatry from its pandemic spread around the world is the economic factor: locking up someone in an asylum is expensive for the state. Otherwise, psychiatrists have sunk so deep into the madness that they would be ready to declare all citizens mentally ill and send them all to a psychiatric hospital! Also, psychiatrists are forced to divide the population into two groups: patients too dangerous to be left at liberty, and those, less dangerous, that can be left at liberty, while keeping them under control. I tell you, my friend: psychiatrists are not nearly as cruel as the members of the Inquisition who claimed that all humanity bore the responsibility for original sin committed by Adam and Eve to the earthly paradise. Luckily, unlike crazy monks, doctors from psychiatry studied in schools where did they enlighten, and therefore where they were enlightened and therefore bright thoughts sometimes visit their blurred consciousness. Therefore, I was able to turn to the mind of Serge Lunatic and apparently he understood me.

Boris reluctantly agreed with good reason. – And he is just an executioner who is forced to do his job to feed his family. Although unlike the executioner, he is endowed with a conscience and has the right to choose.

This allowed Voldemar to take a breath and he, clinging greedily to the bottle of cognac, fell into a swamp of new thoughts:

– The approach of psychiatrists against humanity can also be compared to that of the communists who in the twentieth century invented the notion of "international duty" in order to imprison the people in a new dogma, which replaced, so to speak, that of the Church. The non-respect of these dogmas has been a good pretext, in the case of the Inquisition, to send to the stake the heretics and as far as communism is concerned to send the freethinkers to the Siberian camps. Moreover, the repression of the Americans against the Communists is often called the "witch hunt"! Of course, all psychiatrists do not share the extreme idea that all men are crazy and good to send to the asylum where they are wiped out with psychotropic drugs. And this is the case of the brave Dr. Lunatik.

– Count, –Boris interjected– with all that you just told me I think that, if they had the possibility, the psychiatrists would not hesitate to put on you the straitjacket to silence you! I imagine what once you will be caught and locked in an ultramagnetic cage ultra secure and wearing a mask to prevent you from speaking as Hannibal Lecter!

— You do not think so well, my friend! —Voldemar exclaimed.

The count laughed a little forced, as if the words of Boris had awakened a certain fear in him.

— But do not worry about me, my friend, —Voldemar said— It is impossible to catch me because as it is written in the Bible "my name is legion" and I am only part of the Force that was created for evil, but is forced to do good. Many of the people want to reign evil on earth but no one can stop us. On the other hand, my brother Jesus is not safe from the malevolence of men who have already put him on the Cross. It must be said that if he is the Son of God, then he is also the Son of Man, which makes him far more vulnerable than me. Today, he knows that if he returned to earth, he would be arrested again but this time it would not be on the Cross on which he would finish its second coming but in a psychiatric hospital. To be honest, I think that a few small sessions of electrotherapy would not hurt him! But enough talking! Young witches are already waiting for us at the Castle of Garoupe because Boris Berezovsky, the owner, has also agreed to house my guests. Between the holidays in the estate Baron Munchhausen and that of the Castle Garoupe we will have enough time for slutty girls to welcome everyone! Ah, I can not wait to find these charming witches and to devote myself with them to carnal pleasures around a good glass of wine! As they say, "love is ageless" and believe me I can still satisfy a woman as in the good old days when I established my quarters on the French Riviera.

– Count, I'm not going to blame you for wanting to enjoy the benefits of earthly life! —Boris commented— I do not understand you to well! But I warn against the use of Viagra because the body of the master Pole works at the last limit and you can suddenly die riding a passionate girl!

– So I'm immortal! —Voldemar exclaimed.

I am telling you about the worn-out body that you use, in order to avoid disrupting the main celebration scheduled for the night of May 1. And Viagra can trigger a myocardial infarction or cerebrovascular accident... —Boris said with a serious look, but then laughed when he saw that his warnings scared poor Voldemar.

The days that followed at the Chateau de la Garoupe were devoted to all sorts of unbridled festivities between excess of vintage wines and orgies unleashed. But shortly before May 1 a phone call came to interrupt the festivities: Serge Lunatik wanted to talk again with Boris. The magician wondered what the psychiatrist wanted but however, he went to the second interview. Upon entering the office he saw at once that Serge Lunatik was uncomfortable even though the doctor was trying to look good and had a forced smile. Boris wondered if Lulu and Zozo had not made a night visit to the psychiatrist as they had done with Mr Rode and his deputies. After all, he did not know how Voldemar went about trying to convince the doctor not to send him to an asylum for crazy people.

— So, doctor, why did you want to see me again? —Boris asked him.

— I just wanted you to sign an attestation stating that you are well aware of your illness. —Serge Lunatik said— You understand, it is to make sure that nobody will come to question my diagnosis...

The doctor threw to the magician a look of beaten dog cornered under the blows evil master. Boris realized that the psychiatrist found himself between the malle and the anvil. One side, he had to undergo some pressure from the bus station manager or the authorities who must have been very unhappy that Serge Lunatik had not sent Boris to a psychiatric hospital. And on the other hand, the poor psychiatrist was swept by Voldemar and the company.

— Dear doctor, —Boris replied— we both know that I do not have bipolar disorder and that if I went to your diagnosis it was to avoid a much worse situation primarily for you. But I am not an evil person and am always inclined to search for a compromise solution.

The psychiatrist had a small grin of annoyance at Boris's truth. The latter thought that the psychiatrist, if he had not been bound by an agreement with Voldemar, then would have decided to submit to the authorities and send Boris to an asylum. Also, the magician preferred to reassure Serge Lunatik immediately:

— However, I imagine that our arrangement must cause you some inconvenience. I know how it feels to be hunted because I am suffering the same thing as you. Also, I do not wish to cause you more trouble and I agree to sign your paper so that it can shelter you from the repression of the authorities.

The psychiatrist immediately handed Boris a document which he picked up took the time to read before putting his signature on it.

– There, doctor, you have nothing more to fear. –Boris concludes– I will not come to you, unless the State refuses to pay me my allowance. I also hope that if one of your colleagues in future not questions your diagnosis.

– It will not happen, Mr Lvov! –Serge Lunatik said– Everything is in order now.

Boris took leave, and the psychiatrist escorted him to the door of his office. The magician noticed that Serge Lunatik seemed relieved as if he were relieved of a heavy burden on his shoulders. Boris would not have gone so far as to say that the doctor was happy but he thought he saw in the psychiatrist's faded blue eyes a spark of gaiety that was not likely to illuminate Dr. Lunatik's melancholy gaze. Boris himself felt some relief after reading black and white that his condition did not require internment.

"It seems I cured the poor doctor of depression! And now he will not be so sad!" –Boris thought over and smiled politely at his executioner.

After his interview with the psychiatrist Boris returned to the Castle of Garoupe where he was awaited by a horde of witches eager to resume their passionate antics with the beautiful magician. At least, these moments of debauchery allowed Boris to completely erase image of Margot from his mind and to relegate to oblivion those sweet memories that had long tormented him.

Unlike the neighboring Castle of La Croe that had often changed hands before ending in those of Abramovich the Castle of Garoupe had experienced fewer different owners and was therefore haunted by fewer ghosts. There was still the specter of Pablo Picasso who during the nights of the full moon was pleased to browse the spacious rooms of the house.

If the first time that Boris had spent the night at La Garoupe on the occasion of the festival at the Castle of Croe, Anna Gelman, the mother of Mr Berezovsky, was absent, but this time it was well in the owned by his son, which the who was in exile in London. Old Anna had resumed her good old habits and was preparing a hearty breakfast for Voldemar every morning. Maybe making pancakes – delicious, by the way – and tea for the Count made up for his son's absence. In any case, Voldemar seemed delighted by the attentions of the old lady and this probably explained why he had stayed many times at the Castle of Garoupe.

Boris understood Voldemar's attachment to this house for he himself felt safe from the hustle and bustle of modern society. However, the Count had explained to him that this serenity was often disturbed by the impromptu visits of the Marseille public prosecutor and the police who investigated the malpractices of Boris Berezovsky. In the beginning, Anna Gelman was terrified by these police raids and over time she got used to it and even enjoyed it seeing the opportunity to break the boredom of her solitary old age. Each time she saw the envoys of the French Themis, she rejoiced as once in distant childhood the next performance, which these funny Frenchmen arranged. The old woman screamed joyfully, clapping her hands with joy:

-- My little Voldemar! You need to hide well from these serious uncles! And then they will again rummage everywhere in search of a safe with compromising material!

—Well, how much longer can they look for him? —Lazily Voldemar answered her-- After all, it is impossible to constantly look for what is not!

—So they have such a job! This is in the era of Stalin, people in black could come at night and not only take away property, but also life. And now, they follow the procedures, that is, they fool around with fools, and then all the same, my son's house will be taken to the state treasury.

—What are you saying! - For the sake of decency, Voldemar was always surprised at the words of his beloved grandmother Anna.

—Sometimes even now they do not perform formalities, and break into the sleeping people at night! - The old woman lamented. -- For example, most recently, the same judge from the Marseille prosecutor's office, who catches my son Boria and searches there, decided to arrest our neighbor Ilya Kokarev on false charges. So his bandits broke the door by force at night and arrested Ilya, his wife and daughter. All but the hamster, which already sat in its cage. They, too, searched for a safe with compromising evidence, and then arrested ilya him for three months in Marseille prison where he nearly died of exhaustion and torture.. For two years now, he has not been able to return to Moscow.

—Yes! No one is immune from mistakes! Voldemar every time it said that to maintain a conversation. At the same time, he did not forget to eat another pancake and drink a cup of tea insured in the Russian manner, and the old woman Anna put raspberry jam on him.

This time, at the end of April 2005, the old lady rejoiced to have of about fifty witches settled at the Castle of Garoupe had fun was far more entertaining than the police with the cold visits. The usual tranquility and silence of the estate were broken by the cries of joy and the hysterical laughter of the witches. To the old witches' gossip came the yapping of the young novices who were half-naked. Everywhere resounded songs with obscure words, such as:

"Parvati, Ganesh and Kumara!
Show us the way! Ah, ah, ah!
Shiva, Brahma and Vishnu!
Come back! Wow, wow, wow! "

Boris was the only man in the world of the living among these cohorts of witches and he was therefore very much sought after by the young novices like a stallions to project the mares of the flock. The magician did not reluctant to fill the desires with these girls who, moreover, did not hesitate to indulge among themselves lesbian pleasures. Encouraged by Voldemar who seemed to amuse himself like a little fool Boris was caught in a whirlwind of debauchery and intoxicated with this life of sin.

He did not know was that the merry team and of which he was a part that had invested lots of fun in the castle Garuppe, was closely watched from outside. Indeed, the appearance of the master Polyus at the conference of Nico Sinister in Paris had made a great noise and President Jacques Rusé was quick to be notified. At this news, President Jacques had almost fallen down on the floor: how could it be that Polyus whom he had placed in a retirement home under strict surveillance and who was supposed to be in a coma could present himself, in good shape, at the congress of the UMP? President Jacques had summoned his successor Nico Sinistre to the Elysée to express his fears: the president was afraid that Polyus wanted revenge for the fact that Jacques had sent him to a sordid retirement home, this which could be interpreted as treason by the great master. Hearing the confidences of President Jacques, Nico Sinister had said he could take advantage of the situation: he had explained to Jacques that indeed Polyus had perhaps wanted to send a kind of warning to the president Jacques had been shocked and Nico, falsely sympathetic, had told him that he could perhaps intervene on his behalf with Polyus and ensure his protection in exchange for a small service: he wanted the president to appoint him minister of the Interior in his next government and give him full support in the upcoming presidential campaign. The president, too distracted and scared by what Polyus could do to him had no choice but to accept the conditions unconditional surrender which imposed on him and he put up a white banner!

Nico Sinister, not a little proud of having managed this blow difficult opponent, asked his agents to report to him everything Polyus did. He was not much surprised to learn that the grand master had taken up residence at the Castle of Garoupe but he could not help but release some exclamations of surprise when on the morning of April 30 one of his agents made him on the phone the following report:

– Yesterday evening, in the middle of the park of the Castle of Garoupe, a huge bonfire was lit around which naked girls began to dance. A helicopter bearing the coat of arms of the Principality of Monaco brought several old ladies on the estate, among whom I recognized Rosa, the secret adviser to President Jacques. These old ladies swallowed some sort of potion and as if they had regained their former vigor they too began to dance. The circle around the bonfire was faster and faster when suddenly all the women collapsed on the ground. In a sort of trance their bodies twisted in every direction. Then they spread their hands towards the sea above which appeared a gray cloud that suddenly exploded in a sheaf of silver sparks like fireworks. From this glittering smoke arose the great master Polyus accompanied by his assistant Boris, the Russian who performed a magic ritual at the bus station in Cannes and was arrested at the Palace of Monaco before he escapes the vigilance of the guards. The witches, young and old, then rushed to the feet of the two men. Then Polyus shouted something in a language unknown to me and threw the contents of a flask into the fire that suddenly intensified. Tongues of fire seemed to lick the sky. The witches got up again and started dancing again while chanting incomprehensible songs. It was then that the whole field was plunged into a phosphorescent light. I remember that I felt a shiver run down my spine and I had the impression that strong hands were pressing my shoulders. I must have fainted because when I regained consciousness this morning I was lying on the ground on the rocks where I had been posted last night for secret surveillance of the object. That is, until the moment when the giants kindled a giant bonfire.

As soon as I regained my senses, I called you to tell you everything, Mr Sinister. That's done! I still have the head that buzzes as if a swarm of bees had taken up residence in my skull and I want you to know that I did not drink anything but water last night. I assure you that all that I have just reported to you is not the fruit of my imagination. By the way, this morning you could still see in the middle of the park the glowing ashes of the bonfire. So I did not dream: everything I saw last night was real! That same morning of the 30th of April after the boozed evening of the day before, Boris woke up with a hangover. He joined Voldemar on the terrace to have breakfast. Enjoying the aroma of black coffee with the addition of good Scotch whiskey and cream, the magician asked the Count:

– Why did you want to do a dress rehearsal for tonight's Sabbath? Yesterday, the witches seemed to know very well what they had to do!

– My friend, it was not really a repetition. –Voldemar answered– But, you see, this Sabbath has a particular flavor for me: this is the last time I will take possession of Polyus's body which I was used to and I will have to say goodbye to you, Boris. I am sad to leave you. Also, it seemed to me that one night of Walpurgis was not enough to honor our friendship and our good old Polyus! That's why I preferred to start the festivities yesterday.

It seems to me that it will be less difficult for me to leave you. Next night I'm going back to hell but I want to thank you, my friend, for those wonderful times we spent together. Our discussions allowed me to better understand humans and especially why they indulge in the weakness of loving. I do not pretend to have understood what love was but thanks to you I perceive the power of this feeling better. But do not fall into nostalgia and take advantage of the time we have to spend together. My friend, add one more a tear of whiskey to your coffee! You will have to be in shape tonight because I am sure that the coming night will bring us many surprises!

Chapter 15 - May 1 Sabbath

— Oh! Grand Voldemar, it has been a long time since we had seen you here on the French Riviera! —Young witch cried happily who had just arrived in her private helicopter, that had been offered to her by US President George W. Bush. All the participants in the Sabbath of May 1 came to greet in turn Voldemar who greeted them with a benevolent smile. The sun had disappeared into the horizon behind the mountains of the Tanneron Massif and the red Moon had taken up quarter in the starry sky overlooking where for celebration the Sabbath glade in which most of the guests were already assembled. Priestess Rosa who had made an appearance the night before at the Garoupe Castle had not yet arrived as well as President Jacques. The secret adviser to the head of state and the president had to be held at the Elysee Palace to settle some matters of vital importance for the country. Although being late is a privilege that could have been granted to such important personalities that evening it was not possible to wait for them. At midnight Voldemar solemnly declared that the Sabbath could begin. This coven of witches and magicians was of particular value to the participants because it was an opportunity to celebrate the nascent spring the solidarity that reigned in the world of magic but also, and the proletarians of the whole world, who could not lose anything except their chains. It is curious that the Orthodox Passover also celebrated on this pleasant spring evening. Although Jesus, the Son of God, chose another way in his eternal life, but he was still the brother of the master of hell and had contributed through his miracles together with other supernatural phenomena to the rise of witchcraft in the terrestrial world.

Once Voldemar had the attention of the whole assembly, he waved his copper cane and the wind which usually blew hard at this spot on the mountain fell at once skirting the clearing. All of witches present were able to admire the Mimosa valley below and, in the vicinity, the estate of Baron Munchhausen, owned by Rashid Selimovich who had welcomed the most eminent members of the magical community according to the Russian tradition, bread and salt, as well as several boxes of vodka brand Stolichnaya. On the outskirts of the witching glade sheltered were also little huts, made of branches, which the novices had built, for their lower rank had not allowed them to be entitled to a room in the Selimovich manor or in the Castle of La Garoupe.

Luckily, in the long stables of the estate of Baron Munchhausen wonderful Arabian horses were found thanks to which the issue of fresh meat for modest food and horse skulls for cheap table wine was successfully resolved. It is known that from time immemorial horse skulls served as a ritual cup, and and witches preferred horse meat and only occasionally goat meat., which was the main food of the Sabbath meal were also distinguished. Kind women decided not to sadden the heart of Rashid Selimovich and therefore secretly slaughtered all his horses, as well as his guests from the Moscow club of gentlemen of Russia, who decided to celebrate this day the solidarity of the oligarchs and other capitalists - oppressors.

Boris had a thought with anxiety for his friend the Homeless Poet that his already weakened mind can not survive this surge of witches with all their mysterious practices.

In the past, witches went to Walpurgis' night by flying on brooms which was possible thanks to a special ointment with which they brushed the handle of the broom. Other witches, of lower level, moved on goats or wild boars. Today they arrived by taxi or by helicopter the most influential. And the flying brooms served only to amuse the young novices who took pleasure in practicing this ancestral custom. However, some witches still came on the Sabbath on horseback, often to mark their superiority. Also, no one was surprised when hoofbeats were heard and the priestess Rosa appeared very dignified riding on the shoulders of the President Jacques who seemed far less comfortable compared to the race mule. According to the established tradition, his work as horse-drawn transport it was his annual fee to his mistress. The arrival of the priestess and head of state was greeted with applause which delight Rosa because she knew that many ministers, deputies and senators were present at this celebration, even if they tried to be discreet in hiding on the edge of the woods bordering the clearing.

Rosa found them all ridiculous and joyfully exclaimed:

– Why did they hide themselves like this? Everyone in the world already knows that they had used spells to gain access to the high office of the state!

But now, that all the participants had arrived, the witching ceremonial could begin. Voldemar, who had donned a costume from another era, sat down in a large armchair that looked like a throne. Each of the witches took turns approaching the head of Hell to greet him and tell about his great achievements in witchcraft for the benefit of the victory of World Evil they had done over the past year. Voldemar complied with this tradition but it was clear that he found it boring. After a while, the Count waved his hand and invited everyone to sit around the large tables that had been set up for the occasion.

Once all the guests were seated, the meal could begin. A fire had been lit to cook the meat. One would have thought that during this kind of meeting the followers of the black magic indulged in cannibal feasts, after having sacrificed young frightened virgins. After all, human flesh had been a feast for the Crusaders when the Christians had decided, in the name of God, to take the Holy Places from the Muslims, or Orthodox, during the great Soviet famines. But John Paul II subsequently forgave the acts of cannibalism of survival. It must be said that forgiveness had been a fixed idea in this brave Pope, since he had been constantly asking for forgiveness for all the heinous crimes committed by the

Catholic Church over the centuries. Be that as it may, there was no human flesh on the menu tonight but horse meat cooked to the heart that the witches and magicians let down in their throats with the help of a table wine served in skulls of horses, which they circulated around the table. Once the guests were sated, the fire was fanned until the flames rose high in the sky, and the witches began dancing an infernal armband around the fire. Their bodies were drawing sensual and provocative movements that thrilled wizards and devilish followers of the devil such as President Jacques and other politicians who finally came out of the woods at the edge of which they had hidden, joining the magicians to wait patiently, as spectators, the moment when the excited witches would offer themselves to satisfy sexual appetite. Usually excited young bacchanal women were already indifferent to what age their partners were during this bacchanalia. The witches wore wooden shoes from cedar Lebanon more precisely which slammed at each step of their dance on the stony ground of the Tanneron massif which created a rhythmic din.

Meanwhile, in Monaco the witch Margot arrived at the front door of the residence of her former rival, Princess Jeanne. The two women had recently ignored their differences for they shared the same sadness with regard to the imminent death of the great master. Indeed, soon after Polyus had been in a coma since it had been discovered that a magical ritual had been accomplished the two women had not been allowed to go to the bedside of the grand master.

Retirement home where he had been placed his room being well guarded by a brigade of secret service agents and therefore both women very sad. However, Margot was very surprised when she received a call from Princess Jeanne asking her to come to her home as soon as possible. Margot rang at the door which Princess Jeanne opened at once to warmly welcome her:

– Hello, Darling! Here you are!

– Hello, Princess Jeanne! –Margot answered– I admit to being a little surprised that you asked me to come to your place in the middle of the night.

– Because I received our invitation a little late. –Jeanne explained.

– Our invitation? –wondered Margot, who did not understand what the princess was referring to.

– Well, yes, our invitation to the Sabbath of May 1! –Jeanne added– It is explicitly stated that we must go both together.

Margot was petrified at this announcement, so she did not move an inch when Princess Jeanne opened the door wide to let her in.

– Well, Margot, –Jeanne said to her– do not stay there on the threshold of my door! Come in!

Margot shook her head as if to wake up and entered the home of Princess Jeanne, who took her to the salon. As she sat down in the comfortable chair that Jeanne had pointed out to her, Margot spoke again:

– I did not expect to be invited to the Sabbath this year after everything that happened with Polyus.

— You should rejoice that we have not been left out of these celebrations. —Jeanne said— Rather than make this burial head. What's bothering you, darling?

— Since we're both invited. —Margot said hesitantly— I'm wondering if Boris was invited too.

— Do not worry about that! —Princess Jeanne reassured her— Speaking of Boris, he had left a bottle of Smirnoff No. 57, that vodka with fifty degrees of alcohol. Do you want a drink? Or do you prefer cognac?

— Yes, I'd take a glass of Smirnoff. —Margot said— I always had fun watching Boris chew on gherkins while drinking vodka.

— Sorry, darling, but I have more pickles! —Jeanne retorted, laughing.

The princess filled two glasses of Baccarat crystal and handed one to Margot, saying:

— It was written on the invitation we would be picked up here at my home to take us to the place of the ceremony.

The Princess Jeanne smoking a Davidoff cigarette, of which she was a great consumer and drank a few sips of vodka just as Margot remarked to her:

— This invitation is still curious. Midnight has passed and the Sabbath must have begun.

Margot was soon to have the answers to her questions because she had just finished her sentence that the front door slammed and that Lulu appeared like a tornado in the living room under the dumbfounded eyes of the two women. The newcomer smiled at Margot and Jeanne then, seeing the bottle of vodka on the table, grabbed it and emptied it all at once right down the throat. She put the empty bottle down, wiped her mouth with the back of her hand and exclaimed:

— So, ladies! It's time to move your buttocks! Our driver is not going to hang around for hours in front of the door!

The two women got up and followed Lulu outside. The Rolls-Royce was parked just outside Princess Jeanne's home, and Zozo was standing next to the back door, already open.

— What a beautiful specimen of a male! —Jeanne exclaimed, detailing the demon from head to toe.

Zozo laughed and reached out to the princess to help her get into the vehicle. Jeanne grabbed the hand of the demon who did not fail when she rushed into the cockpit to give her a light tap on the buttocks. The princess gave a little chuckle of pleasure. Then, regaining his seriousness, Zozo turned to Margot and bowed respectfully before her, before opening the door in front.

— Mademoiselle, —Zozo said solemnly— you are the queen of the Sabbath and I ask you to sit at the front where you will be more comfortably settled.

Margot did not understand why the demon was so kind to her but she did not ask questions and lifting her black dress slightly sat in the passenger seat. Zozo supporting her delicately by the elbow. For her part, Lulu had sat in the back seat next to Princess Jeanne and had already opened a bottle of vodka which she handed to her neighbor after drinking a large swig. Zozo closed the two doors and took a seat on the driver's seat. As he started the engine, he announced:

— A helicopter is waiting for us at the landing field of Monaco, to take us as fast as possible to the massif of

Tanneron, where the party is in full swing. Everyone can not wait to see the Queen of the Sabbath arrive!

With that the demon pushed the Rolls-Royce forward at full speed. Zozo's mysterious allusions began to annoy Margot who asked him curtly:

— Can you explain to me what rhymes all this masquerade?

— Divine Margot, —Zozo replied as he drove— this night the gates of the earth are to open and the most daring dreams will come true... And it is your great honor to see your dearest desire come true first.

Zozo satisfied with his tirade turned his head to Margot and said smiling:

— Not bad my little welcome speech, huh? I think I could start a career as a poet!

— Look at the road rather than say nonsense! —Margot exclaimed.

Zozo looked in front of him and saw that a car coming in front was making headlights because Rolls-Royce drove into the oncoming lane. Zozo whirled and restored the vehicle to his path, narrowly avoiding a collision with the car coming in front which honked violently.

— Oops! —Zozo exclaimed— Forgive me, dear Margot, this kind of misconduct rarely happens to me. Your presence beside me troubles me.

Margot sighed with annoyance and did not say a word anymore. Anyway, the two drunks in the back seat were responsible for livening up the trip. When they arrived at the heliport, the pilot came to greet them and led them immediately to the helicopter, stamped "Heli Air Monaco" and equipped with high—tech instruments. Princess Jeanne, Lulu, and Zozo took their seats in the cabin while the pilot helped Margot get on her side in the cockpit.

Once everyone was seated, the pilot started the craft and the screws started turning. Then, the helicopter took the height and went like an arrow in the dark and cloudless night. Margot tried to chase away all the questions that tormented her to take advantage of the landscape that lay before her: the lights of Nice and neighboring towns glittered in the darkness like a cohort of fireflies stretching along the Mediterranean Sea. The city lights were reflected in the sea waves shining with a thousand lights like so many shimmering precious stones. It was really beautiful and Margot thought she understood why the French Riviera attracted so many tourists both by its beauty and its mysterious side.

The witch, overwhelmed by the landscape, did not see the time pass, and she was surprised that the pilot announced as soon as they would soon land. Margot then saw an immense bonfire that illuminated the heart of the Tanneron Massif. Naked female silhouettes fluttered around the fire in a frantic and jerky dance.

The helicopter landed smoothly in the clearing and the screws had not stopped turning already, already witches were rushing to greet the newcomers. Margot was surprised to notice that she was the object of attention and once the pilot had helped her get off the cabin the witches threw themselves on her to cover her with kisses then dragged her away. To the chair where Voldemar sat such as Baal who on his throne adorned with precious stones reigned from top Mount

Tsafone. Boris, who had not yet seen Margot, concealed by the cloud of witches that surrounded him wondered who could arrive in this helicopter. But he quickly turned away from the excitement that this emergence had created to contemplate the few naked dancers who had remained around the fire and moved in all directions under the eager eye of wizards and politicians. If Boris had been allowed to sit next to Voldemar's chair right next to the bonfire the other men were still standing a little apart as if waiting for permission to approach.

Suddenly, Boris saw that the group of witches who had gone to meet the helicopter was getting closer to Voldemar. So, he turned his head and, intrigued, understood that the witches were pushing a person towards the Count. The latter than took a few steps forward and raised her head: it was Margot! Recognizing his beloved Boris almost fell from his chair! He just caught himself and gaped staring at Margot. Nothing could turn him gaze away from her not even the naked dancers who were taking enticing poses, so much had he thought he would never see the his lover again. Margot, on the other side, stared at Voldemar identifying him as Polyus whom she thought was in agony in a miserable retirement home. The witch did not know what to think and felt herself completely lost. Suddenly, the bonfire intensified into a crackling sound that made a sheaf of sparks flies. Everyone jumped and turned reflexively their heads towards the fire, including Boris. But the magician recovered quickly and he wanted to see his beloved but, alas, she had disappeared in a split-second carried away by the crowd of witches.

Boris bit his lips in annoyance: he had found Margot scarcely but she was flying away again already! The red flames of the fire were still gaining height, as if they were being fed by pouring oil on the pyre. Above the blazing fire silhouettes were outlined in the glowing sky: it were strange birds with the demonic appearance and ghosts such as Boris had already seen at the Castle of Croe and the Ritz, except this time they were much more.

The men, wizards and politicians, left their position in retreat to join the assembly of witches. The living then faced the dead who were still circling in the sky.

Voldemar rose from his chair and took a few steps forward. Boris wanted to get up from his chair still in shock at the appearance of Margot but he was held by an invisible force and plated on his seat. Turning to the crowd of living creatures that formed a semicircle around him Voldemar spoke in a powerful voice so that everyone could hear him:

– Dear guests, we are here tonight to celebrate eternal life! While some ignorant men spend their lives waiting for the return of the Son of God back to earth with all the Apocalypse will bring about as catastrophes, you have chosen to enjoy every moment of your earthly life. So, let's dance, drink and have fun! Glory to life!

– Hooray! Glory to life! –The assembly exclaimed.

When silence reappears, Voldemar returned to his chair. He watched the crowd for a moment and shouted:

– Where is the Queen of the Sabbath? Bring her to me!

The crowd moved aside to let Margot pass who was pushed forward by Priestess Rosa. The beautiful witch finally emerged from the crush. Boris opened eyes more wide: his beloved was completely naked and her body coated with ointment shone by the light of the fire. Boris tried again to get up but an invisible power still held him on his seat.

Margot approached Voldemar and instead of bowing before him she raised her arm ready to give a powerful blow to the face to the master of hell. Priestess Rosa and President Jacques intervened in time to stop the blow. Rosa caught hold of Margot's raised arm while Jacques wrapped his arms around the waist of the furious witch and girded her vigorously. Margot who was prevented in this way continued to struggle like a beautiful devil and shouting:

— You are only a dirty liar! I cried about you all the time when I was thinking you were in agony! With young novices! Traitor!

Boris stuck in his chair was hurt to find Margot had not even looked at him and had focused all his attention to the one she thinking was Polyus.

Boris thought: "She never loved me! She only did the orders of her lovely grand master. How could I be so stupid as to believe her feelings to me were sincere?!"

This thought was so painful for Boris that he had the impression a dagger was being thrust into his heart. However, he could not let Margot misunderstand Voldemar's identity. Although he could not move, he still could use the words and he decided to intervene as soon as Margot was able to get rid of the influence of Jacques and Rose. The young witch rushed to Voldemar and wanted to hit him when Boris shouted:

– Margot, stop! It's not Polyus! It's Voldemar! It's the Devil! He took possession of the body of Polyus!

At these words, Margot suspended her gesture and let her arm fall.

Frightened by what she had just know she looked at Voldemar and stepped back a few faltering steps. Then she turned her head to Boris and shaking with sobs exclaimed:

– Boris, why did you disappear? Where have you been during all this time? I waited for you!

Margot's eyes rolled back and her legs bent. Helpless Boris saw Margot fainted. Fortunately, President Jacques had time to take Margot in his arms to accompany her fall and put her gently on the ground. Boris, wriggling in his chair, felt that the invisible force released his pressure and managed to get up. He rushed to Margot and knelt beside her, stroking her face.

Margot quickly regained consciousness and saw the worried face of Boris leaning over her. She smiled at him and whispered:

– You broke my heart, Boris, but I'm glad to see you again...

Boris would have liked to find something to answer her but he was all back by the words of his beloved: why did she think he had disappeared? It was she who had fled the morning after the ritual! At the same time, Boris had not looked for her either because he had been taken over by Voldemar. And for Margot it would be difficult to get him, even if she tried to find him, because Boris was on a journey... organized by Voldemar! It was easy to believe the Count had planned all their trips just to prevent the two lovers to meet again!

Boris turned his head to Voldemar and gave him a suspicious look, which clearly meant:

"Don't you do everything to make Margot and I separate? ".

Boris's eyes met those of Voldemar and the magician immediately understood that something abnormal was happening: the Count's left eye, the one who seemed to be wearing a black prosthesis was sometimes tinged with an opaque veil like the blind eye of the master Polyus when Boris went to visit him at the retirement home. Suddenly, Voldemar collapsed on the ground and rolled writhing in all directions like a snake in full molting. The Devil began to scream like a wild beast. His screams were so frightening that the assembly of witches and magicians took a few steps back. Even demons and ghosts, twirling in the sky, seemed to take a little height.

Finally, Voldemar's wild roar stopped. The Count sat up and struggled to stand up facing the crowd. His face seemed to have more wrinkles than usual. Voldemar shouted in impeccable French without the accent point with which the Count spoke and his voice had resumed the chafing of that of Polyus:

— There is nothing more beautiful than love!

He gave a look filled with paternal affection to Boris and Margot. The beauty being lying on the ground supported by the magician.

— I declare Boris and Margot are the King and the Queen of Walpurgis night! —Voldemar cried, still with the intonations of Polyus.

These words about love tinged with romance astonished witches and magicians and even more demons and ghosts.

Never had any of them heard the lord of darkness say such things. But, of course, nobody dared to make a comment out loud. Boris helped Margot to stand up and, holding her by the shoulders, whispered in her ear:

– I think Polyus has taken over for a moment Voldemar to give us his blessing.

Margot smiled at Boris to signify she agreed with him. Then the magician tenderly kissed his beloved.

– Long live the King and the Queen! —Voldemar cried clapping his hands like a child.

The crowd felt obliged to go in the direction of their master and bowed to the embracing couple. Suddenly, Voldemar fell to his knees on the floor. His left eye became black again and his voice regained its accent and clear hue as he spoke as in a dialogue with himself:

Polyus, stop shaming me! I promise you that as soon as dawn breaks you will recover your body so that you can leave the earthly world in good conditions. And you will see that I have reserved a nice surprise to welcome you in my hell... But I can not tell you because it's a surprise! Be reasonable! Do not spoil the Sabbath of May 1! ... Yes, it is promised: as soon as the ceremony is over I give you back your body!

Apparently, Voldemar's words convinced the great master Polyus because the Count got up without difficulty and had regained his usual appearance: he had regained full control of the body of Polyus.

Voldemar sank into his chair and shouted to the assembly:

— It is time that you do honor to all earthly pleasures! Drink and make love until you are exhausted! Long live the night of Walpurgis! And bring me some champagne!

As the witches went closer to Satan's wizards and politicians, and as the bodies began to brush against each other, a young witch hurried to bring Voldemar a frosted bottle of Dom Perignon. The Count looked at the her with an interested eye: considering her young age he was obvious that she was still a virgin. He grabbed the bottle of champagne, put it on the floor and opened his arms wide to invite the young witch to snuggle in which she did in hesitant gestures. As he closed his arms around the frail body of the novice Voldemar snapped his fingers and immediately the back of his chair lowered back offering a layer on which the Count and the girl lay down. Obviously, Voldemar had decided to deflower the witch! He tipped the novice so that she found herself lying back against the diaper and took a position above her. The witch completely inexperienced in terms of sex seemed not to know what to do, so Voldemar used himself to spread her legs and at the same time he unbuttoned his pants. Then the Count penetrated the novice and began to go back and forth brutally under the envious glances of other witches who would have liked to be in the place of the novice. Having a relationship with Lucifer made the lucky one climb the witch hierarchy! When the first drops of blood stained Voldemar's armchair, demonstrating that the girl had just lost his innocence, the crackling of the fire intensified sparking sparks of sparks above the crowd that uttered a loud cry of joy. Even the ghosts and demons made joyous antics in the starry sky before reaching the ground and mingling with the frenzied witches' dances. Laughing, moaning and roaring sound disturbed the tranquility of the Tanneron Massif. This green paradise looked like an antechamber of hell. Priestess Rosa had dragged President Jacques into the dance who was struggling to catch his breath as the old witch had energy to spare. So, Jacques went away for a moment and picked up a few strands of mimosa. Then he returned to Rosa and while bowing handed her his humble bouquet, to apologize for not being able to keep up the hellish pace. The priestess took the strands of mimosa; she had tears in her eyes and was very touched by President Jacques's attention. Rosa then proposed to the head of state to walk a little in the clearing.

While they were making their way through the dancers Rosa and Jacques passed close to Voldemar who after deflated young novice had dressed, had straightened the back of his chair to resume a sitting position.

Rosa thought it was a good time to talk to the Count about something that was important to her. She asked Jacques to wait for a moment and approached Voldemar. After greeting the Count she asked him:

– Lord of Hell, have you thought about what I suggested the last time we saw each other?

– And what was your suggestion, Rosa? – Voldemar asked, just to make the old priestess angry because he knew exactly what he was doing.

– Make my foal Manu the president of France! – Rosa exclaimed, annoyed.

Voldemar let a few seconds pass before answering:

– Well, yes, do you imagine that I have followed the progress of your foal! And I must admit that you have been right: he is an excellent candidate for the presidential post. However, I still find him a little young. And you know that the results of the next elections have already been planned. I can not go back to the agreements I made.

Priestess Rosa pouted. She was disappointed because she had taken under his wing the young Manu and had bet on him a lot. To see his recruit arrive at the highest office of the state would be a consecration for her.

Voldemar amused herself with the priestess's deceit and let her marinate a little longer before adding:

– Rosa, I give you my word that your Manu will become the President of France in twelve years!

Rosa could not restrain a cry of joy imagining her next hour of glory. When Manu will be president, she would have control over the higher spheres of power, much more than with President Jacques who was a real weather vane and did not hesitate to betray those who had always supported him.

Priestess Rosa bowed to Voldemar and joined President Jacques with joyful steps to drag him into the woods that bordered the clearing.

Meanwhile, Boris and Margot had withdrawn from the festivities. They had a lot to say to each other. They discussed it the rest of the night, and it was not until the first light of dawn that they drew near the bonfire which was beginning to lose its intensity. The cries of witches and wizards had also faded away making the Tanneron range feel tranquil. Around the fire which was only trembling with a few flames it was a tangle of bodies asleep or exhausted from that night of orgy.

It was not the rooster's singing that woke up all this beautiful people, but the engine sound of a Hummer off-road vehicle that popped into the clearing like a wild animal. Boris was surprised to recognize behind the wheel the face of the Homeless Poet. Next to Vadim could one see the ruffled hair of the passenger.***

The roar of the powerful engine made the whole assembly rise. Voldemar was anxious to see a small Caucasian descending from the passenger door. It was Rashid Selimovich, the owner of the Baron Munchhausen estate not far away. He held a Kalashnikov assault rifle in his hands and carried a double barrel shotgun across his back. A Colt pistol and a scabbard of a Caucasian dagger hung on his belt. It was obvious that Rashid Selimovich was angry! The night before Vadim had come to tell him that the funny women who were staying at his house had taken horses from the stables and slaughtered them before cutting them up. Seeing this scene, the frightened homeless poet remained in his room on the second floor of the stable, and only when the women left for the clearing did he leave his room and went to tell everything to his former boss. The Caucasian had gone into a rage and had asked Vadim to take him to the clearing the next day at the first hour, as soon as the esoteric ceremony there was finished. While Rashid Selimovich defied the assembly with his weapons, Vadim frightened remained in the vehicle's armored salone. Suddenly there was the sound of other car engines. Several off-road cars appeared in the clearing from which armed men dressed in military uniform descended who lined up in front of the assembly of the followers of Lucifer. One of the new arrivals was even equipped with a grenade launcher. At the same moment, a rooster was heard singing in the distance, and the morning sky turned pale shades of dawn. Suddenly, a green glow pierced the horizon.

Voldemar, paying no attention to the armed men, yawned and stretched before declaring:

— My friends, it was a wonderful ceremony! But it's time for me to find my hell again.

At these words, witches hastened to revive the fire, so that Voldemar and the beings from hell could return home. As soon as the flames had regained sufficient power, the ghosts and demons as if they feared to be trapped on earth, hastened to jump into the inferno where they instantly disappeared. When the last hellish being had taken the fiery gate into hell Voldemar stood up and collapsed to the floor. The body of the great Polyus master was shaken by a few jolts and came out a spectral silhouette which Boris recognized at once. Iit was the same form that he had seen at the bus station on the morning of the ritual.

The ghost of Lucifer looked at the body of Polyus lying at his feet and exclaimed:

— I do not say goodbye, my friend Polyus! Because I know that you will join me very soon! Voldemar's spectral voice resembled the creaking of a chalk on a blackboard, which made Boris shiver and lift the hairs of his arms. The magician saw, with the smiles that the other adepts showed, that all had felt the same unpleasant sensation.

The demonic specter turned to Rashid Selimovich, to whom he said in Russian, with a slight Baltic accent:

– Rashid Selimovich! You will receive a compensation for the horses that were taken from you. But beware: if you continue to amass an inordinate amount of money and exploit your employees, like the poor Homeless Poet that you do not pay for the work he does in your stables, then your entire empire will collapse and you will soon join my hell!

Then, Satan's ghost signaled Boris and Margot to approach him. The two lovers complied and, when they reached his height, the Devil stared at them. His left eye, the black one, suddenly brightened up and pulled out a ray of light that lit up the faces of the magician and the witch. Lucifer did not say a word but the crowd understood, to the smiles of Boris and Margot, that he had transmitted a telepathic message to them alone. Finally, the Devil plunged into the flames of the fire, in which he disappeared immediately. At that moment, the bonfire exploded, making incandescent splinters fly. The flames had gone out at once: the door of hell had closed. Witches rushed, equipped with cauldrons and pots, to recover the infernal embers that were still glowing. As the devotees of Satan worked to clear the clearing of the various detritus left by the Sabbath ceremony, Boris suddenly saw one of his old acquaintances: the seer Tamara Evgenevna, whom he had rubbed shoulders with in Cannes. He approached her and, seeing that she was holding a cauldron filled with embers, asked her:

– Tamara Evgenevna! What are you doing with all these embers?

— Yes, you're right... —answered the old woman, a little confused to be surprised in this situation— I do not really need those ashes. But, you understand, my neighbors are very noisy and rot my life. I was planning to cast a spell on them with these embers...

— Beware, Tamara! —Boris retorted, smiling— As the saying goes: "Whoever throws nettles at his neighbor's will see them grow in his garden."

Boris and Tamara were interrupted by Rashid Selimovich, who shouted to his men:

— By car! We have nothing to do here! The gunmen climbed into their all-terrain vehicles, which set off at full speed, poisoning the clearing of their exhaust fumes. They passed not far from the Jeanne princess, who, drunk dead, had fallen asleep at the edge of the woods.

At the same moment, awakened by the rumbling of the engines, the grand master Polyus straightened up. He seemed a little lost and felt all his limbs before getting up, surprised to walk, he who had not been on his legs for a while already.

As no one paid attention to him, witches and magicians being busy cleaning everything, Polyus took the opportunity to discreetly join the wood. He passed beside the sleeping Jeanne princess, but not wanting to disturb the repose of his old friend, he contented himself with watching her with amusement. Then he rushed into the forest. The grand master knew that he did not have much time left in the terrestrial world, and he absolutely wanted to see for the last time a place that was dear to his heart: there, in these woods, he had made his declaration to his well-beloved Gretchen, in the middle of an undergrowth covered with lily of the valley and bordered by a stream. Even if it had been a long time ago, when he was going through the fairs to sell printing machines, he remembered that moment well. While he and Gretchen were walking in the forest, they had discovered this place dotted with lily of the valley, one of the favorite flowers of Ostara, the goddess of the rising sun. Bewitched by the sweet scent of lily of the valley, he had picked a bouquet he had offered to Gretchen as a pledge of his eternal love. Having wandered a long time in the forest, Polyus finally found the place where he had lived the best moment of his life. He was surprised to find that the place was still sprinkled with lily of the valley, as in his memories. He sat on the floor and gently caressed the white bells. A deep melancholy seized him and tears came to his eyes. Shortly after this idyllic moment spent with his beloved, he had met Voldemar, with whom he had made a pact, as Faust had done before him with Mephistopheles. Alas, to fulfill his market share, Polyus had to give up Gretchen. This lily of the valley was, for the grand master, the symbol of broken hearts. Polyus had tried to get in touch with Gretchen but, like Faust's who had preferred the executioner's ax, his beloved had chosen to flee rather than live under the evil influence of Voldemar. Polyus did not hold it to his Gretchen; she was too pure to pervert her soul. And then, while Polyus was slowly aging thanks to the action of Voldemar, Gretchen had suffered the pangs of time and left the earthly world. Polyus picked a few sprigs of lily of the valley and carried them under his nose to get drunk with their perfume. Then he advanced towards the stream, where he drank a few cups of refreshing cups with his hands, which relieved his dry throat. Finally, he lay on his back on the edge of the stream and lost his gaze in the contemplation of the sky he could see through the canopy of trees. Suddenly, he thought he saw a green gleam pierce the blue of the sky. Intrigued, Polyus straightened up on his elbows, discerning a silhouette that shot out of the green light. The tall master narrowed his eyes and, as the figure drew closer, he distinguished the graceful forms of his body, which seemed to be sculpted by the expert hands of an ancient artist, with blond, curly hair. Then his face with delicate features: it was his Gretchen! Suddenly a light breeze arose and brought him a sweet melody; he recognized without difficulty the voice of his beloved who said to him:

— My beloved, it's time to follow me!

Polyus would have liked to answer him, but he felt his strength leave him and sank to the ground. As his eyes struggled to stay open, he saw the diaphanous figure of Gretchen walking among the lily of the valley bells. She leaned over him and stroked his face, smiling at him.

Polyus stared into the turquoise eyes of his beloved who shone with a strange light and, while his heart was emitting its last beat, he found the strength to say:

— Are you surprised that Voldemar has reserved me! I am ready, my beloved! I will follow you to hell!

Epilogue

The body of the great Polyus master was found in a forest of the Tanneron massif, the day after the commemorations of the victory of France and its allies during the Second World War. This time, Polyus was indeed dead.

A few days later, on May 11, 2005, the police department again landed at the Garoupe Castle, property of Boris Berezovsky. But this time, they grabbed important documents and hard drives from computers found in the office of the disgraced oligarch. The police claimed that the seized items provided evidence of Boris Berezovsky's wrongdoing. Following this statement, Mr Berezovsky made the following comment:

– There was nothing important in my office at the castle Garoupe! The computers carried away were used by my wife Galina. As for the documents, I do not see what the police could find other than the drawings of my daughter and the notes, in Russian, that my son took during his lessons with his private teacher. My mother, who is eighty years old, now lives on this property. For my part, it's been four years since I went to France.

Eleven years after these events, while reading the newspaper, Boris came across an article, "Thank you, Dad", mentioning that Russian billionaire Rashid Selimovich had married his daughter Victoria for the modest sum of ten million dollars:

"The wedding took place in a former nineteenth-century castle in Prague. The bride and groom had chosen a "satanic" atmosphere, which was unusual for a wedding, since the guests were received by hostesses with fangs to the Dracula and smeared with fake blood. The dress code was, of course, the color black. On the tables draped in black, bunches of red roses came to enhance the brilliance of the crockery crystal. Among the guests, there were a number of celebrities, such as: violinist Vladimir Spivakov, pianist Denis Matsuev, soprano Hibla Gerzmava, designer Izet Hajiyeva, actor Anton Tabakov, supermodel Sara Sampaio... British singer Robbie Williams and Norwegian band Madcon were chosen to lead the evening."

It was stated in the article that the guests were prohibited from posting wedding photos on social networks. However, it seemed that some photos had filtered through the press and Boris, comfortably seated on a deck chair facing the Mediterranean Sea, was watching them slowly. Suddenly, the magician jumped: on one of the photos, one of the guests, a man with white hair, seemed to be wearing a black prosthesis in his left eye... This detail immediately made him think of Voldemar. And he said to himself, with a touch of nostalgia:

"Ah! We still had fun, with Voldemar, on the French Riviera!"

As for the Homeless Poet, after a few years of slavery in the stables of the Baron Munchhausen estate, he had finally come to the obvious: Rashid Selimovich would never take him back to the manor. Also, he had left the Tanneron massif to settle in a town near Versailles, where he worked as a scouter. Inner voices always tormented him, but he had made the decision to seek treatment.

***The icing on the cake.

One day in 2018, on a beach on the French Riviera, Boris, while walking, picked up abandoned newspapers on the sand. The magician was at first a little irritated that we let drag trash in such a beautiful place. Then, mechanically, he glanced at the headlines and finally sat down on the sand to read the newspapers. One of the articles was about President Manu's comments some time ago about rumors his love life. It must be said that these remarks were memorable and had marked the spirits:

"It's unpleasant for Brigitte, who wonders how I do physically. She shares my life from morning to night. And I have never paid for it! If, in the dinners in town, you are told that I have a double life with Mathieu Gallet, it's my hologram that escaped me."

As he read these lines, Boris thought back to a remark Lulu had made thirteen years ago about the manners of future President Manu. The magician burst out laughing, then, regaining his composure, immersed himself in reading another article on the Benalla affair:

"On May 1, 2018, during clashes between protesters and police, a man, wearing a visor helmet like the police, was filmed molesting a man and a woman. A month and a half later, on July 18, his identity was revealed by the newspaper "Le Monde": it is Alexandre Benalla, mission manager at the Élysée, who was not authorized to participate in CRS interventions. This revelation shook the Head of State because Benalla was very close to President Manu. The latter paid Benalla an exorbitant salary, at the expense of the taxpayers, put at his disposal a luxurious company car, equipped with emergency lights usually reserved for the police, and housed him in an apartment at Quai Branly, in the former residence of the mistress of President Mitterrand. Many documents suggest that Benalla was of all presidential, official and private trips. A blur persists as to its exact function in the organogram of the Elysée. Benalla is a Freemason initiated in the French National Grand Lodge. He also holds the rank of lieutenant—colonel in the gendarmerie's citizen reserve, as a specialist in security issues. Note that this grade is purely honorary. President Manu returned to this case by stating: "Alexandre Benalla has never held the nuclear codes, Alexandre Benalla has never occupied a three hundred square meter apartment, Alexandre Benalla has never had a salary of ten thousand euros and, incidentally, Alexandre Benalla is not my lover. [...] The only person in charge of this business is me and I. Alone who has trusted Alexandre Benalla, it's me. a leader, he is in front of you, let them come and get him. " This last sentence has not gone unnoticed and has provoked strong reactions, which only feed a climate already fraught with social tension."

After reading this news, Boris thought:

"I wonder if Voldemar is still happy with Manu, the rookie of priestess Rosa. In any case, I have no doubt that it is he intervened to get rid of the importunate Benalla... As wrote the poet Aeschylus: "What must be will be". " The article Boris had read was not wrong, because a few months later, the revolt of "yellow vests" broke out. It was at this time that Boris composed a song that seemed to him to be blown by Voldemar:

"I've been told that Paris is too noisy
Because of the yellow vests that go to the Elysée
to kick the ass of Manu the president!
He told them to come and get him!

Yo, yo, yo! It's a nightmare!
But we must always look for the woman,
the one who has done a damn mess
by putting Manu in the palace of Paname!

Greed makes so many victims,
While the rich ministers and deputies
Only eat dishes from "Maxim's"
With truffles and vintage wines!

But, one day, it will be the end of these intrigues,
the bees will refuse that one steals their honey to them!
And sound the knell of the reign of the prodigal son
who will only have to pray to reach the sky!

Bibliography

The first Russian version of the novel.

cover design: Andre Lwow

The first French version of the novel

cover design: Andre Lwow

Table of contents

Printed in Great Britain
by Amazon

36073000R00219